LITTLE LIES

New York Times Bestselling Author **HELENA HUNTING**
writing as
H. HUNTING

LITTLE LIES

ALL THE LITTLE LIES (you tell yourself to fee better about the truth)

I don't want you.
> *You mean nothing to me.*
> *I never loved you.*
> I turned my words into swords.
> And I cut her down. Shoved the blade in and watched her fall.
> I said I'd never hurt her, and I did.
> Years later, I'm faced with all the little lies, the untruths, the false realities, the damage I inflicted, when all I wanted was to indulge my obsession.
> Lavender Waters is the princess in the tower. Even her name is the thing fairy tales are made of.
> I used to be the one who saved her.
> Over and over again.
> But I don't want to save her anymore.
> I just want to pretend the lies are still the truth.

LITTLE LIES

ACKNOWLEDGMENTS

Husband and kidlet, you are my favorite people, thank you for your love, I wouldn't be me without you.

Deb, I adore you. Thank you for matching my weird and being my trampoline.

Kimberly you are awesome, and I love your brain, your cheerleading, your insight and your friendship.

Sarah, you're incredible and wonderful and I absolutely couldn't do this without you. Thank you for knowing what I need before I even need it.

Hustlers, you're my cheerleaders and my book family and I'm so grateful for each and every one of you.

Denise, thank you for your hockey knowledge, for your insight and your willingness to share it with me. You're incredible and I'm honored to have your support.

Tijan, you have the most incredible heart and I'm blessed to have your friendship.

Jessica, Christa and Julia, thank you so much for working on this project with me and helping me make it sparkle.

Sarah, Jenn, Hilary, Shan and my entire team at Social Butterfly, you're fabulous and I couldn't do it without you.

Sarah and Gel, thank you for being graphic gurus. Your incredible talent never ceases to amaze me.

Teeny, thank you for not only your ability to make the insides glorious with graphics, but also for your friendship.

Beavers, thank you for giving me a safe place to land, and for always being excited about what's next.

Deb, Tijan, Kelly, Ruth, Kellie, Erika, Marty, Karen, Shalu, Melanie, Marnie, Julie, Krystin, Laurie, Angie, Angela, Jo, Lou; your friendship, guidance, support and insight keeps me grounded, thank you for being such wonderful and inspiring women in my life.

Readers, bloggers, bookstagrammers and booktokers, your passion for love stories is unparalleled, thank you for all that you do for the reading community.

For the ones who feel everything so intensely that it makes the world as painful as it is wonderful.

Don't Let the Monsters Get You

LAVENDER

Age 6

"IT'S SUPER FUN in there, Lavender. You're going to love it!" my big brother Maverick assures me with a grin and a wink.

I smile back up at him. He thinks everything is fun, and most of the time he's right.

"The mirrors are the best!" Kodiak announces. He's Maverick's best friend, but he's my friend too. "We'll make sure you have a great time."

I nod and wrap my arms around myself, trying to keep my shiver of worry inside, but it doesn't work.

"Lavender, honey, are you cold?" Daddy asks. "Where's your jacket?"

Mommy checks her purse. "We must have left it in the car. I can run back and get it. I'll only be a minute."

"Ah, man," Maverick mutters. He's quiet enough that our

1

parents don't hear, but I do. His frustration is a thick blanket, heavy on my shoulders. Maverick doesn't like to wait, and they've already spent five minutes trying to convince me to come with them.

"It's okay. She can wear my hoodie." Kodiak unties it from around his waist and holds it out to me.

I take it with a small smile and slide my arms through the soft fabric. It's warm and smells like laundry detergent. The hoodie has the hockey logo from the team my daddy coaches and Kodiak's daddy plays for. I slip my hands into the pockets, and my fingers brush candies and a few empty wrappers. Kodiak always has Jolly Ranchers. They're his favorite. My favorite are the marshmallows in Lucky Charms, even though it's really cereal, not a candy.

"You're sure you want to go?" Mommy asks quietly as she helps me roll up the sleeves.

I nod, but don't use my words. I don't trust my voice right now. Besides, Mommy said we could have funnel cake after the fun house, and I don't want to be the reason we don't get to.

Mommy and Daddy look at each other. They talk without words all the time. Me and River do that too. It's different because River is my twin, but also the same in a lot of ways. We don't always have to use words to know how the other feels, which is good since sometimes my words get stuck in my mouth.

"River, you keep hold of Lavender's hand the entire time, okay? That's your job," Daddy says in his firm voice. "You hold her hand the whole time."

It's the voice he uses with River a lot, but he never uses it with me.

"I hold Lavender's hand. I don't let go. I keep her safe," River repeats.

Daddy nods solemnly and turns to me, his expression shifting. His face is like a fresh marshmallow, softening, so much nicer. "You tell River if you don't like it in there, okay? Robbie, Mav, and Kody will be with you."

I nod and whisper *okay*. Daddy kisses me on the forehead and grips River's shoulder. "Take care of your sister, and stay with your brothers."

River nods and holds my hand so tight, it almost feels like the bones are bending. I want to tell him it hurts, but everyone is running toward the fun house, and I don't want to ruin it, even though I'm already frightened.

Everything scares me.

Too much noise. Too many people. Especially too many people I don't know.

There are a few people and things that make me feel safe.

Most of the time River is one of them, but tonight I feel like I'm on a merry-go-round and there's no way off. I want to have fun. I want River to have fun. But the noises and the people are too much.

I stick close and hold his hand tight. My palm is damp and slippery. I feel cold and hot.

I should tell him I want to go back and stay with Mommy and Daddy, but it's too loud and my voice is stuck. I remind myself that after this, there will be a treat, and I'll be back where I feel the safest. And I like how proud Daddy looked when I said I wanted to go inside the fun house.

Robbie, Maverick, and Kodiak rush ahead, moving through a maze of mirrors. Kodiak looks over his shoulder, brows pinching together. He grabs Mav's shirt and tries to get him to slow down, while River rushes to keep up with them. Maverick laughs and disappears around a corner. Kodiak hesitates, looking back one last time before he disappears too, and River urges me to move faster.

I bump into my own reflection and grip River's hand even

tighter. We're reflected all over the place. River's eyes are bright with excitement, his smile wide. "You're okay, right?" he asks, eyes still focused ahead, to whatever lies around the corner.

I nod, because there's loud music and he won't be able to hear me. When we move away from the mirrors, some of the fear disappears, but then we have to walk through a bunch of what look like Daddy's punching bags in our gym at home, except they have clown faces on them. I don't like those, so I close my eyes and let River pull me along. I bump into things, and someone bangs into me from behind. I stumble and lose my grip on River, falling to my knees. Someone trips over me and a foot hits my side, so I scramble to get out of the way.

There are flashing lights in here, and every time they flicker on and off, it makes it hard to figure out which way I'm supposed to go. The hanging clowns swing above me, knocking me over when I try to stand.

River is calling my name, but my fear makes the world murky and unclear, and I feel like I'm underwater. I can't breathe, or see, or speak anymore.

This is why Daddy wanted River to hold my hand *the whole time*. When I get scared, my words get stuck, and I feel frozen. It makes it hard to find me, especially in a place like this. The panic monster gets bigger in my head, taking up all the space, and I suck in shallow breaths. I try to remember all the things my art teacher, Queenie, tells me to do, but my mind is racing, racing, racing, and all I want is my mommy and not to be here anymore.

I scramble away from the feet and the bigger kids stomping and pushing their way between the hanging clowns. I bump my cheek on something hard. It brings tears to my eyes, but when I look up, I see a door with a sign that reads EMPLOYEES ONLY. I don't know what that means, but I decide I would rather get in trouble than stay in here. I turn the knob and peek through the crack. It's a hallway and stairs. I glance over my shoulder at the hanging clowns. I can't go back through there.

I step out into the hallway. I feel better and worse. I just want my mommy. I want to go home and snuggle in bed with her and Daddy where it's safest.

The walls in the hallway are yellow and dirty. People have written on them in marker. I hurry toward the stairs and stumble again, falling on my bottom and sliding down a few of the steps. They're dirty and wet, and now so are my clothes. Tears prick my eyes because my mommy made me this dress, and I don't want it to be ruined.

There's a big door at the bottom of the steps. It's red, but the paint is flaking, exposing brown underneath. It looks like dried and fresh blood. In the corner is a chipmunk, scratching at the door, trying to get through a small crack. We have chipmunks up at the cottage where we go in the summer. We feed them peanuts, and they're so friendly, they climb right in our laps to get them. But my mommy always makes sure we don't touch our faces, and we wash our hands after we feed them. I think this one is too scared to be friendly. He wants out, just like me.

"Hi, little guy." My voice is barely a whisper. "I can open the door for you."

I push on the bar, but it's heavy, and my arms are shaking. The chipmunk huddles in the corner, and my tears come faster because now I'm afraid I won't be able to get out, and I don't want to go back up into the fun house where the hanging clowns are.

If I can just get the door open, I can get back to my mommy and daddy, and then I'll be safe. The door finally clicks, but a thick chain keeps it from opening all the way. The chipmunk rushes outside, and I squeeze through the narrow gap. My dress gets caught, tearing at the bottom. *Oh no.* I don't want my mommy to be upset with me.

It's noisy out here, lights flash and people scream and laugh. I suck in a big lungful of air, which tastes like cigarette smoke. The door closes behind me with a loud click.

I feel frozen, stuck to the spot. I don't know where I am or how to get back to everyone. My daddy always says if I get lost, I should stay where I am or find a person I trust to help me, like a police officer, but there's no one back here except me. I don't know which way I'm supposed to go to find my parents, and I worry River is still inside the fun house, looking for me.

I try to use some of the calming exercises Queenie taught me, but my mind is a jumbled mess, and I'm scared.

"Cali, is that you?" A big man appears out of the darkness.

I stumble back a step and trip over a rock, landing on my bottom. My glasses fall off and hit the ground. The man crouches down. His eyes are empty wells, hollow and dark. He smells wrong, like the stuff my mommy puts on my scrapes that burns.

"Are ya lost, little girl?" His words blur together. "You look just like my Cali." He tosses an empty bottle away, and it lands in the grass with a thud.

He's scarier than the hanging clowns. And my parents tell me never to talk to strangers. I feel around for my glasses, but I can't find them.

He reaches out, and I scramble back, but there's a garbage can behind me, and I hit my head so hard, it makes stars explode behind my eyes. I want to yell for my mommy, but my throat is all locked up.

"Are you alone? Where's your family?" He crowds me. "You look just like her. You could be her." His breath makes my eyes water. "I can take you home."

My tummy feels upset.

"Come on now, you're safe with me." His smile is missing teeth, like mine.

I don't want to go with him, but I'm scared out here in the dark.

He slides his hands under my arms and lifts me. My knees are shaky, and I don't like how dry my mouth is. "Don't be scared. I'm not gonna hurt you." He takes my hand. "You're exactly like my Cali." He pulls me along, and I stumble, looking back over my shoulder. I think I hear my name, but I don't know if it's real or not. Instead of moving toward the shouts and the rides, we're moving away from them. I slip my hand in the pocket of Kodiak's hoodie and pull a candy out, dropping it on the ground. Like Hansel and Gretel with the bread crumbs.

I try to dig my heels in, but he yanks my arm and moves faster. I trip over something and lose my footing. He drags me back to my feet. He's not smiling anymore, and his empty-well eyes remind me of Kodiak's dog, Brutus, when he finds a squirrel in the backyard he wants to chase.

"Don't make a sound. Not one," he says as he opens a door.

I drop another candy on the ground, and he pushes me into the darkness. I stumble and fall forward, landing on my hands and knees. The floor is hard and cold.

"You stay here and stay quiet, Cali, or you're never gonna see your momma again," he growls.

The door closes and clicks.

I want to tell the man my name isn't Cali, but I'm afraid if I say anything, I really won't see my mommy again. It's dark like a cloudy, starless night at the cottage and smells like the stuff my daddy puts in the boat to make it run. I slip my hand in the pocket again and feel for the candies there. There are only two left.

I wish I hadn't tried to be brave.

7

I wish I were anywhere but here.

I start to cry, and it's hard to keep the noises from coming out. I clamp my mouth shut and dig my nails into my palms. They bite into the skin, little silent screams.

I tuck my face inside Kodiak's hoodie and try to breathe in the scent of detergent and his watermelon candies.

I'm afraid to move, because if I make noise, the man is going to come back.

I feel around on the floor. It's hard and cold, and my teeth are starting to chatter. My bottom is wet from falling down, and the smells in here make my tummy feel bad.

I reach out, brushing my fingers over the things close to me. I don't know what any of the stuff in here is.

I find something soft beside me. It feels like a stuffed animal. I hug it to my chest and stand. My legs are wobbly, like they're made of Jell-O. I shuffle forward and hold a hand out in front of me until my fingers touch something cold. I can hear the sounds of the carnival, but just barely. There's a loud fan in here that makes everything outside seem far away.

I feel along the cold surface until I find a bump. I think it's the door. I don't understand why that man left me in here. I turn the knob and try to push, but it doesn't budge.

I want to be home.

I want my mommy and daddy.

I want River to know I'm okay.

I want to be able to give Kodiak his hoodie back.

I hope he isn't cold like me.

I try the door again, but it's still stuck, and I'm still here, all alone.

I don't know how long I'm in the dark, but after a while, I think I hear someone calling my name. I hear it again, more than once this time, and it sounds closer. I press my ear to the cool metal.

I think I hear Kodiak and my daddy.

Someone bangs on the door, and I stumble back, falling to the floor.

"Lavender?" There's banging and banging, and then suddenly the door folds in and Daddy and Kodiak are right there.

I don't know where Mommy is, and all my words are trapped in my throat because the fear is holding on to them.

"Oh my God. Thank God. What happened, baby?" Daddy scoops me up, and Kodiak's eyes are so, so wide. He's holding the candies I dropped on the ground and my glasses. "I have her! I found her!" Daddy's running, and it makes my tummy jump and twirl. Kodiak runs after us, and we burst out from the darkness, back into the noise and lights of the carnival.

"Oh thank God!" Mommy wraps her arms around me in a hug so tight, I feel like a jelly donut that's being squeezed too much. "What happened, baby? Where did you go?"

Daddy tells her where he found me, and finally my words start to work. But all I can get out is *a man* before I get all choked up again.

"A man took you?" Mommy's voice is a siren.

I nod, and then there are more questions and my head is so full. I'm still scared he's coming back. I cry and cry.

Daddy finds security, and they call the police.

Kodiak's daddy comes and takes him and my brothers away.

There's a policewoman in the room with me, and her eyes are soft and kind and sad. Mommy has to explain that I'm shy and have a hard time talking around people I don't know. I just want to go home, but they ask me questions about the man, and I try to answer them.

They give me a blanket, but it's scratchy on my legs.

I have an apple juice box and a sugar donut and an apple. I

don't like apple juice, because it tastes like metal, but I'm thirsty, so I drink it anyway.

The policewoman asks me questions that make my tummy hurt.

I throw up the donut, and that makes me cry even more.

Mommy tells me it's going to be okay, but I don't feel like it is.

Finally they stop asking questions. I'm glad because I don't like them. Then someone takes pictures of all of my bruises. I don't really know how I got them all. Daddy is angry, and Mommy tries to hide how sad she is.

I'm glad when they finally say we can go home.

Daddy carries me out to the car, and Mommy sits in the back seat with me. I snuggle into her hair, breathing in her shampoo, trying not to let the memories or the smells come back. I want to put on my favorite pajamas and hug my stuffed beaver and never leave my house again.

I want to feel safe.

Daddy carries me upstairs, and Mommy starts a bath for me. Daddy sets me on the stool beside the bathtub and kneels in front of me. I only have one shoe on. I don't know what happened to the other one.

My dress is filthy, covered in smudges of dirt. Kodiak's hoodie has a tear on one side, and there's crusty brown stuff all over the sleeves. I start to cry again, because everything is too much. I dig my nails into my palms, so I don't make any noise.

"Hey, hey, hey." Mommy pries my hands open. My palms are crusted in dried blood, and fresh blood wells in the cuts I've opened up. "Lavender, honey, who did this?"

"He said if I made a sound, I'd never see you again, so I screamed into my skin."

"I'm so sorry, sweetie. We'll never let anything bad happen to you ever again."

"What if he comes back?" I whisper. "What if he takes me again?"

"He won't, honey. I promise that's not going to happen."

I want to believe her, but the memories are still there—like a bad dream that doesn't go away. He lives in my head now, the biggest monster in there.

Later, after I'm all cleaned up and in fresh pajamas, Mommy makes me a snack. But I'm not hungry, and all I want is my bed and to make sure River is okay. I want to tell him it wasn't his fault that he couldn't keep hold of me.

I want everything to be the same as it was before.

But it isn't.

And I don't think it ever will be.

1

First Day Fuckery

LAVENDER

Present day, age 19

"HEY, LAV!" MY brother's fist slams against the bathroom door, and half a second later it flies open, scaring the living shit out of me as it bashes into the wall.

I jab myself in the eye with my mascara wand, and coffee sloshes down the front of my white tank. I was attempting to multitask. I should know better. "Ow! What the hell, Mav!" I cover my burning eye with my palm and drop my mug in the sink. The handle breaks off. "Goddammit! That was my favorite freaking mug. And I could've been naked!"

Maverick makes a gagging sound. "I just ate breakfast. Don't say things like that if you don't want me to hurl."

"Screw you, fuckboy." I try to close the door on him, but it's useless, since he's a damn giant and standing in the middle of the doorway. "And looking at your face makes me lose my appetite."

13

Much to my parents' dismay, Maverick is a certified manwhore. A monogamous one, but a manwhore nonetheless. Based on what I've learned from the girls who like to stop by our house—there are many—he hangs out with the same girl for exactly four weeks. And by "hang out," I mean, bones as often as possible.

My brother is not an ogre—far from it. Maverick looks like a damn supermodel with his wavy dark hair and ridiculously chiseled features. Girls and women fawn all over him. It's annoying.

"What are you doing busting into my bathroom at seven freaking thirty in the damn morning? I'm trying to get ready for class." Even though I'm a sophomore, it's my first day at a new school, and I'd like to start my second year of college on a positive note. Poking myself in the eye with my mascara wand is not very positive.

"Riv has to be at football practice, and I need to be at the arena in like, twenty. Have you seen my car keys?"

"Why would I know where your car keys are?" I drop my palm and glance at my reflection in the mirror. Awesome. Now it looks like I'm part raccoon with the mascara smeared around my eye.

"Mav, we gotta roll out or we're gonna be late," my twin brother, River, yells from somewhere in the house.

Maverick runs his hand through his hair. It falls back into place as though it's made of perfectly obedient soldiers. "Where are *your* keys?"

"You can't take my car." I prop my fist on my hip. "Take River's."

"Some chick puked in the back seat last night, and it needs to be detailed." Mav taps on the doorframe, impatient.

"And that's my fault, how?" I do not want to know the how and why regarding the puking girl. River isn't quite as bad as

Maverick, but he still has a ridiculous number of girls fawning all over him at any given time—and that's even with his less-than-glowing personality. Or possibly because of it.

Maverick glances to the right, just outside the bathroom door, and a sly smile turns up the corner of his mouth. He snatches my keys from my dresser and dangles them from his finger. "We'll owe you one, sis."

I jump up, trying to grab them back, but my brother is over six feet, and I'm five one and a quarter—that quarter is very important to me—so there is absolutely zero chance I can reach my keys when he's holding them over his head. "You can't leave me without my car!"

"You can walk in a straight line, Lav. You'll be fine." He strolls down the hall, and I scale his back in an attempt to reclaim my keys, but my contact lens is burning. It's distracting and means I can only hold on to my brother with one arm while I press my palm against my watering eye. He hits the first flight of stairs and takes them at a jog, bumping me around on his back.

I somehow manage to jam my big toe into one of his belt loops, and it gets stuck there.

He drags me along like an awkward sloth he can't shake. "My class is all the way across campus. It's a half-hour walk, and it starts at eight thirty!"

"It's not that far. You'll be fine."

The doorbell rings as we pass through the living room.

River stands in the kitchen, shoving half a bagel slathered in cream cheese into his mouth while texting. He frowns—this is his most common facial expression—and glances from the door to Maverick to me still hanging off his back. He crosses the room in two angry strides and throws the door open. He spins around, pinning our older brother with a disgusted look and thumbs over his shoulder. "This asshole has to sit in the back seat so I don't have to look at his face."

Standing in the doorway is Kodiak Bowman, more commonly referred to as Kody by everyone other than me. We all grew up together, basically, and probably know one another better than we should. Like the place he was conceived, Kodiak possesses a rare kind of arctic beauty. His hair is almost black, his eyes a pale green that doesn't look quite natural, and his features hover between severe and exotic. But when he smiles, there's a dimple in his left cheek that makes him look boyish and melts the panties of anyone with double X chromosomes. And a lot of XYs as well.

He's not paying attention to my twin, because he's too busy staring at his phone. Probably arranging a lunchtime blowjob.

Both he and Maverick are here at school on hockey scholarships. Not only is Kodiak an incredibly talented player like his dad, he's also a genius, like his mother. But unlike his mother, who is a saint, Kodiak is an asshole.

My twin harbors a particularly severe disdain toward him. Because of me.

Something happened involving Kodiak two years ago, which was so devastatingly embarrassing for me that I wish I could scrub the memory from my brain. River received the stripped-down version of events, and I made him promise to never, ever speak of it. He never asked any more about it, and I never offered any further details. However, now River can't stand Kodiak, and he wasn't his biggest fan in the first place.

Kodiak ignores River. "We gotta roll, Mav, or we're gonna be late."

Maverick peels my fingers from his shoulder. "Can you get the fuck off me, please?"

My toe is still caught in his belt loop, so I fall back, and because I have no coordination or balance—thank you so much for that, Mom—I smack my head on the floor. I also shriek because my toe is bent at a very unpleasant angle. Maverick stumbles back a couple of steps, trying to figure out how I'm still attached to him.

"My toe is caught! Oh my God! You're going to break it!" I scream at the top of my lungs.

It's ironic, because when I was a kid, I didn't talk much. River used to do a lot of the talking for me because I was shy and got all tongue-tied around people I didn't know. He was trying to be a good brother. Unfortunately, it made me reliant on him for a lot of things for a lot of years.

I've also been highly insulated by my family. It's like living inside a bubble, viewing the world from behind a screen and never fully participating in it. For someone raised in a highly stable, incredibly supportive, loving—albeit weird—family, I'm pretty damn messed up.

Maverick manages to get me untangled from his belt loop without breaking my toe. I jump to my feet, and because my embarrassment hasn't hit epic levels yet this morning, my boob pops out of my tank.

"For the love of God, Lav! Put your tit away!" Maverick yells.

"It's not my fault it fell out!" It's genetics.

Kodiak glances up from his phone as I tuck my boob back inside my tank. His expression remains flat, as if he's completely unaffected by the fact that my nipple was just eyeing him.

Because he is. Completely unaffected.

Unlike me. I can't even form a full, coherent sentence around him anymore.

I'm sure my face is red and blotchy with humiliation. Again.

Kodiak always seems to have a front-row seat to these awful moments.

"I hope you all sprain your groins at practice." I spin around and head for the stairs.

"I'll find you in the quad after your first class, okay, Lav?" River calls after me.

"Whatever." I stomp my way back up to my room.

I should've fought harder for on-campus housing. Even the all-girls dorm would've been better than living with my damn brothers. But there was no chance my parents would ever let me live in a dorm—too many unknowns and uncontrollable variables. And River, being the overprotective twin that he is, had a meltdown over the idea that I would even *consider* the dorms as an option.

The only reason my parents conceded to me moving away from home is because I'm living with my brothers, and I'm only about an hour away. Once high school was over, we packed up our house and moved to what used to be our cottage on Lake Geneva, in Wisconsin, which is much closer to Chicago than Seattle was. And don't be fooled by "cottage"—it's really a huge house on a lake.

And now, after years spent avoiding Kodiak—apart from that one, horribly mortifying incident—I'm going to have to deal with him again. Probably on a regular basis.

So I'm here, feeling a lot like I'm moving backward instead of forward. Because instead of fighting for what I wanted, I've let everyone else's fears dictate my choices.

2

And the First Day Fuckery Continues

LAVENDER

Present day

THANKS TO MY brothers, I have to rush to get ready for my first class. I also end up having to wear my glasses instead of my contacts because the eye I stabbed with my mascara wand won't stop watering.

I pull one of my handcrafted dresses over my head—I make all my clothes and have since I could operate a sewing machine. I slip my feet into a pair of flats, grab my backpack, and speed-walk all the way across campus to get to class on time.

I don't take Uber or cabs because I won't get into a vehicle with someone I don't know. I also don't like public transit because there are too many people I don't know in a small space. Most of the time, it's not a problem because I have a car, or I can get a ride with my brothers, if I need one. Except when my brothers screw me over like they've done this morning.

On the upside, I'm starting today with a class I'm looking

forward to—costume and set design. Unfortunately it's at eight thirty on Mondays and Wednesdays. Usually only drama majors are allowed to register for this class, but because of my transcripts, my heavy involvement in both school and community theater, and the letter from Queenie, who is still my therapist, I was able to enroll. I was also granted special permission to take a visual arts class, thanks again to Queenie and my dad's generous donation to both the school hockey team and the arts department. It doesn't hurt that my dad is a hockey legend.

Is it nepotism? Sure. Do I feel bad that I'm potentially taking a spot from someone? Sure. But I worked hard for this, and the only reason I haven't declared my major yet is because my parents thought it would be better for me to stick to general classes until the end of my sophomore year. Had my parents not been so adamant, I would be a theater major already.

I don't necessarily disagree with taking a little bit of everything if you're uncertain of your future path. Maverick's already changed his major twice. He started in physics and then switched to chemistry and eventually decided he wanted to go the kinesiology route. All his courses have really long names, and the textbooks are so thick, they could stop a bullet. I may have forgotten to mention that while Mav is a fuckboy and a hockey player, he too is shockingly smart. Maybe not as smart as Kodiak, but pretty damn close.

But I, unlike my brothers, already know exactly what I want to do. My goal this year is to appease my parents, who are afraid attending college away from home is going to overwhelm me. They also don't want me to lock myself into something too specific and close any doors before they think I'm ready.

I love them, but the overprotective bullshit can be a lot to handle. I get it, but it's still tough to deal with at times.

I jog up the steps of the art building with only five minutes to spare. Of course, because I'm in a rush, I trip halfway up. My glasses, which I try not to wear unless I'm in the privacy of my own home, slip off and land facedown on the steps. It would be fine if my knee didn't then land right on top of them. The crunch is ominous and telling.

"Crap."

I scramble to right myself as a pair of hands slip under my arms and someone helps me to my feet.

"Are you okay?"

The voice belongs to a guy. *Awesome.* Today can suck a set of old man balls.

"Yeah, being top-heavy makes walking tough," I mumble. Of course those are the first words out of my mouth. Sometimes I wish I were still as tongue-tied as I was when I was younger.

"Pardon? I didn't catch that."

"I'm fine, thanks. Just embarrassed." I smooth my skirt and tip my head back. I'm short. I always have to look up. At everyone. Except for small children and pets.

The guy in front of me is only mildly blurry. It's possible he may be cute. He's tallish, maybe around six feet, although to be fair, almost anyone seems tall to me. His dark hair is cropped short and he's wearing thick-rimmed black glasses. And a Hufflepuff T-shirt.

He bends to retrieve my glasses with a grimace. They're in two pieces, and the lenses are scratched to hell. "I think you have a casualty."

"I have spares at home." Because I'm clumsy and this isn't the first time I've landed on my own glasses—not that the spares are going to help me during this class. At least I have a break between this one and the next, so I can go home and grab a backup pair. I shove the broken glasses in the front pocket of my backpack. I don't know why I don't toss them in the trash. It's not like there's any hope of fixing them.

"Are you heading in?" My savior inclines his head toward the doors.

"Oh, yeah." I slip my hand into my skirt pocket—all my dresses have pockets, because it's convenient and prevents me from hand-talking—and pull out my phone. I have to bring it right up to my face to make out the time. "Crap, I have four minutes to get to class."

"What're you taking?"

"Costume and set design."

"Really? Me too. We can go together."

"Sure. Great, thank you. I'm so freaking blind without my glasses, I can't read the numbers on the doors unless my nose is almost pressed against the wall." That's a slight exaggeration, but not much.

My new friend taps his glasses. "I'll be the eyes for both of us. I'm Josiah, by the way."

"I'm Lavender."

"That's a cool name." He smiles blurrily. "It's nice to meet you, Lavender."

"You too, Josiah."

We rush the rest of the way up the steps. Thankfully, our class is close to the entrance, and we slip in with a minute to spare. It smells like rich fabric and the metallic tang of electricity, sewing machines, wood, and paint.

"Oh my God," I half moan in a whisper. "I wish I could see this room clearly. It smells like heaven."

I follow Josiah to the blob of students arranged in a semicircle on one side of the room. We take the last two seats at the edge, and Professor Martin starts calling names. As usual, I'm last on the list.

Once roll has been called, our professor reviews the syllabus. Luckily, I have a tablet, and Josiah lends me his glasses for a minute so I can make the font huge enough to take notes I can read. Basically it's a sentence a page, but it's better than nothing. We spend half the time playing icebreaker games, and in the last twenty minutes, we have to write a couple of paragraphs on what we hope to get out of this class.

Most of the students in this course are super outgoing. I'm the exact opposite, since all I ever want to do is hang out backstage or work behind the scenes, but I survive.

"Are you a theater major?" Josiah asks when we're on our way out the door.

I shake my head. "I'm undeclared until next year."

"Really? How'd you manage to get in that class? It's supposed to be for drama majors only."

"Uh, usually that's true. I have special permission. I did a lot of costume and set design in high school and community theater, so they let me take it." It's partly the truth.

"Oh, well that's . . . cool. What other classes are you taking?" He sounds genuinely interested.

"Um, hold on . . . I'll show you my schedule, and you can tell me if we have any together, since I can't see anything right now." I set my bag on a bench, retrieve my binder, and pass it over to him. It would be nice to know someone in more than one class. The whole getting-to-know-people thing is stressful, and I'm always inclined to say dumb, embarrassing things when I'm nervous, which is a lot of the time.

"Looks like this is the only class we have together. But I'm meeting some friends for coffee now, if you want to come?"

"Oh, I would really love to, but I have to go home and pick up my spare glasses. Otherwise I'm going to have a killer headache by the end of the day." I tap my temple. "Maybe if you're going after class on Wednesday, I could come with you?"

Josiah smiles. "Yeah, sure. Should we trade numbers?"

"That'd be great. You'll have to add yours for me, though." I pass my phone over as it vibrates.

23

"Uh, Twinsie is texting you?"

"That's my twin brother."

"You have a twin? That must be kind of cool."

"It can be. It can also be a giant pain in my ass."

I use the text-to-speech function to find out where River is hanging out between classes. He's all the way on the other side of campus, still with his football buddies, and Maverick has my car keys.

Thank the Lord for speech to text. Mav is in the quad, which isn't far away, and Josiah, being the nice guy he is, offers to walk me over since I can't see well enough to make out the names of buildings, or read any of the posted signs unless I'm six inches away from them.

As we draw near, Maverick's laugh can be heard through the entire quad, along with the sound of simpering girls. At least River isn't around to act like a rabid, angry guard dog, snapping at Josiah's heels. He's adept at scaring off guys.

"Thanks so much for being my guide," I say.

"It's really no problem. I'd be in the same predicament if I broke my glasses." Josiah pushes his up his nose.

"Holy shit, Lav!" Mav shouts and is suddenly all up in our personal space. He grabs Josiah's hand and starts pumping it. I half expect water to come spraying out of his mouth, it's so vigorous. "This is so exciting! You made a friend!"

"Oh my God, will you shut the hell up?" If I could see properly, I'd kick him in the nuts.

He finally lets go of Josiah's hand and wraps his arm around my shoulder. "I'm just so proud of you. I'm Lavender's embarrassing-as-fuck older brother Maverick."

"I'm sure he's already figured out the embarrassing-as-fuck part. Can you lower your voice and turn your younger-sister-humiliation dial down from a ten to a more respectable two or three?" As annoying as this outburst is, Maverick is probably the least overprotective of my family members.

"I can maybe take it down to a five, at best. You gonna stage a formal introduction, or what?"

"Maverick, this is Josiah. I tripped this morning and broke my glasses, and Josiah has graciously lent me his eyes so I could find you, although I'm sure he's very much regretting that now."

"Just imagine how much more he'd regret it if it was Riv he was meeting."

He has a point.

I turn to Josiah. "Anyway, thanks so much for helping me out today. I know you're meeting friends, and I don't want to hold you up." I'm 100 percent giving him an out and hoping he takes it before Mav says something else embarrassing.

"Honestly, it's no problem. I'll see you on Wednesday?"

"For sure." I nod.

"Nice to meet you, Maverick."

"You too, man." He waits until Josiah walks away. "Look at you! Making new friends on day one. Just don't introduce him to your feral twin, and you'll be fine."

"I don't know what was worse, living at home last year or living with you two now."

While River went to Chicago and lived on campus, where literally everyone we know is, I got to live at home in Lake Geneva with my parents and take a general year at the local college. In hindsight, I think it was the right move for me. Did it suck to miss out on all the stuff that comes with living away from home? And was it hard knowing that pretty much my entire network of friends and cousins were out here? Yup. But it was nice being away from my overprotective brothers. I even had a boyfriend that no one threatened to murder. It was an experience I needed and wanted. That relationship only lasted a few months, but I managed to get in some great experimental learning since he had his own room on campus.

"At least now you have some freedom." Mav tosses my keys at me. They fall to the ground because I can't see them, and my ability to catch is questionable on a good day with glasses.

"I can't see to drive, Mav." I point to my face and nearly poke myself in the eye.

"Oh, shit, right." He bends to retrieve them. "Huh, well, I have class in ten. I could take you after that?"

"You know what? It's fine. I'll walk."

"I'll take her." Kodiak's deep voice makes the hairs on my arms stand on end.

"See, perfect? Thanks, K." Mav is all smiles and cluelessness as he pats Kodiak on the back, slings his backpack over his shoulder, and takes off.

"You don't have to drive me home. I probably have a spare pair in the glove box," I mutter. I'm sure my face is on fire. The humiliation from the last time I was alone with him comes flooding back, like blood rushing to a fresh wound.

"You're gonna need to know where the car is parked, regardless." He's so close, it's hard to breathe.

I'm glad I can't see him clearly. I want to tell him to go fuck himself, but the words get trapped in my throat. It didn't used to be like this. For a long time, Kodiak was my safe space. We used to tell each other everything. I thought he was my soul mate—until I screwed everything up and made him hate me, and then he went and made sure I hated him back.

"Let's go. I don't have all day."

I practically run to keep up with his long strides.

I want to make some kind of cheeky remark, but the last time I spoke to Kodiak, the results were less than desirable, so it's better for me to keep my mouth shut. Besides, there's a good chance I'll trip over my words like I trip over my feet.

Tears of frustration and embarrassment prick at my eyes. I feel stupid. Clumsy. Unwanted. A nuisance. Girls whisper his name as we pass, and one falls into step beside him, asking about some party on Friday.

He barely acknowledges her, aloof as always.

"Who's your friend?" she asks.

I don't bother to look at her or give any indication that I'm aware I'm being talked about as though I don't exist.

"No one you need to concern yourself with. See you at the party on Friday." He snaps his fingers at me, like I'm a dog. "Come on, pick up the pace."

I follow him across the parking lot, teeth clenched, fighting the urge to scream or cry. This is so humiliating.

My car beeps, and I rush around to the passenger side, but Kodiak has only unlocked the driver's side door, so I yank on it twice and then have to wait until he feels like hitting the button a second time.

"Please let there be glasses in here somewhere." I slide into the passenger seat and flick open the glove compartment, pulling out the manual and insurance papers in hopes that I'll find something, anything. Even an old pair with the wrong prescription would be welcome. Or forgotten contact lenses.

Kodiak opens the driver's side door and bends over to slide the key in the ignition and roll down the windows before he closes the door again and leans against it, talking to yet another girl.

Suddenly my car is filled with sound. But it's not music. It's one of my audiobooks. Specifically, a smutty audiobook. And it's right in the middle of a particularly smutty chapter. Because that's what I was listening to last night when I went to bed, and my phone automatically syncs to the sound system.

Some people read books or listen to music before bed. I listen to sexy books. It's way better than porn. The guys are always super attentive, and the women always have seven billion orgasms. And the hero always gives great oral. It's the ultimate fantasy. Except last night I decided to try out a new genre: reverse harem. It seemed like it might be female-empowering, which is alluring when you're me—not the actual reverse harem-ing, but feeling empowered.

"You wanna ride our cocks, baby?" the very sexy, gritty male voice blasts through my amazing sound system. "Both of our cocks?"

"Oh my God." I frantically search for my phone, but it falls to the floor and slides under the seat. Of fucking course. I slap blindly at the dash, trying to find the volume button, but instead of turning it down, I turn it up, right as graphic penetration happens.

I finally find the volume control and mute the damn thing, but it's too late. Anyone within a mile radius has heard the literary porn. My mortification is extreme. I sink down in the seat, hiding behind my hair, the sound of laughter outside the car like needles under my skin.

I feel like I'm a kid again—standing in the middle of the playground, someone making fun of me, calling me weird. *Why doesn't she talk above a whisper?* Everyone looking at me. Laughing. Until River stepped in. Or Kodiak, before he hated me.

But River's not here. And Kodiak can't even stand to look at me. Why he offered to drive me home is another huge question mark. Unless he's just looking for an opportunity to torment me.

My face is on fire. My entire body breaks out in a cold sweat. I can't get out of the car, not with all these people around. It makes me feel trapped, and I hate it.

Kodiak finally opens the driver's side door. "You find your spares?"

I shake my head, refusing to look at him.

"Is that a no?"

I purse my lips and remain silent.

Kodiak sighs. "I gotta take this one home. See ya Friday."

He gets in, closing the door with a slam. He takes his time adjusting the mirrors, and it hits me how close he is. Some things haven't changed in the past two years: same deodorant, same body wash, same cologne, same hair product, same asshole.

My eyes burn with the threat of tears, but I refuse to let them fall. I will not give Kodiak the satisfaction of seeing me cry ever again. I hate him so much for so many things, but this unnecessary humiliation is currently at the forefront, the things he said to me two years ago a very, very close second.

"Didn't realize you're into the whole tag-team thing." His voice is flat, apathetic.

I focus on remaining still. On breathing.

"Is that what you and all the drama geeks get up to back-stage? You find a nice quiet spot behind the curtains and get yourself good and fucked?"

I want to say something scathing, like I'm surprised that's not *his* thing, since his dad was into threesomes back when he was Kodiak's age. Although, the version of Kodiak's dad I know is a really good guy, and doesn't seem like the type who would bang two girls in a hot tub. However, there's a really, really old video floating around on the internet that proves it's true.

There are also about a thousand pictures of *my* dad with his tongue in different women's mouths. Apparently he didn't sleep with all the puck bunnies, he just made out with them in public. Including my mom. Having a famous parent can be a real pain in the ass, and far more informative than is normal.

My throat is tight, and anything I say is going to come out a pathetic whisper, if at all. So instead, I clench my fists to keep from fidgeting and try not to focus on Kodiak's hurtful words, or the memories being close to him incite.

"You got words for everyone else, but none for me?" he taunts.

I stare straight ahead, unwilling to look at his horrible, beautiful face. I weigh my response before I speak, trying to inject some steel into my spine, so it doesn't come out a weak whisper. "Why would I give you my words when all you do is twist them into something ugly?"

"Still living in the past?" Real emotion hides under his ire, a waver in his voice that I recognize: anxiety.

I let the things I want to say sit on my tongue like bitter pills and finally ask, "Why are you doing this?"

"To remind you nothing has changed, Lavender," he grinds out.

The boy I used to love never would've embarrassed me or talked down to me like this. And his current actions prove that what happened two years ago wasn't a mistake. He meant to hurt me then, and he means to hurt me now.

He pulls into the driveway, and I yank on the door handle, but it doesn't open, because the child locks are still engaged. "I hate you." I spit the words like nails.

He leans over the center console until he's so close, his face is clear and beautiful and so, so hideous in its perfection. His pale green eyes burn with emotions I don't understand, and the flecks of gold shine like refracted sunshine. "I don't believe that. Otherwise you wouldn't have gotten into this car with me."

I can feel his humid, minty breath on my lips.

He drapes his arm across the back of my seat, and his fingertips brush my neck. I jerk back and slap his hand away.

Kodiak frowns and grabs my wrist, prying my fist open.

I hate the way my body responds to the contact, a shiver

working its way down my spine, soothing but igniting at the same time.

"What the fuck?" He twists my hand so I can see what he does. "You really haven't changed at all, have you?" There's something in his voice that doesn't quite match, an emotion I can't put my finger on—maybe because he's touching me and I hate it as much as I crave it.

Four crescent-shaped marks line my palm, and I'm mortified all over again when thin lines of blood well from the fresh cuts. I yank my hand away. "Let me out." It's barely a whisper.

"Lavender." Dismay lurks in my name.

I find my voice, finally, and its strength is fueled by my anger. "Let me out. *Now*."

"I should've known better," he gripes and hits the unlock button.

I throw the door open and clamber out, slinging my backpack over my shoulder.

Kodiak cuts the engine and gets out of the car, calling my name again.

I give him the bird without looking back. He doesn't deserve any more of my words.

3

Too Far

KODIAK

Present day, age 21

LAVENDER STALKS UP the stairs to the front porch, jabs in the code, and disappears inside the house. The door slams behind her.

She leaves a bloody smear on the doorknob.

I glance down at the back of my hand, also streaked with her blood. It takes me back to when we were kids and makes my stomach turn.

Instead of acting like a normal human being, I humiliated her. Again.

Publicly this time.

And she took it out on herself.

Nothing ever changes with Lavender. Except that's not entirely true. She's definitely not a gawky, gangly teenager anymore. That much is obvious.

I scrub my face and debate my options, which are limited. I

knew this was coming. Just before high school, my family moved across the country. Since then, I've spent more than half a decade avoiding every possible situation in which I might inadvertently run into Lavender. It was easier when we weren't living on the same street, going to the same school. And I was managing fine, until the holidays two years ago when she showed up drunk, dressed like goddamn Wonder Woman.

At the time, I'd stupidly thought I could handle seeing her after years of nothing. I'd obviously been wrong. The last time I'd seen her—prior to the Wonder Woman fiasco—she'd been a middle schooler, and I'd been on the verge of starting high school. A lot changes between the ages of twelve and seventeen, and that was extra true for Lavender.

It was my only huge slipup in all those years. But I never fully recovered from it—obviously still haven't, considering I just drove her home and made her feel like shit because I can't control my mouth.

For years, I managed to have something important to do during get-togethers with the Waters. I'd cry anxiety, skip the dinner/family/social garbage, and tell my mom I had to study, or a paper was due. I found ways to spend time with Maverick without subjecting myself to Lavender. It was better that way—for both of us, but mostly for her.

My mom knew there was something else going on. She always knows. And because everyone believes Lavender is fragile like glass, she let me get away with it. Until two years ago. The aftermath from that was a downward spiral that took months to come out of. Thankfully, I was in college already, away from home, so I could mostly wallow in my own self-loathing without parental observation.

There's no avoiding Lavender anymore, though. Not with her living in the same house as my best friend, away from her parents.

I'd grown complacent with time, secure in my self-control. But today is a reminder of exactly what I'm facing again, and it pisses me off. I don't need this bullshit—her weakness, her dependency on everyone around her.

She's going to be there every time I turn around, with those blue eyes and those pouty lips. A constant reminder of all the ways I've fucked up. It's a nightmare.

I'm betting River is the reason she's here. I know twins have a thing, but the way he is with her is borderline psychotic—more so than the way things used to be with her and me. And that was pretty messed up.

I don't have the energy to deal with more of Lavender, so I grab my hockey equipment from the trunk of her car and slip the keys in the mail slot. Then I walk to the house three doors down, where I live with Quinn Romero, one of my fellow hockey teammates, and BJ Ballistic. Our fathers have been friends our entire lives, and it made sense for them to pool resources and buy a house for us to live in while we're here.

They all played on the same NHL team for a while, and when they retired, they decided to start a foundation—a hockey training program that subsidizes the costs for kids who otherwise wouldn't be able to play competitively. Hockey is expensive and time-consuming.

When I enter, Liam, one of the Butterson twins and Maverick's older cousin, is chilling in a gaming chair, one earbud dangling loose, messing around with a set of metal rings —I think it's some kind of brainteaser, or a sex toy, who knows? He lives a few blocks over with his twin brother, Lane, but he spends a lot of time with Quinn, which explains why he's here. BJ, otherwise known as Randy Ballistic Jr., is passed out in the lounger, one hand cupping his junk.

Quinn is sitting on the couch, playing a video game, with some blonde girl I've never seen before all up in his space. He's on the rebound and taking the breakup particularly hard, from what I've witnessed. The girl's wearing a pair of tiny shorts and a crop top. Based on the way her nipples are saluting everyone, she's not wearing a bra. A broken necklace of purple hickies decorates her throat. She glances up from her phone, and her mouth drops open. "Oh em gee! Kody Bowman! You are so flip- ping hot."

Quinn pauses the game and gives her a look that would bury most people. "Could you be less chill?"

"Geez. It's just an observation." She makes this face like she can't believe he'd get upset about the comment.

"You were all over me less than half an hour ago. Give it a few hours before you go after my roommate." It half sounds like he's joking, half not.

Liam makes a noise, as if he's waiting for shit to go down.

"So, you guys do share, then?" The blonde twists the end of her ponytail around her finger. When we all just stare at her, she tacks on, "And you're hot too, Quinn, just . . . different hot."

Quinn rolls his eyes and tosses aside the controller. "I gotta roll out. Enjoy my friends." He stalks across the room, brushes by me, grumbling about bad choices, and slams his way outside.

I can already predict where he's headed: the garage. There's a gym out there with a punching bag, which we've had to replace more than once because Quinn uses it a lot. He's a good guy with a big temper, which he tries to control with nonharmful outlets.

The blonde sits there, eyes wide, and repeats, "It wasn't an insult."

"It kinda was, though," Liam says.

I don't stick around to hear her flawed defense. Instead, I head upstairs. I want to shower again before my next class because I had practice, and I don't like the showers at the arena. Technically there's nothing wrong with the facilities, but I have issues with public showers and bathrooms and their questionable cleanliness. I have issues with a lot of things, actually.

I unlock my door—it's always locked unless I'm in my room. I might like my housemates, but I don't necessarily trust anyone they bring back here not to go snooping around—see the girl downstairs for details. My dad taught me that one.

I have two hours before my next class, so before the shower, the first thing I do is sit at my computer desk and open the bottom drawer of my filing cabinet. I lift the false bottom and sift through the contents until my fingers close around a stack of old photos.

I freeze at the sound of a soft knock on my door.

I don't even have a chance to say anything, such as *fuck off and leave me alone,* before the knob turns, and I instantly regret not locking it. A blonde head appears. Obviously this girl is clueless. Or desperate. Or both.

I drop the photos and close the filing cabinet on an annoyed sigh. Turning the key, I slip it out of the lock and toss it in the top drawer of my desk, sliding a few miscellaneous items over it before I close that too.

I spin in my chair as she steps inside and shuts the door behind her. She scans the room, taking in my personal space. I don't like people I don't know in my room. I don't like people much period.

The list of humans I tolerate and who tolerate me on a regular basis is fairly short.

"Wow. Your room is really clean." She lets go of the doorknob and crosses over to my bed. Taking a seat on the edge, she smooths her hand over my comforter. "Is this a king?"

"What're you doing in here?"

She lifts a shoulder and lets it fall, gaze shifting from the hockey posters on my wall to the raw canvas I never bothered to have framed, and back to me. "I was curious."

"About?" I bite, even though it's essentially pointless.

"You."

I remain silent, because that's not really an answer.

She crosses her legs. They're long and toned, and mostly bare because her shorts cover very little. Her top leaves the vast majority of her tanned stomach exposed. There's nothing particularly unique or compelling about her features. I guess she would be considered attractive in the general sense of the word. But her desperation is unappealing.

She drags a single finger along the neckline of her top purposely drawing attention to her cleavage. Compared to Lavender's, it's pretty unimpressive. Which is something I hate myself for thinking.

She gives me what I imagine is supposed to be a coy look. "Can I tell you something?"

"Seems like that's your plan."

Her laugh is high-pitched and nervous, her bravado faltering. "I wasn't really interested in Quinn."

"Probably shouldn't have hooked up with him then, huh?" What's with this girl?

She licks her lips. "I really came here for you."

"Is that right?" I don't feel like entertaining this after what happened with Lavender.

She nods. "I don't have class until five."

It doesn't take a genius to see where she's going with this. "You were just with my roommate."

"He said I could have fun with his friends, though, and I'd like to have some fun with you."

Her persistence isn't a turn-on. Not for me. Liam isn't interested in the bunnies, so if she propositioned him, I'm pretty sure he said no. BJ might bang her, even if she's been with more than one of us, but she'd have to wake him up, and he sleeps like the dead.

"You realize that would basically make you the house bunny."

She bites her lip. "I kind of figured that would be the case. And I don't mind, so long as I get to fuck you."

I'd like to say this kind of behavior is uncommon. But it's not. And unfortunately, Quinn, who is not very discerning as of late, has made a habit of picking up exactly this kind of girl.

"Are you high?"

"No." She laughs. "Do I look high?"

It's my turn to shrug. "Not particularly, but it's always a possibility."

"I know exactly what I'm doing."

I run my hands down my thighs, noting the dried streak of Lavender's blood still staining my skin. Driving her home was a reckless mistake. I should know better than to think I have control when it comes to her. All I want is to get her out of my head. "I don't have condoms."

She stands and digs into her pocket, tossing a few foil packets on my bedspread. "I came prepared."

4

And I Thought This Morning was Bad

LAVENDER

Present day

I T TAKES ME twenty minutes to find my glasses, in part because the second I close—and lock—the door, leaving Kodiak standing in the driveway, I lose my shit. As in, I start bawling like a toddler who lost her favorite binkie.

A lovely panic attack ensues, because I'm terrified I won't be able to stop crying now that I've started. I don't like tears. They exacerbate my anxiety, which is often present, and once the spiral hits, it can be tough to get out of.

Also, trying to find a pair of glasses while crying isn't easy, especially since my vision is crap to begin with. Eventually, I manage to get myself together. I put in some eye drops, wait for the redness to abate, and pop in my contacts.

My left eye doesn't feel like it has sand in it anymore, so I'm thinking I might be able to get away with contacts for at least a few hours. I have to reapply concealer and fix my makeup, thanks to the tears, but at least I can see again. And if nothing else, my car is mine for the rest of the day. Screw my asshole brothers.

I hate that Kodiak, who used to be the answer to calming my attacks, now incites them. I hate that he affects me at all, and that I *don't* affect him.

"You and me? We're toxic together." I rub my temples and squash the memories, packing them into the box in my head where I store all the things I don't want.

The worst part is, he wasn't wrong then, and he isn't now. Five minutes trapped in a car with him, and I'm already a mess. Thinking I'd be able to handle seeing him again was stupid. If I'd stayed at home for one more year, he'd have graduated by the time I got here, and I wouldn't be dealing with any of this.

I make sure I have my contacts case and a spare pair of glasses. It's a lot easier to find them when I can actually see more than a blur. I have forty-five minutes before my next class. I toss a few granola bars into my backpack so I have something to snack on and find my car keys downstairs on the floor under the mail slot. At least Kodiak didn't leave them in the ignition. I nab them from the mat and lock up behind me.

My stomach somersaults as someone steps out onto the front porch three doors down, which incidentally is where Kodiak happens to live with my cousin BJ—short for Balls Junior—and Quinn Romero. Quinn and Kodiak play hockey for the college team, as do a lot of the other guys who live on this street. So basically, I live on hockey row with a bunch of guys I'm related to—apart from Quinn and Kodiak, the latter of whom I loathe with the fire of a thousand burning yeast infections.

I'm instantly relieved the person on the front porch isn't Kodiak, or one of my cousins. It's just some girl. Probably a puck bunny, which is another thing I'm going to have to get used to again. Last year was a nice break from my brothers and their gaggle of endless girls.

I can only imagine what it would have been like if I'd come last year. River moved in with Maverick and my oldest brother, Robbie, and even I can admit my brothers have good genes and are easy on the eyes. This place probably had a revolving door of girls. So nasty. Robbie's now spending a year abroad, working on his master's, and I took his room.

River's football cleats are on the floor in the back seat, which accounts for the aroma of stinky feet in my car. I'm not sure how I missed it earlier—other than I was too busy being mortified. I pick them up by the laces and walk around the back of the house so I can leave them in the garage, which smells like sweat and stale sports equipment. However, there is a separate washer and dryer out here for their crap.

When I return to my car, the girl who was on Kodiak's front porch is strutting down the sidewalk. She's wearing heels, tiny shorts, and a crop top that barely covers her underboob. Her neck is dotted with purple suction marks, made all the more obvious on account of her haphazard ponytail. She's wearing earbuds, and apparently she's on a call and has no idea how loud she's being.

"Oh my God, you will never guess whose bedroom I was just in!" She barely takes a breath before screeching. "Kody Bowman, bitch! And oh em gee, he's so f'ing hot up close." She snaps her gum. "I know, right? And the best part? There's a party on Friday night, and we are so going." She glances in my direction, giving me a once-over before dismissing me as irrelevant. "I heard the whole team is gonna be there. It'll be a free for all."

My stomach feels like a lead weight has dropped into it. I shouldn't be the least bit surprised that Kodiak humiliated me, made me feel like a bag of shit, and then went back to his place and hooked up with some random girl five minutes later.

I don't want it to hurt.

But it does.

The nice boy who protected me, stood up for me, who honestly and truly cared is long gone, and in his place is a man I have no interest in knowing.

I watch the girl's retreating form and realize this is going to be my life this year. I wonder if I can still get on a list for the dorms.

5

Let Me Bury You in Crap

LAVENDER

Present day

WHEN I GET back to campus, all the parking lots are full. It takes half an hour to find a damn spot, so I have no time to grab coffee or food before my next class, which happens to be psychology. I'm well versed in things like cognitive behavioral therapy, so this class should be okay—except for group assignments. I hate those, because it often means talking to, and working with, people I don't know. Josiah was an anomaly this morning. I don't usually make friends easily because I can be shy and quiet and people mistake that for standoffishness. Hence, the majority of my friend base is made up of my extended family.

We didn't all end up here by accident. It started with Quinn and Robbie, who both happened to apply and get accepted. Then Liam and Lane followed, also ending up in

Chicago. By the time Maverick was submitting college applications it had become a running joke that we'd all end up in Chicago. Except both him and Kodiak were accepted too. Then Lacey, Lovey, and BJ all applied. By the time it was mine and River's turn it was assumed that we'd come out here, too, if we were accepted. Only I deferred my acceptance for a year.

After psych class, I meet up with my twin cousins Lacey and Lovey since I have some time to kill before my next class and no desire to go home. At least River, Maverick, and I aren't the only ones with odd names in our family. They're sisters to Liam and Lane, who are also twins.

I find them sitting in the back corner of the campus café, and of course, they're not alone. My cousin BJ is lounging in one of the chairs. His long legs are stretched out, and his head is tipped back, mouth hanging open, because he's passed out cold. There are three pencils stuck in his man bun, and someone's decorated his forehead with a row of reinforcement stickers.

"Lavy!" Lacey hops off the couch, jumps gracefully over BJ's legs, and pulls me into an enthusiastic hug. It means my face is almost mashed into her chest. Lacey and Lovey are willowy, and very nearly identical. There are subtle differences, but unless you know them well, it's almost impossible to tell them apart. They look very much like Barbie dolls come to life and are the kindest, most genuine girls I know. I'm so glad I'm going to school with them this year.

Lacey and Lovey are in their junior year, both studying public relations. They pledged the sorority and live off campus in a house with six other girls. They're involved in pretty much every fundraising event there is, and they're super outgoing. They invited me to pledge, but the idea alone makes my mouth dry, so I declined.

Lovey waits until I've made it past BJ before she gets up to hug me. "I love this dress! Do you think I can borrow it?"

Lovey is almost six feet tall, so I'm thinking the skirt would be a micro-mini at best, but if she's cool with her underwear showing, so am I. "If you want, sure."

They pull me down, so I'm sitting in the middle of the couch, sandwiched between them while they volley questions at me.

"How are you?"

"What's your schedule like?"

"Are your brothers driving you nuts yet?"

"Are there any cute guys in your classes?"

"Have you seen Quinn? I heard he got into a fight this morning *before* the guys even got on the ice," Lovey says, eyes wide and thumbnail between her teeth.

"Quinn is always getting into fights." Lacey rolls her eyes. "There's a party at our house this weekend. You should come and sleep over at our place! It'll be so fun!"

I make a time-out sign before they can launch any more questions. "Overwhelmed," I whisper and then realize, with horror, that I'm on the verge of tears and not sure why.

Well, that's not entirely accurate. Today has been a cluster-fuck, and I still have one more class before I can go home and eat all the marshmallows out of a box of Lucky Charms.

"Oh no!" they both whisper back, and suddenly I'm engulfed in a hug from both sides. "We're so sorry."

"We know better."

"Take deep breaths."

"I'm okay," I mumble, not wanting to draw more attention to myself.

They release me, but both shift at the same time, pulling one leg up so they can turn toward me, the movement synchronized.

"You don't seem okay," Lovey says softly and tucks my hair behind my ear.

"It's been a long day. And to answer your questions, yes, my brothers are driving me nuts, my schedule isn't bad, but today is heavy, and I didn't know about Quinn and the fight. It's not really a huge surprise, though." I adore Quinn, but he has a short fuse. "There's a nice guy in my costume and set design class who might be cute, but I couldn't see him very well because I didn't have my glasses, and let me think about the party. A sleepover would be fun, but we'll see if I can deal with the meeting new people part."

"The girls in the house are really chill, and the guys who come to our parties don't hang out with the hockey team, so you won't have to worry about your brothers showing up, or anyone else." Lacey chews her bottom lip and glances furtively at BJ, still passed out in the chair. He can literally sleep anywhere.

"Maybe."

Lovey grins and claps her hands. "Maybe is almost as good as a yes."

"And there will be tons of cute guys." Lacey waggles her brows.

I laugh and shake my head. "We'll see. As much as cute guys sound awesome, I'm not sure my brothers are going to make dating very easy this year."

"Hopefully they're too busy with sports and classes to pay attention to what you're doing." Lovey twirls the end of her hair around her finger. "Thankfully Liam and Lane live closer to hockey row, so they can't interfere with our dates."

Lovey and Lacey are the youngest of six, and they have four older brothers to my three, so they sort of understand where I'm coming from, but not completely.

"They're also super chill," I point out.

"This is true." They nod in tandem.

As much as the *idea* of a party excites me, the reality isn't at all the same. I want to be social, to have lots of friends like they do, to join clubs and be part of things, but I get so stressed out when there are too many people around. People think I'm weird.

Which I am, but in those situations, I end up looking weirder than average.

My stomach growls loud enough to startle me. I glance at the line of students. There are at least ten people waiting to order.

"Are you hungry? Do you want me to grab you a coffee? Something to eat?" Lovey offers.

"I can wait."

"I was about to get a tea. Tell me what you want, and I'll order it for you."

Even lines make me anxious. Sometimes people try to talk to me, and then I have to make polite conversation with strangers, and I don't have the energy left for that today.

I give her a grateful smile. "Okay. I'll take a decaf, coconut-milk latte and a scone or a muffin."

"That's it? They have sandwiches."

"A muffin is good."

"Nothing with raisins, though, right?"

"Right."

As soon as Lovey gets in line, she strikes up a conversation with the guy in front of her. She isn't even flirting. She's just nice.

Lacey and I talk about class schedules while we wait. Every few minutes someone stops to say hi. Lots of girls give BJ a sly second glance when they pass him. Like Lacey and Lovey, he's a junior, but unlike most twenty-one-year-olds, he's sporting a full, lush beard, better suited for someone at least five years his senior. He's also sporting a sizeable tattoo that spans from his wrist to his elbow, and he has plans to continue the art until he has a full sleeve, exactly like his dad. In fact, BJ is almost the spitting image of his father, apart from his chocolate-brown eyes, which are very much his mother's.

The other big difference is that instead of being into hockey like his dad, BJ is a figure skater—a tattooed, bearded figure skater, who hangs out with a bunch of hockey players. He gives off a zero-fucks vibe at all times. Since our mothers are half sisters, we've always spent a lot of time together, particularly during holidays.

When Lovey returns with food, BJ's eyes pop open. He yawns loudly and stretches. "Lavender? When'd you get here? How long have I been out?" His voice is low and raspy with sleep.

"A while ago." I help Lovey unload the tray of food. She was smart not to let me go up and order myself. There's no way I could carry the tray without spilling something. I'll never have a serving job; that's for sure.

BJ leans forward to scope out the goods. Before he can reach for something, Lovey shifts to block him, her hands on her hips. "What do you think you're doing?"

"I'm hungry," he says gruffly.

"And? You think you can pick whatever you want without even asking?" There's as much amusement in her tone as there is annoyance.

"I was just looking. Besides, the one thing I really want to chow down on is you, but you keep denying me."

"Oh my God! You're disgusting!" She shoves his shoulder.

BJ flops back in the chair, his grin full of mirth. Lovey's face is completely red as she huffs and throws herself back down on the couch, as far away from BJ as possible.

It doesn't matter that we've all grown up with him, or seen him in a full sequin leotard, he still hits on Lovey all the time.

BJ isn't related to the twins, so it's not quite as squicky as it would be if he flirted with me like that. I can't decide if he does it because it always gets a reaction or because he's a compulsive flirt. Then again, he doesn't do that with Lacey.

Before I can take a seat in the middle of the couch again, BJ grabs me by the waist and yanks me into the chair with him.

"What're you doing?"

"I need you to save me. A girl I hooked up with last semester walked in, and she's a stage-five clinger. Pretend like you're into me."

I make a gagging sound and try to get out of the chair, but the springs in the seat are shot, and my knees are practically at my chest. "Seriously, BJ, that's just wrong. We're related."

"She doesn't know that. Just stay put until she's gone." He wraps his arm around my shoulder to keep me seated.

I'm not sure if I'm embarrassed or entertained or both. BJ is ridiculously charismatic, and girls throw themselves at him on a regular basis.

A tall, blonde girl with her hair pulled up in a ponytail, fastened by a pink glitter bauble more suited to a six-year-old, wearing uber-short-shorts, a spaghetti-strap tank, and four-inch espadrilles sashays over, popping pink bubble gum. Interestingly, she looks a little like Lovey and Lacey, but a lot less wholesome.

She glances at me, eyes narrowing slightly, then turns a creepy, megawatt, lip-glossed smile on my cousin. "BJ! How are you? You remember me, right? We hooked up at that party at the end of last semester. I texted you after, and then left you a voicemail, but maybe you didn't get the messages."

"I got the messages." BJ's tone is flat.

"Oh." She twists the end of her ponytail around her finger. "I get it . . . end of year, you got busy with stuff."

"Uh, not really. I figured it was a one-off, so I didn't think calling or responding to text messages would give the right impression."

I don't know whether to be embarrassed for this girl and her obvious desperation or horrified by BJ's easy dismissal.

"Oh. Yeah. Totally." She nods a bunch of times. "I thought maybe you'd want to hook up again, but, like, maybe you're involved now, or whatever." She shoots me another scathing look. "Anyway, I heard there's a party this weekend, so if you're there, and you're, like, not attached, then we could hang out again or something . . ." The offer hangs in the air like a hot fart after taco Tuesday.

"It's probably not gonna happen. But you know, I appreciate the offer."

More nodding from the girl follows. "Okay, well, you can always text if you change your mind." And with that, she flounces off to the barista.

I shudder in disgust. "I can't believe that just happened. That was harsh."

BJ shrugs. "She's tried to screw every single guy on our street, so don't feel too bad for her. Three days ago, she tried to hook up with Liam when she was at our place, and when she realized he had a twin, she thought it would be fun to see if they were both game."

"Please don't share the outcome of that story."

"You know that's not Liam's style. Laughlin, maybe . . ."

Laughlin is their older brother, who has the personality of a vampire and the social skills of a gnat. It's crazy because Uncle Miller and Aunt Sunny are quite literally the nicest people on the face of the earth.

I shake my head. "Still, I don't know how you guys don't all have raging cases of incurable STIs at this point."

"Condoms are the answer to all of life's problems," BJ muses.

"Or you guys could choose *not* to screw the same girls." I try to pull myself out of the chair, but I'm wedged in.

"Yeah, but then you run the risk of getting emotionally involved, and I'm not ready for that."

BJ is unapologetic about his prolific sex life, and he never leads girls on. They just can't help but fall for him. The beard, the tattoos, the fact that he's a figure skater? He's also ridiculously well endowed, which I've been unfortunate enough to confirm with my own eyes, thanks to his lack of modesty.

The bell over the door tinkles, and a ripple of excitement moves through the café. I don't have to look to know who's graced everyone with his majestic presence because I can sense him, like a shadow darkening my already-shitty day. Again.

"Fuck my life." I stop trying to get out of the chair and try to sink farther into it instead. I keep my eyes trained on BJ's outstretched legs and will them to stay there.

"Ballistic, we need to talk." Kodiak's voice comes from my left. He's close enough that I can smell his cologne.

"Aboot?"

Like my dad, BJ's mom is Canadian, and for whatever reason, there are a few words where that accent bleeds through.

"Who you let into the house."

BJ shifts beside me, his arm stretching out across the back of the chair. "You weren't complaining this afternoon, from what I heard. And she wasn't mine; she was Quinn's."

I don't want to be here. I want to disappear. I don't want to listen to this, to be this close to Kodiak and hear him and BJ talk about the girls they have sex with. Particularly when only minutes before the girl currently in question, he was driving me home, making me feel like nothing. Then he hammered home the point by screwing a bunny right after.

"How would you know since you were passed out in the living room?" Kodiak counters. "And I talked to Quinn. I know it was you who brought her by. There are better ways to cheer him up."

"Says the guy who filled the hole Quinn didn't on our houseguest," BJ scoffs.

I'm almost glad I haven't had a chance to eat much today. I'd puke all over BJ's brand new trainers, otherwise.

"BJ, have some class!" Lovey hisses.

"Sometimes the truth is dark and dirty. Isn't that right, Bowman?"

I stiffen when Kodiak's hand lands on the arm of the chair, his fingers curling around it, the tips going white with the pressure. There's a brown smear on the back of his hand. He's a compulsive hand washer. Sometimes when he was younger, he'd wash them so much, his skin would crack and bleed.

"You have no idea what the truth is, and you really don't want to push me today."

A heavy silence weighs down on me. BJ traces a figure eight on my shoulder, and suddenly I can't breathe. It's purposeful. An intentional reminder that BJ knows the history Kodiak and I share in ways most don't.

"What's eating you today, Kody?" he asks. "You must've taken the extra-strength dickhead pill this morning."

"Fuck you, Balls."

"You're not really my type, but thanks for the offer."

"You're treading a thin line, and you know it." Kodiak moves away, but the heaviness in the air is slow to dissipate.

"Dude's got problems," BJ mutters and gives my arm a squeeze. "This isn't on you, Mini Waters."

I finally pull myself out of the chair. "I should probably get going. My class is on the other side of campus." I grab my latte and muffin, aware that class doesn't start for another half hour, but I need to get away from Kodiak and the inevitable questions I'll get from my cousins if I stick around. I can see Kodiak in the reflection in the windows, standing in line, making small talk with some starry-eyed girl.

No one calls me on bailing, because they know better. All of them know at least a little about my tumultuous past with Kodiak. But no one knows how bad things got, or how it all imploded, except him and me.

6

Locked Closet

KODIAK

Age 11

I'M SWEATY AND stiff from standing in the same place for long minutes. It's dark in this room, and I'm tired of being stuck behind this curtain. It's been too long. My hiding place is too good. Maverick is never going to find me.

Just as I think this, the door opens and the light flicks on, sending shadows up the walls. Maverick's footfalls are barely audible, but my heightened senses mean I can hear every tiny creak. I hold my breath, and a bead of perspiration trickles down my spine; anticipation makes my heart race. I need to take a deep breath to calm myself, but there's a chance Mav will hear me if I do.

I want to win, but anxiety slithers down my spine, making my skin itch. I always feel like I want to burst out of it when it gets bad—like I want to be outside of my body. I wish my brain would shut off every once in a while.

I don't think I can handle being stuck here with my thoughts if he moves on to another room without finding me. I missed a goal last night at hockey, and we lost. I can't stop thinking about what I should have done differently. I feel bad about it, and it's making me edgy.

I want to be still and silent inside, like Lavender is on the outside. Just thinking about her usually makes the spinning thoughts calm, but right now, it sends another uncomfortable jolt through me. *I'm done*, I decide. I move three inches to the right, causing the floorboard to squeak. Silence follows for a few agonizing seconds, and finally the curtain shifts to the side, light pouring in. I shield my eyes with my hand.

"Found him!" Maverick yells.

"It's about time. That took for-freaking-ever," BJ grumbles from the doorway.

I swipe my arm across my forehead. "You suck at this game, Mav."

"Whatever. This is boring and I'm hungry. Let's get a snack."

I follow Mav down to the kitchen with Lacey and Lovey, the Butterson twins, tagging along, their matching pigtails swinging. Their family and BJ's are visiting because it's a holiday. That's how it's always been; all of our families get together and celebrate.

Mav peeks around the corner, checking to see if anyone's looking, before he sneaks into the pantry and grabs a box of cookies and a bag of chips without asking the nanny. He tosses each of us a can of soda.

All of our parents are out for dinner, and that means the nannies get together and watch movies with the little kids while we get the run of the rest of the house. My mom would be mad if she knew I was eating chips and cookies after nine, but she's not here right now. I'll probably tell her later, though, because I don't like the way guilt feels. It gnaws inside my head and makes me restless.

We sneak back upstairs, creeping past Robbie's room. The door is closed, but we can hear the TV from the hall, and it smells like the inside of a gym bag or a science experiment.

Once we're safely back in Maverick's room, Lovey and Lacey cram themselves into the single beanbag chair and BJ sprawls on the couch. Maverick stretches out on his bed, and I take the gaming chair on the floor.

We pass around the cookies first, cracking sodas and munching on sugary treats. We polish them off in less than two minutes. Well, the twins are still nibbling theirs, but the rest are gone.

"Where are Lavender and River?" I ask, passing BJ the bag of chips.

"Probably watching a movie with the littles," Mav says, swiping through pictures on his phone.

"So you found them?" I press. That prickling feeling under my skin spreads, blanketing me.

"Yeah. I found River where he always hides."

In his room, under his covers. He only plays because we force him to and because Lavender likes hide-and-seek, even though she always picks the most obvious places to hide.

"And Lavender was with him?"

"Huh?" Maverick looks up from the screen.

"Lavender was with River?" I repeat. "You found her too?"

"No, but she always hides under the bed, so there was no point in checking." He rolls his eyes, annoyed with his siblings' predictability.

"Right." I can't swallow. My throat is suddenly all locked up. My palms sweat, and my hands ache. I push out of the chair and head for the door.

"Where you goin'?" Mav asks.

"Just to check." I pad down the hall to River's room, but he's not in there. I check under the bed, in case Lav fell asleep while she was hiding. It's happened before.

I move on to the next room and knock on the door before I peek inside. Lavender's room is peaceful chaos. Her artwork is tacked all over the walls, and her sewing machine sits in the corner, a pile of fabric on the table beside it.

Lavender is beyond talented. Everything she feels she puts on canvas and paper or binds together with a needle and thread.

But she's not here, and that horrible itch under my skin grows until I want to claw myself out of my own body. I run down the hall, taking the stairs too fast and sliding down the last few on my butt. I sprint to the media room, grip the doorjamb, and scan the seats and mats laid out on the floor where all the littles are. My baby sister, Aspen, is curled up facing the movie screen, but her eyes are closed. My younger brother, Dakota, is right beside her.

River is sitting in the front row, but there's no Lavender. I spin around and head for one of the other places I might find her—the art room. I take a deep breath to prepare myself for the overwhelming visual stimuli before I flick on the light. Every surface is covered in her ideas. Her thoughts are laid out in vibrant colors, pretty paintings, and designs that swirl and blend together. She told me once it's what she feels like inside most of the time, but usually darker.

I call her name and cross over to the closet because the door is open a crack, but it's empty too. Panic makes everything tight, and I try to think about where else she might hide, what her other favorite places are in the house. I rush back upstairs to the spare bedroom at the end of the hall that looks like it belongs to a princess, and push the door open. It slams against the wall with a startling thud as I call out, "Lavender, the game's over. Are you in here?"

A sound so feral, it makes the hairs on the back of my neck stand on end comes from the other side of the room. It's followed by an aggressive slam that makes the closet door rattle on its hinges.

I slide across the hardwood floor and try to turn the knob, but it's jammed or locked or something because I can't get it to turn. "Lavender? It's Kodiak. I think the door is stuck. I'm gonna get it open, okay?"

She wails from the other side, sounding more animal than human. I don't want to think about how long she's been stuck in there. Lavender hates the dark; she's afraid of the things she can't see. Ever since she was taken three years ago at a carnival. A lot of things changed after that night.

Lavender isn't just quiet anymore, she's something else— missing, even though she's here. She doesn't really remember what happened, but dark and small spaces make her nervous. And sometimes she has bad dreams that make her look tired.

I keep trying to turn the knob, but it won't budge. Once my baby sister locked herself in the bathroom, and I had to figure out how to get her out. I run into the bathroom and yank open the vanity drawer, searching for something I can use to pick the lock. I find a safety pin and prick myself trying to straighten it out. My hands are shaking, and the door keeps rattling, like Lavender's slamming herself against it. I try to jam the pin into the tiny hole, but it's hard with how slippery my hands are. I finally manage to slide it in, and I hear and feel the faint click and release.

I turn the knob and Lavender tumbles out, knocking me down. We land on the floor with a thud and an *oof*.

"It's okay, it's okay, it's okay," I repeat, sitting up and rearranging her stiff, shaking form. She curls into a tiny ball, her entire body convulsing with silent sobs.

Her hands are fists, and I can't see her face. Her auburn hair is a wild, tangled mess. I try to smooth it with my palm, like I've seen my mom do with my baby sister when she's upset. I register the wetness in my lap, the smell of urine and something metallic. I wrap my arms around her and rock her, telling her she's safe—reassuring myself as much as her.

Lavender is nine.

I've known her my entire life.

She is my secret best friend.

We're the same but different.

We're connected by invisible threads. I always seem to know when she's sad or scared. But no one really understands, so we don't try to explain. I feel sick with guilt that she was stuck in that closet with the monsters in her head.

Her panic is so big, it fills the room and seeps into me too. I rock with her, trying to make it better with my words, but that's not fixing it.

I shift so I can tip her head up and ask her to look at me, like my mom does when I have a hard time settling my bad thoughts. Her eyes are wild, distant, and filled with fear. Tearstains streak down her cheeks, her lids puffy and red from crying. But that's not the part that scares me the most. It's the streaks of blood on her cheeks and across her forehead. It's the teeth marks that have cut through the skin in her bottom lip and the fresh blood seeping from the wound, trickling slowly down her chin.

Dread wells inside me. I'm terrified they won't let us all hang out together anymore because of this, scared they're going to take her away from me, scared she's locked inside her head forever and I'm never going to get my friend back—that she'll be here, but totally gone now.

But I lock all the panic and the fears down in the box in my mind, like my therapist tells me to, because right now, Lavender needs me to be stronger than my fear. I take her blood- and tear-streaked face between my palms, wishing I knew if the cut on her lip was the only place she's hurt.

"Lavender, look at me. I'm right here," I whisper. "You're safe now." I repeat it until her gaze slowly meets mine.

Her whole body shakes every time she drags in a shallow breath.

"I'm right here," I reassure her.

"I-I-I," she stammers.

Lavender's words sometimes get stuck, like a beat skipping. It used to happen to me, but I outgrew it.

"It's okay," I reassure her. "I know you were scared. I'm sorry we didn't find you sooner. I can help, though." When I was really little and the worry got too big, my mom would always make it better. She said it was a distraction from the monster living in my head, and that when I didn't give the monster attention, it got smaller, and then it wasn't as scary anymore. So I do the same thing for Lavender, hoping I can make her monster small again. She's too upset to talk, though, and I can't do it the way my mom would, so I improvise.

I take her small hand in my clammy one. "Can you open for me?" My voice shakes with nerves.

She uncurls her fist. She's dug her nails into her skin so hard, there are weeping, crescent-shaped cuts spanning her palm.

Before she can see it, I press her hand against my chest and keep my own on top. The blood soaks through my cotton shirt. It's black, though, so it will disappear.

"Do you feel it?" I whisper, not needing to explain. She understands what I'm asking: Does she feel how fast my heart is beating? How scared I am too?

She gives me one jerky nod.

"Your fear is my fear," I say, just like my mom does when my heart is beating out of control and the panic takes over. "I feel what you feel."

Lavender blinks at me, eyes watery. She starts to bite her lip but flinches.

"It's okay. It's a little split. It'll be fine." It might be a lie, but I don't want to feed her monster. "We just breathe it out, okay? We just breathe." And that's exactly what we do; we breathe until my heart isn't racing anymore and she's not shaking like she's inside her own personal earthquake.

I want to clean up all the blood on her hands and her face, but if she sees the damage, it's probably going to make the panic come back. So we sit and breathe. With every inhale, I draw a figure eight on her back, and then repeat it on the exhale. It helps distract me from the panic, so I hope it helps Lavender too.

My legs lose their feeling.

My heart slows until all I want to do is sleep.

Calm. Calm. Calm.

Lavender sways into me. Her hand grows lax over my heart and slips down, landing in her lap. I always sleep for ages after the panic monster has been tromping around in my head. I lean against the wall, legs asleep and neck already cricked, but I don't want to disturb Lavender.

So I wait for our parents to come home.

And I fall asleep too, because anxiety and fear are exhausting.

7

Into The Spiral
We Fall

LAVENDER

Age 9

I WAKE UP to shouting. My body hurts so much, and I'm confused. I'm not in my bed. I'm in the spare room, and suddenly I'm dumped on the floor.

"What did you do to her?" River is screaming, screaming, screaming.

River has a big temper sometimes, the kind that explodes out of him in ways that make my entire body break out in a cold sweat. Mostly he gets mad when someone does something to upset me. He's like an angry, rabid dog right now, barking and lunging at Kodiak.

I try to find my words, but I can only make one sound. "I-I-I." I hate it when my brain and my body don't work. And I'm so tired. So, so tired.

"She got locked in the closet! She was scared and couldn't get out!" Kodiak's voice is loud and strained and unsteady.

The floor vibrates under me as more people come rushing down the hall.

"Hey! Boys! That's enough fight—oh my God." My mom skids to a stop, hazel eyes wide, hand coming up to cover her mouth. She pushes past Kodiak and River, dropping to her knees in front of me. Her hands hover in the air like scared birds before they finally cup my cheeks. "Lavender, baby, what happened?"

I open my mouth, trying to find words, but her fear is my fear, and it all gets stuck again. Kodiak's mom, Lainey, appears in the doorway, eyes bouncing around the room, taking in the way Kodiak and River are facing off against each other.

"River, Kody, what happened?" Lainey asks in a tone I've never heard before.

"He did something to Lavender!" River shouts and points a finger at Kodiak.

I cover my ears with my hands and shake my head. My hands hurt. I don't understand what's happening.

All of a sudden Daddy is in the room too, and he is angry—angrier than River. His voice is a sonic boom. Kodiak bursts into tears. And there is yelling, yelling, yelling.

And I am scared all over again.

I can't breathe.

I remember smells and sounds and being scared, but I can't connect them to anything but the darkness and how badly I wanted out of the closet and how it felt like I would be there forever.

It's Lainey who cuts through the noise with a shrill whistle. She doesn't yell like everyone else. Instead, she says, "Everyone out except Violet, Lavender, and Kodiak, please."

When Daddy starts to argue, she holds up a hand and says, "Your anger is a trigger for both of them, and we cannot get the story with you here. If you're not part of the solution, you're part of the problem. So please, help us help them."

"Please, Alex," Mommy whispers brokenly. Her palm is damp as it smooths my hair away from my face. "Lainey's right."

He backs out of the room, taking a still-uncontrollable River with him, and then there's just the fear monster in my head and the salty sadness left hanging in the air.

"Kodiak, can you tell us what happened?" Lainey asks softly.

He stumbles over his words, desperate to purge them. "We w-were playing hide-and-seek. Mav was it. He found R-river first and t-took a l-long time to f-find me." He sniffs and swipes under his nose with the back of his hand, but his voice grows steadier as he speaks.

I want to be strong like Kodiak. I want to know how to make the monster in my head smaller.

"When Mav found me, we decided we were bored with t-the game, and we went to get a snack. But then I asked if he'd found Lavender, and he said she always hides in the same place, which is true most of the time. But I had that feeling—the one that makes my stomach feel off. Y-you know, the one you told me not to ignore?"

"Your instincts," Lainey says.

He nods. "So I went to check, but Lavender wasn't with River, and I know she likes this room, s-so I came looking for her. The door must have locked on her so she couldn't get out. I got it open, and then I took her fear and made it mine like you do with me." His voice cracks, and he shakes his head like his monster inside is growing too fast. "I would never hurt Lavender. I would never do anything to hurt her, not ever. Please, Mom, I w-would never."

"I know, honey. It's okay. You did the right thing. It's okay."

She opens her arms, and he steps into her embrace. She cups the back of his head and turns toward Mommy.

They share a look that makes my stomach hurt.

After everyone is calm, Lainey takes Kodiak home, and Mommy takes me to my bathroom and draws me a bath. I sit on the closed toilet lid while she wipes my face with a warm, wet washcloth. I don't really understand why since I'm getting in the tub.

Now that it's just the two of us and no one is yelling anymore, I get my words back. "Kodiak was telling the truth."

"I know, baby. Kody isn't a liar." She gives me a soft smile, but her eyes are sad. Big, fat tears well, and she blinks a lot, like she's trying not to let them fall, but they do anyway.

I lift a hand, wanting to wipe her sadness away, but I stop when I see my palms are crusted with dried blood. "I hurt my hands." I did it before, when I got lost at the carnival.

Mommy covers them with hers gently, her bottom lip trembling. "It's okay. That's my fault. I should've trimmed your nails for you earlier this week." She stands and presses a kiss to the top of my head. "Let's get you in the bath and ready for bed."

"I'm sorry I had an accident," I mumble as we peel off my still-damp pants.

She tosses them into the corner. "You don't have anything to be sorry for, baby." The cracks in her voice scare me.

I don't want her to be upset with me or Kodiak. I finish getting undressed, and she helps me into the tub. Everything hurts, and my hands sting when the warm water hits them. I start crying again, because now that I'm not as scared, the hurt is bigger. Little bubbles of memory float to the surface and pop before I can hold onto them. Queenie says it's okay not to remember, so I don't chase the memories because I think there are monsters hiding in them.

Mommy lathers up a cloth and washes my back. She tries to sing one of my favorite songs, but her voice keeps breaking, so I tell her it's okay. I usually get changed on my own at bedtime, but tonight, she helps me into my jammies when my bath is done. She puts antibacterial ointment on my hands and my lip, which is sore too. She winds gauze around my hands. The sides are bruised from banging on the door.

"You must have been so scared," she whispers, brushing my hair back again.

I nod. "I thought the monsters were going to get me. I thought all I would have is the dark and what was inside my head. I kept trying to scream, but the fear ate all my sounds."

She hugs me so tight, it's hard to breathe.

She gives me Tylenol and asks me where I want to sleep tonight.

"Is River okay?"

"Should we go see him? I know he's worried about you."

I want to hold her hand, but mine hurts so I settle for rubbing the edge of her sleeve between my fingers. It's damp from my bath. "Maybe I could stay in his room tonight." I already know he feels bad, and for some reason there's an uncomfortable weight making my chest heavy. It's not the worry monster clogging my throat. It's more like that feeling I get when we sneak cookies before dinner and then we aren't that hungry for good-for-us food. It feels like I've done something wrong, but I haven't.

Mom knocks on River's door and pokes her head in. "Is it all right if we come in?"

"Sure." It's Daddy who replies, not River.

Mom slips in the gap, and I follow, my stomach churning as I see River, curled up in his bed with Daddy. It looks like he's been crying. His hair is all messy, and his eyes are tired. He has a line between his eyebrows that deepens when he's upset, and it's there now, deeper than ever.

River doesn't cry often. He gets mad and throws things, breaks his toys and then feels bad about it, but tears aren't that common for him, which is how I know he's really upset about what happened.

He sits up, eyes filling again. He swipes at them irritably. "I'm sorry."

I cross the room, gravitating to my other half. "It's okay. It's not your fault."

He shakes his head furiously but opens his arms, pulling me against his wiry, hard warmth. "I should've known you weren't okay," he says into my hair. "I should've been the one to find you. I'm supposed to be your trampoline."

That's River's way of telling me he loves me. He's my trampoline—with him I know I'm always safe to fall. He's going to beat himself up over this—not just because they forgot about me, but because it was Kodiak who found me and not him. Being a twin is tough sometimes. We're connected in ways people don't understand. I feel his anger and frustration. I feel his guilt. We know when things aren't okay with each other.

So I understand why he blames himself right now. It's like being half of a whole. You're your own person, but you're not. Everything about me is tied to River, and everything about him is tied to me.

He's fiercely protective.

"Can I stay in here with you tonight?" I ask.

He nods and squeezes me so tight, it makes my ribs hurt, but I don't say anything because he already feels bad enough.

There are two beds in River's room. We've only had our own rooms for the past six months. We decided it was for the best because all my art supplies are a lot to handle. Plus Mom said when we get older, we'd have to have different rooms anyway, because boys need privacy and so do girls. But we left the other bed because sometimes I don't like being in my own room by myself.

Daddy cuddles with me for a few minutes and inspects my bandaged hands and my arms. The fronts of my forearms are starting to turn colors—yellows, greens, and darker blues and purples. He takes my chin between his thumb and his finger, gaze shifting to Mommy. "That's a pretty deep split."

"I know. Do you think it will heal on its own?" Mommy wrings her hands, eyes wide and nervous.

He's quiet for a few seconds before he finally answers. "Probably." The way he breathes hard through his nose tells me it upsets him, so I say I'm sorry.

"Oh, Lavender, honey, I'm the one who's sorry. You must have been so scared."

"I'm okay now, though," I say, because even though he's right and I was scared, I don't want River to feel worse than he already does.

Daddy tucks me into the bed next to River's, and Mom grabs my stuffed superhero beaver. It used to be hers. He wears a cape and he's cuddly, and she's a grown-up, so she let me have it because I think beavers are funny animals. They're cute but mean, and when we visit Daddy's family and friends in Canada, we always get flat donuts coated in sugar called Beavertails.

I hug the beaver to my chest and curl up on my side, facing River. His mouth is set in a thin line, halfway to a frown. He waits for the sound of Mom and Dad's door closing down the hall before he throws his covers off and swings his legs over the edge of the bed.

"Can I see?"

I want to tell him no, because I don't want him to get upset all over again, but I think doing that might make it worse, so I nod. Moving makes my body hurt, and I wonder if it will be better or worse in the morning as I sit up and the covers fall away.

River turns on the lamp on the nightstand between our beds and hops up beside me. I hold my hands out so he can inspect them. He drags a finger gently across the edge of the bandage. "What'd you get cut on?"

"My fingernails," I whisper.

His gaze lifts slowly. "You did this to yourself?"

"I guess. I didn't know it happened until after I got out of the closet."

"Does it hurt a lot?" His voice is soft and shaky.

"It's not so bad."

He tips his head to the side. "Don't lie, Lavender."

"My nails were too long. Mommy wanted to cut them yesterday, but I was busy painting and we forgot." I don't acknowledge his accusation. I don't need to. He knows when I'm telling the truth.

She trimmed them all the way back right after my bath and filed them short, almost until there wasn't any white left.

"Maverick feels really bad. Not as bad as me, but he was crying, and Mom and Dad grounded him."

"They grounded him?"

Maverick doesn't get in trouble much. He's too busy with hockey and trying to keep up with schoolwork.

River nods. "He's not allowed to play hockey for the rest of the weekend. You should've heard Daddy; he was so mad. He took Mav to his office, and I could still hear him yelling."

Daddy and River have the same temper. Sort of. Daddy's fuse is long, and he never yells at me. Ever. Sometimes he raises his voice with Mav and River, but not usually Robbie because he mostly does what he's supposed to. He likes to study a lot and has a greenhouse in the backyard that he spends a lot of time in.

69

But Mav and River get saucy, and Daddy doesn't like it when they don't listen to Mommy or do what she asks them to—like cleaning up their rooms and stuff. And there was the time he got mad at Mav for the way he was playing hockey. Mav got a penalty for fighting, and Daddy said he was a better player than that. We use our brains to solve our problems and not our fists.

I feel bad, though, because Maverick was right. I always hide in one of three spots, and usually under River's bed. But I'd already hidden in all three, and Mav is good at finding me, so I did something different this time.

I want to ask about Kodiak, but I don't want to make River more upset. Sometimes they don't get along, and I know it's because of me. Kodiak and I understand each other. We both have worry monsters that live inside us. He likes to be perfect at everything. Sometimes when he makes mistakes, he can't handle it. That's when the monster inside gets so big, it takes over.

Even though we're twins, River doesn't understand what that's like. He wants to, but he can't, and that makes him angry.

"Is everyone else okay?" I ask.

River shrugs. "Mostly. Lovey and Lacey were really upset and wanted to see you before they left. BJ too. Kody had a big meltdown 'cause Daddy was so angry."

A spike of panic makes my throat tight.

"He was okay before they went home, though. I know he was just trying to help," River rushes on, his eyes darting away for a second. "Everyone was okay, just worried about you and feeling bad 'cause you got stuck."

I nod and yawn. I'm so tired, and all the worries seem to be seeping back in. I want to fall asleep before they make it impossible.

River goes back to his own bed, flicks off the lamp, and we

lie facing each other. I close my eyes and focus on trying to sleep, but the dark reminds me of the closet, and the panic makes it hard to swallow. And I'm worried about Maverick now too. River's breath has evened out. He never has trouble sleeping.

I slip out of bed and push the door open. I check over my shoulder to make sure River is still asleep before I pad down the hall toward Maverick's room. I have to pass Mommy and Daddy's room on the way. Their door is open a few inches, a light still on.

"It'll be okay, Vi."

"I don't know if it will, Alex." Her voice cracks, and she sucks in big breaths. She's crying. Because of me.

"We'll call Queenie in the morning and up Lavender's sessions with her."

"She was so scared, Alex." She hiccups.

"Shhh, baby, it's okay," Daddy says. "It'll be okay. I'm sorry I lost it. I just thought . . . I don't know what I thought. It took me right back to when she went missing."

I peek through the crack in the door, my body full of energy I don't like. Daddy keeps wiping Mommy's eyes. He looks so sad. They both do.

"It was exactly the same for me. All I could see was what she looked like when you found her. I feel so awful. Kody was just trying to help. That poor kid. Those poor kids. River was losing his mind."

"I know, but he's okay. They both are. We're not going to fix the problem tonight, Vi."

She's quiet for a few seconds. "I want to protect her from everything. I want to keep her safe from the world and everything that can hurt her."

"We all do. C'mere, baby, let's try to sleep."

The light extinguishes, and the sound of sheets rustling follows.

I don't go to Maverick's room. Instead, I head back to River's. My parents' conversation makes me uneasy. I don't like it when they talk about the night at the carnival.

I crawl back into bed and try to sleep, but the dark makes me feel alone, even with the sound of River breathing close by.

All I want is for things not to change. But they always do. And every time, I lose something. Pieces of memories disappear, and new fears creep in and live in those holes. I can never get a handle on things. I can't keep up. And no matter how much I wish time would stand still, it keeps moving forward, pulling me and everyone else along with it.

8

Misinterpretation Nation

LAVENDER

Present day

"**H**OW WAS YOUR first day of classes?"

I adjust my laptop monitor so my therapist isn't looking at my rack and neck. "*Clusterfuck* would about sum it up."

Queenie nods slowly and folds her hands in her lap. As a kid, when I used to see her, I'd stay busy with my hands, working on some kind of art project while we talked. But now that our sessions are less frequent, I try my best to stay in the moment, even if it's uncomfortable sometimes. We've been working together since I was four years old. Even though she's still in Seattle with her family, she's always made time for me.

There have been times when I only needed to talk once a month, but we decided since I've moved away from home, we'd start my first month with weekly sessions and adjust from there.

This is the one relationship in my life no one is worried about me being too dependent on, myself included.

"Would you like to tell me what made the clusterfuck?"

I give her the abridged version—Maverick taking my car, breaking my glasses, Kodiak driving me home and being a giant dick, him being a dick again at the school café, and me basically holing up in my room after that.

Queenie's expression shifts ever so slightly at my mention of Kodiak being a dick. I never told her what happened two years ago, not the real story. But the way her jaw tics tells me she's unhappy with this news.

I run my finger in a figure eight around my knee, needing to keep my hands busy. "You know what I've been thinking about a lot lately?"

"What's that, Lavender?"

"That time I got locked in the closet. I'm sure it's symbolic, or some living metaphor for my deep-seated trauma or what-ever—like the closet symbolizes my powerlessness and the feeling of being trapped." I stare up at the ceiling for a moment, bits of memories filtering in—ones that aren't related to the time I got locked in the closet. I always recognize them when they come. Sometimes it's a sound and sometimes a smell, like dirt and metal and gas and watermelon Jolly Ranchers. "I felt like that today," I continue, "when I was trapped in the car with Kodiak. Powerless and insignificant."

"How did he make you feel insignificant?"

I sigh, debating how much truth I want to share. "He said I hadn't changed at all."

Queenie tucks her hair behind her ear, wedding ring glinting in the sunlight from the window behind her. "And how would he come to that conclusion during what you've said was a five-minute drive home?"

I keep my hands clasped in my lap to hide the damage to

my palms. The upside of a video session is that she won't see what I've accidentally done to myself. I don't want it to raise red flags, or for my parents to come to the conclusion that this is already too hard for me. "I refused to speak to him and told him he didn't deserve my words because all he'd do was twist them around."

She chuckles softly and smiles. "Well, that doesn't sound anything like the Lavender who was locked in the closet, does it?"

"No, it doesn't." I'm definitely not the helpless little girl I used to be. But the state of my palms tells me she's still inside, and I don't want to go back to that.

"Maybe Kodiak is projecting, and it's not you who hasn't changed, but him."

"Maybe." I don't really know if that's true or not.

I've learned a few very important things since the night Kodiak found me trapped in the closet when I was nine:

1. The path of least resistance might be more alluring, but it certainly isn't always the best choice.
2. Dependency goes both ways, and I developed a very strong, very unhealthy dependence on my brother's best friend.
3. That event triggered a savior complex in Kodiak that only got worse over the weeks and months that followed.

I didn't realize at the time how destructive that would prove to be, or how much damage needing one person could do —not until I was forced to relearn how to manage my own fears.

DAY TWO IS SLIGHTLY BETTER than day one, primarily because I'm able to avoid Kodiak. And I have a three-hour evening class I'm excited for.

I had an opportunity to pick an additional elective, and there were lots of cool courses, so I chose an English course that focuses on myth and folklore. I've always loved fairy tales, and I figured a semester reading about gods and spirits would be awesome.

I climb the stairs, confused that the class is not in the Arts Building. But maybe they ran out of room or something. I find the classroom and search for one of the left-handed seats. It's really annoying when righties sit in them, because there are so few available in most lecture halls. Luckily I'm able to grab one in the back. I hate sitting near the front because I feel like the professors are more likely to call on you. Even if I do know the answer, I always end up stumbling over my words.

There are still about fifteen minutes before class starts, so I pull out my laptop and log into my email account. I had some issues with it because they'd used my middle name instead of my given name for my email address, but I finally managed to get it sorted out yesterday. This means I haven't had a chance to connect with professors yet, but I have my schedule and most of my textbooks, so I'm feeling pretty okay about things. Was it stressful getting it sorted out? Sure. But I managed all by myself without having any kind of panic attack, so that's a win.

After a few minutes, the professor ambles in and sets up his laptop. The screen at the front of the class lights up and the course code appears, along with the name of the class. And it's not an English class at all. I pull out my schedule, feeling suddenly hot because it's obvious I'm in the wrong building, or something has gone incredibly awry.

I check the code on the screen against the one on my schedule. They match. I quickly log into the course calendar, positive there must be some kind of mistake, even though it's clear there is not. I assumed that anything starting with an *E* would be an English course, but I see now that I botched the registration, and I'm sitting in Intro to Macroeconomics—which is basically another form of math, and my least-favorite subject in the entire history of the universe.

Both of my parents are good at math. My mom is a math wizard. She was actually a mathlete in high school and won all sorts of championships. My dad built her a math-trophy shrine in our basement. She can do triple-digit multiplication in her head. And my dad may not be a super math genius or anything, but he's good with numbers and has a freaking degree in English and another one in kinesiology.

My oldest brother, Robbie, is studying to become a botanist, and he's currently on a fellowship in Amsterdam. He's planning to follow in my grandfather's footsteps and work in medical marijuana research and development.

Maverick is probably the most like my dad. He's studying kinesiology, but he's already been drafted. That doesn't necessarily mean he'll ever play in the NHL according to my dad. Some drafted players never make it.

River is ridiculously smart and tries at nothing. Unlike my dad and Maverick, he has zero interest in playing hockey. Well, that's not exactly true. I think he likes hockey, but he decided he wanted to play football instead, maybe so he wouldn't have to compete with Mav.

And then there's me. I'm decent at school, but I always had to work harder than everyone else to get the same kind of grades. My anxiety doesn't help the situation. And I suck at pretty much everything with numbers that isn't measuring fabric, so the fact that I'm sitting here is a big old punch to the tit.

I grumble profanity under my breath.

"Excuse me?" the guy in the desk closest to me asks.

I give him what is probably a horrible grimace and motion to the empty seat between us. "Sorry. Just talking to my imaginary friend."

"Right, okay." He shifts in his desk and angles his body away from me.

Awesome, Lavender. Of course you had to say something weird. I drag my palm down my face. Why couldn't those words stay in my head like most of them do?

I spend the next three hours trying to manage my mounting panic. I'm too embarrassed to get up and leave. What's even worse is that we round out the end of the first class with a freaking assessment quiz. I avoided all the business courses in high school because they all included some form of math. When I took the *required* math courses, I was always in River's class. My parents made sure of it. I probably should have taken the easier math, but with River there, I could copy most of his work, barely pass the exams, and still manage not to totally obliterate my average. But now I'm on my own.

After class, I arrive home to find Maverick, River, and BJ hanging out in the living room, playing video games.

"Where've you been?" BJ asks.

I drop my backpack on the floor and head for the kitchen. "It's this thing called class. Maybe you should try it."

"What's up your ass? Other than Kody's tongue?" BJ shouts after me.

I grab an orange and stalk back into the living room. "That's disgusting!" I lob the orange at him. Unfortunately, unlike my brothers, I have shit aim and miss him completely. Mav nabs the orange out of the air before it hits a lamp three feet away from BJ's head.

River pauses the game, his expression stormy, which is not unusual. "What the fuck?"

I want to give BJ shit, but it'll just give River more of a reason to be angry. "BJ's just being his usual gross self."

River looks from me to BJ and back again with a shake of his head. "Don't buy it. What happened?"

BJ shrugs, playing it off like it's nothing. "Other than Kody getting his rocks off on some dirty bunny yesterday, not much."

"Wait, what? When did that happen? I thought he was driving you back here to get glasses." Maverick seems confused.

"He did. I guess he fit it in—quite literally—between dropping me off and whenever his next class was." I try to come off as blasé, but this whole conversation makes me feel exposed.

"Hold the fuck on." River's eyes flare, and he sits up straighter. "Why were you in a car with Kody, and why am I just finding out about this now?"

"Uh, because I didn't see you yesterday." And even if I had, there's no way I would have told my twin any of this—see his current reaction for details. "I broke my glasses and needed to come home to get my spares. He drove the car. I sat in the passenger seat."

River's eyebrows pull together into his customary angry-pensive expression. "Did he say anything?"

"Are you asking if we had a nice chat? A little stroll down memory lane, back to the days when I used to have regular meltdowns at school and he used to have to come save me?" Man, I am fired up tonight and not in the mood to deal with any more bullshit.

River blinks a bunch of times, his lips thinning. It's been a long time since I've had a public panic attack. I've learned how to control the cyclical thoughts and physical breakdowns until I'm alone. It's easier to fall apart when no one's looking.

"You two haven't seen each other for more than a couple of minutes in years. You must've talked about something," Maverick presses, a hint of disbelief in his tone.

"It's not grill-Lavender time," I announce. "I've had a day, and the last thing I need is the two of you getting on me about Kodiak, when you and Mav are the goddamn reason I needed a ride yesterday in the first place! I wouldn't have been in a damn rush if you hadn't taken my car, and then I wouldn't have broken my glasses and needed to go home and get new ones."

"Shit, calm down. It was just a couple of questions," Maverick gripes.

"My car is being detailed, and I'm getting it back in the morning," River offers.

"How nice for you."

Mav cocks a brow. "You really are in a mood."

"Yeah, well, I just came from a three-hour macroeconomics class, so I think I have a right to be."

BJ makes a face, and River scrunches up his nose. "Why are you taking economics?"

"I don't know! I didn't think I was. I thought it was folklore, not a math course in disguise, and then I get there and they might as well be speaking a whole different language."

"So go to the registrar's in the morning and see if you can get it switched. I mean, it has to be some kind of mistake, right?" River has resumed playing Xbox, so he doesn't even bother to look away from the TV as he speaks.

"I should've said *screw it* and pushed for living on campus." I whirl around, done with this conversation.

"You'd hate the dorms. You'd have to share a bathroom," Mav calls. "Shark week would be a nightmare!"

I fire the bird over my shoulder on the way out of the living room and make a stop in the kitchen for a box of Lucky Charms. I stomp up to the third floor and my loft in the attic. Like every room in this house, it's huge and spacious, but it has the added benefit of angled ceilings and skylights and a balcony that overlooks the backyard.

I close my door, put my earbuds in, and shove my hand into the box of cereal, picking through it for all the marshmallows. I derive an inexplicable amount of gratification from eating them all and then putting the box back for my brothers.

I consider texting Lovey and Lacey since we have a group chat, but it's already ten thirty, and I have to be up early in the morning.

I stare at the ceiling for a few minutes, trying not to let myself fall back into memories I don't want.

I'm saved from myself by a knock at the door. I know it's River because he raps twice, pauses for a second, and raps once more before repeating the sequence—like a heartbeat.

I sigh. Looks like I'm not getting out of a conversation that easily. "It's open." I lock it before I go to sleep every night.

The doorknob turns, and he pokes his head in. He waits until I wave him over. River is tall, so he has to stay in the middle of the room to avoid hitting his head on the slanted ceilings. He's very much a hybrid of our parents. He has our dad's dark hair, but our mom's waviness. His eyes are hazel, and he and I share the same mouth, but he has our dad's nose.

Where Maverick is rugged, *GQ* modelesque, River is . . . pretty. He's obviously masculine, but his angles aren't as severe. Everything about his face is softer, which contradicts his personality. And because he's constantly scowling, he looks like he wants to murder the entire world, but he'd be pretty doing it.

River crosses the room and stands beside my bed, scrutinizing me. I scoot over and pat the empty space. He sits and stretches out, his massive body taking up more than half of my queen-sized mattress.

"No houseguests tonight?" I decide to break the heavy silence with humor.

"I have an early class, and practice tomorrow."

"How responsible of you." I tip the box of cereal in his direction.

"I'm good."

I shove my hand in the box, fishing around for a marshmallow. They're getting harder to find.

"You know it drives Mav insane when you put the box back and there are no marshmallows left, right?" River is clearly struggling to say what he wants to.

"Yup." I produce a rainbow and pop it in my mouth.

River grabs my hand, and I drop the box, cereal spilling over my bed. He sits up in a rush as I curl my fingers into a fist and try to hide the crescent moons scored in my palm. But River is strong, and I'm no match for him, so he pries my fist open—gently—and sucks in a breath.

When he looks at me, his expression is tortured. "What happened, Lav?" He runs his callused fingers across my palm. The cuts aren't deep, but they exist, and that's enough.

"It's nothing." I pull my hand free.

He rolls to his side and props himself up on one elbow. "Why are you lying to me? You always lie to me about him. Why?"

Because we had something you'll never understand. Because even though I hate him, I'll always love him. Because he used to get me in a way I don't think anyone ever will again. Because he could save me without smothering me. "It's complicated."

"I wish I'd known about the glasses situation. I would've come to get you."

"I should've walked home—or done anything but get in the car with him. But that was the choice I made, and only I get to regret it." I link my pinkie with his.

"I don't like that he does this to you," River says softly.

"I do this to myself."

"Because of him."

"It's been a lot of years, River. It was a shock to my system." That's a partial lie.

River chews the inside of his cheek to the point that I wonder if he's making it bleed. "I shouldn't have pushed you to come to school here and move in with me and Mav. It was a mistake. My mistake. I thought it would be better 'cause, like, we're all here, and I didn't want you to have to stay back with Mom and Dad for another year. But I feel like I'm making your life harder, not easier. It was selfish of me."

"You didn't force me to come here. It's where I wanted to be." That's mostly the truth. I didn't want to miss out on being where everyone else was.

His pinkie curls tight around mine. "I always wanted to keep you safe, Lav, but I kept fucking up. I couldn't even keep you safe from Kody. Even now, I can't."

I squeeze his pinkie back. "I don't want you to keep me safe from Kodiak. That's my own cross to bear, not yours."

He's quiet for a long time before he finally exhales a long, slow breath. "I couldn't keep you safe from a lot of things."

After all the damage that's been done over the years, I have to wonder which of us has suffered more.

9

Additional Suckage

LAVENDER

Present day

THE NEXT MORNING I get up early and make a stop at the student housing department so I can get myself on the list for a dorm room. It might be a long shot, but it certainly won't happen if I don't try. Turns out, there's a pretty extensive waiting list, but if I don't mind shared accommodations, I have a better chance. At this point, I'll take about anything other than a cardboard box.

Unfortunately, when I head over to the registrar's office right after, I'm even less successful. Apparently I need the macroeconomics course, and switching it to next semester isn't an option unless I'd like to lose my elective. At least it's only once a week. I guess it's a good thing I stuck around for the quiz, although I don't have much faith that I've managed to pass it.

As the week unfolds, I'm glad to report that the rest of my classes are awesome. So the upside is that I get macroeconomics out of the way at the beginning of the week. The downside is that the coursework for that is going to take me more hours than I would like to complete.

On Friday, the house starts filling up with random people early in the afternoon. It's a gorgeous day and still gloriously warm as we approach the last week of August. By three o'clock, girls upon girls in skimpy bikinis are draped all over my brothers and their hockey and football friends.

Fortunately, I have plans to meet Josiah for coffee, and Lovey and Lacey are still trying to persuade me to come to their party. I pass through the kitchen, stopping to toss a few snacks in my backpack on my way out the door.

Two of River's teammates—they immediately announce that they're football players—start chatting up my boobs. Granted, I'm wearing a sundress that draws attention to them, but still, they don't even attempt to keep their eyes above my neck.

The beefcake on the right belches loudly and skims one of my straps. "You got a bikini on under there?"

I shake my head and shift away from his unwelcome contact. His nails have dirt under them, which is nasty. I glance around, hoping one of my brothers will appear and tell this guy to back off. I usually keep to myself and my room when they have a lot of people over.

Instead of Maverick or River coming to my rescue, Kodiak pushes his way between the two beefcakes and slings an arm over each of their shoulders. A beer bottle dangles from his fingers and his eyes slide over me, expression full of disdain. "Who let you out of your ivory tower?"

I roll my eyes and flip him the bird.

The football players laugh, and the one on the right smirks at his friend. "I like this one."

Kodiak's lip twitches. "There's a do-not-touch policy on *this one*, so find another set of tits to eye-fuck." He tips his beer back, draining half of it in one long gulp, his gaze still trained on me. He swipes the back of his hand across his mouth as he steps forward, into my personal space. My heart rate kicks up, and my breath gets trapped in my lungs—like I'm stuck underwater.

Kodiak's hard glare stays locked with mine as he bends down, our noses almost brushing. His breath smells like beer and more faintly of something sweet. His fingertips glide up my arm and wrap around the back of my neck, his thumb sweeping up the side, causing goose bumps to rise on my skin. He tips his head, bringing his mouth to my ear. "Still such an attention seeker, aren't you? You should leave before you embarrass yourself." He drops his hand and steps back.

"I hate you." I spin around and head for the front door.

"Keep telling yourself that until it's true," he calls after me.

In the driveway, I run into River, who's arriving home from practice. He nods to the backpack slung over my shoulder. "I thought you didn't have class today."

"I don't. I'm meeting a friend from my costume and set design class, and then I'm probably going to meet up with Lovey and Lacey."

He rubs the scar under his bottom lip, which almost matches mine. Except his teeth went through his bottom lip when he was playing football. Mine is from a childhood panic attack during which I bit my lip hard enough that I should have had stitches. But I'd already been so traumatized, my parents didn't want to risk taking me to the hospital.

"You're gonna stay there tonight?" he asks.

"Maybe." I hadn't planned on it, although I also hadn't

planned on dealing with Kodiak, either, so I'm leaving my options open.

"Okay, might be a good idea. Based on the noise level already, it's gonna get rowdy here, and Lovey and Lacey's place is chill."

In other words, he won't have to worry about making sure I'm okay or comfortable.

River takes my bag and unlocks the car door. Sometimes he can be ridiculously kind and thoughtful. He pulls me into a hug so tight, it's nearly suffocating. "I'm sorry about the party. Message later so I know you're safe, okay?"

"Yeah, of course."

He waits until I pull out of the driveway before he goes inside.

What the hell have I signed up for this semester? And how much of Kodiak can I tolerate before I break?

I meet Josiah at the quad. He greets me with a hug and huge smile. "How was your first week?"

"Goodish. Good. I made it through, so that's what counts."

His right eyebrow lifts above his black-rimmed glasses. "Uh-oh, *goodish* sounds more like not good."

"It was okay." Cue internal eye roll. No one likes a Negative Nancy. "Living with my brothers is an adjustment."

"Ah, right. Maverick seemed all right, though?" It's posed as a question.

I fall into step beside him. "He's the easier of the two for sure, but he plays hockey for the school team, and my twin plays football, so it's jock central there right now."

Josiah makes a face. "Oh man, that sounds like the opposite of your jam."

"Uh, yup, pretty much. The dudebros are bad enough, but the girls are the worst. It's desperation nation over there. When

I left, there had to have been about twenty girls in thong bikinis wandering around the backyard."

"What about the shirtless jocks?" He waggles his brows.

"They're nice to look at, as long as they don't open their mouths and speak to me." My cheeks flush at the memory of River's football friends chatting up my chest before I left.

"There has to be at least a few of them who aren't total dirtbags, though, right?"

"Probably—not that it matters. There's zero chance I'd ever date one of those guys."

"Who says you have to date?" He gives me a knowing smirk.

I scrunch my nose. "You mean hook up with one of them?"

"Sure. Why not? Those guys have great bodies and wicked stamina."

"My twin would murder any of his teammates who so much as looked at me the wrong way, so a hookup is out of the question, and also not my style."

"Hmm . . . I can see how that might be a problem, then." Josiah opens the door to the Identity and Inclusion Center. It's marked with a safe space symbol. "Well, if you ever need a wingman at one of those house parties, you let me know. I'll be the Goose to your Maverick."

"Oh my God, you did not reference *Top Gun*."

"The opening was there. How could I not? My mom watched that movie all the freaking time."

"So did mine."

"I used to fantasize about Goose and Maverick hooking up in the locker room."

"But Goose's mustache." I scrunch my nose.

"A little tickle for your pickle." Josiah waggles his brows and I burst out laughing.

"Anyway, I was obsessed with that movie for a while, and

fighter planes, but mostly with young Tom Cruise." He makes a heart with his fingers and holds it up to his chest.

"Here's an interesting fact: My mom was on a Tom Cruise kick when she was pregnant with Maverick."

"So she named him after the character in the movie?"

"That she did. There are conflicting stories about who picked mine and River's names, but he most definitely drew the short straw. I mean, River Waters?"

"River?" His eyes flare and he coughs once before he says, "That's a movie star name."

"He's pretty enough to be one, and moody too." I take in the very cool, very open lounge area. Students congregate in small groups, seated on couches and chairs.

A group standing by the pool tables waves Josiah over, and I'm introduced to his friends. They're easy to talk to, welcoming me in. Which means I've made my first genuine friends here.

THAT NIGHT, I stay over at Lacey and Lovey's. The sleepover is both a good and bad idea. Good, because it means I don't have to deal with my brothers' jock friends. Bad because I end up getting drunk and developing a horrible case of verbal diarrhea. I'm almost positive I bitched about Kodiak to some random guy who may or may not have been flirting with me.

Post-night with Lovey and Lacey, I do everything I possibly can to avoid running into Kodiak. It's not all that difficult. I can hang out with Josiah and his friends between classes. I spend time with Lovey and Lacey at the café. I study anywhere but at home, which means I find all the best, quietest spots in the library, and I eat an unprecedented amount of dry cereal and granola bars as a result.

It's hellishly inconvenient, but it also means I don't have to deal with my brothers or any of the other shit that comes with living with two guys who throw a lot of parties and have a constant rotation of embarrassingly desperate women in the house.

Regardless, I'm managing, and I've made a few friends of my own, so those are all wins and what I'm trying to focus on— at least until I get the pop quiz back from macroeconomics class.

Of course I've failed. With 25 percent. The note at the bottom of my test suggests I visit student services and set up tutoring to help me with the basics, since this test is the foundation for the rest of the semester.

Student services has been closed for hours by the time class ends on Tuesday evening. It's warm tonight, and I'm aware that we only have a few more weeks before the weather turns for good, so I figure I'll go for a swim when I get home and clear my head. Plus, the physical activity helps my anxiety. During my video session with Queenie yesterday, she suggested I take advantage of the pool while it's still open. She was pleased that I'd made new friends, and even that I'd gone to a party. I left out the part where I got drunk, obviously.

Being uncoordinated means there aren't a lot of sports I'm good at, but I love to swim. The water is the one place where I feel like my body isn't awkward. And it's quiet, peaceful— which is something I don't feel very often. Especially not recently. It also tends to help me sleep, another thing I haven't been doing well lately.

I almost throw up in my mouth the second I step into the front foyer and trip over a pile of nasty-smelling sneakers. I cover my mouth and nose with my palm and leave my shoes on.

I don't trust that they won't get lost under the other ones, and I don't want the smell contaminating them.

The living room is blissfully empty, the low drone of ESPN playing in the background. No one is watching, though, and I soon discover that's because they're all outside.

There have to be at least two dozen people in the backyard. Lots of them girls. On a Tuesday, for shit's sake. I spot BJ, so I have to assume the rest of his housemates must be out there too. It's very likely that Kodiak is among them, despite his dislike of social events that aren't hockey games.

So much for a peaceful, quiet swim.

I make a pit stop at the fridge, debating whether I should make myself a sandwich, when the French doors open and the sounds of girls screaming and someone cannonballing into the pool stream in. I don't bother to check who it is, since I don't particularly care. I need food, and then I can disappear into my bedroom and forget about this crappy class I can't get out of.

No one addresses me, so I assume it's one of the girls coming in to use the bathroom. I grab the ham, lettuce, and mustard and set them on the counter, letting the fridge fall closed. I groan my annoyance when I spot the loaf of bread on top of the fridge. My brothers seem to think this is the logical place to keep carbohydrate products.

My height makes it exceedingly difficult for me when they put things up high. And they probably do so on purpose. Maverick thinks it's hilarious when I have to jump to get stuff, likely because my vertical is abysmal. They also constantly buy whole grain bread—never the nice, plain, soft, stick-to-the-roof-of-your-mouth white stuff.

I push up on my tiptoes and mash my chest against the stainless steel door, reaching for the end of the bag. It's just beyond my grasp.

"Say please and I'll get it for you."

I spin around and find Kodiak standing less than six inches away. His pale green eyes are fixed on me, but the only emotion in them is passive disdain. I will my own eyes to shift to the side and not down, but they don't obey.

As a child, I saw Kodiak in swim shorts all the time. Our families were always together for barbecues, birthday parties—any excuse for our parents to hang out meant our nannies also got together with us.

Kodiak has always been a bigger-than-average kid. He hit his first growth spurt at eleven, and by the time he was fourteen, it was clear he was going to be more than six-feet. At nineteen, he was six-three. He was a lanky teen, but tall and with broad shoulders that promised to fill out in time.

Time has done its job. And so has Kodiak's rigidity and his obsession with being the absolute best. He's ripped—all hard edges and cut muscles. Broad shoulders, defined biceps, thick veins roping down his forearms. A chiseled chest and six-pack abs leading down to the slice of V that disappears into his basic, black swim shorts.

Fuck. I'm ogling him. My heart stutters in my chest, and color explodes in my cheeks as he leans in.

He's so close that his wet hair brushes my temple, and I can feel his hot breath and the cool radiating from his skin. "You look hungry, Lavender."

I recoil, hating the way my body reacts to his low, taunting tone. I'm aware he's making fun of me, that he knows he's physically appealing and I'm not immune. I hate that it hurts to be so horribly dismissed over and over again by someone who once meant so much to me.

I take an unsteady step back and hit the counter. He moves forward, one hand landing beside me, the other gripping the fridge door. His gaze moves over my face and drops to my mouth. My immediate response is to suck my bottom lip between my teeth and hide the scar.

Something in his expression shifts, and his voice drops to a whisper. "Nothing has changed."

"You're right. I still hate you, and you're still an asshole."

He grins, the dimple in his cheek popping. "Only one of those things is true."

The French doors open. "Kody? Are you coming back out? 'Cause if you wanna go, I'm cool with that too."

I glance past him to the tall, lithe, bikini-clad girl. She's not the girl from the first day of school, although I have seen that one since. She's been here, in the pool and all over Kodiak, during their many parties.

I hate that relief is the first thing I feel. Her eyes narrow when she sees me, and it's my turn to sneer. "It's kind of embarrassing that you're so used to bunnies falling all over you that you've forgotten how to act like a human being," I note, meeting Kodiak's eyes. "I guess it's good that you don't have to rely on your winning personality to get laid."

The only sign I've gotten to him is the slight tic in his cheek and the way his expression goes flat.

"Kody? Why are you talking to her?" Her jealousy is a green-eyed monster.

I leave the sandwich stuff and grab a box of cereal from the counter, wanting to get away from Kodiak before he hits me with another low blow.

"I live here." I throw a fake smile her way and elbow past Kodiak. "And don't worry, I'd rather choke to death on a rotten hot dog than let him put his hands on me."

I head for the stairs, aware that Kodiak isn't going to follow me or antagonize me any further when there's some girl vying for his attention. I rush up the steps, nearly tripping on the first landing. I manage to catch myself and make it to the third floor without falling on my face. I close my door and lock it from the inside, but I don't turn on my light.

Since my room is in the attic, I have windows that look out on all sides of the house, plus the balcony that overlooks the backyard and the pool. I drop the cereal and my bag on the bed and cross to the other side of the room. Flipping the lock on the sliding door, I open it enough to get my body through, which is wider than I'd like, thanks to my boobs. I close it silently and drop down, staying hidden behind the towel I left hanging over the railing yesterday.

I scan the lit-up pool. I spot River with some girl hanging off him while he basically ignores her. It always surprises me how willing girls are to bask in his high-level surliness on the off chance he might give them a shred of attention.

I love my twin, but how he manages to attract the opposite sex confounds me.

Maverick is sitting at the edge of the pool, making out with someone. He's been dating her for the past two weeks, I think, which means she won't be around much longer.

It takes me a while to find Kodiak. He's in the shadows, sitting on one of the stools behind the pool bar, forearms on the bar top, his expression grim. The blonde is nowhere to be found. He's wearing his ball cap now, so I can't see his face, but it feels like his eyes are on me. Although it always feels that way when he's around.

The blonde appears out of the shadows and drapes herself over him. I watch every muscle in his body tense for a few long seconds before he finally gives her his attention. She lifts his ball cap from his head and puts it on her own. She shimmies her way between the bar top and the stool and rests her forearms on his shoulders.

And of course he lets her. Why wouldn't he?

I don't stick around to see more.

I may always be a silent observer, but masochism has never been my jam.

I tell myself this is a good reminder.

The only person who can save me from myself is me. No point in wallowing in the past and the things I can't get back. I probably shouldn't want them anyway.

10

Nope

LAVENDER

Present day

THE NEXT MORNING I get up early, but my brothers
are long gone. Despite the fact that they were up late last
night, Mav is already at hockey practice and River is likely on
the football field.

I pull one of my favorite dresses over my head. I have lunch
plans with Lovey and Lacey after my morning class.

I start with a visit to student services, embarrassed that I
have to solicit help to make it through the most basic economics
class a college can offer. Back in high school, I once used the
school tutoring services. I was paired with this sweet, nerdy girl
named Michelle who was in love with Maverick, so most of the
two tutoring sessions we had revolved around her asking questions about my brother, rather than helping me. I decided it
wasn't worth the hassle and had River do my homework for me
instead.

The guy sitting at the student services desk doesn't look anything like the nice, nerdy girl who tutored me before. That he's a he, not a she, is obviously a factor. However, so is the fact that he's built like a brick shithouse. His sweatshirt has RUGBY stamped across the front, so I'm guessing he's on the school team—not a hockey player, which is an automatic thumbs-up in my book. Interestingly, his name does not match the rest of him.

"Hello. Welcome to student services. How can we be of assistance?" Merlin asks.

I look around for another person to complete the "we" component, but there doesn't seem to be anyone but him in the office. I have to clear my throat so I can speak above a whisper. "Uh, hi. I was told I could access tutoring services for economics here."

He smiles and laces his fingers together, propping his forearms on the desk. They're thicker than my thighs. "You sure can! We have a variety of students in senior-level classes as well as master's programs who may be able to assist you. Do you have a copy of your schedule so I can check availability for you?"

Wow, he's super nice. And extra friendly. Maybe this won't be so bad. "Oh, yeah, of course." I let my backpack slide down my arm and plop it on his desk, nearly knocking over his coffee mug.

He moves it out of the way and motions to the chair behind me, still smiling. "You can have a seat. It might be safer."

"Oh, right. Yeah. Thanks. Sorry." I drop down in the chair and rummage around until I find my schedule. I smooth out the rumpled paper and pass it over. I guess I could've just as easily showed it to him on my laptop, but I always have a paper copy in case of tech fail.

He scans my schedule, his smile easy. He has a big chip out of one of his front teeth. "You're freshmeat?"

"I'm sorry, what?"

His gaze lifts. "A freshman?"

I must be hearing things. I'm blaming it on lack of sleep. And living with a bunch of jocks. "Uh, sophomore. I transferred this year, but I have a first-year class I need to complete."

"Ah, makes sense. How are you liking it here so far . . . Lavender? Is that your real name?"

"Um, yup. My mom likes purple and uh . . . so far I like it okay—aside from economics, anyway." I clasp my hands together to keep from picking at my nails.

"I like purple too." He gives me a flirty wink. "And econ can be a tough one. I'm a history major, so the numbers I deal with are mostly dates, you know?"

I nod. My mouth is dry, and my hands are clammy. I don't deal well with blatant flirting. Especially not from jock types, because they might look nice, but they're often players, and full of themselves.

When I don't offer any words to go with my nod, Merlin turns to his computer. "Let me see who matches your schedule availability." He clicks away for a minute and mutters something under his breath that sounds a lot like "lucky fucker." But I could be paranoid and hearing things.

"I think I found someone for you." He spins around in his chair and brings his fingers to his lips, whistling shrilly. "Hey, Bowman, I got a new student to introduce you to!"

My already-dry mouth feels full of sand, and a bead of sweat trickles down my spine. "Bowman?"

It's a fairly common last name. There's no way Kodiak has time to tutor students. And definitely not Intro to Macroeconomics. That would be a colossal waste of his incredibly huge, brilliant, asshole brain.

Merlin nods, but his gaze is trained on the doorway. My attention shifts to his reflection in the window—where I note that his friendly, nice-guy smile has turned smarmy—and then to the hulking figure now standing in the doorway.

Dressed in a school hockey T-shirt and a pair of dark jeans is Kodiak.

I guess it's not so common a last name.

His hair is still wet, likely because he came from practice. He's holding a massive apple in his equally massive hand. His gaze shifts from Merlin to me. I can't imagine what my expression must be—somewhere between disbelief and horror, I'm sure.

His lip twitches, and he grabs the schedule from Merlin. Aside from being freakishly intelligent, Kodiak has a photographic memory. All it will take is thirty seconds with my schedule for him to remember every single course code, date, time, building, and room number.

I sit there, helpless, as he scans it. His lips barely move, but I know the mental trick he's using to memorize it, likely so he can torment me some more, as seems to be his MO recently, and during the holidays two years ago.

He showed me his true colors then, none of them pretty.

"I don't usually tutor economics." His gaze finally lifts to me.

"I'm sure you can manage for an hour a week." Merlin gives him a wide-eyed *what-the-hell* look, like he can't believe Kodiak is passing up the opportunity.

I would like to be flattered, but mostly I'm disgusted, and sadly, not surprised. It's not my face that gets the attention; it's my rack.

I flip Kodiak the double bird. "I would rather fuck a cactus than have you tutor me." I push out of the chair and nearly trip over my backpack in my rush to escape. I nab it from the floor and hurry out of the student services office. As I go, Merlin asks Kodiak what that was about, and Kodiak says something about obsessions.

I loathe him so much.

It looks like I'm going to have to bug River to help me, either that or deal with failing the course.

I go to class, feeling less than awesome about this new development, as well as the fact that Kodiak still has the paper copy of my schedule. I would like to think it doesn't matter, but he's proven to derive great pleasure from making my life difficult, and I have a feeling this is only going to help his cause.

After class, I meet up with Lovey and Lacey for lunch in the student cafeteria. I choose to drown my sorrows in coconut-milk ice cream—I'm not above using food as an emotional crutch, but actual ice cream will create more problems since I'm lactose intolerant.

"That's your lunch?" Lovey asks when I take the seat across from her with my giant sundae. Her plate is full of salad and some kind of vegan casserole. The cafeteria here caters to everyone, so they have great nondairy and plant-based options.

"Don't judge," I say through a mouthful of ice cream and cookie bits—those are also vegan. Who knew? The marshmallows and gummy bears, however, are not.

Lacey slides into the seat beside Lovey, her plate almost matching her twin's. "Ooooh, looks like someone is eating her feelings. What happened?"

"I failed a test." I pop a mini marshmallow into my mouth. I love them when they're frozen because they remind me of the Lucky Charms marshmallows.

"Oh no," they say in unison.

"It gets worse, though." I stab my spoon into the ice cream, digging out a gummy bear.

Their eyes flare.

"Worse how?" Lacey whispers.

"I went to student services to see about an econ tutor."

"They didn't have anyone available?" Lovey asks.

"Oh, they sure did. But it was Kodiak."

Both of their faces fall. "Oh."

"And I said I'd rather fuck a cactus than be tutored by him, so obviously I won't be going back there."

Lovey choke-coughs on a mouthful of spinach, and Lacey pats her on the back. "Oh my God, did you really say that?"

"Yup." I'm equal parts mortified and impressed with myself. It was witty, but also highly inappropriate. My mom would probably be proud.

"That's awesome, but I guess that means he's still being a jerk." Lovey props her chin on her fist. "I don't get it. You guys were so close when you were kids. He would do anything for you."

I shrug and dig back into my sundae. "People change."

"I guess," Lacey agrees.

"Except BJ, he's always a flirt and a player." Lovey rolls her eyes, but her cheeks flush. "Anyway, back to this tutor thing. We might know someone who could help."

"Really?" I perk up. Most of Lovey and Lacey's friends are really nice.

A bright smile spreads across Lovey's face, and she claps her hands. "You remember Dylan? You met him at the party at our place?"

I deflate. "Oh, yeah." The guy I bitched to about Kodiak while I was drunk off cheap coolers.

"Well, he's majoring in, like, some kind of business program. I don't really know what it is, but he does all the financial stuff for the fraternity, so I bet he'd help you out."

"I don't know if that's such a good idea."

She frowns. "Why not? He asked about you after the party."

It's my turn to frown. "Really?"

She nods vigorously. "Oh yeah, he said you were really pretty, and funny."

"He said I was funny?" I'm parroting her now, but I'd thought I made a total ass out of myself. I perseverated about it for two days, running over the things I could remember saying, wondering if I sounded like an idiot. It's the reason I try to avoid parties in the first place.

"You are funny," Lacey says and takes a bite of her casserole, chewing slowly.

Maybe he was as drunk as me and doesn't remember all the asinine things I said.

"Lacey's right. You are, and maybe he can help you with econ *and* you can get to know each other better." She gives me a hopeful look. "You're not living with your parents anymore, so you can have a little fun, right? Meet someone new? Maybe date and stuff?"

"I dated last year." I even lost my precious virginity. He was nice, and I liked him, but it wasn't an earth-shattering experience. Still, it felt good to be wanted and to finally have some experience that had nothing to do with a freaking silicone pleasure device gifted to me by my grandmother. "Besides, I may not be at home, but I still live with my brothers."

"Well, they don't have to know, do they? And it's just tutoring. So what if the guy who wants to tutor you also thinks you're pretty and funny?"

I dig another marshmallow out. "Okay. You can give him my number or whatever. If nothing else, I need the help, and it's flattering to have someone say I'm pretty."

"Yay!" She claps again, causing the cherry tomato on her fork to pop off. It flies toward me, and I put my hand up, surprising all of us when I deflect it before it beans me in the head. Unfortunately, my flailing arm smacks into someone walking by, and a tray goes clattering to the floor. Something warm splashes my leg.

Lovey and Lacey cringe, and I shudder at the high-pitched shriek behind me.

"Oh my God!"

I don't want to turn around, because then I'll be able to see how many people are staring at me. As it is, the entire table in front of me has turned around to see what the commotion is about. I can't do *nothing*, though, because it's my fault my leg is covered in someone else's lunch. Judging by the temperature and texture, it's likely soup.

I turn slowly, feeling wet warmth trickling down my calf, ready to issue an apology and offer to pay for the lunch that's now on the floor. But my voice gets caught when I realize the girl is familiar. She's the one who was talking to her friend on the phone about Kodiak after she'd been with him that first day. Even worse, one of the other girls is in my art class.

"Aren't you going to apologize?" Her lip curls, and her eyes narrow. "Do I know you?"

"I'm sorry. That was totally my fault," Lovey says.

The girl's eyes shift from me to her, and then to Lacey. "It's your fault this klutz spilled my lunch all over the floor?"

As if some kind of karmic god has heard my prayer, BJ drops down at the table between Lacey and Lovey. He slings an arm over both of their shoulders. "It's my favorite set of twins." He turns his face into Lovey and rubs his scruffy beard all over her cheek.

She shrieks and pushes him away.

"Hey, BJ." The girl from the first day tosses her hair over her shoulder and gives him a simpering smile. Apparently the dropped soup and my missing apology are totally forgotten.

BJ glances at me, concern coloring his features for a moment before he turns his megawatt smile on the girls behind me. "'Sup, Bethany."

"Are you guys having a party this weekend?" she asks.

BJ shrugs. "Dunno."

"Well, if you are, me and my girls are up for some fun."

"I'm sure you are." BJ nods, but I can tell he's fighting not to laugh, or say something incredibly malicious.

"Okay, well, hopefully see you around." She and her friends strut down the aisle, leaving the broken bowl and a puddle of soup at my feet. It's actually spread all the way to my backpack. I pick it up off the floor and set it on the seat beside me. I nab a napkin and wipe the soup off my leg. It must have been some cream variety because it looks like a cross between puke and jizz. It's also all over my favorite pale purple Chucks, which means I'll need to wash them when I get home.

BJ blows out a breath. "That girl is off her tits."

"What's her deal?" Lacey asks, lips pursed as she watches her walk away.

BJ shrugs, reaches around Lovey's shoulder, and grabs a cucumber slice from her salad. "Dunno, but based on what I've seen, she's been bouncing around the hockey team circuit like a ping-pong ball." Instead of dropping his arm, he pulls Lovey in closer and pops the cucumber in his mouth.

She rolls her eyes and elbows him in the side. "Why is it okay for guys to sleep with whoever they want and girls get labeled as sluts if they do?"

"I'm not calling her a slut. I just don't think it's smart to try to hook up with guys in the same friend group. It creates unnecessary drama." He raps on the table. "Anyway, I got to get to class. Just wanted to stop by and say hi. I'll see you later, Lav?"

"Probably?" The only place I tend to go other than home is

the library or Lovey and Lacey's, so there's a pretty solid chance I'll see BJ later.

I use a handful of napkins to mop up the puddle of soup before we take our trays over to the garbage and head out. Lacey and Lovey both have class. While we're walking, Lovey sends Dylan a message asking if he's interested in tutoring a friend in economics.

He responds right away, asking which friend.

Lovey throws me a saucy smile as she types my name. Less than fifteen seconds pass before a new message appears:

> **When and where? I have time this afternoon.**

Which is how I end up at the library less than an hour later in one of the study rooms with Dylan. He suggested a café, but that would feel too much like a date, and I'm less likely to run into any of my family members in the library.

The first few minutes are a little awkward, because I'm nervous and can't remember everything I said to him when we were talking at that party. But he's really nice and seems totally happy to help me out. He's tall and lean with blond hair, gray eyes, and a nice smile. I pull out the test I failed.

"Oh wow, did you take this hungover?"

I'm pretty sure it's meant to be a joke, but not really.

I smooth out the paper, feeling heat creeping into my cheeks. "Unfortunately no. I just really suck at all the calculations, which is kind of ironic because my mom's an accountant." I'm afraid I'm about to start rambling. "Anyway, we only have this room booked for an hour, and clearly I need a lot of help, so . . ." I trail off.

The way he smiles at me makes me nervous. "I don't mind. Let's figure out where you went wrong, so we can get you back on track."

An hour later, I sort of understand where I messed up, but I don't think Dylan has ever tutored anyone, and he tends to skip a lot of steps by saying *magic happens*. As far as I can tell, there isn't any magic, just a lot of stuff that makes my brain hurt. I'll consider myself lucky if I pass this course.

It's overcast when we leave the library, so Dylan offers to drive me home. It's not far, but on the off chance the threat of rain becomes real, I agree. My palms start to sweat as soon as I get in the car. I know him just well enough to make the ride possible at all, and now that I'm alone with him, my mouth goes dry.

A few minutes later, he pulls onto my street, and that tight feeling in my throat starts to ease up, which is good. He's been so helpful, and I don't want to ruin it by acting weird. I surreptitiously breathe in and out to the count of four, willing myself to stay calm and not say or do anything embarrassing or stupid.

"Whoa, these houses are huge," Dylan says.

"Yeah," I agree.

Compared to the house I grew up in, they're not, but I'm aware they're bigger than average. We pass BJ and Kodiak's place, and I point to the house up the street. "I'm right here, number forty-four." Three cars are parked in the driveway, meaning my brothers must be home.

"Holy shit." Dylan whistles. "You live here?"

"Um, yeah."

He turns down the radio, which means we can hear the music coming from the backyard. Judging by the bass, it's Maverick's playlist.

"Sounds like there's a party."

I wonder if this is his way of asking me to invite him in. "My brothers probably have friends over."

"Right, you said you live with them." He runs his hands over his thighs.

"Yeah." Awesome, I'm down to one-word answers.

"Are they, like, cool with *you* having friends over?"

He's definitely looking for an invitation. "Uh, I guess?"

Back in high school, some of my drama friends would come over in small groups, but the guys were usually in the friend zone, because, well . . .

"They're a little protective."

"Like, protective meaning they'll grill me and do a background check to make sure I don't have any speeding tickets?"

I think he's trying to make a joke. "Um, that would probably be on the tamer side of things. My twin can be a lot to deal with."

He glances at the house. "Right. Okay. Well, maybe next time we could study at my place?"

I'm relieved that I've managed to get myself out of a potentially awkward situation, at least for now. "Oh yeah, sure, maybe we could do that." I unbuckle my seat belt, wanting to get inside before someone spots the car—namely River.

"Um, Lavender?" He's gripping the steering wheel like he's trying to choke it.

"Yeah?"

"There's a party next weekend at my fraternity house. It'll be pretty chill if you want to come. I could tutor you first or something?" He looks hopeful.

I don't want to hurt his feelings, so I go with noncommittal. "Can I message you and let you know? I think I'm supposed to do something with Lovey and Lacey."

"Oh, you can totally invite them to come too."

"I'll talk to them." I want to get in the house before

someone comes along and sees us here. If it's River, he'll flip his lid, and if it's Mav, he'll embarrass me. I'm leaning against the door, feeling around for the handle.

"Okay, sounds good. I had a good time today." He leans in, and I realize he's coming in for a hug.

At the same time, a loud bang on the window right beside my head startles us both. The car rocks back and forth violently, and I jerk forward, bashing my face on the side of Dylan's head.

BJ shouts, "No boning in the driveway!" The door is wrenched open, and I tumble out, smacking my head on the concrete. Stars burst behind my eyes, turning the world black and white for a few seconds.

"Oh shit, Lav, are you okay? I had no idea it was you in there."

I blink through the pain and find BJ, Liam, and Lane standing in a semicircle around me. Liam and Lane are finished with college, but they still live in the city and hang out with Quinn and BJ. All three of them are staring down at me with confusion and concern. My legs are still in the car.

I open my mouth to speak, but the words are stuck, either from shock or from hitting my head. BJ slides his hands under my arms and hauls me up as Dylan opens the driver's side door.

His head pops up over the roof, eyes wide. "Are you okay?" He scans the massive wall of man behind me, and the color drains from his face.

"I'm fine." I don't know whether to rub the back of my head or my lip, because both hurt. I go with my lip because it's easier to reach, swiping my fingers across the bottom one. BJ grabs my wrist. "Shit, you're bleeding."

"You scared the crap out of us, and this is the result." I motion to my face. My heart is pounding like I've run a marathon, but I feel like I'm managing this unfortunate situation pretty well, all things considered.

I motion to the three of them. "Dylan, these are my cousins BJ, Liam, and Lane. Guys, this is my friend Dylan who was just dropping me off."

My cousins grunt out a variety of greetings.

"Hey, guys." Dylan raises his hand in an uncertain wave.

"Thanks for driving me home." I need him to get out of here so I can be alone with my embarrassment.

The front door swings open, and the never-ending nightmare that is this day smacks me in the face like a long-expired sausage. Kodiak stands in the doorway wearing only a pair of swim shorts, wet hair sticking out all over the place, water dripping on the damn floor. But God, is he ever glorious. Muscle layered over muscle, thick biceps flexing as he holds the doorjamb, a mischievous grin popping the dimple in his left cheek.

My heart seizes and gallops. I miss this version of him: the one that smiles and doesn't hate me.

He ruins everything a moment later by bellowing, "Who's fucking in the driveway?"

His gaze moves to Dylan, who looks as horrified as I feel, but as it shifts to me, his smile drops and my stomach tightens.

"You should really go," I tell Dylan.

"I'll see you around." He disappears into his car and barely has the door closed before he's backing out of the driveway and screeching down the street.

I adjust my backpack on my shoulder and head for the house, steeling my spine and my nerves because Kodiak is still standing in the middle of the doorway, his face a mask of indifference. I try to brush by him, but he stays where he is, making it impossible.

I sigh, exhausted beyond belief. I just want to go upstairs

and have a good, cathartic cry. I try to mirror his apathy. "Can you move so I can get into my house?"

His brow furrows as his eyes move over my face. He lifts his hand, like maybe he's thinking about touching me. There's no way I can handle that. I jerk back and swat his hand away. "What are you doing?"

"Your lip is bleeding."

"Don't act like you actually give a shit, Kodiak."

"Tell me what happened." His voice is low and soft, and for whatever reason, that makes me even angrier, so I lash out, wanting to wound him the way he keeps wounding me.

"You, Kodiak. You happened, and you ruined my goddamn life. Now get the hell out of my way." I elbow past him, almost tripping over several sets of running shoes.

I head straight for my bedroom and lock the door behind me. I slide down the wall until my butt hits the floor and close my eyes, taking deep breaths.

I imagined the concern in his voice.

I imagined the pain that sat heavy behind his eyes.

We see what we want to, not the truth, especially when it hurts.

11

Dependency is a Dangerous Addiction

LAVENDER

Age 10

I LOVE AND hate Halloween. *Hate* is a strong word, and Mom always tells me not to use it, but I feel strongly about Halloween. I love the dressing-up part, and Mom always makes me a costume. We sit and flip through picture books and look at pretty princesses and fairies and decide which one I'm going to be.

I like that part a lot.

My costumes are always bright and fun, so I stand out. I like clothes that make it easy to pick me out in a crowd, even though I don't like crowds and try to avoid them.

But I *don't* like that some kids dress up like monsters and try to scare one another. I'm always afraid they're going to try to scare me too, and then I might cry in front of other people. This makes my worry monster grow inside me like ivy, choking out all the good feelings.

This Halloween, I'm dressed like the princess from *Brave*. Mom did my makeup and everything. Robbie's in high school now, so Mom says this is his last year trick-or-treating. He still dresses up though, and he's going as a mad scientist. It's sort of a costume and sort of not, because he loves science—only he's not mad. Maverick is a hockey player, which isn't much of a costume at all since that's what he does all the time, and River is going as Batman. It means he's wearing all black, a mask, and a cape.

Robbie and Maverick get to stay out later, because they're older and don't have to go to bed as early. I only like to do our street, and then I come home and give out candy with Mom while Dad follows the boys. But he's not allowed to walk *with* them because they get embarrassed.

Our street is busy with kids, and a lot of the houses give out really good treats like full candy bars instead of the mini ones. Queenie, who lives on the same block, gives me a special present to go with my favorite chips. It's a felt pouch sewing kit, and now all I want to do is go home and put together the cute little yeti and beaver pouches, but I don't want to make River come in with me because he's still having fun.

Whenever there's a scary costume, River flings his arm out wide and wraps his cape around me, shrouding me in darkness until the threat has passed.

Kodiak lives three houses down from us, so when we stop there, he joins Maverick and Robbie, and they walk ahead of us. Things have been different with us since the closet incident. It's hard to explain. We're closer but farther apart.

On nights like this, I feel like he's a million miles away, and the invisible string that connects us is brittle and thin.

Sometimes I can feel him watching me, like he's waiting for me to fall apart so he can piece me back together. It's happened a bunch of times since I got locked in the closet—me falling apart and him picking up the pieces for me. He always really wants to do it.

I know I shouldn't rely on him. Just like I know I shouldn't eat ice cream because it makes my stomach hurt. But I do it anyway, because in the moment, it makes me feel better. Later I have guilt for not being able to handle it on my own.

"We're gonna skip the next house." River's arm swoops up behind me, and I'm suddenly enveloped in darkness.

"What's going on?" A shiver runs down my spine. I can hear Kodiak's voice to my right, and Mav and Robbie laughing.

"It's the haunted house, the one you don't like."

"Oh." Another shiver. "Okay." I want to be brave enough to go to the haunted house, but after that carnival, Halloween has never been the same. Maybe it never will.

After a few more seconds of darkness, River drops his cape and guides me to the next house. This one has cute pumpkins with happy, toothy grins. I glance at the haunted house and then away. There are too many flashing lights and ominous, ghoulish sounds.

When we reach the door, River is the one who knocks. A lady opens it, and River says, "Trick or treat."

I manage to whisper the words.

She smiles at us, and her kind eyes focus on me. "Aren't you the most beautiful princess I've ever seen."

"Our mom made her costume," River tells her, even though I probably could have if I tried hard enough.

"Well, it's beautiful just like you." She tosses a handful of candy into my bag and turns to River. "And who might you be?"

"I protect the princess," River says.

"Is that right? Well, in some fairy tales, the princess slays her own dragon." Her smile isn't as soft now; it holds something else.

River tugs on my hand, but I stay where I am. I open my mouth once, twice, but nothing comes out. The third time I find my voice. "I would like to be that princess."

"I'm sure you will be," she says with a smile.

I want to believe her, but I'm afraid of cartoon dragons, so I don't think I'd ever be able to slay a real one.

I thank her for the candy and follow a scowling River down the walk. He looks over his shoulder and at the same time three huge clowns with makeup that reminds me of horror movies come running down the path, making lots of noise.

I stumble back a couple of steps, trip over my own feet, and land on my butt on the cold, damp grass. My mouth opens in a scream that doesn't reach my throat. I'm sucked back into the fun house with the hanging clowns, and the big teenage boys who were pushing, and the hollow-eyed, gray-toothed man. I curl into a ball and cover my head with my arms.

I should do one of my calming exercises, but it's loud, and River is yelling for our dad, and there's a ghostly soundtrack playing in the background. It's all too much. I can't focus on anything but the panic as it sinks its teeth in and takes hold.

Someone tries to touch me, and I kick out, scrambling away from the hands.

"I can help. Let me help."

I feel the thud of knees hitting the ground beside me. "Lavender, it's Kodiak." Warm breath that smells fruity like candy hits my cheek, and I shiver violently.

"It's okay. I got you. I'll make it better." His voice is deeper than it used to be, like he's hovering between kid and teen. His palm settles on the nape of my neck and curves around it.

The wave of relief is almost instantaneous. It takes so much less effort to calm down when Kodiak is here. I know it's not good for me. Queenie and I talk about how relying on another person to calm the anxiety, even my mom or River, can be dangerous, but it's hard not to let him help when it's so much easier.

"It's just stupid boys wearing masks. You're safe right here with me. Just breathe, and when you're ready, I'll walk you home," he murmurs in my ear, his cheek almost touching mine as he speaks, reassuring me that it's fine, to focus on his voice. He takes my hand and presses it against the side of his neck so I can feel his pulse slowing. His other hand stays anchored against the back of my neck, and his index finger draws figure eights on my skin. The pattern is lulling, like his heartbeat, and it slows as our breathing does. As the anxiety settles, a new emotion creeps in: embarrassment.

I had a panic attack in the middle of someone's front walk because boys dressed as clowns scared me. Usually when I have one, there isn't an audience, or at least not one like this. My parents and brothers and maybe my cousins might be witnesses, but not the neighborhood kids who will whisper about me. And this will be another reason for River to be over-protective, and for me to want to hide from the world.

As if he knows what I'm thinking, Kodiak whispers, "We made a wall around you. You're protected, Lavender. The boys are gone, and no one knows you're here. We can cut across the front lawn and go back to my house, if that would make it better. I can show you what I made the other day when I was at Queenie's."

Kodiak has anxiety too, so he also goes to see Queenie. But he's better at managing his most of the time. He has other things that make life difficult, though, like always wanting everything to be perfect, including himself. Mom says it's impossible to be perfect, so he's always setting himself up to fail, and it makes me sad.

Kodiak gets straight A's all the time, but if he gets one question wrong on a test, he has a meltdown. They're not the same as mine. He folds in on himself, a broken lawn chair. Beats himself up. Pushes himself too hard until he cracks, like a chip in a windshield that spiders out until the whole thing threatens to shatter. He usually manages to pull himself back together before it gets to that point. But not always.

Kodiak slips his hands in mine and pulls me to my feet. River nudges him out of the way and puts his arm around me, hiding me in his cape. All I want is the calm Kodiak brings, but now I have River's possessive anger and his guilt because he didn't see the boys with the masks before it was too late.

Sometimes it's hard to balance the things I want with the things that make me feel bad, like River's guilt and his overprotectiveness. And how much I like the attention from Kodiak.

12

Exposed

LAVENDER

Present day

"**H**AVE YOU TRIED talking to Kody?"

I have video therapy with Queenie today. Usually my sessions are more spread out, but with all the changes that have come with a new college and living away from home for the first time, we decided to add a few. "I don't know that talking would be particularly helpful," I tell her. I produce a heart marshmallow from my box of Lucky Charms and eat it.

"Why is that?"

"Because so far, every conversation I've had with him has reinforced all the reasons he stopped talking to me in the first place."

Queenie turns her head to the side, staring off at something in the distance. Her jaw tenses briefly, and she taps her lips. Sometimes I wonder how hard this is for her, because she knows both sides of this story. I'm not sure if she still talks to

Kodiak the way she does me, but for a lot of years, she treated both of us.

"My relationship with him was like an untended garden," I blurt out.

She turns back, a small smile tipping up one corner of her mouth. "That's an interesting comparison. Would you like to elaborate?"

"Well, if a garden is left untended, the weeds creep in and take over, don't they? No matter how careful you are, if you don't take care of it, they'll choke out everything beautiful, suffocate the delicate blossoms and replace them with hardy, ugly, impossible-to-eradicate parasites."

Queenie nods. "What other principle does this apply to?"

I think for a moment, putting together all the pieces of my past with Kodiak. "Dependency." I fish another marshmallow out of the box and flip it between my fingers. "Kodiak became my drug. I did things I knew would send me into a tailspin. And I didn't use any of the strategies we'd worked on because I wanted *him* to help me."

"To be fair, it wasn't one-sided," Queenie says softly. "But eventually you learned to depend on yourself again."

"I know."

Kodiak was complicit in our demise, determined to save me every single time.

For me, someone who felt powerless most of the time, it was a terrible, wonderful, heady feeling.

But it was me who single-handedly obliterated our friendship. He was the delicate flower, and I was the clinging vine. It was me who broke the beautiful, genius boy with a savior complex—one he could never satisfy, because the harder he tried, the worse it got.

Until it all came crumbling down.

THURSDAYS END WITH ART, my favorite class along with set and costume design, and I'm done by five thirty, which means my weekend officially starts in three hours.

Sure, I have lots of homework to tackle, but Maverick has an away game this weekend, and River has football, so I'll have the entire house to myself. No smelly boys, no video games, and best of all, no random girls and no Kodiak.

I enter the art studio, my mood buoyant and rising further when I see the easels set up. I didn't think we were going to be using them for another week or two, so this is an awesome surprise. In the middle of the room is a beautiful, black velvet chaise lounge.

Professor Meyer greets me with a wide smile.

"Human subject?" I ask, then shake my head. "I'm sorry. I'm just excited. How are you today, Professor?"

"No need to apologize, Lavender. And yes, human subject. We have a volunteer whose schedule isn't very flexible, and today worked, so here we are." Her smile and expression are ridiculously gleeful.

I glance around, noting the absence of palates and paint-brushes. "Are we sketching?" I'm a little disappointed. I love working with paint. But any opportunity to work on a human subject is a great one.

"We are. Why don't you get set up and choose a seat?"

I pick a spot near the front and set everything up, giddy with excitement. The fact that I get to end my week with some-thing I love is awesome. Maybe the rest of the weekend will be just as good. Even economics homework won't get me down.

The seats around me fill with students, all of whom seem as excited as I am. Once we're set up, Professor Meyer takes her place in the center of the room. "I know this is unexpected, but we had a rare opportunity present itself and a model offered to come in this week. Today we'll focus on sketching and shading. I urge you to pay close attention to detail. Your goal today is to capture the raw authenticity of the nude male form."

A quiet murmur goes through the room. I glance to my right and make accidental eye contact with the girl beside me, who also happens to be one of Bethany's friends. Her name is Elise. She's never been particularly friendly to me, but she's been even more sour since the cafeteria incident. She's also an art major and doesn't like that I'm not and still managed to get into the class.

She loves to offer harsh critique of everyone's work, especially mine. Last week she called my use of pastels juvenile and uninspiring. I think my silence also pisses her off, because I've never actually spoken to her.

"Please come on in." Professor Meyer's attention shifts to the back of the room, and the class turns as a group.

My excitement drains as our male model enters the studio, wearing a white terry cloth robe. *This can't be happening*, is my first thought, immediately followed by, *of course this is happening*.

And I am 100 percent certain it's happening because of me. I don't understand why Kodiak feels the need to remind me at every turn that I'm nothing to him and never will be.

I turn to face my easel, uninterested in watching everyone else fall under his spell. Kodiak is exactly like the place he's named for—exceptional, rugged, cold, unique. As much as I hate him, it's impossible to deny his stunning beauty, or to avoid being sucked in by it.

White terry cloth passes on my right. I don't want to look up, but I realize I have to. For the next three hours, he's going to be my primary focus. Even worse, I have to sketch him. Naked. In a room full of my peers.

I'm also aware that this entire thing is—or at least used to be —far outside his comfort zone. He used to get anxious before games when we were younger because it meant so many people would be watching him, and he was always afraid of failing. But he learned how to compartmentalize the anxiety, how to push it down and put it in a box so he could play without distraction.

Maybe he's learned to like the feeling of being watched. Maybe he's learned how to feed off it instead of letting it feed off him. Whatever the case, he's about to drop that robe and expose himself to a room full of strangers.

God, does it ever make me angry. And that anger makes me furious, because I don't want to feel anything about him, or for him. At all. I want to give zero fucks. It's clear that's where he is, so why can't I be?

His hand goes to the tie at his waist and stays there for several long seconds. Why isn't he disrobing? Maybe he's having a panic attack. Maybe he isn't as okay with this as he pretends to be. *Maybe he needs me like I used to need him.* The thought is fleeting, childish, and entirely too romantic. Kodiak doesn't need anyone. I lift my eyes. His jaw tics as I meet his eyes, the palest green. His pupils are pinpricks. *Acute anxiety.*

But that's what he was waiting for—my eyes on his. He pulls the tie, and I don't look away. We're locked in some kind of odd stare down. I don't understand what he's doing. What's the point of baring himself to me in front of everyone? Is it another way to humiliate me?

The robe slides over his heavily muscled shoulders and down his arms, piling on the floor at his feet. A collective intake of breath follows. A feminine giggle comes from somewhere behind me and is quickly covered by an embarrassed cough. And then silence.

Kodiak doesn't break eye contact as he steps back and drops down on the chaise. Which is when I realize what exactly has elicited the inappropriate giggle. Aside from the fact that Kodiak is built like a Greek god, carved out of marble by the most talented of hands, he's also unapologetically sporting a semi. At half-mast, he has a lot going on, so I don't want to think too hard about what the deal is when he's fully erect. Or why he's hard in the first place. It's possible he gets off on my misery these days.

He doesn't make a move to hide his erection. Instead, he reclines and stretches his arm across the back of the chaise. The way he positions himself seems almost careless, but I can see that it's not. Every muscle is tense, vibrating with disquiet. He bends one knee and the other stays on the floor, which means every person in the room has an excellent view of his ample junk.

He's uncircumcised, which I didn't know until today. Although I'm very aware that my dad is also in that category of male. My mom used to talk about the Snuffie and Super MC when I was younger. Eventually I figured out she was referring to my dad's penis. Yes, I'm scarred for life.

Yes, it's also kind of hilarious.

Or it was, until I realized all the tube-shaped superhero costumes she'd made had a use. There are some things you should never, ever know about your parents.

Kodiak could easily shift his hand and employ some modesty, covering some of the show he's putting on, but instead, he splays his hand on his upper thigh, palm down. Again, it seems casual, but it's what he used to do when he was trying to keep his knee from bouncing.

And still, he's staring at me, and still, I'm staring back.

I thought I hated him before, but it has nothing on how I feel about him now. I want to kick him in the balls, which incidentally, are resting on the plush velvet seat. Looks like that will need a steam clean after this.

A cough comes from my right. I glance at Elise, and she widens her eyes at me. I don't know what message she's trying to send, but it distracts me from my rage-glaring. I exhale my frustration and prepare for the torture of having to look at my least favorite person in the entire world for the next few hours. While he's naked.

I pick up my pencil and get to work, sketching first the outline of the chaise and then Kodiak's form. I avoid looking above the neck. Even with as little direct contact as we've had recently, I can draw every detail of his face from memory. However, I don't take the literal route with this particular project. Instead, I take a few artistic liberties.

Halfway through class, we take a ten-minute break, and Kodiak, whose semi has deflated—and whose unerect penis is still annoyingly impressive—shrugs back into his robe. A few of the bolder students, who obviously know who he is, giggle and titter as he passes them, flashing his dimpled smile.

I wait until he leaves the room before I finally relax. I need to pee, badly. Instead of using the bathroom on this floor, I go down a level so I can avoid running into Kodiak in the hall. Of course he's standing out there, surrounded by girls, his smile fake and uneasy.

Kodiak was always good with small doses of interaction, but he never did well with being surrounded, especially by people he doesn't know. Not that I care to save him. This mess is his, not mine.

A few minutes later I return to my easel, and Elise shifts in her seat, eyes narrowed and homed in on me.

"What's the deal?" She motions to the empty chaise.

I give her a *what-are-you-talking-about* look.

She rolls her eyes. "He's been staring at you the entire time."

"He plays hockey with my brother."

"So, you're a thing?"

"No."

"I don't believe you. He's been looking at you like he wants to either stab you or eat you for dinner."

"The former is more likely than the latter."

"You know Bethany already has dibs on him. Plus, I've heard he's kinky as hell. Likes to watch and stuff."

I don't respond. I have nothing to say to that.

The class trickles back in, and Kodiak drops his robe again. At least he's not hard anymore.

I spend the second half of the class working on the details above his neck and between his legs. Professor Meyer stops behind me. I wouldn't be the least bit surprised if I end up with a failing mark for this, but there's so much gratification in the end product that it will be totally worth it.

She clears her throat, and it actually sounds like she's trying not to laugh. "That's an interesting perspective, Lavender."

"Just embellishing the subject, so it lines up with my vision."

"I look forward to hearing all about it in your write-up." She moves on to Elise and calls out, "Ten minutes left. Please put the finishing touches on your piece."

I add extra shading, taking liberties by adding a hint of color until Professor Meyer calls time and we all have to put our pencils down. Elise looks over, forever trying to compare us when we have completely different styles. Besides, I'm going to spend my life sewing costumes, not creating masterpieces on canvas or paper. This is my therapy, not my career.

She's in the middle of a sip of water, which she sprays all over her drawing and the floor. "Oh my God!"

All of a sudden, I have the attention of the entire class. I'm actually surprised the students behind me didn't notice until now, or maybe I was covering the head with my body.

Curiosity must get the better of Kodiak, because he shrugs into the robe and comes around to look at my piece. He coughs a couple of times. "Wow, that's—"

"Astoundingly accurate," I supply.

I drew a half-erect penis where his head should be, and where the head of his actual penis should be, I drew his face—a tiny, very detailed version, red and angry, with horns, like the devil.

It's actually one of my better drawings.

13

The Secrets We Keep

LAVENDER

Present day

POST-ART CLASS, I spend the night at Lovey and Lacey's, not wanting to go home to the possibility of having to face Kodiak. He's always at our place. I don't know why they can't hang out over at his and BJ's house. I love seeing BJ, but Kodiak is always with him.

I don't tell the girls why I don't want to go home until after I've had two coolers. And then my motormouth kicks in and I spill all the half-hard-on beans. They're equally as mystified by the fact that he posed for my class as I am. It's completely out of character for him. I also tell them what happened with Dylan and how I'm not really interested in another tutoring session, and I doubt he is either.

I sleep like crap and dream about Kodiak lounging in that freaking velvet chaise—except in the dream he's clothed and I'm the one who's naked, straddling his lap, my classmates sketching us as he tells me over and over that he'll never love me.

Even in my dreams I'm pathetic.

I don't head home until early afternoon on Friday. Lacey and Lovey tell me I can stay over again, but there's a sorority party, and Dylan might be there. I'd like to avoid him for as long as I can.

When I enter my house, BJ's passed out in the recliner—I think he likes it more than his own bed. Three guys fill the leather couch, wearing what are probably wet swim shorts, drinking beers, and playing video games. One of them is Quinn. He's not here often. He's getting his master's in physical therapy. He's a second-round pick based on his reputation, since his anger issues are a red flag for the scouts.

One of the guys calls out to me, and Quinn shoots him a glare that would make me pee myself if I didn't know him. "She's a Waters. Do not talk to her unless you want to lose precious body parts."

I roll my eyes. "Please don't castrate anyone on my behalf. Blood is really hard to get out of the carpet."

"I'd do it in the backyard to avoid the mess." He gives me a wink and brings the bottle to his lips, tipping his head back and draining the contents.

"Not sure if I should be grateful or concerned that you've already thought that through." I salute him, grab a box of Lucky Charms from the cupboard—checking to make sure it's not one of the three I've already eaten all the marshmallows out of—and hoof it up to my room. I lock the door and shove in my earbuds, pulling up a heavy album to drown out the music blasting from the outdoor speaker.

I move across the room and run my fingers over the satin-and-velvet skirt hanging from my dress form. It's a project for my costume and set design class. It isn't due for another month, but since I love sewing more than Lucky Charms, I started it right away.

It's complex and layered, with lots of ruching, an intricate lace overlay, and detailed bead work. I'm in the middle of a particularly tricky part when there's a knock on my door. I'm inclined to ignore it, but the knocking continues—two raps, a pause, one rap. It's River.

I finish the line of stitching, set the dress aside, push my chair back, and stand slowly. My shoulders are sore from hunching over, and my right foot is stiff. I hobble to the door and open it a crack.

"Hey, can I come in?" He looks over my head, as if he's expecting someone to be in here with me.

The only people who come up to my room are Lovey and Lacey, and that's only happened a couple of times.

"Sure. 'Sup?"

He steps inside my room and closes the door behind him. His expression is pensive, and serious, as it is most of the time. "This kinda sucks for you, doesn't it?"

I wait for him to elaborate, but he just stands there, frowning. "My earbuds drown most of the noise out," I finally say. I have to assume he's referring to the party happening downstairs and outside.

"I don't mean the noise. Well, I do mean the noise. But it's more than that. It's everything—all the jocks, the girls, the people, the mess."

I shrug. The mess isn't much of an issue. River and Mav aren't the tidiest, but we have a cleaner who comes every Monday.

I sigh and thread my fingers through his, squeezing. "I don't need to be babied, River. I can handle the parties and the noise and everything that comes with it. I might not want to partici- pate all the time, but I don't mind being a silent observer. This is normal college-kid behavior. And we have a sweet house with a pool, and you and Maverick have lots of friends. I don't want you to think you have to shoo everyone away because you're worried about me."

He flips my hand over and skims the faint crescent scars, *most* of them faded. "I feel like a shitty brother. I'm the one who pushed you to move in with us, and I'm hardly here. And when I am, there are always people to entertain, and you're stuck up here."

"It's my choice to be up here."

He nods, but I can tell he wants to say more. Instead, he drops his head and sighs. "I'm going over to a friend's house tonight, and I'm probably gonna stay there."

"A friend?" I quirk a brow.

"I'm not feeling the party vibe, and I have practice tomorrow morning." He's focused on his fingernails.

"Okay. Do I know this friend?"

He makes a face and ignores my question. "You want me to take you to Lovey and Lacey's or something?"

Maybe he's finally met someone he actually likes. That idea hurts a bit, because River and I don't keep things from each other. Not often anyway, though anything involving Kodiak has been the exception to that rule. I let it go for now. "Mav has an away game tomorrow, right?"

River nods, dark hair flopping over his right eye. He's freshly showered, and he smells faintly of cologne. I also note that he's wearing his stylish jeans, his favorite running shoes, and a shirt I once told him made his arms look awesome.

"I'm good here," I tell him. "I'm working on a dress, and I can sleep in if the house is quiet and empty in the morning."

"Okay. Just keep your door locked. Some of those guys down there are douchebags."

"Sure."

He pulls me into a rare hug. It's tight and hard and full of pent-up emotion. "I'll always be your trampoline, Lav, even if you don't need me to be."

"I know I'm always safe to land."

"Always." He kisses me on the top of the head and slips out the door, waiting for me to turn the lock before he taps on the door and descends the stairs, leaving me to wonder what secrets he's keeping.

14

Burn It All Down

LAVENDER

Present day

I WAKE UP to the sound of a door slamming at the ass-crack of dawn. Maverick's game is in the afternoon, and the bus ride is two and a half hours. They won't get back until this evening. I can wander around in my jammies and eat cereal out of the box without anyone getting on me about it. I can also watch TV in the living room on the huge screen instead of the small one in my room. But first, I'm going to sleep in.

I pull my covers over my head and snuggle into my pillow. However, after what feels like a handful of minutes later, I'm woken again by the obnoxious blare of a siren.

I bury my head under the pillow to block it out, but it's not stopping. At all. In fact, it sounds like it's right outside the house. After thirty seconds of pervasive sirens, I finally throw my covers off, drag my ass out of bed, and peek through the blinds. A haze hangs in the air, smoke coming from somewhere close by.

I rush to the next window—the one that has a view of the top of BJ and Kodiak's house and a bit of their backyard. Smoke billows into the air, and the flashing lights of the fire truck out front make my chest suddenly tight.

"Shit. *Shit.*" Everyone should already be on the bus, except for BJ—who sleeps like the actual dead.

I wrench open my door and rush down the stairs. I'm not fully coherent yet, my body in flight-or-fight mode. My coordination is bullshit on the best of days, so I skid down the first set of steps on my ass, slam into the wall on the landing, and then hurtle myself down the second set. For sure I'm going to have bruises, but all I can think of is BJ in that burning house.

I bolt through the living room and come to an abrupt halt when I see BJ stretched out on one of the recliners, mouth open, a hot dog hanging out of the right side like an unlit cigar. He's surrounded by empty food boxes. It smells like stale farts and sour sleep breath, but I have never been so freaking happy to see my cousin in my entire life.

I rush over, trip on a half-empty carton of Ramen noodles, and land on top of him. The hot dog slides out of his mouth and down into the chair somewhere. He grunts, but otherwise doesn't rouse.

I shake his shoulders until his eyes pop open. It takes me a moment to find my voice through the panic. "There's a fire!"

His confusion morphs into concern. "What? Where? Here?"

I give my head a violent shake and clamber out of the chair, stumbling backward. BJ is quick, though, and he grabs me before I land on my ass.

"Your place. Come on." I grab his wrist and tug, making him follow me outside.

Instead of a clear, bright morning, we step out into a cloud of acrid smoke.

"Holy shit!" And now it's not me pulling BJ along, it's him pulling me.

I stumble, barefoot and light-headed. BJ wraps an arm around my waist and hauls me up so my feet aren't touching the ground. He cuts across the lawns to get to his house, but police stop him. There's already a crowd of students congregated across the street, watching smoke billow out of the windows on the first floor.

"Hey, hey, you can't go in there," an officer tells us.

"That's my house. What happened? Was there anyone in there? Is there anyone in there?" His panicked gaze darts to mine, the same fears reflected there.

"Game." My voice is a whisper I'm sure he can barely catch over the sound of people shouting and the spray of water.

"Shit. Right. Thank God." BJ runs his free hand through his sleep-messed hair.

The police officer nods in confirmation. "The house is empty. The fire started in the kitchen. You said you live here, son?"

BJ scrubs his palm over his face and motions to me. "Yeah. I crashed at my cousin's last night."

The police officer looks from him to me and back again. "Your cousin?"

It takes me a few seconds to understand why he's wearing a confused expression. BJ is dressed in only a pair of low-slung jogging pants. His entire lean, somewhat wiry chest on display, along with his tattooed arm, which is mostly a colorful burst of flowers. Lilies to be exact, because that's his mom's name, and he loves the freaking shit out of her.

Beyond the shirtlessness, based on the way his jogging pants hang, and the outline at the front, he's commando. I'm dressed in a pair of sleep shorts and a tank top. It's black, thankfully, so it hides my nipples, but I'm braless, and there's a lot of cleavage. BJ's arm is wrapped around my waist, presumably to keep me from tripping over my own feet.

"Yeah. Cousin. She lives just there." BJ thumbs over his shoulder and then points at the smoking house. "How bad is it? Do you know what happened? My dad is going to shit a brick." BJ is all over the place, but I can understand why since his house is currently on fire.

"Hard to say. We'll know more soon, but it looks like the fire was confined to the kitchen for the most part. You have roommates?"

"Yeah, two, but they play hockey for the school team, so they're away until tonight." He looks to me. "This is gonna be bad. We're gonna have to call everyone."

I shake my head. "I'm not calling Quinn's dad." Lance Romero scares the crap out of me. He's a nice guy, but when he gets pissed about something, he's a lot like my dad. The fuse gets lit, and he goes off. I've only seen it a few times, but that is more than enough. "Do you think it'll be better if we call your mom or your dad first?"

BJ strokes his beard like a magic genie is going to appear and blows out a breath. "Dunno who's gonna be less volatile. I'd say my mom, but man, I can't see her being happy to hear the kitchen went up in flames. I really hope it was faulty wiring or something."

Since there's nothing we can do but stand around and watch the firefighters do their job, BJ and I head back to my house so I can change and find him something to wear from Maverick's room. I pull a T-shirt from my brother's closet, unwilling to look inside his dresser. There's a distinct possibility I might find things I don't want to, if the tub of lube and box of condoms decorating his nightstand are any indication.

When I return, BJ is sitting at the kitchen table, his phone in front of him, his hands in his hair. I toss the shirt at him and turn on the Nespresso machine.

"Coffee?"

"Please."

Neither of us talks while I prepare lattes; mine is coconut milk. I grab a box of Lucky Charms from the cupboard and tuck it under my arm. "We should probably go back out there."

I don't know what purpose it will serve, other than to remind us we're lucky the house was empty and BJ likes to sleep on our recliner.

"Yeah." He's still staring at his phone.

"Did you call your parents?" I pop a crunchy marshmallow into my mouth. "You don't want them to see it on the news first."

"Shit, you're right. It's gonna be everywhere." He waffles between his mom and dad and finally settles on his dad.

BJ video calls him. When his face pops up, it's like looking in an aging mirror. BJ has his mom's dark eyes, and his hair is darker than his dad's salt and pepper, but they are essentially replicas of each other. Uncle Randy's grin falls as soon as he sees BJ's serious expression. "What's wrong?"

BJ explains what he knows so far—that there was a fire, and it started in the kitchen, but they have it under control now. Uncle Randy throws a million questions at him, so we end up walking back over to the house so his dad can talk to someone in charge.

Of course when the police and firefighters realize it's *the* Randy Ballistic, former NHL player, they all lose their cool.

Like my parents, BJ's live an hour or so away. They bought a piece of property on Lake Geneva a few years ago, and when our dads—along with my uncle Miller—decided to start their own training camp, they moved out there too. It didn't hurt that some of their former teammates and friends had also moved back to the area.

So of course that means BJ's parents are coming to assess the damage. Within the hour, I have a call from my mom, telling me they're coming too, along with the Romeros and the Bowmans.

BJ and I end our respective calls, during which there is no room for argument, and both exhale the same, long, distressed breath. It sucks that we're the only ones here to deal with this.

"My parents aren't going to tell Mav before the game," I report.

BJ yanks on his beard a couple of times. If he keeps doing that, he's going to start pulling it out. "Yeah, but, like, everyone on the block has seen the spectacle, and for sure people were recording it out there and posting it. Someone's gonna send something to the guys."

I bang my head on BJ's biceps. He's right. It's going to get back to them. "I guess it's better coming from us?"

"Probably."

"I'll call my brothers?" River might be at practice, but if he catches wind that BJ's house caught on fire, he'll be worried because those two are pretty tight. I make a face like I've sucked on a lemon. "You can call Quinn and Kodiak? Or Mav can tell them?"

BJ nods resolutely and pulls up his contact list while I call Mav and tell him what happened.

"Oh shit, Kody's gonna flip his lid." Is pretty much all Mav has to say.

After that, I call my twin. I assure him everything is okay and he tells me he'll be home in a couple of hours.

BJ and I sit on my back deck, where the nosy bastards who are filming and posting on social media can't see us. There's now a police barricade at the end of the street to keep people from driving by. Neighbors are throwing porch parties, watching the fire crew clean up. It seems like the worst of it has been taken care of, but the air is sharp with smoke.

"Everything is going to smell like a freaking campfire. Kody is going to lose his mind." BJ keeps rubbing his beard.

I tip my head back and look up at the sky. "Do you think he'll have a meltdown?" Kodiak has always been very particular about his things.

"Absolutely." BJ laces his hands behind his head. "He's being a fucking idiot."

I glance at BJ. "What do you mean?"

"He'll for sure have some sort of massive attack, and it won't be pretty because he's Kody, but I'm not talking about the house. I mean with you. He's being an idiot. I know he's been nothing but a dick to you."

"He really hasn't been *anything* to me since we were kids." Such a stupid lie.

"If you want to play it that way, you go right ahead. But I've known both of you my entire life. You two were tight, like it was . . ." He shakes his head. "I remember being jealous as a kid."

"Jealous? Of what?"

"I don't know exactly. It's weird. Everyone wanted to protect you all the time, and I get why, because you went through a lot."

Like everyone else, BJ talks *around* the carnival incident.

"River has always been the worst, and I understand why, 'cause he's your twin, but Kody, man, he lived for you, and you were the same. You had this thing no one could touch. It drove River fucking insane."

"Everything drives River insane, and we were kids."

"Nothing drives River more insane than the way Kody was with you, and you know it."

I nod because it's true.

BJ crosses one leg over the other. "I get that we were kids, but like I said, it's weird shit. We all knew it was something way bigger. Like, I'm tight with Quinn and River as much as anyone can be, but you and Kody were an extension of each other. He's never been like that with anyone else. He even keeps Maverick at arm's length. But back when we were kids, when you moved, he moved. You were completely in sync with each other. It was like watching a perfect-ten pairs performance on the ice."

I've watched BJ skate pairs competitions before. He's absolutely amazing, and it's easy to see why pretty much every partner he's ever had falls hopelessly in love with him. He pretends it isn't happening.

I consider how my relationship with Kodiak must have appeared to our friends. BJ's right; Kodiak and I always had a very strange kind of connection.

"Everyone thought it was so cute, but after that night you got locked in the closet, things changed." BJ looks away from his smoking house, all sorts of questions in his eyes.

No one really talked about the closet incident after it happened. For about a week, Maverick went to Kodiak's house and he didn't come to ours, but it wasn't because of me. River was the issue. Lainey and my mom had closed-door conversations, and I saw Queenie every day during that time.

The longer they kept us apart, the worse my anxiety got, and I started having nightmares about being locked in the closet. I slept in River's room, and still the nightmares kept coming. Eventually they gave in and let Kodiak come over when River was out with friends. I still remember how hard it was not to rush up and hug him, to soak in the balm of his presence like a sponge.

He'd looked so tired, like me. And worn out, like me.

That event had flipped a switch in both of us. We recognized exactly what we could do for each other, and it became . . . addictive. I can see now how dangerous that probably was. Power wielded over each other has the ability to both build and break.

"Kodiak was only trying to help me. That's all he was ever trying to do. It just became unhealthy for both of us." At least that's what our parents eventually decided.

BJ stays silent for a while. "But then something happened two years ago with you guys, when he was a sophomore here."

My head snaps in his direction. "Nothing ha—"

I stop, because he's giving me the BJ *fuck-off* look. "He spiraled after winter break. So whatever happened was big. Kody went dark after that. He didn't eat for days, and he's always so rigid about everything. He spent hours at the gym, like he was punishing himself. And girls started talking. Like, he'd never been big on hookups, but there were rumors . . ."

I don't want to think about Kodiak with an endless stream of girls, but I can't help but be curious. "What kind of rumors?"

"Like, he wouldn't let anyone touch him." BJ blows out a breath. "I should not be telling you this shit."

"What do you mean he wouldn't let anyone touch him? I've seen girls put their hands on him plenty of times."

"I don't know. It's just rumors."

"Which are usually built on a grain of truth."

"All I'm saying is whatever happened or didn't happen between the two of you over winter break that year really messed him up—more than he already is, anyway. I can't imagine what it's like to live inside his head. It's bad enough that he's an elite athlete, but to be that smart too? It's like he can predict his own mistakes before he makes them. It would drive me mental."

I nod. "His panic attacks used to be legendary."
"They still are; he just suffers silently now."
I don't ask what that means.

15

No Empty Spaces

LAVENDER

Present day

A LITTLE WHILE later BJ and I realize that with the parents descending, we're going to need the house *not* to look like a complete man cave sty so we rush around, cleaning up the worst of the mess. It takes us an entire hour to manage the kitchen and the living room.

The backyard could be better, but there's not a lot we can do with the limited time we have. BJ tosses the empties and the Solo cups into garbage bags before the doorbell rings.

The second I open it, the air is crushed out of me, thanks to my mom's hug. I sink into her, absorbing her love. We've always been close. We love a lot of the same things—minus math—and being the only girl, the youngest, and having some massive social anxiety has made me a bit of a mama's girl. Which I'm totally okay with.

"I am so, so sorry, sweetie," she whispers into my ear.

I pat her back. "We're okay."

She gives me another squeeze and mutters, "No, I meant that Gigi and Pops are planning to stop by this afternoon, and she's bringing you a present. I tried to tell her now is not the time, but she insisted, and honestly, you kinda want it because it's awesome, but I'm still sorry. Just don't open it in front of everyone." She holds me at arm's length, her expression somewhere between empathy, amusement, and worry.

"Thanks for the warning." My gigi is awesome. She's also very, very liberal. I've amassed an entire drawer full of personal pleasure devices because she wants to make sure I know my own body before anyone else does. The message is a good one, but it can be embarrassing when she hands these things to me in front of my family.

"I didn't want you to walk into that scenario unprepared." Mom cups my face between her hands. "You look tired. Are you sleeping okay? How about eating? Have you been moopy? I brought a new bottle of lactose pills for you."

"I'm fine, Mom, really."

She nods and scans the space beyond me, which leads to the kitchen. "What about the boys? Are they being slobs? They're not having too many parties, are they? Are they being careful about who they invite over? Do you have mace? Maybe we should go out and get some, or you could take a self-defense class refresher. That might be a good idea."

"Mom." I squeeze her shoulders. "Take a breath."

Her eyes fall shut for a few seconds, and she and I breathe a count of four and out again. When she opens them, she looks like she might get weepy on me. God, I miss her. She has always been in my corner, doing everything she can to help me be comfortable in my own skin.

"I'm so glad no one was in that house." She exhales another long, slow breath.

"Me too."

"Lainey must be beside herself. She and Rook should be here soon."

I nod. "Aunt Lily and Uncle Randy left about the same time you did, so they shouldn't be far behind you."

"And Lance and Poppy just had to pick up the girls from a friend's house and then they were heading out, too."

"I'm surprised Aunt Charlene and Uncle Darren didn't come along for shits and giggles." I'm only half joking. Charlene and Darren aren't technically my aunt and uncle, but our families are so close we might as well all be related.

"Darren had to run a hockey practice for your dad and Charlene had to take Rose to rehearsal, otherwise they'd be here, too." She fiddles with my hair. Her nails are a glittery purple, the color of my name. "How are things with Kody?"

I shrug noncommittally. "I don't really see much of him. The guys are always at practice, or games, or class, and so am I. I've been hanging out with Lacey and Lovey a lot, though." I shift the conversation, because talking about Kodiak with my mom is never easy, and I don't want to lie to her.

She doesn't have a chance to ask any more questions because the front door swings open again. "How's my baby girl?" My dad swoops in and picks me up like I'm a toddler, folding me into a ridiculously tight bear hug.

"Oh my God! You're going to break my ribs, Dad!" He gives me a stubbled kiss on the cheek and sets me back on the floor.

"I missed you, kiddo." He holds me by the shoulders, and his lips thin. "Have you lost weight? You look tired, honey. Are the boys being a problem?"

"Everything's fine." I wrap my arms around his waist. "And I miss you too."

I let him hug me for a while. Me going away for college has

been tough for him. He tried to bribe me with a really awesome car to get me to stay in Lake Geneva. Then River's head nearly exploded when I suggested I'd live in the dorm, so here I am. I still got a cool car out of the deal, though, because my dad didn't want me to be without my own transportation. Obviously I haven't mentioned to anyone that I signed up for the student housing waiting list. No need to invite unnecessary drama.

There are more people waiting on the steps behind him, so we move out of the foyer. Lainey greets me with a huge hug. Kodiak is such a mix of his parents. He has his mother's dark hair, almond-shaped eyes, and full lips, but he has his dad's dimple, rugged jawline, and size.

"You've really grown up, haven't you?" She squeezes my hands.

I shrug. I'm severely lacking in height, but I'm not the gawky little girl she probably remembers. "Happens to all of us, I guess."

She laughs and her eyes soften. "I hope my son has been treating you well."

I fight to keep my smile in place. "I don't see too much of him."

A shadow of sadness passes behind her eyes. "Really? I thought with him living down the street, you'd see more of each other."

I swallow past the lump in my throat. "Well, they're all so busy with sports and classes."

"Right. Of course."

Fortunately, Uncle Randy and Aunt Lily arrive to end that uncomfortable conversation. I can't tell Lainey the truth.

By midafternoon, all of the parents are gathered on the back deck. My dad wanted to shock the pool, but my mom told him to hold off until right before they leave. He did, however, clean the hot tub. He was not impressed by the condom wrappers he found nearby.

Lance and Poppy, Quinn's parents, are the last to arrive, and they bring his younger sisters along. Heather is fifteen, and Celeste is thirteen, and I adore them. We jump in the pool while we wait for the guys to get home.

Just as my dad and Rook head to campus to pick up the boys, Gigi and Gram-pot show up.

"I have a special present for you!" Gigi hands me a small, wrapped box. Upon closer inspection, I realize the design on the paper is cartoon penises with faces. Thankfully, the presence of Heather and Celeste means I can put off opening it, and I run it up to my room.

My dad and Rook pick up takeout on the way home from getting the boys, and when they return, we all sit outside on the back deck, stuffing our faces while our parents figure out how to deal with the situation.

Kodiak sits on the far side of the deck, beside his mom. His knee bounces a mile a minute, a sure sign he's anxious. Not that I blame him. The kitchen in their house is destroyed.

"I talked to a contractor friend on the way over, and he's saying it'll take at least a few weeks for the house to air out and the kitchen renovations to be done," Uncle Randy says.

"Yeah, I made a few calls too, and everyone I talked to said the same thing," Rook adds.

"Should we look at renting the boys a place?"

"I can stay at a friend's place for a while," Quinn says.

His dad gives him a look. "What kind of friend are we talking about?"

"Just someone from class."

His mom gives him a look. "A female someone?"

He shakes his head. "Just a buddy, don't worry, Ma."

"BJ can stay with us," Liam suggests, and Lane nods his agreement.

"You have an extra bedroom?" Uncle Randy asks.

"There's a game room in the basement with a murphy bed," BJ replies. "It'll be fine for a few weeks."

"Well, that's two out of three sorted," Uncle Randy says.

"What about the spare room here? Kody could stay with us. There's already a bed and a dresser in there," Maverick suggests.

My dad and Rook exchange a look. "I don't know if that's a good idea," my dad says.

"It's perfect, right, K?" Maverick's eyes are alight with excitement over the idea of having his best friend in the room down the hall. "Then everyone has somewhere to stay, and you don't have to deal with a rental. Besides, it's only for a few weeks."

A few weeks of Kodiak in the bedroom under mine. A few weeks of potentially running into him in the hall, or the kitchen, or anywhere really. A few weeks of his constant awfulness. What if he brings girls home? What if I have to listen to him banging them through the vents?

"Lavender, honey?" My mom squeezes my knee.

"Huh?" I glance around to find everyone looking at me. Including Kodiak. His expression is flat, but his knee bounces a few times before he spreads his hand over his thigh to stop it.

"Are you okay with that?"

I shrug, going for apathetic. "It's only a few weeks."

How bad could it be?

But based on how things have been so far, I know it has the potential to be really, really bad.

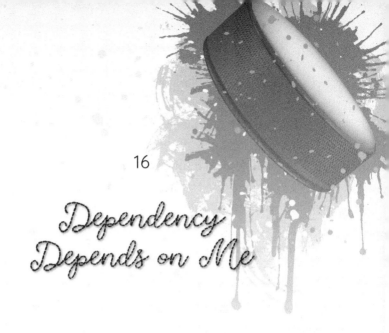

16

Dependency Depends on Me

KODIAK

Age 13

LAVENDER AND RIVER got cell phones for their eleventh birthday. I didn't get one until I turned twelve, but Lavender is a girl, and her parents worry about her a lot. They wanted her to be able to contact the people in her support network, so they gave in and got them both one.

It's supposed to help with her independence.

It also means we can text each other.

Which is good, because sometimes she needs me and not everyone understands. It makes me anxious when I can't be there to calm her down. I know what it's like to be trapped in my head, unable to get away from all the spinning negativity. Once I'm in the spiral, it's hard to get out.

On the way to hockey practice, my phone pings, so I flip it over and check the screen. It's Lavender.

I used to have a photo of her attached to her contact. It was

147

her at Queenie's, our therapist, working on one of her pieces of art. Her hair was pulled up in a messy ponytail, and she was wearing a dress she made. Her expression was fierce with concentration.

I changed it to an infinity symbol and switched her name to a boy's because I don't want my parents to know how much we message each other. I don't think they'd like it, since it's every day. I erase all the messages after we're done chatting, because my mom and dad check my phone sometimes and go through all my conversations with friends. Most of the time, I talk about hockey and school, but with Lavender it's different. We talk about other stuff, and I won't betray her trust, because she confides in me.

She tells me how sometimes River makes things hard for her. Or how everyone is so protective. I'm protective too, but Lavender doesn't seem to mind as much with me.

When she first got her phone and my dad saw how much we were messaging, he sat me down and talked to me about how Lavender is still mostly a little girl, and I'm a teenager, and I'm starting to grow up, but she's not there yet. I didn't want to hear it, even though I know he's right.

Lavender and I have always been close, and I don't want anyone to take her away from me, so I promised him it wasn't ever like *that*. I told my dad she's like my little sister, only she doesn't annoy me like Aspen.

I understand why he's worried, though. Sometimes at hockey practice, the older boys who play before us talk about their girlfriends and the stuff they do.

Maverick kissed Abby Saunders at a party last month, and her braces cut his lip. But he still said he'd do it again anyway.

I'm too focused on hockey to deal with girls right now. Lavender is the only girl I like hanging around with, and she's the only one who really gets me, just like I get her. I don't understand most girls. Or most people. I don't like having to pretend I'm interested in what someone is saying, and most of the time people like to fill the silence with nonsense.

Lavender doesn't have a lot to say when we're in big crowds, but when we're alone, or with people she's comfortable with, like her cousins, she's animated and fun and funny and introspective.

My mom says she's going to be a knockout when she's older and finds her confidence. Secretly, I don't know if I want that to happen, because then she might not need me anymore.

Lavender is what my mom calls an old soul. She sees people for what they are, and she feels everything really intensely. I think it's why she has such bad anxiety attacks—the kind that make it impossible for her to get words out, because the fear chokes her.

I know how to make that better. Not even Queenie is as good at calming her down as I am. Or River. And if I'm honest, I like that Lavender relies on me. I like that she needs me, that I'm the only person who can fix things for her when she's out of control. It makes me feel like *I'm* actually in control, because most of the time my head is a big, jumbled, uncomfortable mess.

The only time I really get any peace is when I'm on the ice, or when I'm helping Lavender. Occasionally my sleep is peaceful, but lately I've been waking up from dreams that make me feel bad, even though I don't have control over my thoughts when I'm unconscious. I never tell Queenie about them. Or anyone. I know they're wrong, so I keep them to myself.

Sometimes my sessions with Queenie overlap with Lavender's by a few minutes, and I get to see what she's been working on. Mostly I'm early because the possibility of being late stresses me out, but it also gives me a glimpse inside Lavender's head, which is a fascinating place. She's brilliant; not in the same academic way I am, but she understands the world on a different level.

I understand logic and math and reason. She understands people and feelings and emotions. I don't know which one of us is more tortured because of it.

My mom tells me we perseverate. I've learned it's a nice way of saying we're obsessive and overthink everything. The hard part about being a genius is knowing all the fundamentals but not being able to talk to anyone about anything mundane without sounding like an asshole.

My mom sounds sweet and kind and genuine. I sound like I hate everyone. Because mostly I do. I like Maverick because he gets me, and we both love hockey. I like my dad because we share the same passion, and he pushes me to be better. I love my mom because our brains are the same, and she feels the same level of guilt I do when I'm not entertained by people. And I revere Lavender because she's all the things I'm not. She's sensitive and aware, kind and sweet, and she's soft and compassionate. But she's also a warrior.

She knows how to exist in this world without always having to be part of it. Sure, she falls apart, but if she didn't, I wouldn't have the same role in her life, so I live for those moments when she needs me.

I glance over at my dad, but he's focused on driving. I key in my passcode and tap the message. Lavender knows my hockey practice schedule since I play with Maverick.

> ru at the arena
> yet

> heading to
> practice, sup?

I wait for a response, but one doesn't come right away. Finally the dots appear, and then disappear and appear again. That familiar unsettled feeling makes my legs restless, like there's an itch under my skin I can't get to. I force my feet to stay planted on the floor and my knees not to bounce.

> u ok?

> Everything ok,
> talk ltr

I stare at those four words, willing them to shift and change into the truth. Lavender doesn't usually message until later in the evening, especially when I have practice.

> don't lie 2 me

The dots appear again. This time the message is more jumbled, as if she's having trouble typing, which happens when she's having an anxiety attack and her fingers won't work the way they're supposed to.

> ill b ok, msg me after prctace

I want to call her, but I can't with my dad right beside me. I don't want another one of his lectures about how it's not good for me and Lavender to rely on each other like this.

> where are you

> drama clb at scool

Lavender helps paint the sets because it's what she's really good at. She can sing, but she doesn't like it when there's too much attention on her. *Any* attention really. Teachers know not to call on her in class—not because she doesn't know the answers, but because she can't stand all of those eyes on her, and she can't respond when everyone is looking.

She loves the drama club, but lately she's been having a hard time because there's a girl who isn't very nice to her.

> Courtney messing w u?

> she wont leve me alone

Our school is close to the arena. I check the clock. We can stop, and I can fix whatever is wrong and still make it to practice on time.

I take a deep breath and fight the panic creeping down my spine over the little lie I'm about to tell. "Oh crap!"

My dad glances at me, brow furrowed. "What's wrong?"

"I left my math binder at school, and we have a test on Friday I need to study for."

"Don't worry, kiddo. We'll stop at the school and pick it up on the way home from practice."

I let my knee bounce and run my hands up and down my thighs. "Can we stop on the way to practice? Sometimes they lock the doors to the hallway my locker is in before five, and then I can't get to it. It's an algebra test, and I got a few questions wrong on the last assignment. I don't want to mess it up again."

My dad looks at the clock and then down at my shaking legs. The little lies make my throat feel tight. We do have an algebra test, but I almost always have perfect scores on my math. But if my dad thinks it's going to make me anxious during practice, he's more likely to stop for me. He doesn't understand my worry the way my mom does, and he doesn't read my cues the same way either.

My mom would know I'm faking it, and she'd make me use my strategies to help calm down. My dad always goes right into solve-the-problem mode.

"You can't be late for practice." He grips the wheel, obviously considering it.

"I won't be late. It'll just take me a minute to grab it. Please? I really need to study tonight." My voice cracks, because some of my anxiety is real. I need to get to Lavender, and if he doesn't stop so I can, I'll end up having a real panic attack. Practice will be a mess, and it'll be a huge downward spiral that will take me hours to get out of.

I'll feel guilty that I let down my team, and I'll feel even worse that I couldn't help Lavender. The sooner I can get to her, the better everything will be.

"Okay, but you run in and grab your textbook and that's it." He taps on the wheel, frowning.

I nod vigorously. "I'll be super fast."

He pulls up to the front doors of the school, and I jump out before the car even comes to a full stop. As soon as I'm inside, I text Lavender to tell her I'm here and on my way to the theater.

She doesn't ask any questions, like how I managed to get here when I have practice.

in the prop room

I burst through the door that leads directly to the stage. I know the drama room well, even though there's no way I would ever be part of any kind of production.

I search for Courtney in the group of kids standing around, but I don't see her.

I head for the hall leading to the prop room, and one of the boys calls out, "The gym is on the other side of the school."

The drama teacher, Miss Garrett, calls my name, but I ignore her. My whole body breaks out in a cold sweat. I'm going to get in trouble for this—from Miss Garrett and definitely from my dad when I'm not back in two minutes—but I don't care. Lavender needs me.

It's dark behind the curtains, like a starless night sky, because the walls are painted black. As soon as I start down the hall, the noise of the students on the stage disappears, replaced by Courtney's nasal voice.

"What's wrong with you? You just do this to get attention. You know no one likes you, right? Everyone thinks you're a weirdo and a loser. They're only nice to you because of your brothers and Kody."

I rush toward her voice and the plaintive, low sound of Lavender trying not to cry. When I finally reach them, I find not only Courtney, but two of her other friends too. They form a wall in front of the prop room, blocking the way out. The room is dark, but the glow of a phone illuminates the girls' faces and the fact that one of them is covering the light switch with her hand.

They don't notice me, so I approach quietly, waiting until I'm right behind them before I growl, "What the hell do you think you're doing?"

Courtney shrieks, and the other two girls gasp and spin around. I slap the light switch on the wall, bathing the prop room in a harsh fluorescent glow. Rage makes my blood boil when I see Lavender backed into a corner, curled in on herself on the floor, forearms pressed against her ears to protect her from their words, face tucked into her knees, hands clenched into fists.

Courtney raises her hands, eyes wide, feigning innocence.

"Kody! Oh my gosh, Lavender's having one of her meltdowns, and we were trying to help."

I get in real close and drop my voice. "By calling her a weirdo and a loser? Get outta my way, *now*."

I push between them and crouch down in front of Lavender, acting as her shield. "Leave us alone," I snap, running a gentle hand over the back of her head and softening my tone. "It's okay, I'm here."

A full-body shudder runs through her, and she makes a sound, but there aren't any words yet. I wrap her in a protective hug and whisper the calming words that help bring her back down.

"Just ignore them, Lavender. It's you and me right now. I got you." I put my hand over one of hers and encourage her to unclench her fist so I can put her palm against the side of my neck. This helps the most, for her to feel how much her panic is mine too, and then we breathe together until she's calm again.

Her palm is damp and slick, and her nails bite briefly into the side of my neck as I flatten it there. I'm worried she's hurt herself. It happens sometimes when the panic gets really bad, like that time she got locked in the closet.

The sound of heels coming down the hall barely registers as Lavender drags in deep, gasping breaths, struggling to match her breathing to mine.

"What's going on back here?" Miss Garrett demands.

"Lavender's having an episode. We were trying to help her, but you know how she gets, Miss G," Courtney lies.

"You should've come to get me instead of trying to handle it yourself," she chastises. "Kody? What are you doing here?"

"I'm helping. And Courtney is a liar. They were bullying Lavender, calling her names and making things worse." I don't bother looking over my shoulder when I address the teacher.

Suddenly Courtney and her friends are loud, defensive, calling *me* a liar.

Lavender scrambles to get closer, to hide more of herself. She's tiny, the smallest girl in her class, and I'm already five-seven, so I dwarf her and cover her almost completely, keeping her safe from Courtney and the other mean girls. She buries her face against my chest, trying to muffle the desperate sounds that leak out of her.

I keep telling her it's okay and that I'm here and no one can see her while Miss Garrett orders the girls to go to the office.

"Kody, I need you to let go of Lavender, please," Miss Garrett says.

"Just give me a minute. I can make it better," I tell her.

Miss Garrett touches my shoulder. "I know you're trying to be a good friend, but this isn't appropriate."

"She needs me!" I snap.

"If you don't do as I ask, Kody, I'm going to have to get the principal."

Lavender takes a deep breath and lifts her head, those bright blue eyes meeting mine. She mouths the words *I'm sorry* and drops her hand from the side of my neck.

I don't want to let her go, but I also don't want to get in trouble with the principal, and I'm already going to be in shit with my dad over this. There's no winning, Lavender is going to be embarrassed, and there's a good chance she won't be at school tomorrow as a result.

"Oh my goodness, Kody! Are you okay?" Miss Garrett's eyes are wide with shock, and her horrified gaze is locked on the side of my neck.

I don't understand, at least not until I rub my sweat-damp skin and look down at Lavender's palms, which are decorated with crescent-shaped cuts, oozing blood because her nails are too long again. She curls her fingers into fists to hide the damage.

"It's fine. I'm not hurt; Lavender is," I tell her.

"Did those girls do this to you?" Miss Garrett crouches down beside us.

Lavender shakes her head, eyes darting between me and Miss Garrett.

"It happens when she's really upset; she can't control it," I explain, encouraging Lavender to open her hands.

Miss Garrett's hand comes up to cover her mouth, but she quickly schools her expression and clears her throat, her eyes soft. "We need to get you to the office so we can get those looked at, Lavender."

Now that the panic is over, for both me and Lavender, I can see how big the problems are here, and now I'm worried about a lot more than hockey practice and my dad being mad that I lied. I'm worried about Lavender getting bullied even worse because of this, and what Queenie is going to say when I have therapy later this week. But I shove that into the box in my head and lock it for now. I'll have lots of time to worry later.

"Can we clean up her hands first, please, Miss Garrett?"

She purses her lips and nods slowly. "Of course." I can tell she's unsure about leaving me alone with Lavender, but she pushes to a stand. "I'll be right back."

As soon as she's gone, I turn back to Lavender. "Has it been this bad for a while? And don't lie; I'll know if you're not telling the truth."

She licks her lips, her tongue running over the scar on the bottom one. "I was handling it okay until today," she whispers. "I'm sorry."

"Don't be sorry. It's not your fault."

"You're going to be in trouble."

I shrug, like it doesn't matter. She's already upset enough.

She doesn't need more things to worry about. So I lie, not wanting to send her back into the panic. "It's gonna be fine."

Miss Garrett returns with damp paper towels, and we clean up Lavender's hands and the side of my neck. We're on our way to the front office when it finally registers that my phone is buzzing in my pocket. I'm scared to answer it, aware my dad is going to freak out. I don't have a chance to figure out what I'm going to tell him, though, because he's in the office when we arrive.

My dad is a really big guy. He's over six feet tall with wide shoulders. He's mostly calm, and he doesn't get mad about much. My mom calls him her big teddy bear. It's kinda gross the way they are with each other. But my mom is right; my dad is soft, and the second he sees Lavender, head bowed, shoulders curled in like she's trying to hide herself from the world, the anger drains from his face and empathy settles in its place.

Sometimes it bugs me how different my dad is about Lavender and my mom's anxiety than he is mine.

His gaze shifts between Lavender and me as all the pieces come together, but it's Miss Garrett he addresses. "What's going on?"

Her smile is strained and questioning. "There was an incident, and Kody was trying to help."

"Lavender, are you okay, honey?" my dad asks softly.

She wrings her hands and nods, peeking up at him. "I'm sorry. I don't want Kodiak to get in trouble."

His face softens even more, and a sad smile pulls at the corner of his mouth. I don't like the way it makes my stomach feel. "I know that, sweetheart."

Miss Kay, the guidance counselor, appears in her office doorway, and she and Miss Garrett exchange a look as Lavender wordlessly moves into her office. She glances over her shoulder once more, expression full of uncertainty.

I spend the next half hour in the principal's office with my dad and Miss Garrett, explaining what happened. I don't really know Lavender's side of the story, but I tell them mine—how I know Courtney has been saying things to Lavender for a while, that I didn't know how bad it was, and that I overheard them saying mean things to her when I found them trapping her in the prop room.

Eventually they ask me to have a seat in the office and wait while they talk to my dad. There are no devices allowed in the office, so I ask if I can use the bathroom. While I'm in there, I delete all the messages between Lavender and me. It's going to cause me trouble, and there will be consequences, but I don't really care at this point.

I have unanswered messages from Maverick too, but I leave them alone for now. He'll find out what happened eventually, and he's still on the ice, where I should be right now. I splash cold water on my face and try to calm my breathing. There isn't anything I can do about it now, so I try not to focus on all the what-ifs.

By the time I get back to the office, my dad is waiting for me, grim-faced. He's silent on the way to the car, and my unease grows until it feels like I'm choking. I climb into the passenger seat, but all I want to do is run, to shut my brain off and stop it from racing. My mouth is dry, and my palms are sweaty.

My dad holds out his hand, palm up. He doesn't have to say anything for me to know what he wants. I slip my phone out of my pocket and set it in his palm. I was smart enough to change Lavender's contact back to her name while I was in the bathroom. I even put a picture of purple flowers on it.

He stares at the empty message screen for a few seconds before he holds it up for me to see. "Erasing your conversation with Lavender tells me you have something to hide, Kodiak."

I plant my palms firmly on my thighs, to keep them still and avoid fidgeting. "I didn't want to get her in trouble."

I can feel his eyes on me. I bite the inside of my cheek until I taste blood and keep my head down.

"Well, that's part of the problem, then, isn't it?"

I look over at him, confused.

"If the content of your messages with Lavender could get her into trouble, that's an issue in itself, not to mention that you lied to me outright about leaving your math book at school. I don't even understand what your plan was. You had to know I was going to find out."

I throw my hands in the air. "You wouldn't have stopped at the school if I'd told you why!"

"You're absolutely right. I would've called the school and had an adult—namely her guidance counselor—find her so they could deal with the situation at a school level. I also would've called Violet or Alex to let them know there was an issue. You are thirteen years old. You cannot make yourself her savior."

"You don't understand what it's like! I make it better for her! I can help when no one else can."

"You lied to me, knowing full well I was going to find out. This is a real problem."

"But I was right. Courtney was bullying her! You didn't hear what she said to Lavender."

"A teacher would have intervened," he says.

I scoff. "Yeah, right. You know what happens when Lavender panics. She can't even talk, so how was anyone going to help her?"

My dad is quiet for so long that I sneak a peek at him. He's rubbing his forehead, head bowed in something that looks a lot like defeat. "What happens when you're in high school next year, and she's still in middle school?"

I don't want to talk about next year. "River will be there."

It's weird. They're twins, but he can't help her when she's in that state. She says it's because she feels his frustration at not understanding.

"He wasn't there today, and it wasn't him she messaged, was it?" my dad asks.

"Maybe she messaged him before me, but I answered first."

"Maybe, but I have a feeling that's not what's been happening. This is getting worse, not better, and it has been for some time now."

I bite the inside of my cheek again, not wanting to acknowledge the truth.

"What happens if she messages you next year, looking for your help? What are you going to do when your high school is miles away from here?"

My legs start bouncing, even though I try to push them down and keep my feet flat on the floor. My head is spinning, my thoughts out of control. All I can see is Lavender curled up in a ball somewhere I can't get to her—a black void I can't reach into and pull her out of.

Suddenly it feels like all the air has been sucked out of the car. I clench and release my fists, aware there are things I can do to stop this, but I'm unable to find the will to use any of them. Instead, I let the panic take over, washing through me like a toxin.

"Shit," my dad mutters.

He puts his hand on my shoulder, but I shake him off and yell, "Don't!"

By the time we pull into the driveway, I'm itching to get out of my skin. My dad barely has the SUV in park, and I'm already running through the garage. I want to be alone with my thoughts so I can spiral in peace.

But my mom is right there, blocking the way up the stairs.

Her expression makes the guilt almost unmanageable. So much disappointment.

And fear.

I don't know what the fear is about. Is she scared *of me, for me?*

I press my palms against my temples—the headache already starting—screw my eyes closed so I can't see her face, and grip my hair. Anything to distract me from the jumble of thoughts slicing through my brain.

What if I'm not there next year?

What if they separate us?

What if I stop being able to fix things?

What if someone else is better at helping her than me?

Black spots form in my vision, and I keep fighting to breathe.

"Kodiak, honey, you need to sit down." My mom grabs me by the shoulders. "RJ, your help, please."

Two strong hands grip me under my arms, and I sink to the floor.

My head is swimming. It's too full. I just want Lavender to be okay.

"This is out of control," my dad says.

"Queenie's on her way over." My mom's warm palm rests against my cheek.

"What about—" My dad doesn't finish the sentence, but I think he wants to know about Lavender, and so do I.

My mom doesn't answer the unasked question directly. "I don't know what to do anymore," she says. "I don't know how to help them."

17

Seven

Kodiak

Age 13

I DON'T GO to school the next day. My session with Queenie was exhausting, and I had a hard time sleeping. I don't get up until late, and still feel tired. I want to know how Lavender is doing and make sure she's okay. My parents have confiscated my phone, so I have no way of getting in touch with her without going to her house. Maverick is my best friend, so I'm there a lot, but I worry that's going to change.

And I'm right to worry.

I come downstairs and find my parents and Lavender's parents sitting around the kitchen island. Their whispered conversation stops as soon as my mom addresses me. "Morning, sweetie, did you sleep okay?"

I shrug. I had bad dreams where I kept finding pieces of Lavender's dress and her broken glasses in front of a door I couldn't open. Every time I tried to call her name, all that came out was a whisper. It feels like I haven't slept at all.

My mom pushes out of her chair and comes around the island so she can pull me into a hug. Usually I'd be embarrassed because we have company, but this morning I need it. I don't like it when my parents are upset with me, and last night they were. I'm already taller than my mom, so I have to hunch. When she lets me go, her eyes are bright and shiny, as if she's trying not to cry.

"What's going on?"

She brushes my hair away from my forehead. "We all need to have a talk."

"We did that last night, though." My stomach feels off.

"I know, but we thought it would be best if we were all present, and Queenie will be here too."

I glance over where everyone is sitting. They look tired and sad. "What about Lavender?"

"Queenie's going to bring her. You should get dressed, because they'll be here soon. I'll make you some toast, okay?"

"Okay." I nod numbly and go back upstairs to change. Everything feels wrong.

Twenty minutes later, I'm sitting at the table with a glass of orange juice and buttered toast I don't think I can eat with how nervous I am—especially since Lavender is seated across the table from me, her parents situated to the right of her, just like mine.

There are dark circles under her eyes, making the blue even more vibrant. She clasps her hands on the table, and her teeth run along the scar on her bottom lip, over and over again. Her lips are red and raw.

Queenie sits at the head of the table, with us on either side. Her eyes are soft and full of compassion, but today she also looks nervous and slightly uncomfortable.

"Do you know why we're all here?" she asks.

"Because of me," Lavender says quietly.

Her mom puts her hand over Lavender's but doesn't squeeze.

"This isn't just about you, Lavender. If it were, only you would be here," Queenie explains. "What happened yesterday made us very aware of how out-of-hand this situation has gotten. We cannot rely on another human being to make our anxiety better."

"But it's only when it's really bad," I argue. "And I make it stop."

"Lavender's panic attacks have increased in frequency and severity over the past several months," Queenie says.

"That's because Courtney is bullying her. And middle school is different. It was hard for me too, when I started," I counter.

"I agree that middle school is different, and Lavender's told me about the bullying, which we're going to deal with. But it's more than that, Kody. You're hiding things, and that's not good for either of you."

"I'm not hiding anything!" But it's hard to swallow, because that's a lie.

Queenie nods to Lavender's dad, who produces a thick folder. Inside is a stack of white paper. He flips it open and fans the sheets out. His gaze meets mine; he doesn't look angry, but he doesn't look happy either. "These are the text messages between you and Lavender for the past two weeks."

I look at Lavender. Her chin quivers, and I can see the apology in her eyes. She didn't remember to erase the messages, or maybe her parents kept all the message receipts. I disabled mine, but didn't think to do the same for Lavender.

Tears stream down her cheeks, and her shoulders shake as

she curls in on herself. Her mom takes her hand, probably so she doesn't hurt herself again, although her nails have been cut.

"I know you care about Lavender, Kody, and you would never do anything to hurt her, but this"—her dad has to clear his throat—"talking almost twenty-four-seven without anyone knowing. It isn't good for either of you."

My anxiety spikes as I think about all the messages we've sent, the things we talk about, the times where some girl has said something mean to her, and I've told Lavender the girl is jealous because Lavender is prettier. Her dad has read them all. He knows sometimes we message late at night when she's having trouble sleeping, and that our messages are constant, starting first thing in the morning and continuing all day. We're each other's lifelines. Why don't they understand that?

"She's my friend," I say. "I just want to help."

My mom squeezes my hand. "We know, honey."

"I think it would be good to establish some boundaries," Queenie says gently.

Lavender's expression reflects the panic I feel.

"Boundaries?" she whispers.

"You two need some space from each other," my mom says.

Queenie looks at my mom, lips pursed, and I can tell she's doing that thing where she's really thinking about what she wants to say. "This dependency is becoming unhealthy. It's not good that you're hiding things from your parents." Queenie takes Lavender's free hand. "You were doing so well, Lavender. I know middle school is different, but we can't go backwards in life; we can only keep moving forward, or what happens?"

"We get stuck in bad patterns." Lavender's gaze shifts briefly to me and then away again. Two tears drop onto the tabletop. "I can do better. I'll do better. I'll work on my strategies. Just please . . ." Her voice breaks.

"I know you can, and it will be easier to do if we set some boundaries for the two of you. We'll try—" Queenie says.

"I really think it would be best if they had some time apart," Lavender's dad interrupts. "Kody will be in high school next year. Lavender, he's not going to be there to help you."

"But he can still be my friend, even if we're not in the same school." Lavender's eyes are wide, darting from her dad, to me, to Queenie.

"Of course he can, but you can't only rely on Kody to get you through the panic. You have to rely on you," Queenie says.

Even though I don't want to see it, acknowledge it, believe it, Lavender's dad is right.

I won't be there next year. And then what? How will she manage without me? I've been damaging Lavender without even realizing it. Setting her back instead of helping her move forward.

My stomach turns at the thought.

But Lavender was so helpless yesterday.

"You need to be able to cope without a human crutch," Queenie explains.

Lavender goes into a full meltdown.

All I can do is watch it happen, knowing how much worse I've made things for her.

I want to save her from her demons, and me from mine. But they always catch up. No matter how hard we try to outrun them.

Something dark settles in my gut. Anger I've never felt before bubbles up and mixes with despair, because I finally realize what everyone else seemed to know already: Lavender is better off without me.

18

Live with Your Choices

KODIAK

Present day

"HOLY FUCK, MAN, check out that ass," says some freshman jerk-off, who's had one too many beers, to the guy beside him.

I knew this was a bad idea, but I still let it happen. Maverick wanted one last party before we close up the pool, and then he went and disappeared upstairs to his room with his girl of the month, leaving me to manage things.

It was only supposed to be a few of the guys, but then a few people told a few more people, and it snowballed from there. I'd have to say there are more than fifty people out here. And it's only eight o'clock. I'm sure Mav will be back down in an hour, but until then, I have to deal with people, and that's pretty much my least favorite thing to do.

If my house weren't currently under construction thanks to some faulty wiring that shorted out the toaster oven, and the kitchen weren't completely gutted, I could leave him with this mess. But since I live here for the foreseeable future, I don't have much of a choice. On the upside, we'll have a sweet new kitchen whenever it's done.

Fortunately, River is out for the night, so I don't have to manage him glaring holes through me. And Lavender is likely hiding in her room, which is pretty much all she's done since I moved in after the fire. Her room is directly above mine.

Her bedframe squeaks at night when she's restless. The hum of her sewing machine is a relentless drone in the wee hours of the morning when she can't sleep. She sings in the shower all the time. But the worst are the nights when I mutter some heinous comment to her, meant to remind us both what a horrible fucking person I am. And later, I get the confirmation I'm looking for when I hear her fighting for breath. I used to be the one to save her. Now I'm the reason she falls apart. Those are the nights she sews for hours.

As the party rages, I distract myself by scrolling through my messages. My mom called an hour ago to check in on me. I lied and told her I was studying at the library, but that I would call her tomorrow.

"Oh shit." BJ sets down his beer, which he's been nursing for the past hour. It has to be piss warm by now. I glance at him, but my phone pings again; IG this time. I'm bored. I wish Lavender would stop hiding so I'd have something to occupy my brain.

"Someone distract Clarke so I can introduce myself." Freshman Jerk-off knocks back the rest of his beer and slams the plastic cup down on the railing, causing it to crumple.

"I'm on it," another freshman says. "But it means I get your sloppy seconds."

"Maybe she'll be down with tag-team action."

"Fuck, yeah." They fist bump each other.

"I would seriously consider shutting the fuck up," BJ says.

Freshman Jerk-off's brow furrows. "Why? Look at her—that bathing suit screams bend me over and slap my ass while you ride me from behind."

"Because that's my cousin, and if you so much as breathe in her direction, I'll use your nuts as a bow tie at my next formal event."

That gets my attention. I follow Freshman Jerk-off's gaze toward the pool and nearly ram my fist into his face when I realize who he's talking about. "What in the actual fuck?"

Standing at the edge of the pool, smiling at Clarke—a senior and one of the dirtiest players on the team—as he hands her a shot, is Lavender. It's bad enough that she's way underage—although more than half the people here fall into that category—and that she's wearing a goddamn white bikini, the top of which barely covers her nipples. The bottoms are a thong. Her entire ass is on display, including the strawberry birthmark that very much resembles a heart. I saw it once, by accident, when we were kids. Her butt had been eating her bathing suit at the time.

Obviously I never fucking forgot.

Is she the only girl out here in a thong? Nope. But she should know better than to put herself on display like this. If Maverick and River were here to see, they would lose their goddamn minds. And clearly the responsibility is going to fall on me, considering the way BJ is smirking.

"Lavender, get over here!" I shout.

Her smile widens, but she doesn't look away from Clarke. Instead, she raises her hand in the air and fires the bird in my direction.

BJ barks out a laugh.

"Fuck this bullshit." I slam my beer down on the closest surface, and because it's mostly full, it acts like a geyser, splashing me and everyone within a three-foot radius, including a few bunnies who are standing close by, eavesdropping on our conversation—or waiting for the right moment to rub their tits on whoever they're interested in hooking up with tonight. Three girls have done that to me already tonight, including that chick who came into my room in August and offered me her sloppy seconds.

All I can see is red as Clarke reaches out and fingers the end of Lavender's ponytail, conveniently resting about two inches away from her right boob. Which is what he's staring at. And so is every other guy out here. Or her ass.

Obviously this is payback for the art class. The major difference is the presence of alcohol and a lot of testosterone-fueled jocks. I'm not sure she really, truly thought it through before she came out here dressed the way she is. Because as much as she's smiling and laughing, her skin is turning red. It goes blotchy at her chest first and works its way up her shoulders and neck, slowly moving down her torso.

It's not something most people would notice right away. But I do. Because it's Lavender. And as much as she doesn't want me to know all of her deep, dark, painful secrets, I still do.

"Touch her again and you'll be minus more than just your front teeth," I call out as I approach.

I'm making a scene—one I'll probably regret because it's going to get back to Mav and River. But if they were here, this wouldn't be happening.

Lavender finally looks my way. "You can go back to your bunnies, Kodiak. I don't need a bodyguard or a babysitter."

Clarke laughs and smirks at me. "You heard her. We're good." He slings his arm over her shoulder and pulls her into his side. I'm pretty sure her ass cheek is pressed up against his leg, and his fingers dangle perilously close to her boob.

My control slips. The frustration over not being able to

have what I want is wearing me down. Everyone has an opinion on what's good for me—how I have to manage all the impulses, how I can't let the obsessions rule me the way they often do. But this is more than I can take. It's been weeks and weeks of fighting the need, of being an asshole because the alternative is to dive right back into that fixation—and if I do, I'm very worried it's going to consume me. And her.

But we're living in the same house. And she's right above me every night. Close enough to hear and too far away to touch.

All the rational parts of my brain short out. I slam my palms into Clarke's chest, and he stumbles back. Losing his footing, he lands in the pool with a massive splash.

Lavender throws her hands in the air, her anger nowhere near as vicious as mine. Not yet anyway. "What is your goddamn problem, Kodiak?"

"You are my fucking problem. You're always the problem," I snap.

A flash of hurt crosses her face, but she rolls her shoulders back. "You could solve your problem pretty easily by leaving, since this is *my* house, not *yours*."

She's right. Of course. I could have stayed in a million different places while my house is getting a new, uncharred kitchen, but I didn't want to. I wanted to be here so I could torture her the way she's tortured me for years without even realizing it. Turns out, I'm a bit of a masochist.

Clarke pulls himself out of the pool, spluttering and fuming. "What the hell is up your ass, Bowman?"

I point a finger at him. "Stay out of this. It's not your business, and she's not for you."

Lavender's mouth opens, but no words come out. A sick feeling makes my stomach twist. I'm doing this in a public place, something she hates so much. All this attention on her, and she's mostly naked.

I'm done with the audience. I try to take her hand, but she swats me away. I slip an arm around her waist and haul her up against me. She kicks and flails, making it difficult to avoid her thrashing limbs. I drop down on one knee, wrap my arm around her legs, and toss her over my shoulder. She shrieks, high-pitched and clearly shocked. I stalk toward the house, gripping her thighs tightly, because the last thing I want to do is drop her on her face.

She sucks in a gasping breath and wheezes my name, "Kodiak!"

Her tits bounce against my back as I jog up the stairs, past Freshman Jerk-off, the desperate bunnies, and BJ, whose brow is raised like he's in on a secret.

"BJ!" Lavender shrieks, extending her hand, but he's way too far away to reach.

He grins, shakes his head, and raises his hands in surrender. "Sorry, Lav, I can't help you now."

She grabs the edge of the doorframe as we pass through the French doors. I have to give it to her; she puts up a decent fight —not like when she was a scared little kid.

"Down!" she says, loud and squeaky and pissed.

I turn, not to acknowledge her, but to pry her fingers free. When I hit the first step on the way to the second floor, she slaps my ass, hard. And then she does it several more times, so I do it back.

She shrieks, obviously not expecting my retaliation.

"You might want to think twice before you do that again," I warn.

"You're an asshole, Kodiak!"

"You're just figuring that out now?" My skin prickles as I pass the second floor bedrooms and head for the attic, where we keep Princess Lavender.

The sharp sting of her teeth sinking into my side makes me

almost miss a step. My grip on her thigh tightens further, and I turn my head, biting the soft, hot flesh next to my ear. She tastes like things I shouldn't want.

"Ow!" she screams.

I release her skin from my teeth, barely resisting the urge to suck and leave a mark that will last. She kicks her door open for me, and I almost groan as I'm submerged in everything Lavender—posters on the walls, sparkling sewing needles, and the smells. There's fresh fabric, lavender candles to calm, and peppermint oil to stimulate for studying. The smell of her shampoo also hangs heavy in the air.

I've been in here a few times, even though I shouldn't— mostly as an experiment to see if I could handle it. I can't. My knees almost buckle as I breathe in the familiar scents, so much stronger up here. All around her room are pieces of random art and photographs of her with her family and friends.

There is nothing of me. Not one picture. Not a single memory.

I made it this way. I did this.

Because I didn't want to smother her. Because I didn't want her to rely on me. Because relying on her was dangerous for both of us. Because I knew the lines were always going to be blurry, and my ability to separate her from the obsession might become impossible. I could never let go of the fact that I'd let her down, even as I tried to help, and my mistakes had altered her, and us, irrevocably.

I cross over to the bed and drop her on it. Her boobs bounce, along with the rest of her. I'm going to burn this bikini. Light it on fire and watch it go up in flames.

She scrambles to her knees, face red and beaded with sweat, eyes blazing. "What the hell is wrong with you?" She rubs her ass and looks over her shoulder, probably checking for marks.

"What's wrong with me? What the hell is wrong with you coming down there dressed like this?" I fling a hand out toward her, eyes raking over all that bare flesh. That Clarke was eyeing like his next meal. That Freshman Jerk-off was going to try to get a piece of.

Her eyes flare, and her lip curls in a sneer. "Are you kidding me? You were butt-ass naked in front of my entire goddamn art class for three hours, and you're coming at me with this load of crap?"

"It's not the same fucking thing at all!" I shout back.

"You're right. It's not. I'm actually wearing clothes, and you were wearing *nothing*. And for what purpose, other than to remind me, yet again, that I'm inconsequential to you?" She motions to her chest. "Every single girl down there is dressed exactly the same. I was trying to fit in."

Not even remotely true, but she's spitting mad, and so am I.

My body is reacting in ways it really has no business doing right now, and all it does is make me angrier. "Is that what you want, Lavender? To be a bunny like the rest of the vapid lemmings down there? Gonna make your rounds through the team, minus the guys you're related to? Then maybe you can start on the football team when you're done."

"And so what if I want to?" She props her fist on a curvy hip. "Who are you to dictate what I do and with who? You sure as hell enjoy the perks of all these parties. Why shouldn't I?"

I don't know what kind of rumors she's heard, or what she thinks she knows about me, but I'm doubtful it's accurate. I'm not a saint, but I'm not like Maverick or BJ. Regardless, the mere thought of her hooking up with one of my teammates, let alone *more* than one of them, makes my brain short out, and I become the worst, most heinous version of myself.

"This is a ploy to get my attention, isn't it, Lavender? Did you want to get me alone again and see what would happen?

Haven't we done this before?" I take her face in my hands, warm and alive and so fucking beautiful, it hurts to even look at her. But I lean in anyway, the torture of being this close to her better than the alternative, which is Clarke or some other asshole getting his hands on her. "Nothing has changed, Lavender. I still don't want you." Lies. All lies.

A flash of hurt mars her features, but she covers the reaction quickly, and her full lips twist into a sneer. "Are you sure about that?" Her fingertips connect with my chest and goose bumps flash across my skin. She holds my gaze as her hand drifts down, the challenge in her eyes apparent. I naïvely assume she doesn't have the balls to go there, until she does. She skims my erection and cups me through the thin fabric. "How screwed up must you be now, Kodiak, that manhandling me gets you all jacked up?"

I grit my teeth against the desire to stop the lies and end this torment. Instead, I do what I've programmed myself to: be an asshole. "You're practically naked. You're all tits and ass and bare skin, just like the last time. Have some goddamn self-respect, Lavender." I release her and stalk out of her room, slamming the door behind me.

I loathe myself for the things I said and the way I handled her.

I wish things were different, that I hadn't brought us here, to this point where she believes I hate her, when it's really myself I can't stand.

19

Fuck this Bullshit

LAVENDER

Present day

I DON'T MOVE for long minutes after Kodiak leaves, unsure what to make of his reaction and his actions versus his words. I'm so confused.

I flop down on my bed, feeling a lot like an idiot. I wanted to get him back for art class. I guess that's what I get for taking advice from Lovey and Lacey after they've been drinking coolers. I hadn't accounted for all the drunk jocks pawing at me. I mean, I realized I was going to draw some attention, just not quite as much as I did. But dealing with Kodiak and his asshole behavior is exhausting.

I'm definitely going to regret this tomorrow. More than I already do.

THE NEXT MORNING I'm busy working on a new costume piece. I already handed in my costume at the end of last week and offered to start something new. A loud thud makes me jump and almost prick myself with a needle. I tug my earbuds free, and the sound of loud male voices filters through my door. I push back my chair and stumble a few steps. I'm stiff from having been in the same position for the past several hours. It takes me a few seconds to get the lock to turn, since my eyes are still adjusting from having been staring at tiny stitches.

I rush down the stairs and find the source of the noise. "What's going on?"

River is on top of Kodiak, aiming punches at his face. "I told you to keep your fucking hands off her!"

"She was drunk and talking to Clarke!" Kodiak has quick reflexes and blocks every shot, which makes my brother even angrier.

How does River know about last night when he wasn't even here?

I don't have a lot of time to think too much about that, because at the rate these two are going, there's going to be missing teeth and bloodstains on the carpet if someone doesn't do something to stop it. And apparently that someone has to be me.

I latch on to River's arm, but he's on the down swing and drags me to the floor beside Kodiak. When I'm elbowed in the neck, I quickly conclude I've made a mistake getting in the middle of their fight.

Then suddenly the fighting is over, because I'm flopping around on the floor, holding my throat and gasping for breath. I remind myself of a dying fish, but man, that really hurt.

"Oh my God! Are you okay?" River reaches for me, but I kick at him, because no fucking thanks.

The fighting resumes.

"Look what you did now!" River yells at Kodiak.

"You attacked me! And you're the one who dragged her to the floor!" Kodiak shouts back.

"Stop!" I wheeze.

They both do that weird man thing where they don't know what to do to help, so they push each other back and forth, trying to get ahead of the other, I guess.

I roll over and get to my feet, clutching my throat protectively. At least now I know what my defense maneuver will be, should someone ever attack me. "What is wrong with you two?" I rasp.

River shoves his phone in my face.

I snatch it away so I can see whatever the damn problem is. "Where did this come from?"

It's a picture of me, slung over Kodiak's shoulder. I'm flailing, and he looks like he's on the verge of murder.

"Someone took it last night," River growls and spins toward Kodiak again. "I told you not to put your hands on her!"

"You think it would've been better if Clarke had gotten his hands on her? That guy's is a colossal douche!" Kodiak yells back.

I am so damn tired of this. "Are you serious with this?" I shout. It's the only way to be heard over their bickering.

Both of them turn around.

"First of all, I'm not an idiot. I know Clarke is a douche, and I would never, ever be stupid enough to end up in a room alone with him. Secondly, do you hear yourselves? I'm not a child. I'm an adult. If I want to drink an idiotic amount of alcohol, wear a thong bikini, and flirt with a dickhead, that's my goddamn prerogative." Although saying it out loud, I can see every single flaw in that terrible plan. "I get to make my own damn mistakes, just like the rest of you. The double standard around here is ridiculous! Maverick has a new 'girlfriend' every month, and bunnies are constantly hanging off the two of you. But I talk to one freaking guy, and Kodiak becomes a damn caveman, and now the two of you are going to what? Punch each other out over it?" I throw my hands in the air. "You know what? I'm done with this. I cannot and will not be defined by something that happened when I was six years old. I don't need a set of bodyguards."

They're both heaving and angry, and now so am I. I shove past them and head back upstairs.

"I was trying to stop you from doing something you'd regret!" Kodiak calls after me.

I spin around. "No. You weren't. You were being a dick, and I'm done with it. And you"—I point a finger at River— "need to chill out and take the *Flowers in the Attic* down a few notches. I get that you want to protect me or whatever the heck you think you're doing, but Kodiak isn't the only villain out there. He just happens to be the one you target." I stomp back up to my room and slam the door.

It's just after ten. I start jamming things into my backpack. I need to get out of here before I seriously lose my shit. I'm supposed to meet Lovey and Lacey for lunch and tell them how my idiotic plan went.

Honestly, I should've gone to their place last night and avoided all of this. I shove my econ textbook into my bag. I also grab a change of clothes, because there's a solid chance I'm going to spend tonight at Lacey and Lovey's. All this testosterone is driving me crazy.

The door clicks quietly. I don't have to turn around to know it's my twin.

"I don't need a lecture or a bodyguard."

"Are you okay?" His voice is soft, low.

"I'm fine."

"I should've been here last night."

"You being here wouldn't have changed anything. I did something without thinking it through, and that picture was Kodiak overreacting as a result. If it wasn't him, it would've been you or Mav." I turn to face him.

He's frowning, as usual. He still looks angry, but he also looks something else . . . Confused? Sad?

"I don't get why you would do something like this in the first place. You hate the attention, and it's really not like you. And since when do you own a thong bikini?"

I answer the easiest question. "Since Gigi took me tanning before we went to Cancun last year." She said it would be better for avoiding tan lines. I ended up with a seriously burnt ass. I have fair skin, and apparently when a butt has never seen the light of day, it's more susceptible to sunburn, even with sunscreen.

"It still doesn't explain why you'd wear it in public, though."

"Because I'm tired of the bullshit."

"You mean Kody?"

"I mean all of it. The double standards, the never being able to date without you guys attacking whoever it is like starved, angry pit bulls. I need a break from this."

"I should've said no to him moving in here."

"It's not just him."

"But he's part of it."

"He's going to be here no matter what, River. He's Mav's best friend. They play hockey together, and he lives down the street."

"It never used to be like this with you two."

I rub my temples. "It's been a lot of years since it was like anything."

He drops his head and nudges my foot with his. Like the

rest of me—apart from my boobs—my feet are small. His are ridiculously gigantic. "Can I ask you something?"

"Sure, but I reserve the right not to answer if I don't feel like it."

He nods once. "Did I fuck that up for you? Am I the reason it's like this?"

"No, River. I'm the reason it's like this."

He pulls his bottom lip between his teeth, looking more kid than boy-man. "When we were kids, I hated him."

I laugh. "I don't think much has changed."

He shrugs. "I didn't like that he always seemed to be there when you were falling apart." He's quiet for a few moments, but I wait, aware that he's not done. "And now, I don't know. I feel like maybe I made things worse."

"Why would you think that when you have nothing to do with it?"

His gaze remains focused on our feet. "I kinda do."

"Can you explain that, please?"

He blows out a breath. "I overheard Mom and Dad talking after that thing happened at the middle school. When Kody got in trouble for lying to his dad and missing hockey practice?"

It's funny how we all experienced that event differently. "Because of me. He got in trouble because of me."

"You'd been having such a hard time, and I knew you were talking to Kody a lot 'cause he got you in a way I couldn't." He pauses, the furrow in his brow deepening. "I hated that too, that I couldn't understand and couldn't help."

"I know, but there was a reason no one wanted me relying on Kodiak to get through the panic. Even he understood it." And they were right.

"That's what I heard Mom and Dad talking about, 'cause you were so sad and they didn't know what to do. But Mom said some things, and I twisted them around because I wanted to think it was Kody who was making you worse. I wanted it to stop, and I thought maybe you'd rely on me more, instead of him."

And there it is. The guilt he carries around like an anchor. Now it's for thinking he's the reason Kodiak and I are such a mess. "First of all, me relying on you instead of Kodiak wouldn't have made anything better. The problem was me relying on anyone other than me. And I still don't see how this makes what happened your fault."

"So, I did this thing with your text messages."

"You did what thing?" This whole conversation is making my head hurt.

"I blocked his contact on your phone so you wouldn't get them."

"You what? When did you do that? Why?" My throat is suddenly tight.

"Just after Kodiak's family moved to Philly at the end of sixth grade. I knew it would only make it harder on you if he kept texting when he was so far away, so when he messaged after they moved, I saw it before you did and I messaged back."

"As me?"

He nods. "At first I know it was hard for you, but you were better without him. Every time he messaged, you cried *and* had another meltdown, so I told him it was too hard to be friends with him and he needed to stop messaging. I knew it was wrong, but it was so hard to watch you struggle. I just wanted it to stop. And I know it got worse for a while, but then you got better, and I thought I'd done the right thing."

I hold up a hand, feeling sick. "You had no right to interfere."

"I know, Lav. I'm sorry." He runs both of his hands through his hair.

"Right now, you're not forgiven." I sling my backpack over my shoulder and push past him.

"Where are you going?"

"Away from you and the rest of the stupidity happening in this house." I don't even know how to process what's going on, or whether it means anything anyway. It doesn't change the fact that Kodiak's been horrible to me. But maybe it explains it. I don't know.

Kodiak calls my name as I pass his room, but I ignore him and keep going.

The living room is empty for once. No Maverick, no random dudes, not even BJ passed out on the lounger. I shove my feet in my shoes and am out the door, cutting off the sound of feet pounding down the stairs as I slam it shut. I hit the automatic start button and thank the karma gods that I remember to unlock it before I reach the car. I yank the door open, toss my bag on the passenger seat, and practically dive inside, pulling the door closed behind me and slamming my finger on the lock button.

I get my key in the ignition and my seat belt on as the front door opens. I remember I also need to turn the key to be able to get out of here, and when I do, the car is filled with the sound of another damn audiobook. Thankfully this time it's not in the middle of a sex scene.

Kodiak stands on the front porch in a pair of sweats. I can tell he's yelling something because his stupidly gorgeous mouth keeps opening and closing. He grabs his hair with both hands and spins around as River joins him. I catch a glimpse of a teeth-mark-shaped bruise on his side. I must have bitten the shit out of him last night.

I shift into reverse, wishing I'd been smart enough to back in so my getaway could be smoother. I pull onto the street and fire the bird at them as I drive away.

I'm not supposed to meet Lovey and Lacey until eleven thirty, so I make the impulsive decision to stop at the housing office. There were at least ten girls already on the housing waiting list, but people drop out all the time. The last time I went in for an update, there were still four girls ahead of me. My luck seems to be pretty crap, but it doesn't hurt to check.

When I arrive, a middle-aged woman sits behind the desk, looking less than impressed about whatever is on her computer screen. I catch the reflection in her glasses and realize she's on Facebook. She types furiously for a minute and stabs the enter button aggressively before she gives me her attention. I focus on remaining calm by counting all the yellow things on her desk.

She forces a smile. "How may I help you?"

"Hi. I'm on the waitlist for the dorms. I know I'm supposed to get a call when something opens up, but I was passing by and thought I'd stop in to see where I am."

A hint of annoyance makes her cheek tic, and a hot feeling creeps up my spine. I hate irritating people.

"Let me have a quick look. I'll need your name and your student ID."

"Thank you so much. It's Lavender Waters."

She glances at me. "Lavender? That's a pretty name."

"Ironically my parents aren't even hippies."

She smiles, and this time it's friendlier. Thank you, Mom, for the weird name. I give her my student ID number, and she taps on her keyboard for a minute.

Her eyebrows shoot up. "Oh! It looks like you're next on the list. Well, that's good news for you." More tapping ensues. "And it seems a spot has opened up in the co-ed dormitory."

"That's great! How soon can I move in?" Thank you so much, karma, for not being an asshole today.

She clicks a few more buttons. "Seems to be available

immediately. I'll have to double-check with the residence team, but you could potentially move in as early as this afternoon."

"Seriously?"

"It looks that way. I can call now and find out, if you'd like."

"That would be great. Thank you." I take a seat and wait while she makes a phone call. I can't believe my luck. Sure, River might be upset that I'm moving out, but after all the crap that's gone down recently, I need a little separation and some independence. I won't live in the shadow of my past like this, or allow the rest of my family to keep influencing my decisions because their guilt weighs us all down.

It turns out I can, in fact, move in later this afternoon. I fill out all the required paperwork and then realize after the fact that I'm going to have to call my parents and tell them what I'm doing. Legally, I'm an adult and can make my own choices, but I didn't tell them I put myself on the waiting list, thinking I'd never get the call. Plus, I'll have to either use my savings to pay for it or see if my parents are willing to pick up the tab.

My excitement wavers as I return to my car, preparing to make the dreaded call. Video chat is probably the smartest way to go, even though it makes me feel like hurling. I take a few deep, cleansing breaths, pull up my mom's number—she's the more reasonable of the two—and hit call. She answers on the second ring, her face appearing in the small screen.

Her hair is pulled up into a messy ponytail, and she's wearing a pair of bifocals. She's in her office/sewing room, based on the background. "How's my favorite daughter?"

I smile. Being the only girl awards me the favorite-daughter title. "I'm good. How are you?"

"Also good. Just working on a project." She makes a face. "Are you in your car? Is everything okay?"

"Uh, yeah and yeah. Everything is fine. Sort of. I need to tell you something."

She sits up straighter, and something clatters to the floor. My mom and I have the same clumsy genes. "Did something happen?"

"It's nothing bad," I reassure her.

Her eyebrow rises. "Then why do you look like you're going to chew your lip off?"

I free my lip from my teeth. "I need a better poker face."

My mom laughs. "Sorry, sweetie, you got all my best and worst traits." Her expression softens and grows serious. "You can talk to me. You know that, right? Whatever it is, I'm always going to be on your side."

I nod and glance up at the roof. There's some kind of stain above my head. I don't want to know what it is or how it got there. "So, you know how we decided I'd live with Mav and River so I could get settled this year instead of moving into the dorms?"

"Let me guess, living with your brothers is a nightmare?"

I blink a few times, shocked by her reaction. Although maybe I shouldn't be. This is my mom we're talking about. She and I have always been a united front against the endless testosterone and smelly sports equipment. Or Robbie's horrible science experiments. "Um, well, it's not exactly what I would call fun."

"Because they're overprotective slobs who like to party too much and the house is always full of half-drunk jocks?" she offers.

"Uhhh . . . yes to all of the above?"

"I figured as much. Your brothers are idiots, by the way. Just between you and me, I follow them on social media under a fake account, and all of their friends, so I see pretty much *everything* they do."

"Oh my God." I slap a palm over my mouth. "How have they not noticed that?"

"Because it's a catfish account. I use stock photos of hot girls in bikinis." She rolls her eyes.

"You're a genius."

"Just sneaky." She tips her head to the side. "So, this hasn't been the dream scenario we all envisioned?"

"Not really, no. I actually put myself on the waiting list for the dorms."

"I can understand keeping your options open."

"And today I got a notification that a room is available."

My mom nods slowly, almost as though this isn't a surprise. "Kody wouldn't happen to be a factor in you wanting out of there, would he? And before you give me a high-pitched *no*, I've already seen that picture of you two from last night."

"Oh shit."

She *hmm*s and rubs her bottom lip. She always does that when she talks to me, probably because of the scar on mine. "It didn't look much like a friendly, ha-ha, let-me-carry-you-into-the-house-so-we-can-get-all-cozy-with-each-other   situation." Her voice is purposely light, but her concern bleeds through.

I sigh. "I pissed him off."

"I gathered. What happened? And was that a thong bikini?"

I can feel the fire in my cheeks. My mom isn't nearly as excessive with the overshares as Gigi, but she has zero problem addressing sometimes uncomfortable topics.

"Gigi got it for me for pre-Cancun tanning."

"Of course. I need to have a talk with her." My mom rolls her eyes. "So, I'm guessing the bare-ass show was meant to get someone's attention."

"Mom."

"Well, you're not much of an exhibitionist, so I assume you were doing it to make a point."

I blow out a breath and explain what happened—not all of

what's been happening, but the part about Kodiak seeing my schedule and then magically appearing in my art class to pose as our nude model.

"Nude as in . . ."

"As in swinging free."

"Really? Kody vomits before games, and he got naked in front of your class?"

"How do you know he pukes before games?"

"Rook and your dad talk, and your dad tells me everything before he falls asleep."

"Oh, well, yeah. He was totally naked. For almost three full hours."

"Huh." My mom taps her lips. "That's an interesting way to communicate your undying love for someone."

It's my turn to roll my eyes. "He was being a dick."

My mom gives me a look and drops her head, snickering like a teenage boy, which is roughly the level of her sense of humor.

"Seriously, Mom."

"Oh, come on! It's kind of funny."

"Well, it might be if he wasn't a complete asshole to me all the time."

That seems to sober her. "It's that bad?"

I shrug. "I know things were messed up when we were kids, but it's been years. I don't get why he needs to keep reminding me I messed up his life."

"You didn't mess up his life, Lavender."

"Well, he's very intent on making me feel that way. And don't you dare tell Lainey I said that. The last thing I need is Lainey telling Kodiak he needs to be nice to me. Then I'm the sucky baby who runs to Mommy when I can't handle it," I snap.

"Talking to your mother doesn't make you a sucky baby."

I kind of love how offended she sounds.

I point at her two-dimensional face on the screen. "Do not tell her."

She scowls. She really, really hates pointing, which I did a lot of as a kid. "I won't, but I wish you'd said something to me before we agreed to let him move into the house, even temporarily. Lainey and I thought we were doing the two of you a favor, and I don't believe Kodiak thinks you messed up his life."

"Well, we can agree to disagree about that. You're not here to experience the warm fuzzies he exudes around me."

"Kody has never exuded warm fuzzies, honey, except with you and Lainey. He's a momma's boy through and through. Kody's brain doesn't work the way everyone else's does."

"I'm aware."

"Are you also aware that he has an infinity symbol tattoo?"

"I'm pretty sure I would've seen a tattoo when he posed nude for my class."

"Unlikely since it's in the webbing of his left hand between his ring and middle finger." Her expression is ridiculously smug.

"How do you know this stuff?"

"Lainey and I talk. He got it two years ago." She sighs before she continues. "Look, honey, we screwed up a lot of stuff when you two were kids—including the way we dealt with the situation when things started to get out of hand. Lainey feels as bad as I do about it. We projected our own fears onto your relationship with him, because we were worried about the future. I don't think any of us took into consideration how severely it would impact both of you, or the extremes Kody would go to in order to keep from hurting you."

"To *keep* from hurting me?" My eyebrows shoot up. "He's

being a grade-A asshole extraordinaire. He makes River's bad moods look like sunshine and rainbows."

My mom makes a face. It looks a lot like she's constipated, which means she's trying to hold back her commentary.

"Just spit it out, Mom."

She sighs and rubs her temples. "I think I've done enough interfering."

"Oh, come on! You can't do the whole temple-rub-and-sigh thing and then decide you don't want to offer your opinion!" I want to throw my hands up in the air, but I'm holding my phone. I secure it in the dash holder so I'm free to flail.

"We made some big mistakes as parents. We wanted to protect you from all the things that could hurt you, and sometimes we took that to the extreme because we'd failed you in the past. You've overcome a lot, kiddo, and your dad and I are super proud of you. As far as Kody goes, I don't think he hates you at all."

"I'll respectfully disagree."

"Do you remember that pencil case you made him for his birthday when you were ten?"

I look away, embarrassed. How could I forget? I'd been so excited. I'd filled it with all kinds of hockey- and science-themed school supplies because those were Kodiak's two favorite things. "What does that have to do with anything?"

"He still has it."

I say nothing, aware the pause is for dramatic effect.

"He always has it with him. The last time he came home to visit his parents, he almost missed a practice because he was having a coronary over the fact that he couldn't find it and wouldn't leave without it."

I don't have the slightest idea how to process any of this. It's such a contradiction to the way he's been with me from the first moment I saw him this year. "So, what are you saying? I shouldn't move into the dorms? I should confront him?"

"If you want to move into the dorms, I think that's exactly what you should do. Kody needs to figure this out on his own, and you showing your independence by moving out might be the kick in the ass he needs."

"So you're okay with me doing this?" I expected more of a fight.

"Yup."

"What do you think Dad is going to say?" Just the thought of his reaction makes me anxious.

"I don't think he thought it through when he pushed for you to move in with your brothers."

"How do you mean?"

"All the parties and such. He assumed having River and Maverick around would create a nice, safe bubble for you, but he failed to consider that while those boys are protective, they're also hormonal."

"I don't want to date their jock friends anyway," I mutter.

My mom makes a sound that isn't a word. "I didn't fight River or your dad on you living with the boys because I thought it would be a good, safe transition. I also thought it might give you and Kody a chance to reconnect, but that obviously hasn't been as seamless as I'd hoped. I'll take care of your dad."

"You're sure?" I have no real intention of dealing with him, but I figure I should at least throw it out there.

"Oh yeah. There's no point in you managing your dad's drama when you already have enough going on there as it is."

She really is my number-one cheerleader and supporter. "Thanks, Mom."

"Anything for you, honey."

I tell her I love her and end the call with a promise to let her know how the move goes.

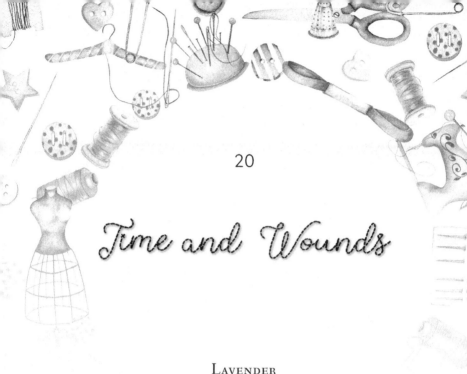

20

Time and Wounds

Lavender

Age 14

TIME IS SUPPOSED to heal all wounds. That's how the saying goes, but I don't know if I believe that. What I do believe is that with enough time, it's possible to reframe every memory into a fairy tale or depressing drama.

Kodiak's family moved to a different state the summer before he started high school, and life moved on without him.

And I've done better. I've learned how to manage the panic attacks. I've realized they're attached to memories I've suppressed. Those have surfaced slowly, and they always seem like they're more dream than reality. I hate clowns and small spaces. But I've learned how to deal with the monsters that live in my head.

I've also found a group of friends who like my weird and my quiet. I take sewing classes in my spare time. I see Queenie regularly. I volunteer at the art center and work with other kids who have anxiety and PTSD. I pour my energy into being productive. I try not to think about Kodiak.

But like a true addict, sometimes I relapse.

I don't text or message. I'm smart enough to know better. But sometimes I creep his social media with the fake account I created. Tonight, I'm restless, missing my old life and the people who used to make me feel safe.

I pull up his profile, and my heart skips a beat. Kodiak is a junior this year, and I'm a freshman. We'd be at the same school again if they hadn't moved. He's filled out in the past two years. He's tall and broad and growing into his body.

Kodiak's nearly jet-black hair sweeps across his forehead, and his northern-light eyes stare back at me. He's not smiling. In fact, he looks more annoyed than anything about his picture being taken. He's sweaty, and the background tells me it's post-practice of some kind. The caption reads: *Missing my boy Mav*, and my brother is tagged.

I tell myself I'm allowed to look at three pictures, and then I'll log out and shut it off. I scroll down, and suddenly all the air and happiness is sucked out of my lungs. I want to unsee this picture.

Because in it, Kodiak is smiling, and there's a girl tucked under his arm. Pretty, blonde, and tall. She looks like a model. I force myself to read the caption. *Date night with my favorite girl.*

And my poor, stupid heart breaks all over again.

But it's the last time I creep on him.

It was bad enough when I saw him kiss that girl the night before he moved away. I'd been working up the nerve to go over there, wanting to keep it together long enough to say goodbye. When I'd decided I was ready, I looked out my bedroom window and there he was, kissing the same girl he'd taken to his eighth-grade graduation dance.

My chest felt like it was caving in then, and it feels the same now. I can't watch him fall in love, not while I live in a bubble created by my overprotective family where I can barely talk to someone of the opposite sex, let alone contemplate dating.

After a restless night's sleep, therapy with Queenie the next day does not go as planned. All I want to do is sew. I crave the satisfaction of creation in the midst of my own personal destruction. All the little lies I told myself to make the truth less painful have finally caught up with me.

I pull out the finger paints—I rarely use them anymore, but they're always my default when I'm feeling particularly volatile.

Queenie waddles over. "Bad day?"

She places her palm on her swollen belly, pregnant with baby number three. Kingston, her husband, has been playing for Seattle forever. He's a goalie and closing in on retirement—at least that's the conversation I've overheard between him and my dad. Kingston has the kind of personality that puts everyone around him at ease. He reminds me of still water, always in motion, but still somehow serene; whereas Queenie is a carbonated beverage—bubbly, effervescent, and always exciting to the senses.

I take a breath, an attempt to quell the storm inside. I don't want to snap at Queenie, and I'm very aware that getting shitty with a pregnant woman will make me feel bad, but I'm on edge today.

So I blurt out the truth. "Kodiak has a girlfriend."

Her hand stills on her stomach, and her eyes flare, which tells me I've shocked her with this revelation.

"Have you spoken to him?"

I can't figure out her tone. She sounds half-concerned, half-hopeful.

I dip my fingers in the lime-green paint, desperate to do something with my hands. "No."

"So how do you know he has a girlfriend?" Her words are careful, calculated, and yet still conversational.

Queenie is an excellent therapist. I've learned a lot from her over the years. She's almost my friend. Almost, but not quite. She's halfway to maternal, because she's only ten years or so younger than my mom. She's also paid to help me, though I'm aware not all of our sessions are billed, because her and her husband are friends with my parents. But I've been confiding in her for over a decade.

Sometimes I wonder if we're too close for this to be as effective as it should be. Queenie is a habit, a source of comfort in a world of complete unknowns. She's a constant in a sea of uncertainty—something my parents aren't willing to take away from me.

I could lie and tell her my brother mentioned it. Maverick still talks to Kodiak all the time. But I don't see the point, and all I want right now is to finally purge him out of my system. "He posted a picture on social media."

She's quiet a moment. "Have you two been in touch at all?"

I turn back to the sheet of paper, swirling the colors together until they're as ugly as my jealousy. "No."

"And how do you feel about him having a girlfriend?"

I dip my fingers into the black paint, not bothering to rinse off the other colors, and rub them together. *How do I feel about Kodiak having a girlfriend?* "It's inevitable, isn't it? That's what teenagers do. They date, experiment, fall and get back up again, suffer their first broken heart, maybe experience other firsts."

Robbie dated the same girl for two years, but then they got accepted to different colleges and broke up. Maverick has had a whole slew of girlfriends already and left a trail of broken hearts in his wake. River always has girls tagging after him, but he's too into football to care.

"That all sounds very rational, but it doesn't tell me how you're feeling," Queenie presses.

"I haven't talked to him in more than two and a half years. I haven't seen him in over two. I shouldn't feel *anything*."

"But you do," she says softly. "And that's okay, Lavender. It's human. You were very close for a long time."

I stare at the swirls and lines on the paper, at the ugliness I've created. "I don't *want* to feel anything. I don't want to be hurt, or jealous, or disappointed. I don't want to feel betrayed." I dip my pointer finger in the red paint and drag it through the mess I've created, splitting it in two so it mirrors my insides.

"I thought I was past all of this, but I'm not, Queenie. He was such a huge part of my life, and then he was gone." I snap my fingers, drops of black and red splattering the paper. "Nobody understands what it was like, what it's *still* like sometimes. And I know it wasn't healthy. I *know* that. But he was *mine,* and then he was nothing. *Is* nothing."

We talked a lot about the loss of that friendship in the aftermath, how it echoed a death. I couldn't imagine how awful it would be to really and truly lose someone. How does a heart recover from losing someone fundamental to its existence? It gave me a new, deeper fear. I obsessed about death for a while, wanting to know where we go when we die. Does our body cease and our mind go on, voiceless and floating in the nothingness? Are we eternally alone with ourselves?

"I'm going to say something," Queenie announces, "not as your therapist, but as someone who cares about both you and Kody."

I still, my breath locked in my throat as I wait for words that will undo this pain. I meet her gaze and see inside her, right to the core of her uncertainty. And in that moment, I learn that adults are not infallible, that they don't always have the answers, and sometimes they fuck shit up.

"No one ever expected things to go this way." Her voice is soft like satin and sad like a funeral.

"Go what way?"

Queenie drops her head, her hand smoothing over her belly in rhythmic circles meant to calm—her or the baby, I'm not sure.

When her gaze meets mine, I feel her regret. "We didn't account for Kody shutting down the way he did. You were both so young, and your bond was so strong. There was concern as to what that might look like in the future."

These are all things I know. Things we've talked about.

And they were right to worry, because we were out of control. I couldn't see it then, but I see it now. Kodiak would have tried to save me forever, and I would have drowned in my own anxiety to let him. I wanted that more than I wanted to get better.

"You did the right thing." I press my palm against the paper. "The only way to break a bad habit is to eradicate it from your life. And that's exactly what he's done. Mission accomplished." I drag my hand down and blur the lines. Everything bleeds together, my creation destroyed. So apt, considering it was me who ruined everything in the first place.

21

Roomies

LAVENDER

Present day

"WHAT DO YOU mean you're moving out?" River follows me down the stairs, nearly stepping on my heels.

I brought Lovey and Lacey with me as reinforcements. I figure I can toss the basics into my suitcase and a couple of tote bins and manage the rest later.

My sewing supplies are going to be an issue. I may have to concede to working on projects here, because they're not quite so easy to transport. But again, I can assess once I'm in my room and have an idea of the space.

"I put myself on the list and a room became available. I decided to take it."

At the bottom of the stairs, he tries to worm his way around me, but I get to the front door first. Lovey and Lacey are behind him with two more boxes. Getting the door open is a problem, though, because I don't have a free hand, and River is crowding me.

I give him a look. "Seriously, River?"

"Why do you want to live in the dorms? You're going to hate it. Girls are catty. You won't know people. What happens if-if-if . . . you have a huge anxiety attack?"

I'm holding a box full of toiletries and crap. It's heavy. It's not like I didn't expect this, but my arms are starting to protest. "Then I'll manage like I have for the past seven years."

"But, but . . ." He flails and flounders. "Is it because of whatever happened last night? Or because I got into it with Kody?"

"That you actually need to ask that question is pretty much the reason I'm moving out. Now back up so I can open the door." I push against his stomach with my box.

The door opens, hitting me in the back and causing me to stumble forward. And of course, because nothing can be easy, Kodiak tries to push his way into the front hall, which was already crowded with me and River and the seven million stinky pairs of shoes on the floor. These guys and their shoes.

"What's going on?" His T-shirt is wet with perspiration. His hair is drenched, and beads of sweat trickle down his temples. He's clearly been for a run. He should look disgusting, but he doesn't.

"Lavender's moving out," River spits. "And it's your fucking fault."

"I can't deal with this." I use their momentary distraction to slip past Kodiak. Lacey and Lovey dance their way around him too.

"How is that my fault? I'm only here for a few weeks, and then I'll be back in my own place," Kodiak scoffs, but he sounds unnerved.

I drop the box in the trunk and turn to face them. River and

Kodiak are standing with their arms crossed, barricading the door. I'll come back for the rest of the things I need tomorrow, when they aren't home.

I pin them with a glare. "I need a damn break from the blame game and all the bullshit." Lovey and Lacey drop their boxes in the trunk, and I slam it shut.

"What about your sewing machine?" River's eyes are wide with panic. "And what about Mom and Dad? Do they know? There's no way Mom is gonna be cool with this."

"I already talked to Mom. She fully supports my decision. As for my sewing machine, I'll deal with it later. Let's go, girls."

We get into the car, and I lock the doors because River is on his way down the steps. He tries to open the driver's side door as I put the car in reverse. He knocks on the window. "Come on, Lav! You can't seriously be moving out!"

I ignore him since there is no other option, and I'm not stopping to discuss this. I'm not giving him the chance to try to convince me to stay. He chases me halfway down the street before he finally gives up.

I'm gripping the steering wheel so hard, the vinyl creaks, and my knuckles are white. It's really to prevent my hands from shaking. I'm aware that this is probably going to make things worse with River and Kodiak, but I can't deal anymore. Pandering to River isn't helping either of us.

"Are you okay?" Lovey asks.

"I don't know," I admit.

"That was seriously badass," Lacey says from the back seat.

"Thanks." I blow out a long breath, trying to find some calm. My cells feel like they're vibrating on a high frequency.

"Kodiak looked like he was going to shit a brick," Lovey says.

"Good for him." I didn't tell either of them what happened last night. Or about the conversation I had with my mom before

I met up with them, or what River admitted to me about blocking Kodiak's number. I still don't know exactly what to think about all of that, other than it shifts my perspective on everything. Kodiak can be very rigid. He's always been that way, unless it's me. I'd been the exception to his rule.

He had a hierarchy, and hockey had always been at the top of that list, followed by his mom, schoolwork, me, and then Maverick—until everything fell apart. And as the pieces of this puzzle fall into place, his behavior begins to make a lot more sense. But it sure doesn't excuse him for acting like a complete asshole the past two years.

We arrive at Hartford House, a seven-story building of apartment-style dorms. I pull into an empty space in the short-term parking, and we each grab a box.

A guy who is most definitely a student sits behind the desk. Based on the way his head is bowed, he's messing around with his phone. It takes so long for him to lift his head that Lovey clears her throat. When he finally looks up, his sour expression turns into wide-eyed surprise. His gaze bounces from Lovey to Lacey and then to me. He fumbles with his phone and drops it on the desk, faceup. He's watching some kind of drunk-fail video. Classy. He quickly flips it over and adopts a casual pose. He's wearing a school branded T-shirt. "Hey. Hi. Hello. I'm Mitchell." He taps his name badge. "How can I help you?"

It takes me about three seconds to find my voice, which doesn't sound long, but when someone is waiting for an answer it seems like an eternity. "I-I—"

"There's a room available here for Lavender Waters. The housing department said she could move in today," Lovey rushes to fill the silence.

I half appreciate it and half hate it. If she'd given me another second, I would've been able to get the words out.

"Oh wow, that's great." He nods a bunch of times, like Lovey has just told him he's won an award of excellence.

I raise my hand. "I'm Lavender."

"Right. Cool name. Let me check on that." He flashes a wide grin and shifts so he's facing the computer. After tapping a few buttons, his grin drops and his expression turns into more of a grimace. "Uh, okay. I found it. You're in a double." He smiles stiffly. "Your roommate is Beth Gull. She's a sophomore."

"Okay. Great. Thanks."

He makes a brief phone call and sets me up with my keys. Two minutes later, a girl named Sydney introduces herself as the RA on my floor and gives me a quick rundown of all the rules. I introduce her to Lovey and Lacey and tell her they're helping me move my stuff in.

"You have to register guests with the front desk. Sometimes people try to sneak them in." Her expression turns disapproving. "But you can get written up for that."

I exchange a look with Lovey and Lacey. "Okay, register guests." Geez, this sounds a lot like a less-fun version of summer camp. Not that I've ever been to summer camp, but my brothers used to go. River loved it until he got into a huge fight with another kid and got sent home for breaking his nose. At least that was the story we got.

The hallways are bland, the doors the same, although some of them are decorated with nameplates, and a few have those whiteboard things fixed to them where people can leave messages. When we get to room 414, Sydney mutters something under her breath and swipes her hand across the whiteboard, erasing whatever was written there.

She knocks and waits a good fifteen seconds before she tries again. More muttering follows and Lovey elbows me, giving me her wide, *what-the-hell* eyes. I shrug. I don't know if this RA is a weirdo, or we interrupted her *Vampire Diaries* marathon or what, but she's definitely in a mood.

She opens the door and peeks inside, shoulders sagging as she blows out what seems like a relieved breath. "Beth must be out." She motions to the space in front of us. "This is your common room. You have a TV, a couch, chair, coffee table, bar fridge, microwave, and coffee maker. You're not allowed to have a hotplate because it's against code. Also, no smoking."

"No smoking and no hotplate, got it," I echo.

The common space is a sty. There are empty food boxes littering pretty much every surface, and used tissues all over the floor. I also think there might be a few condom wrappers under the coffee table, but I'm afraid to look too closely.

"And we routinely do room checks for alcohol. You can get kicked out for that too," Sydney says.

"Right. No booze." I nod my agreement. We're all still holding our boxes, and there's no spot to put them down.

"That's Beth's room." Sydney motions to the door with the KEEP OUT BITCHES sign stuck to it. "And that's yours."

"Cool."

"Do you have any questions?"

"Not that I can think of."

"Okay, well, I'm in room 420 if you need anything. Good luck." And with that, she spins on her heel and busts it down the hall.

I awkwardly prop my box on my hip so I can unlock my room. The door swings open with a creak. I feel around for the light switch and flick it on. Then I drop my box on the desk with a groan. Lacey and Lovey do the same, and we stand there for a few long, quiet seconds, taking in my new bedroom.

"It's . . ." Lovey doesn't seem to be able to find words to finish that statement.

"It looks like a glorified prison cell," Lacey says.

She's not wrong. The walls are cinderblock, painted off-white. There's a basic wardrobe, a dresser, and a single bed, plus a desk and a computer chair that looks far from ergonomic.

"It's cozy." My closet in Lake Geneva is probably the same size as this entire room.

"That's one way to describe it," Lacey mutters.

"Are you sure you want to do this?" Lovey asks.

The answer is *no*. I'm not sure at all. As I stand here, staring at this tiny, ugly room, I come to the conclusion that I'm ridiculously pampered. Growing up with a dad who makes ridiculous amounts of money means we've lived in nice houses and had nicer-than-average things.

I still had a part-time job as soon as I turned fifteen, because my parents wanted me to have the responsibility and to learn how to save money. They also wanted me to be able to handle social situations without having an anxiety attack. Granted, I've always worked in libraries, where quiet is key, and most of the time I'm either shelving or checking out books, but it was still a job and still some forced, controlled social interaction.

"Once I put some of my stuff on the walls, it'll feel homier." It also has a slightly funky smell I can't quite put my finger on.

We spend the next hour unpacking. Even with my comforter and my personal effects, the room is still small and shitty, but it's also away from Kodiak and my brothers, so that's a win.

Lacey and Lovey have some project they need to finish, and I have a freaking economics assignment I need to work on before class tonight, so they take off, promising to check in on me later, and I pop in my earbuds and try to tackle the questions. I get through most of them before I have to leave for class, but I don't even have time to stop and grab dinner so I settle for a handful of Lucky Charms before I'm out the door.

By the time class is over, my head feels like it's going to

explode, and also, I'm starving. In addition, I have seven hundred messages from River that I'm not interested in answering. I return to my dorm, expecting that I might meet my roommate, but our common room is still an empty sty.

I toss my bag on the floor, grab my box of Lucky Charms since the cafeteria is closed, and flop down on my bed with my psych text. I must pass out at some point while reading, because I wake up with a jolt.

It's dark in my room, and the clock reads after midnight. It's not uncommon for me to sleep for twelve hours after I've dealt with some huge emotional thing, so my passing out almost as soon as I got home from class isn't much of a surprise. The whole conversation with my mom about Kodiak and moving out of the house definitely qualifies as emotional.

A high-pitched, feminine voice filters through my door, followed by the low tones of a male voice, giggling and something falling on the floor. Soon the laughing becomes sighs and groans. Awesome. My new roommate is having sex in the filthy living room.

I pop my earbuds back in and crank the volume to drown them out. Every time a song ends, I get a snippet of their sexy times. It goes on for a good half hour before it finally ends. My dorm experience is starting off with a bang.

IN THE MORNING, my anxiety is at a nice, ridiculously high level. At five thirty, the need to pee overrides my desire to never come out of this room in hopes of avoiding a dreaded run-in with my roommate and her boyfriend/fuck buddy. I have to bring my room key with me to our bathroom because my door automatically locks behind me. This isn't super convenient, but I can see why it's necessary.

In addition to the old-food smell, the common room now boasts the horrible odor of used latex and vagina.

I take care of business as quickly as I can and nearly slam into a bare chest on my way out of the bathroom.

"Lavender?"

I lift my gaze from the man nipples to a familiar face. As far as signs go, this isn't a great one. "Oh, hey, Clarke."

He looks super confused. "I didn't know you lived in the dorms." He runs his hand through his hair, eyes moving over me in a way that makes my skin crawl.

I'm wearing one of those bra tank things and a pair of sleep shorts. My nipples are most definitely saluting him. I cross my arms over my chest to hide them. "I guess now you do," is my highly intellectual response.

His eyes flare, as though he's connecting the dots. "Sorry about the noise last night."

"Nothing a nice hard-rock playlist won't drown out." Now would've been an awesome time for my words not to work. "Anyway, bathroom's all yours." I slip past him, desperate to disappear before my roommate wakes up and this gets even more awkward. Clarke is a hockey player, and I'm now concerned my roommate may be one of the bunnies I've had the misfortune of meeting before.

By the time I'm dressed and ready to leave, it's quarter to seven.

I sneak out undetected and head for the cafeteria. It's busy, and I'm not used to communicating with anyone but family this early—and that's mostly in offensive hand signals.

The noise and sheer volume of people is more than I can deal with, so I grab a coffee and a muffin and head for the Arts Building. My class isn't for another forty minutes, so I find a quiet corner, pop my earbuds in, cue up a playlist, and settle in with my coffee and my homework. I have a test at the beginning of next week, and unless I can master these concepts, I won't have a hope in hell of passing. I'm deep into unemployment rates and struggling to understand percentages when a shadow appears in front of me and doesn't move. I lift my head and am relieved to see it's not my brothers, or Kodiak, or one of my cousins.

"Hey, Josiah, how's it going?" He has a hickey on his neck that he's trying to hide with a collared Harry Potter polo.

"Good. You?" He flops down in the chair next to mine.

"That, sir, is a loaded question."

"Uh-oh. What new drama has unfolded in the House of Jocks?"

Josiah lives in an apartment off campus with a roommate named Ali who's in the engineering program and is pretty much always studying at the library or over at his girlfriend's place.

I give him the pared-down version of events—i.e., me being tired of the bullshit. "I moved into the dorms yesterday."

His eyes flare. "Brothers still being overprotective, then?"

"Yup."

"That Kodiak guy still being an ass?"

"Also yup."

"Dude needs to get a clue. How was your first night in the dorms?"

"My roommate brought a hockey player home and banged him in the living room."

"Classy. Wait, how do you know it was a hockey player?" His eyes light up. "Did he say things like *let me show you my stick-handling skills?*"

I snicker. "No, I ran into him in the bathroom this morning. He's been to my brothers' parties before."

Josiah makes a face. "That's awkward."

"Truer facts have never been spoken." I know my room-mate's sex sounds, and I haven't even met her. I poke his neck. "This looks fresh. Potential relationship material or a hookup?"

"Probably a hookup. He's still in the *this-is-just-a-phase* style of thinking." Josiah rubs the spot and looks away. Obviously there's more to it, but I don't want to push. "How's math going?"

I flip the book shut. "I currently have 48 percent in the class and a big test next week that I'm hoping to pass. But unless I can get a handle on this stuff, there's no way that's going to happen."

"Want me to have a look?"

"Sure." I pass him the textbook and flip to the review section for the upcoming test. "I have a ton of practice questions, and every single one is wrong."

He skims through the pages. "I thought when you said you had a math course, you meant actual math, not macroeconomics. I took this last year, so I can probably help you out if you want."

"Are you sure you have time for that? I'd like to say I'll pick it up fast, but I probably won't. Me and numbers have a hate-hate relationship."

"Yeah. For sure. I need to keep my mind off this." He taps the hickey. "And helping a friend would be a great distraction."

I hug his biceps. "I am super willing to be your distraction, but you may regret offering to help me."

He chuckles. "You can't be that bad. And I would've offered sooner if I'd realized I could actually be of some help."

"You underestimate me, my friend, and you may very well be glad you didn't offer sooner."

We gather our things and head to costume and set design class. Since I've already handed in my costume project, I'm working on some of the set design pieces for the fall play. I'm mindlessly painting a brick wall, listening to music, when my professor drops into a crouch beside me.

I pop my earbuds out. "I'm sorry. I was totally lost in my own world."

"No need to apologize, Lavender. Do you have time to meet with me after class?"

"Uh, sure. Is everything okay?" My mouth is suddenly dry, and I have the urge to wring my hands. I hope I didn't screw up my costume project. Maybe it's not as good as I thought.

She gives me a reassuring smile. "Nothing to worry about. But there's an opportunity I'd like to discuss with you. It won't take long, and I think you'll be pleased."

At the end of class, Josiah and I make plans to meet later in the afternoon for tutoring, and I let Lacey and Lovey know I have to bail on lunch, but I'll catch up with them later. My palms are sweaty by the time I reach Professor Martin's office. I pop a mint and take a deep breath before I knock on her door.

"Lavender, come on in." She motions to the empty chair beside her desk.

Posters cling to the walls, books line the shelves, and costume pieces hang from a rack in the corner. It's chaotic and visually overwhelming, but I love it. Kodiak would lose his mind in here. I tell my brain to shut up, because he's the last person I'd like to think about right now.

I take a seat and clasp my hands in my lap so I don't do what my mom always calls the "otter rub," where it looks like I'm trying to warm up my hands by rubbing them over each other incessantly.

She gives me a reassuring smile. "I'm sure you're wondering what this is about."

I nod and manage a quiet *yes*.

"I wanted to talk to you about your costume project."

"Oh." A million worries rain down on me.

She raises a hand. "It's not bad, Lavender. In fact it's quite the opposite."

"Oh. Okay." Some of the tension drains from my body, and I feel less like a sheet of stiff metal and more like one of those soft, squishy plush pillows.

"You're a gifted seamstress, Lavender, one of the best students I've had. I'm aware you haven't selected a major yet, but I'm hopeful costume design is something you're looking to pursue."

I nod, heart thundering in my chest. "That's what I was thinking, yes."

"That's fantastic to hear." She shifts in her chair to face me. "I wanted to talk to you about a special opportunity. Usually it's reserved for senior students, but I felt it might be worth bringing up with you. I'm not sure if you're aware, but we have a connection with a few very exclusive summer internship programs in New York."

"With off Broadway theaters, right?" My stomach churns at the thought of the bustle and energy of such a huge city.

"That's correct. With your permission, I'd like to submit your name."

"For *this* summer?"

"Yes. It's highly competitive, but I think it's worth a shot to at least apply. You'd spend two months in New York City working with some of the best costume designers in the industry. Is that something you might be interested in?"

"Yes," I blurt. "I'd have to talk to my parents about it, but yes, it's definitely something I'd be interested in. Can I have a few days to think about it?"

"Of course! The application deadline isn't until early December, so you have plenty of time to make a decision. I'm aware it's a lot to consider, so I wanted to give you an opportunity to think it through. There are obviously no guarantees, but I believe you have a great shot. Why don't you mull it over, and we can talk next week?"

I leave her office feeling equal parts elated and anxious. I consider who I want to talk to first about this. Usually it would be my mom, but I've put her through the wringer by moving into the dorms and leaving it up to her to talk to my dad—who I have yet to hear from. Although, it's only been twenty-four hours. Mom may have made him promise not to call until he's calmed down about it. That's my guess, anyway.

I decide my best bet is to let the information settle and make a list of pros and cons before I do anything else. This feels like a sign, though. Opportunities like these don't come along every day, and I'd be a fool to pass it up, even if the idea of moving to New York on my own makes me feel like hurling.

The meeting with my professor has made me all sweaty, and I decide it might be a good idea to go back to the dorms, grab a quick shower, and change before I meet Josiah for tutoring. My anxiety spikes as I approach my new room.

I stand outside the door for a few seconds, listening for sounds of . . . things I'd rather not interrupt. When all I get is silence, I unlock the door and slowly open it. I'm relieved to find no one fornicating on the couch.

That relief is short-lived, though, because the bathroom door opens and my new roommate appears. As I feared, I have had the misfortune of meeting my roommate before. Even worse, Beth is short for *Bethany*, and she's the same girl who came out of Kodiak's house on the first day of school, bragging about having been in his room with him right after he treated me like less than chewed gum. She's also the one who spilled soup on my leg.

She's currently wearing a towel on her head. And nothing else.

I keep my eyes on the ceiling as she flounces across the room. "I have a friend coming over in half an hour, so you might want to leave so you don't end up eavesdropping like you did last night." Her door closes with a slam.

I stand there for a few shocked seconds before I finally command my feet to move toward my own room.

I have my key ready, but I come to an abrupt halt when I notice my door is covered in Post-it notes. They take up every last inch of space, and each one cites an infraction I've committed in the past twenty-four hours—from leaving my toothbrush in the bathroom to eavesdropping on her having sex (they were in the damn common room) to trying to steal her boyfriend this morning by offering him sexual favors.

I have the wherewithal to snap a few photos before I hastily lock myself in my room.

I send them to River and ask if he would mind coming to help me move my stuff back home. I also message Josiah and tell him I need to postpone tutoring and will explain why later.

River arrives twenty minutes later with Maverick and BJ. Bethany peeks her head out, and for half a second her eyes flare with excitement, until she realizes they're not here to see her.

"Bethany, I'm sure you remember my cousin, BJ, and these are my brothers Maverick and River."

Bethany rushes over to my bedroom door and frantically peels off the Post-it notes. "It was a joke," she sputters lamely.

Maverick gives her one of his jovial smiles, but his tone doesn't match his expression. "You're blacklisted, sweetheart. I wouldn't show your face at another party if I were you."

It takes two trips to carry all my stuff down to the car.

So much for the full dorm experience. At least I tried.

"I'm sorry it didn't work out, Lav," River says once we're headed back to the house.

"No, you're not," I reply.

He sighs. "The dorms are full of assholes."

"The world is full of assholes, River. You can't protect me from all of them." *Especially the one living in our house.*

"I know." He reaches out and links our pinkies. "But I want to try. And I really am sorry I pushed you into feeling like you had to do this, and that you ended up with that chick as a room-mate. We don't want you to be miserable, and we don't want you to hate living with us."

I sigh. "I love you, and if that's true, maybe we can do a few things differently."

22

I Thought I Was Over This

KODIAK

Age 19 Winter break

MY FIRST THOUGHT is that I shouldn't be here. It's too close for comfort. I'm on edge, and not even some of Mav's grandfather's edibles are going to help calm me down.

There are also way too many fucking people here. I can deal with a packed arena because there's a plexiglass barrier separating us. There is no barrier between me and anyone here. I don't like it—too many unknowns and variables I can't control. Not to mention, almost everyone is drunk off their asses. I can barely tolerate people when they're sober, let alone intoxicated and talking nonsense.

But it's the first day of winter break, and Maverick insisted we throw a party at his parents' place out on Lake Geneva, since they're away.

It's freaking freezing outside, but the hot tub is cranked and packed to the tits—quite literally—with a lot of girls, and there are at least a dozen people out here smoking weed.

Since Mav and I are both on the college hockey team and there are random drug tests, we generally don't partake. But we have two weeks off, so he's all over getting fucked up.

Our parents took a spur-of-the-moment, four-day trip to Mexico for some pre-holiday sunshine, which means we have the run of the house with zero in the way of supervision for an entire weekend. Maverick is supposed to be keeping an eye on River and Lavender, who stayed here so they could hang out with their cousins. Instead of ensuring they stay out of trouble, though, Maverick has invited over every person he's ever met in the area between the ages of eighteen and twenty-two. He figures what his parents don't know won't hurt them.

I'm already worried about things getting broken, what it's going to cost to have the place cleaned, and someone posting pictures on the sly and tagging us.

I move out of the way as two girls in bikinis run by, shrieking at a decibel that's likely to alert every dog in the neighborhood. They cram themselves into the hot tub with the rest of the girls, who keep asking us when we're joining them.

Hot tubs are a petri dish of bacteria and regrets. Also, Maverick was in the hot tub earlier making out with his girlfriend, so there's a high probability that his jizz is floating around in there.

"Do you even know half of these people?" I ask.

Maverick shrugs. "Nope. But if it gets out of hand, I'll just call the police."

"Some of them are underage," I remind him.

"Everyone here is legal to drive and legal to vote. The fact that the drinking age doesn't match those two things doesn't make a hell of a lot of sense."

"Doesn't actually change the fact that it's a law, and we're breaking it dozens of times over." Not that I particularly care. It's more that I don't want Maverick to get himself in trouble over this party. He's social, and I'm . . . really not. People require energy, and I prefer to put mine into one of two things: hockey and school.

Despite that, here I am. And not because Maverick is my best friend and pretty much forced me.

His younger brother, River, appears out of nowhere. He's tall, lanky, and hates the entire world—apart from his twin, anyway. And football. He takes a deep haul from a joint.

"Where'd you get that?" Mav tries to grab it from him, but River ducks and spins out of the way.

"Where do you think? I pilfered it from Robbie's botany experiment." He motions to the greenhouse at the back of the property, tucked behind a copse of trees and dormant rose bushes. It's locked up like Fort Knox, so none of the assholes here can get into it, but Mav knows where the key is, and apparently so does River. He sucks in another long drag and blows it in his brother's face. His gaze slides to me and narrows for the briefest moment before returning to Maverick. "Lav is gonna be here in fifteen minutes."

"I thought she was at some expo thing with L and L," Maverick says.

"She was."

"It's only ten forty-five. Why are they coming back so early?"

River flicks his joint, ash falling to the deck beside my foot. "Mom and Dad gave her an eleven o'clock curfew."

"They're not even here to enforce it."

River looks at him like he's the dumbest asshole alive. He's not; he's drunk and high, so half his brain cells are asleep. "They track her phone." The *duh* is clear in his tone.

That's not exactly surprising. Lavender is the quintessential good girl, and highly unlikely to get into trouble, but everyone is still highly protective over her.

"Why wouldn't she leave it at home?" Mav continues. "Then they wouldn't know."

River's lip curls. "Do you honestly want our seventeen-year-old sister staying out until whatever o'clock in the morning without a damn phone?"

"Point taken," Mav mutters. "You're responsible for keeping an eye on her."

"You know this isn't her scene. Lavender will disappear upstairs, and you won't see her until tomorrow." River pulls his phone out of his pocket and frowns, which is the expression he wears about 90 percent of the time. "Oh, shit."

The front door slams open, and in stumbles a group of girls.

What's confusing, at first, is the fact that these girls seem to think it's Halloween. They're dressed in superhero costumes. And then the reality of who they are registers, and my entire body feels like it's been dipped in fire and ice at the same time.

Dawson, one of the defensemen on the school hockey team, whose family lives about twenty minutes from here, inserts himself into our circle and lets out a low whistle. "Since when is this a costume party? You know what? Who cares? Dibs on the Wonder Tits."

Mav dives in front of River, catching him around the waist when he launches himself at Dawson.

"You touch my sister, and I'll cut your tongue out of your mouth and replace it with your dick," River seethes.

"Whoa, whoa, Riv, calm down." Mav struggles to keep his hold on him.

River might be two years younger, but he's close to the same height, and he's starting to fill out.

Dawson laughs nervously. "Sister? Shit, man. Sorry. I didn't know."

"You breathe in her direction, and I will knock every single one of your teeth out of your mouth, dickhead." He elbows Mav in the side. "Let me go, asshole, or I'll embarrass the shit out of you by kicking your ass."

Mav shoves him away. "Isn't it past your bedtime?"

River takes a deep haul off the joint, flicks the roach at Dawson, and blows the smoke in my face. "She's died enough deaths over you, Kodiak. Stay away from her."

"Twinsie!" Lavender stumbles through the open French doors, tripping over the one-inch lip. She nearly goes down, but River scoops her up and sets her on her feet. She hugs him around the waist.

"What the fuck?" River looks down at his sister, her face plastered against his chest. "Are you drunk?"

"I'm fine," Lavender mumbles into his shirt.

He looks to Lovey and Lacey for an answer. "Is she drunk?"

"We're so sorry," they say in unison. "She had Jell-O cups in her bag, one for each of us, but since Lacey and I are vegan, we can't eat Jell-O, so she ate all three." Lovey wrings her hands.

"Shiiiittt." Maverick kneads the back of his neck. "Well, that explains where the Jell-O shooters disappeared to."

Lovey gives him her best disapproving look. "Jell-O shots are supposed to go in those tiny plastic glasses, not giant pudding-cup containers! How much alcohol was in those?"

"I dunno, like a mickey? I didn't have any of the small ones, and Lav has been on a Jell-O kick like she's seven again, so I figured I was doing the world a favor by recycling. Plus, we're dudes." He motions to me and the other guys. "Pudding-cup-sized shots seem way more reasonable."

"You're an idiot, Mav," River snaps. "Look at her." He motions to Lavender, who's still hugging her brother. "If she pukes, you're cleaning it up."

"Don't be mad, Rivy. I promise I won't puke." Lavender pats him awkwardly on the cheek.

River blows out a breath, his frustration obvious. "You can't promise that, Lav."

"Okay. Well, if I do puke, I'll be really quiet about it." Lavender tips her head back and smiles up at her brother, who's a good head taller than her, although pretty much everyone is.

Even that small movement sets her off-balance, and she stumbles back a step. River grabs her arm to keep her from falling over.

Lavender has never been particularly coordinated. She could fall over an idea. Drunk Lavender is a damn mess.

A damn hot mess.

A damn hot, sexy mess.

Lavender is no longer the quiet, awkward, anxious, knobby-kneed little girl with bruises all over the place and paint in her hair. She's grown up in the years since I last saw her. A lot. She's more woman than girl, and she has all the curves to prove it.

"I'm fine." She knocks her brother's hand away. "Besides, I'm not worried about seeing Kodiak anymore, so that's a good thing." She shivers, and her breath puffs out in white clouds. She drops her voice to a whisper. "Is he still here?" She brushes her hair out of her face and adjusts her headband thing. It's still sitting wonky. "Do I look okay?" She smooths her hands over her hips.

River closes his eyes, exhales slowly, and tips his chin up. When he looks back at her, his expression turns dark and grim. "Yeah, he's still here, unfortunately."

Lavender's eyes go wide, and she twists around, her gaze landing on me. I watch a dozen different emotions pass through her vibrant blue eyes, all of them making me want to slam my head into a brick wall. "Kodiak."

221

My name is more a breath than a word, but I feel it like a hit of cocaine.

"She's seventeen, fuckhead. Don't get any ideas in your dick." River elbows me in the side and puts a protective arm around her, turning her away from me. "Come on, Lavender. Let's get you some carbs and your bed."

"He was there the entire time." She glances over her shoulder, stumbling along beside him as he rushes to get her upstairs. She's too uncoordinated to move at the speed he'd like, so he picks her up and carries her through the kitchen. She doesn't fight, but her body is rigid, and her gaze stays locked on mine until she disappears up the stairs.

Maverick runs his hands through his hair. "Shit, this is bad."

"We'll go up and stay with her," Lacey and Lovey say in unison.

"River isn't going to leave her side now." Maverick's gaze darts to me and back to them.

Lovey props her fist on her hip. "But she's going to need help getting out of her cosplay outfit."

"She can't sleep in it," Lacey agrees. She grabs her twin's hand, and they rush after River and Lavender.

"That's your baby sister, huh, Mav?" Dawson smirks. "So, like, when she's not jailbait, can I take her on a date?"

Maverick's grim expression shifts into a wide smile, but it's not friendly in the least. He clamps a hand on Dawson's shoulder. "You so much as look at my sister, and I'll hold your arms while my brother replaces your tongue with your dick. And believe me, he's crazy enough to do it."

Dawson's eyes go wide, and he raises his hands in submission. "Whoa, dude, I'm kidding."

Maverick throws his head back and laughs, and Dawson joins in. His is nervous though. "Me too," Mav says, grinning and shaking his head no. His smile drops. "Lavender is off limits." His hard gaze shifts my way. "To everyone."

Maverick and I don't talk about Lavender, ever. It's understood that she is not a topic for discussion.

After my family moved to Philly, it was easier to pretend she didn't exist and I hadn't fucked her up by being me. In the five years between moving and now, I've avoided every single family function in which I might've ended up in the same space as Lavender.

Until today.

Because there's no way I'll get out of seeing her over the holidays, so I figure I might as well rip the bandage off and get it over with. Except I'm starting to think that wasn't the best plan. Not after years of nothing.

This must be what an addict feels like when faced with a syringe of heroin and no one to stop him from jamming the needle into his arm.

River doesn't come back downstairs, and neither do the girls. The party goes on until after five in the morning. Maverick disappeared two hours ago with his current girlfriend. BJ is crashed out on the couch with some girl curled up in his lap like a cat. I should call an Uber and go home.

I head down the hall, toward the front door, with my phone in my hand. I hit the button, but the screen stays blank. Shit. My phone is dead. I'm keyed up and exhausted at the same time. My gut twists as I glance toward the stairs. I should look for a charger. Instead, I find myself climbing the stairs to the second floor.

My mouth goes dry, and my hands grow clammy. This is a really bad idea. I've spent years reminding myself of all the damage I did to Lavender when she was too young to comprehend how dangerous I was for her. Five years avoiding. Five years exorcising her from my system. Yet here I am, looking to be possessed all over again, with no real understanding of why.

Well, that's untrue. I know exactly why.

Next year she's supposed to stay here and go to a local college, but the year after that, there's a chance she's going to end up going to school with us in Chicago. Robbie goes to school there, and now so does Mav. River's been talking about the kinesiology program, and the university has a kickass football team too.

I need to learn how to deal with Lavender again, eventually. I can't avoid her forever.

This is how I rationalize my actions. I pass closed door after closed door and stop at the one with the sign fixed to it. It reads:

TEEN GIRLS INSIDE: ENTER AT THE RISK OF YOUR _____.

Followed by a picture of a squirrel holding a set of nuts.

I glance down the hall; no light comes from under any of the doors, including the one I'm standing in front of. I listen for voices, but all I hear is the sound of my own breathing and the pounding of blood in my ears.

I curl my fingers around the doorknob. Feel the heady rush of adrenaline as I turn it, ever so slowly. It's so quiet, I can hear the mechanisms clicking inside, like a bomb preparing to detonate. When it doesn't turn any farther, I push, holding my breath as the hinges creak.

There's no way for me to justify my actions to Maverick, or worse, River, if either one of them found me in here. I wouldn't have a best friend anymore, and after years of separation, it's nice to finally have him back, good to finally be playing for the same hockey team.

But even that isn't enough to stop me, which tells me more than I want it to. I'm so fucked up.

Just so fucked.

I push the door open a little more, quickly this time, to prevent it from creaking. A clock glows on the nightstand between the two double beds. A soft beam of light travels from the bathroom to the bed, cutting a line across Lavender's body. She's curled on her side, facing the door. Most of her covers have been kicked off, and her bare legs are stretched out across pale sheets.

Her long hair fans out in a chaotic wave across her pillow, one arm stretched toward the door, palm up. I don't understand how after all this time I can still feel the same unbearable pull. For years I've had to build walls and detach myself from her, from all the bad choices we made as kids. All the bad choices *I* made. All it takes is seeing her and the sound of my name to storm the gates and force me to my knees.

I don't realize I've moved until the floor creaks under my foot. I'm halfway into the room when Lavender shoots up in bed. She sucks in a gasping breath, and her eyes dart around. She was always a light sleeper—unless she'd had a particularly severe panic attack; then she could sleep like the dead. A full-on party could happen around her, and she wouldn't move for hours.

"Hello?" Her voice is thick with sleep. She squints and leans toward the nightstand, patting around for her glasses. I use the momentary distraction to step back into the hall, pulling the door closed behind me.

I don't stick around to see what she's going to do next. Instead, I rush to the end of the hall, to the last empty bedroom on this floor. The comforter is already rumpled, telling me I'm not the first person to use this room tonight.

I close the door, yank my shirt over my head, and shove my

jeans down my legs. I pull the covers down and slip between them, slamming my head against the pillow. "So fucking stupid."

I don't know what the hell I was thinking, creeping on Lavender. It doesn't serve a purpose, other than to make me more aware that I'm not even remotely over losing her.

I stare up at the ceiling, adjusting to the inky darkness and trying to calm my heart and my breathing. A chandelier hangs above my head, teardrop crystals glinting despite the minimal light. I focus on those, on taming the panic over my reckless actions.

The sound of footfalls in the hallway spikes my already-frantic heart rate. I don't breathe as I wait, unsure if I'm hearing things now. I swear I can *feel* her on the other side. The doorknob turns, and long seconds pass before the door creaks open.

She slips through the narrow gap and closes it behind her. Her breathing is quick and shallow. She's wearing a shirt that hits her mid-thigh. I don't move, focused on keeping my breathing even. It's pointless. She's not an idiot. She knows it was me creeping in her doorway like a desperate douchebag. Eventually she moves away from the door, toward the bed.

I don't know what she thinks is going to happen. Or what I'll do. It's closing in on six in the morning. I've been drinking for twelve hours—not to mention the edible I had earlier in the evening. All of my decision-making skills are flawed at best and damning at worst.

Lavender reaches the end of the bed and comes around the side I'm lying on. Her fingertips travel along the edge of my comforter-covered leg. I jerk my hand away when her fingers brush mine.

"What're you doing in here?" My voice is barely a croak.

She cocks her head, blinking in the darkness. She's not wearing her glasses, which means I must be blurry. "I could ask you the same thing." Her voice is smokier than I remember. Soft, sexy, knowing.

I try to inject some disapproval into my tone. "You should go back to your room."

Her fingertips glide up my arm, causing a wave of goose bumps to flash over my skin. "And you shouldn't have been creeping in mine, so it seems like we're even."

"What do you want?" I snap, frustrated with myself for creating this problem I don't know how to solve.

She chuckles, but it's flat and jaded. "Answers. Acknowledgment. An explanation."

This isn't the Lavender I remember. She wasn't this ballsy. Maybe it's the alcohol. "You're drunk and not making sense. Go back to bed, Lavender."

"Do you think you can still tell me what to do and I'll just do it? I'm not a little girl anymore, Kodiak. I think for myself now. Why were you in my bedroom?"

"I-I was looking for a place to crash."

She scoffs. "And I thought I was the shitty liar." She leans down, long hair brushing over my arm. "Did you want to see what you left behind?"

"You're the one who never came to say goodbye," I bite out. It's really the only thing I have to hold on to now.

She barks a humorless laugh. "I was going to, but you know what made me change my mind?"

My stomach sinks, and I stay silent.

"I saw you kissing that girl, the one you took to your eighth-grade grad dance." Her fingertip moves in a rhythmic figure-eight pattern over my biceps, an infinite loop, mirroring the one I seem to be forever stuck in when it comes to her. I'm not sure if it's meant to calm me or her. "I know she was friends with Maverick's girlfriend at the time. I thought maybe you went with her as a favor. It hurt, but I could understand why you would take her. She was pretty." She sits on the edge of the bed, her hip resting against the outside of my leg. "I looked out the window and saw you there, and for a moment I thought maybe you were waiting for me to work up the nerve to come over. But you weren't. You were kissing her in *our* spot."

"She kissed me." I'd been so angry at the time. Angry that Lavender had given me up so completely. Angry that she'd been strong enough to survive without me.

"You kissed her back." It's not an accusation; it's simply a statement of fact. "And maybe I could've gotten over that too, but it was where *we* used to go when we were kids and wanted space from everyone else. The place *you* used to go when you needed to be alone. You sat there all the time after . . ." She trails off, not needing to finish the statement. *After they took you away from me.* "And then you ruined all of those memories for me."

"Lavender."

"Why, Kodiak? Why there? Why somewhere I could see? Why was she even there?"

Because Maverick invited her. Because he was thinking about himself and what he wanted. But I don't tell her that, because in doing so, I'd be opening a door I can't afford to step through.

A shuddering breath leaves her. "Never mind. It doesn't matter anymore. None of it does." Her hand smooths over the comforter, perilously close to parts of me I have no business wanting her to touch. But I do, and it's messing with my head. We're not kids anymore. We're teenagers, vital and alive, with an excessive supply of hormones to interfere with our decisions.

She reaches the edge of the comforter, and her fingertips find the bare expanse of my chest. She settles her palm over my heart, so soft and warm.

"There you are," she whispers.

My fingers flex beside her knee. "Lavender."

"It's okay. We're okay." My skin burns where her hand rests. "I needed to know if it would feel the same after all this time." Her palm slides up, over my collarbone, along the side of my neck. "I wasn't sure if it was all in my head or not." And there's the vulnerability I remember.

I say nothing, do nothing. I need to tell her to stop, but I don't want to. I want to soak in this feeling, because in a lot of ways, it does feel the same. But it's also so very, very different, because the innocence of childhood has disappeared, and in its wake are feelings that only existed in the periphery before—a whole different kind of need. A new thing to become addicted to. Obsess over.

Something else I can't afford to indulge in.

"This isn't a good idea," I grind out.

"Oh, I know." She shifts, and suddenly she straddles my hips, settling over my erection on a low whimper.

Too far. This is way too far. I understand now what everyone was so worried about. What they all feared would happen over time. Because it is happening, right now, and I don't want to stop it.

Reality hits hard when Lavender leans down, her hair sweeping across my chest, breath washing over my face. She still smells faintly of vodka. There's a chance she's half drunk, despite having been asleep for hours. It would make sense. Lavender generally isn't this bold, at least not the old version of her.

I consider the ramifications of allowing this to happen, whatever *this* is. Lavender is still in high school. I can't feasibly date a high school girl, let alone my best friend's little sister— with whom I already have a tumultuous history.

And that's just stating the really fucking obvious. There's

also how easy it will be for me to drag her right back down into my pit of hell where she depends on me to make everything okay.

We're doomed. I'll ruin her, just like they said I would. I don't want to shatter someone who's already cracked.

I take her hands in one of mine, gently—they're so delicate, so warm, so fucking perfect—and sit up in a rush. "No, Lavender."

I tip my head back, and her lips connect with my neck. "I can feel you, though," she whispers against my skin, rolling her hips. "You want me."

I can't admit she's right. I can't tell her what she wants to hear, because then she'll be under the false belief that one day, we'll be able to be together. And we won't. We can't. If I break her again, I'll never survive it. I barely did the first time around. So I do what I must to save her from me.

I slide my free hand into the hair at the nape of her neck and grip. For a moment I just breathe, aware this is the very last time I'll ever have her like this—close, needy, vulnerable. And I hate myself for being too weak to love her without destroying her.

"I'm nineteen, Lavender. A breeze makes me hard. You show up in my room in the middle of the night, half-undressed, and climb into my lap. All I need is some friction, doesn't matter who it's from."

She stiffens and tries to free her wrists. "You came to my room first."

She's right, but I won't admit it. I drop my mouth to her ear. "What did you think would happen when you came in here? Did you think I would kiss you? Touch you?"

She flinches. "Kodiak, please."

I drag the end of my nose along her cheek, loathing myself

for this, and hating even more that I'm still hard. "Is that a yes, then?"

She swallows thickly. I can feel her throat working, trying to form sounds. Nausea rolls through me as I stroke down the side of her neck with my thumb. Her skin is damp, pulse thrumming violently.

"Shhhh," I soothe and press my lips to her temple. I breathe her in, the sweet scent of her skin, her shampoo, her fucking *fear*, steeling myself for what I'm about to do. "Did you think we would be something to each other after all these years?"

She makes a choked sound, and I release her wrists so I can cup her face in my palms. Everything about the way I'm touching her is a contradiction to my words—tender versus cutting. She tries to turn her head away, but I hold her firmly. Her nightshirt rides perilously high on her thighs. She smells like a grown-up version of the girl I once loved, like lavender shampoo and desire.

And suddenly I'm angry—so full of rage that she still has this kind of power over me and doesn't even know it. I'm pissed because I'll never have the control I so desperately need to be good for her. "Look at me, Lavender."

Her eyes dart around, and she keeps trying to twist her head away.

"Stop fighting and look at me," I demand.

She stills, her breath coming hard and fast. I'm sure she's on the verge of a panic attack, and I doubt she expected this when she came in here looking for me. I didn't expect it to go this way either. Her body trembles. But her eyes, those bright blue eyes that haunt me relentlessly, finally meet mine—so full of fear and more pitifully, weak threads of hope.

I'm about to sever those forever.

Bile rises in my throat, but I force myself to continue. "I reject you time and time again, and still you want me."

Her mouth forms the words *please don't* but I can't stop now. I need to nail the lid on this coffin. I need to be sure this is never going to happen again, because I won't be able to say no next time, and I cannot take that risk with her.

"I need you to hear me, Lavender. Really *listen* to what I'm telling you." I can't stop myself from sweeping away her tears as they start to fall. Her chin trembles, and her teeth sink into her bottom lip, right where the scar is.

I tug at her lip with my thumb, not wanting her to cause more damage—other than what I'm about to do to her heart, anyway. "We aren't good for each other." *I'm not good for you.* "Say it back so I know you're hearing me."

She shakes her head and more tears fall, too fast for me to catch now.

"Yes, Lavender. You and me? Together, we're toxic." *I will poison your pure soul.* "Say it."

She sucks in a shaky, gasping breath. She opens and closes her mouth three times before she finally whispers, so quiet it's barely a sound, "We're toxic."

"That's right." I nod my approval, and my stomach churns. "You're too needy, and I can't deal with it." *I will drown you with my dependency.*

She makes a tortured sound, her face crumpling, and I feel like I'm being stabbed through the heart with every breath she fights for. "I'm too needy." This time it's the shape of the words, with no sound.

I keep pushing, forcing the words out, even though it makes me feel like I'm being skinned alive. "We make each other worse, not better." *I don't know how to love you without hurting you.*

She starts sobbing, soundlessly, as is Lavender's way. Her entire body quakes, and she tries to put her head down. It takes a full minute for her to compose herself enough to stutter out the words. "W-w-we m-make e-e-each other worse."

"Good girl." The praise is in direct opposition to the horrible lies I force her to repeat. "It was bad enough when we were kids. I can't go through this shit again." *I won't survive you leaving me, and that's inevitable.* "I don't want you, and I never will." *I will never get over what I'm doing to you.*

I can feel her caving in on me.

"I need to hear it, Lavender." I fight not to stroke her cheek, not to press my lips to hers.

"Y-y-you don't want me."

"I can't love you." *I will never stop loving you.*

Lavender goes eerily still, and the light in her eyes dies, like a candle being snuffed by the wind. A terrifying calm settles around us. Her breath comes slow and even, unlike mine.

"Do you understand, Lavender?" The words feel like acid in my mouth.

"Fuck you, Kodiak." Her voice is surprisingly steady.

"Not a chance in hell. Then I'll never get rid of you." *I'll never be able to let you go.*

I don't expect the slap across the face. But I relish the sting and the force behind it. It means I've accomplished what I set out to do.

I let go of her, and she clambers off the bed. Her feet get tangled up in the comforter, and she lands in a heap on the floor. I fist the sheets to keep myself from helping her. She picks herself up clumsily and yanks the door open, rushing down the hall, desperate to escape me and the lies I forced on her.

Lavender is everyone's Achilles' heel.

And I just sliced mine to the bone.

23

No Control

KODIAK

Present day

L AVENDER'S DORM EXPERIENCE lasts less than thirty-six hours. I don't ask what happened, and no one offers an explanation. In the almost two days since she moved back in, I haven't seen much of her, but I've heard her.

Her anger comes out in the relentless, aggressive drone of her sewing machine and the music she listens to. I want to reach through the walls and absorb her pain, since I'm the one who created it. I don't know how much longer I can sit here in the acid bath of my regrets without losing my mind.

I check the clock on the TV for the tenth time. She's usually home by now on Thursdays. I don't like that her schedule isn't always predictable. Sometimes she doesn't come home until hours after her classes are finished. I hate that I know her schedule. I hate that I'm an asshole to her, and that she refuses to do anything about it other than tell me she hates me. I hate that I can't handle this, or her, or my own emotions 90 percent of the time, and it all comes out as vitriol.

I try to focus on the video game, but my head is all over the place, so I lose to BJ and toss the controller to River. He grunts, but doesn't acknowledge me with words. He rarely does. Living with him is sort of like living with a porcupine.

Maverick is out with his flavor of the month. At a movie. She insisted he take her on an actual date because all they ever do is hang out in his bedroom. She's not wrong, but based on her conversation skills, I'm going to say there's a good reason for that.

The front door opens, dragging my attention away from the TV screen. Not that I was paying attention to what was going on, since I'm up in my head, as usual. Less than a minute later, Lavender appears. She's wearing jeans and an oversized hoodie with the college logo on it.

She's not alone, though.

The guy who trails behind her is vaguely familiar. He's lanky with thick-rimmed glasses.

"Why are you so late, and why didn't you answer my texts?" River pauses the game so he can glower at her.

Lavender adopts a fake smile. "Hi, twin. It's so nice to see you too. How was your day?"

"It was peachy." His gaze shifts to the guy hovering nervously behind her, and his cheek tics. "What're you doing here?"

Lavender looks like her head is about to explode. "What is wrong with you? You'd think you were raised by wolves. Josiah is my classmate and my friend, so drop your asshole level down to a one or a two, please."

River's gaze darts between them. "Right, yeah, sorry. Hey, Josiah."

"Hey." Josiah raises his hand in an uncomfortable wave, his face turning red as he scans the three of us.

"The bearded one is my cousin BJ."

BJ waves his acknowledgment.

"And that's Kodiak," she mutters, not bothering to look at me. "Anyway, we're gonna go study, so see you all later." She grabs Josiah by the arm, moves him in front of her, and pushes him toward the stairs. She flips the bird over her shoulder at us. I assume it's mostly directed at me, and possibly River.

The three of us watch them disappear upstairs. To her bedroom. Where they're going to "study."

BJ looks at me and then at River, who unpauses the game.

I expect River to shit a brick about Lavender bringing some guy up to her room. Because there is no way they're going up there just to study. She is way out of his league, and I'm 100 percent sure he knows it.

I look at BJ. He raises an eyebrow. I bite my tongue. I can't say anything, or I'll make myself completely transparent.

He finally does me a solid—although I'm not sure he realizes that's what he's doing—and asks the question I can't. "Uh, River?"

"What?" River mows down a hoard of zombies.

"You're cool with that?"

"Cool with what?" He blows up an entire warehouse full of zombies. "Fuck, yeah."

"That." BJ points to the stairs.

River doesn't take his eyes off the screen. "That what?"

"Lavender. That guy?"

"She's nineteen years old. She can bring a guy up to her room if she wants. Besides, they're studying." Another hoard of zombies comes piling out of a doorway and takes his player down. He tosses the controller back to me. "She's her own person. She always has been. I'm going for a run. I can't stand

236

the stench of desperation in here." He pushes up out of the chair and heads for the front door. A few seconds later, it opens and closes with a slam.

I grip the controller and stare at the TV, fighting to remain calm. Why now? Why all of a sudden is River okay with Lavender bringing a guy up to her room? Why am I suddenly a pane of glass that everyone can see through? That familiar feeling of being disassociated from my body takes over, and my knee starts to bounce.

"Fuck this." I toss the controller aside and push up off the couch.

"What exactly are you going to do?" BJ asks, completely unrattled.

"Someone needs to deal with this." I point to the ceiling. "And obviously you and River are useless."

BJ raises one dark eyebrow. "I think you need to figure your shit out."

"This isn't about me."

He huffs a laugh and shakes his head. "Really? 'Cause you're losing it over the idea of someone you apparently can't stand getting action. Look, man, I don't know what the deal is with you and Lavender, or what happened between you to make things how they are, but you need to stop torturing her. This is not you, man. You are not this person." He motions to me. "She doesn't deserve whatever this is."

"You have no idea what you're talking about."

He throws his hands in the air. "You're right. I don't know. No one does because the two of you talk around shit and say nothing. What happened when you were kids? Better yet, what happened two years ago at Christmas? And why are you so determined to make her miserable? Hasn't she already been through enough?"

I can't answer any of those questions. Not with any kind of

honesty. So I don't. Instead, I turn around and head for the stairs.

"You're such an idiot," BJ grumbles, but he doesn't stop me.

I pause outside my bedroom door. I should leave it alone. Leave Lavender alone. But I can't stand the idea of her up there with that guy. If I can't have her, I don't want anyone else to have her either. And that's really what it comes down to.

I made it this way. It's my fault.

I move toward the stairs leading up to Lavender's bedroom. Her ivory tower. The untouchable princess. I take the stairs slowly, avoiding the ones that creak. Because I've come up here so many times since I moved in—sat outside the door, wanting to tell her the truth. Listened to the sound of her sewing machine humming, her soft voice when she sings her favorite songs.

It's almost a travesty that so few people know what a beautiful voice she has. Almost. But I like that I still know so many of the pieces of herself she keeps hidden.

When she moved into the dorms, I broke down again and picked the lock so I could marinate in my own misery like I deserved.

I wrap my hand around the doorknob and press my forehead against the wood. The familiar scent of lavender permeates through. She's always searching for the calm that's so hard to find and hold on to, despite her name.

Her soft laugh makes my heart ache.

God. When was the last time I heard that sound?

Years, I'm sure.

It's followed by silence, and a million scenes float through my head like a flipbook—all of them ones I don't want to be real.

I turn the knob, and the door flies open. This should be the first sign I'm overreacting, but I'm already in panic mode, and rational thought has completely deserted me. All I want is to stop whatever this is—the spinning in my head, the fear that the damage I've done, and continue to do, has become completely irreparable.

Lavender is sitting on her bed, legs crossed. She's lost the sweatshirt, leaving her in a tank top that shows way too goddamn much cleavage. Her back is to the headboard and Josiah mirrors her, elbows propped on his knees, their heads bent together. Her hand on his knee. Touching him.

"This is not happening!" I bark.

Lavender gives me a look like I've gone insane. "What the hell, Kodiak?"

"This right here is bullshit." I point at Josiah. "You are so out of your league, you're not even in the same fucking time zone."

Lavender gapes at me. "Have you lost your damn mind? What do you think you're doing?"

"What am *I* doing? What are *you* doing?" I flail like an idiot, motioning between them. On her fucking bed.

She lifts up her textbook. "Studying for a test, so you should take your meltdown elsewhere."

"Bull-fucking-shit, Lavender." I take another step into the room, submerging in her scent, in her everything. I need him gone, and I'll do just about anything to make it happen. I sneer at her. "Does he know what you're really like?"

"What're you talking about?" Red creeps into her cheeks.

"Does he have any idea what you do when you're alone?" I don't know what *I'm* doing anymore, other than being pissed off and highly irrational.

"Other than sew and avoid you?"

Damn, I love how sassy she can be now. I scoff and hate myself before I've even had the chance to speak, this time to

Josiah. "She's not as innocent as you might think, are you, Lavender?"

It looks like his eyes are going to pop out of his head, and his hands are raised in the air, as if he's being held at gunpoint. Lavender just looks confused.

My next course of action is damning in so many ways. For her. For me. I stalk over to her bed and stop beside the nightstand.

"Seriously, Kodiak, get out of my room." Her voice wavers, a nervous edge to it.

I shake my head, pinning her with a malicious glare. "Don't you think your friend deserves to know what he's dealing with?" I grab the handle on the second drawer down.

In my head, I'm aware this is a terrible move, that it's just going to screw things up even more, that I'm about to humiliate her in a way I probably can't come back from, and that I've completely lost control—what little I had in the first place.

Her eyes flare with understanding and then narrow. "You fucker."

I yank the drawer free and flip it over so the contents spill out, half landing on the bed, the other half tumbling to the floor at my feet.

Josiah's eyebrows disappear into his hairline as he takes in the plethora of personal pleasure devices. The range is actually staggering, particularly when they're not all crammed into a nightstand drawer. There are several small bottles of lube and an array of vibrators, dildos, and some oddly shaped thing I can't figure out.

Lavender slow claps, her expression reflecting her annoyance. "Very dramatic, Kodiak."

I'm actually shocked that she's not a mess of incoherent nerves. In this case, that seems to be me.

Josiah scratches his temple and grins. "Damn, Lavender, you're quite the handful, aren't you?"

She smirks and rolls her eyes, like it's some kind of inside joke. "My gigi is very pro self-exploration."

"I don't know who Gigi is, but I'd love to meet her."

"She's my grandma, and she's awesome—a little too into the overshare, but you'd love her."

I make some kind of sound, sort of like a rabid animal, because this isn't going at all like I'd planned. Granted, I didn't have much of a plan in the first place, but the two of them chatting about her grandmother while surrounded by a drawer full of sex stuff wasn't anywhere on my list of possibilities.

They both glance at me and then each other. "Do you mind if I tell him?" Lavender asks.

Josiah looks appropriately wary now. Whether because he's sitting on a bed covered in sex toys, or because I'm clearly on the verge of some kind of mental breakdown, I can't be sure. Both would be logical. Ironically, he has very little reaction to the confetti of fake dicks surrounding him. Unlike me.

He lifts one shoulder and lets it fall. "I have nothing to hide."

Panic makes my chest tight. Maybe he's been back here before. Maybe there's already more going on than I know about.

"Josiah is not interested in me," Lavender says flatly.

I scoff. "Yeah, right."

No guy comes up to a girl's room to hang out and actually do homework, especially not when that girl is Lavender. She's so fucking beautiful, it hurts. And she has a killer sense of humor, and a huge, amazing heart.

She rolls her eyes. "Josiah would be more likely to want to hook up with you than me."

Josiah raises a finger in the air. "Uh, that's actually untrue."

Lavender gives him her *seriously* look.

"What Lavender is trying to say is that I'm *gay*."

Well, that changes a whole lot of things. Like, exactly how unbalanced I seem right now. And how unnecessary it was for me to come up here and act like a giant dick. Again.

He cuts me off before I can speak. "However, you're an asshole, and I don't care how pretty you are, I would never hook up with someone who treats my friend as shitty as you treat Lavender." He turns back to her. "Do you want to come back to my place or something?"

She rubs the space between her eyes. "I appreciate the offer, but I think I need to deal with this." She grants me a dismissive wave.

"Are you sure?"

"Yeah. I need to handle this situation, and you don't need to witness the shitstorm that's about to go down." She flips her book shut.

He unfolds his legs and carefully steps around the fallen items on the floor. He's a good four or five inches shorter than me, and probably a good fifty pounds lighter, but he rolls his shoulders back and juts his chin out.

I rub the back of my neck. "I, uh . . ."

He shakes his head. "If you're thinking about apologizing, don't bother—especially not to me, because I won't accept it. I'm not the person you should be apologizing to anyway. I don't know what your problem is, but I can tell you from what I've witnessed you don't deserve Lavender or her forgiveness." He turns back to Lavender, who's also now standing amidst the contents of her drawer. He pulls her into a hug, glaring at me over her shoulder and whispers something I don't catch.

Josiah has some serious balls. He's a good friend, and I reluctantly admit to myself that I'm glad she has him in her corner.

She takes his hands in hers and squeezes, pushing up on her tiptoes to kiss his cheek, whispering, "Thank you for being such a good friend. I promise I'll be fine."

The jealousy is almost more than I can handle. But I tamp it down, because I've created a huge mess already. Literally and figuratively. Lavender walks him to the door, and they whisper to each other before she finally closes it with a quiet click and turns to face me. She is seriously pissed, but also exceptionally calm.

She props her hands on her hips. "How many times have you been in my room?"

24

Come Clean

KODIAK

Present day

I RUB THE back of my neck, searching for a way to explain my behavior. There really isn't a good excuse without coming clean. All the way clean. And I'm so exhausted, so tired of fighting against this, of trying to make her hate me, of making myself miserable . . . "A couple."

"So twice?" she presses.

This isn't the Lavender I knew. She was shy and quiet and never, ever called me on my shit like she does now. Although usually I was coming to her rescue, not being an asshole, so the calling out wasn't necessary. "Uhhh, I guess . . ." I swallow as she continues to stare. Not believing me. I think about the times I've sat outside her door just to be close. And the handful of times I picked the lock. "More like a few."

Her right brow raises. She seems to decide the actual number isn't important. Thankfully. "Why?"

"Huh?" It's difficult not to focus on the items scattered across the floor—the ones I dumped there, thinking I'd make some kind of point. It's not helping the thoughts running through my head, which are jumbling up like an off-kilter tray full of marbles.

"Why were you in here? It's a fairly straightforward question, shouldn't be too difficult for your genius brain to manage."

"I just . . . I wanted to see . . ." I flounder, fighting the rising panic.

"See what?" She flails her hand toward her bed. "What I keep in my nightstand drawer? Did you check for a journal? Did you want to see if I was still pining for you? Were you looking for more ways to humiliate me? Coveting them like little grenades you planned to set off every time I needed a reminder of how much you hate me?"

She stalks closer, and I hold my breath, willing her to touch me—shove me, smack me, anything, but she doesn't. Her ocean-blue eyes flash with ire. "Message fucking received, Kodiak. You delivered it perfectly two years ago, and I sure as hell haven't forgotten how that felt. I don't require any more goddamn reminders, though you seem like you're quite fond of delivering them. I screwed up your life. I get it. I was a goddamn child, and I had no idea it was going to get as bad as it did, but I was not alone in those choices, so stop punishing me for something I didn't have a whole hell of a lot of control over."

"That wasn't . . . I don't . . . I'm not . . ." I pace the room, more to keep myself from acting on impulses I can't allow. I accidentally kick a bottle of lube across the floor. It comes to a stop in front of Lavender. She bends to pick it up, flipping it between her fingers.

"Then what was this about?" She lobs the bottle at me. Normally she has piss-poor aim, but it hits me in the thigh, a few inches shy of my junk. I catch it before it can fall to the floor. I try not to think about what she uses this for, but the images are already popping like bubbles in my brain.

"I didn't want you up here alone with him," I admit.

"Why? You've made it clear *you* don't want me. So why are you being such a cockblocking son of a bitch, other than to make me miserable?"

I scrub a hand over my face. "That's not true."

"Oh yes, it is! You've been a nightmare to deal with. Every time I turn around, there you are, making my life damn well impossible. Why can't you leave me alone? Why do you feel the need to torment me so relentlessly?"

"Because I can't have you!" I shout.

Her expression shifts to confusion. "Have you lost your goddamn mind? You don't even want me, so why does that matter?" she shouts back. "Who the fuck are you? What the hell happened to you?"

I don't understand how she can't see what's right in front of her. Why does she have to make me say it all? What happened to when we could just be together and know what the other person was feeling? "You! You happened!"

She throws her hands in the air. "I won't apologize for the mistakes we made when we were kids!"

I'm done fighting this, and her. I can't keep doing this or I'm going to lose my mind, and based on what I've done tonight, I think I'm already halfway there. I can't think, I can't focus . . . All these years of holding this in have eaten away at me, turning me into someone I don't even recognize.

Desperation bubbles to the surface and spills over. "How can you not see it?"

"See what?"

"Don't you get it? All of it was bullshit!" I yell. "I lied!"

Her voice goes eerily calm. "Lied about what, exactly?"

Her frustration at my lack of explanation is understandable, but I've spent so many years avoiding and pushing my feelings down, I don't know how to tell her the truth. I worry I've ruined this, *us*, beyond repair and she'll never forgive me.

And I'll lose her all over again.

"About everything." I run my hands through my hair.

She skims her bottom lip with her teeth, running them over the scar. "Explain that, please," she says, voice barely a whisper.

"After our parents sat us down and told us we needed a break, I was so angry. It hurt to stay away from you. I hated it, but I also realized *I* didn't have control anymore. Not when it came to you. It had to be all or nothing. I was making you worse. I was making *me* worse. I made you dependent on me, and the worst part was that I *wanted* it that way. They were right to try to split us up. I was so fucking toxic."

"That's what you said, we were toxic for each other."

I shake my head. "You were never toxic for me, but I was toxic for you. For a while I didn't see it, but you started to do better. I hated that you were okay without me. I knew if I kept coming back, it would ruin you, and you'd already been through so much." I lace my fingers behind my neck and pace the length of the room. "But that night before we moved, all I wanted was to see you, see for myself that you really were better and that I'd done the right thing."

"You kissed that girl the day you left! I saw it happen."

"I was angry! You didn't come to say goodbye."

Her eyes flash with indignation. It's understandable, but it's terrifying all the same. "You'd barely spoken to me in months. What was I saying goodbye to? And it's not as though you made an effort to reach out *after* you moved anyway!"

"I did try, but you shut me down and then stopped responding!"

"River blocked your messages," she says softly. "I didn't know until recently."

"Of course he fucking did. And you know what? He was right to do it because I wouldn't have been able to let you go otherwise. After we moved, I still missed you all the damn time. It killed me that you were gone from my world, but there wasn't another option. I wasn't going to be good for you. Everyone saw what I couldn't. I was naïve to believe that after five fucking years I could handle being near you again. I couldn't deal at all. All it took was seeing you once and everything came rushing back. I was still going to be toxic for you. And you weren't a kid anymore, which made it worse. Nothing had changed, Lavender. Not for me. I felt exactly the same as I had the day I moved away from you, so I lied." She's silent and unmoving, so I continue, digging my own grave. "That night when you came and found me at your parents'—"

"You mean the night I caught you creeping on me and followed you back to the spare room, and you made me repeat all of those horrible things you said?" Her voice is hard and sharp like knives.

I stop in front of her. "You were seventeen, and I was already in college. If I had done what I'd wanted to, I would have caused us to implode. I wouldn't have been able to manage the distance and not being there when you needed me. I already knew what leaving you felt like. I didn't think I'd survive it again."

"So you told me you didn't want me and you never would."

"I lied to save you from me." My chest aches, and I feel like I'm going to throw up.

She rubs the scar on her bottom lip. "And all the shit you've pulled this year? The horrible things you've said and done? I'm just supposed to forgive you because you decided this was how you were going to protect me?"

"No. Yes. I don't know. I just want you to understand."

248

"You made me feel like *nothing*. You were a huge part of my life, and you abandoned me."

"Because I loved you, I l—"

She recoils and puts her hands up defensively. "Do *not* finish that sentence. You don't deserve to say those words, not with the way you've treated me. From the first day I came here, you made me feel like a nuisance."

"I wasn't prepared for what it was like to be this close to you again."

I was drafted during my freshman year to Vancouver, but my mom and I talked it through with my dad and decided I should finish my degree. I have a great team and coaching staff here, so Vancouver agreed. As much as hockey is my life, I've always wanted a backup plan. Concussions can cause a lot of damage, and I'm screwed up enough as it is. I won't risk my brain for a sweet paycheck.

But the real truth is, I wanted to stay because I knew there was a very good chance Lavender would be here. Some small part of me wanted to prove I was over her, though I knew I wasn't. I didn't have to dig very deep to come to that conclusion. It took one five-minute trip in a car with her to realize I was fucked.

"So you were an asshole instead." She exhales a slow breath. "And Bethany, the girl who came out of your house not half an hour after you dropped me off that first day, did you fuck her right after you made me feel worthless and insignificant?"

"What? No." I don't know how she even knows about Bethany being anywhere near me.

As if she can read my mind, she says, "I was on my way back to campus when she walked by me. She was talking about being in your room and having an in. Might as well tell the truth, Kodiak. All the little lies are piling up and burying you."

"I didn't touch her." I feel sick thinking about that day. How I behaved. What I almost let happen.

"I can hear the *but* in there. Something must've happened. I saw you with her again."

I rub the bridge of my nose. "But I didn't touch her."

"This distinction really seems to matter to you, doesn't it, Kodiak? As if your inaction somehow makes it better. Did she touch *you* that first day, after you humiliated me and drove me home? Did you let *her* put her hands on you, then?"

I shake my head, swallowing past the lump in my throat.

Lavender tilts her head to the side, pensive. Too perceptive. Even after all these years, she knows me too well for my own good. "So what happened then?"

"She wouldn't leave."

"Did you use your words, Kodiak? Seems like you're pretty good at pushing people away when you want to." She turns, giving me her profile, her fingers curl into fists and release. "Have you fucked her?"

"No."

"Has she fucked *you*?" She smiles at the distinction she's making, although it's cynical.

"No." Although she's tried on multiple occasions to make it happen. She's persistent and desperate, the latter of which I'm highly familiar with.

Lavender runs her finger across her eyebrow and rubs her temple, like she's trying to get rid of a headache. "And now you're telling me you want me? That you always have, and you treated me like garbage for my own good?" She glances down at the front of my basketball shorts, which do a shit job of hiding anything. "Are you *turned on*?"

I shrug. "You're fired up, and there are sex toys all over your floor."

"So acting like a dick gets you hard?"

"You giving me hell turns me on." I wave a hand in her direction and give up completely. "And you in general, every-thing about you."

"So what exactly did you think was going to happen when you busted in here and made it rain fake dicks? Did you think I would swoon at the romance of it all and ride yours?"

"I didn't, no. I just thought . . . I just wanted—"

"To come in beating your chest and let Josiah know he couldn't have me? Stake your claim." She motions to my crotch again. "Kinda looks like that was your dick's plan."

"I didn't have a plan. I wanted that guy not to put his hands on you." I spit the words like bitter pills.

"So you could?"

I throw my hands in the air. "Yes. No. I don't know. I told you I lied, that I want you."

"And you sound like you're really ecstatic about it too."

"Maverick is my best friend, and River keeps threatening to murder me if I so much as look at you." And I kind of believe he'd do it. River always seems like he's on the edge of snapping.

She rolls her shoulders back and raises her chin, defiant and painfully beautiful. "Nut the fuck up, Kodiak. You've been an asshole to me for a lot of years. You made me think I was an annoyance and someone you've humored since you became a teenager, and you've done nothing but make this semester miserable for me. Do you have any idea what it's like living here with the three of you? It's a cockblock-a-thon. My entire damn life, everyone's protected me. Who are you to decide what's best for me?"

"Lavender—"

"Shut it, Kodiak. I don't need this dadbro bullshit. You want me? Then do something proactive about it that isn't being an asshole or pounding on your chest like some Neanderthal.

You're a damn genius. Use your brain and figure out how to manage the situation."

I can do that. Be proactive. I take a step forward, but Lavender puts her hand up to stop me.

"What do you think you're doing?"

"Being proactive."

"By doing what, exactly?"

"Uh . . ." I scratch the edge of my jaw. "I was going to start by kissing you."

Lavender snorts. "You think you deserve to kiss me after the hell you've put me through? That's a fuck no, big boy. You want to know what my mouth tastes like, you need to earn it, and everything else."

My erection kicks behind my basketball shorts. "Uh, right. Okay. What can I do? Should I . . . apologize again?"

She drags her tongue across her bottom lip, eyes narrowed as a slow smile forms. "You should sit the fuck down."

I take several steps back and drop into her computer chair, which groans under my weight, since it's made to fit her tiny body, not mine.

Lavender lifts her tank over her head and tosses it at me. Her tits are nestled in a white satin bra. There's a lot of cleavage. Lavender has big boobs. She gets asked if they're fake a lot, especially since the rest of her is so damn tiny. Fun size, really.

"What're you doing?" My voice is about two octaves higher than it should be.

"You seem to think you know what happens when I'm alone up here. So I'm going to show you. And maybe it'll give you a little motivation to figure your damn shit out." She reaches behind her and unclasps her bra.

The straps slide down her arms, and she lets it fall to the floor, exposing her breasts. She grabs them and squeezes, tugging at her nipples. "I bet you want to do this, don't you?"

"God, yes, I really do," I grunt. I want them in my mouth. I want to slide my cock between those full, lush tits. I push out of the chair.

She raises a hand, giving me pause. "Sit down or the show's over."

I drop down and the chair rolls back, hitting her desk, causing the jar of pencils to fall over. She pops the button on her jeans and drags her zipper down. My erection strains, and I grip the arms of the chair to keep from launching myself at her, since the last thing I want her to do is stop. She shimmies the denim over her hips and down her thighs.

She gives me her back, showing off a pair of black cheekies, and bends at the waist as she removes those too. Lavender's ass is fan-fucking-tastic. Round and full and completely biteable. And smackable. I would know, since I've done both of those things.

She falters for a moment, back expanding as she drags in a deep breath. Her arms hang at her sides, and she draws a figure eight on the outside of her leg, like she's trying to calm herself.

"You're perfect, Lavender," I tell her, afraid she's going to lose her nerve and stop whatever this is.

She peeks coyly over her shoulder as she runs her hands over her hips.

I nod in encouragement. "I want to touch you like that."

"I bet you do." She palms her ass, gives it a squeeze, and follows it with a swift slap that makes me jump and her smile.

The thought crosses my mind that she might not be a virgin.

In which case, I'm going to want to dig some graves.

She runs her fingers through her long, wavy hair, pulling it into a ponytail and fixing it with an elastic before she turns around.

I take in all of her, naked and on display. Just for me, not a room full of people who all got to stare at my half-hard cock for three hours because I was trying to get a rise out of her. Because I wanted her but couldn't face the consequences of admitting it. Because I was being an asshole.

I exhale a shaky breath, and the arms of the chair squeak under my grip.

She's almost bare. A thin auburn strip guides my gaze down to the sweet cleft between her thighs. "See something you want?" she taunts.

"Yes," I groan.

"Too bad you've been too much of an asshole to deserve to have me." She skims her lips with a fingertip. There's pink paint under her nails. She drags her finger down her throat, circles her nipples and continues the descent until she dips between her legs.

"I'm sorry," I croak.

"You're about to be." She drops to her knees on the floor, in the middle of the mess of sex toys I dumped out. She grabs a very sizeable, very authentically real-looking dildo, complete with balls, and slams it against the hardwood floor. It's then that I realize it has a suction-cup base.

Without looking, she grabs a bottle sitting by her knee and flicks it open. She pours a thin stream over the head of the veiny fake cock and starts stroking.

Generally I feel pretty good about my size—better than pretty good. But this seems like a lot for someone as small as Lavender. "Baby, I don't think—"

"Pet names? Someone's getting desperate. And you're exactly right; you didn't think, at all—not about how your asshole behavior affected me, not about whether *I* was important too. You used your friendship with Maverick as a cop-out. I'm sick of being ignored and protected. I'm done with the bullshit, Kodiak."

"I was protecting you from *me*."

"Still finding excuses, I see. Pretty dumb for someone so smart." She's kneeling in front of the dildo, so I can't see what she's doing when her hand disappears between her thighs, but the wet sound and her soft whimper are enough to give me an idea.

Her hand reappears, and she lifts her fingers to her mouth, licking up the length of the middle one. "Mmm, tastes like *not* yours."

Half of me wants to dispute that—because as far as I'm concerned, she's always been mine—but the other half, the slightly more voyeuristic side, wants to see where she's going with this. Will she actually go through with it, or is this Lavender trying to push me over the edge?

I should know better.

Lavender has spent years sitting in the wings, behind her brothers, behind a stage, behind a canvas or a sewing machine. Lavender is usually the quiet one, watching the action and not participating—unless she's been drinking.

But she's stone sober right now.

She grips the dildo and slides up the length. She rubs the head over her clit and lines it up with her entrance. Her lids flutter as she sinks down, stretching, accommodating, *fucking moaning*. Her thighs flex as she rises up, and the head appears before it disappears again, and this time she takes more, up and down, in and out, until all that length and girth is swallowed up inside her.

All I can think about is what it would be like if she were riding me like that, tits bouncing, my tongue in her mouth, breathing in her moans.

"Do you have any idea what it's like?" Her fingers dip between her legs, pinching her clit as she slides down the length again. "Being surrounded by all of this . . . ego all the time. Everyone wants to be the best, the biggest, the most, and all I want is to be seen. Acknowledged." She rises up. "You saw me, didn't you, Kodiak?"

No one calls me by my full name. Ever. Not even my parents. It's not even on my school records. Only Lavender has called me that. As soon as she could pronounce my full name, that's what she's always called me.

"Yes. I saw you. I see you."

"But you didn't want to." She lowers herself with a quiet sigh. "Too much of a complication."

"You were seventeen."

"I'm not talking about two years ago." Rise up. "I'm talking about now." Slide down. "It's awful to want something you're not allowed to have, isn't it?"

"I'm sorry. There was so much to lose." I move my hand to my thigh.

"Don't," she snaps. "Don't touch yourself. You need to know what it feels like to be me. Always on the outside." She circles her clit. "Wanting to be wanted." Her eyes fall closed. "But believing the person you want will never want you back."

She shudders, and in true Lavender form, she ducks her head and whimpers quietly as her entire body convulses. Because she's coming.

But she hides it.

Like she hides everything.

Her wants. Her needs. Her anger. Her hurt.

Until tonight.

Silence follows, heavy and thick with lust and something that terrifies me. My dick is so hard, it hurts, but there's no way on God's green earth that I'm going to ask for anything right now.

Slowly, Lavender unfurls, rising up. The wet suction sound is excessive and loud. She stumbles a few steps, finds her balance, and crosses the room. Grabbing her robe from the back of her door, she shrugs it on and flips the lock.

"Get out."

I uncurl my fingers from the armrest and push out of the chair. I have to rearrange myself, and even that contact almost makes me blow my load. "Lavender." Her name is guttural—a plea, an apology.

Her eyes shift from the open door to me, hard and angry. "I hope all the suffering was worth it. If you really want me, I guess you're going to have to find a way to deserve me."

25

Suffer with Me Silently

LAVENDER

Present day

I WAKE UP the next morning, and immediately my mind goes to what I did last night. I might have some kind of weird fetish, considering the way I got off on making Kodiak *watch* me get off. My thighs clench, and I grimace. I'd say I need to do more squats, but I'm unlikely to follow through on that.

I scrub a hand over my face, aware that I have to deal with Kodiak and whatever this new development is in our relationship. I'm still trying to get over the fact that he spent half a decade avoiding me and the past several months being a giant asshole because he was afraid to ruin me. I'm unsure if that's narcissistic, sweet, or something else entirely. Although, when I factor in my conversations with my mom and Queenie, I guess it all kind of makes sense.

I don't have class, but I want to stop by the theater and

work on a project this morning, so I get dressed and prepare to face whoever I may run into in the kitchen. Hopefully everyone is already out of the house or still sleeping.

I should be so lucky.

Sitting at the kitchen table, with a massive textbook laid out in front of him, is Kodiak. He's wearing a Seattle hockey T-shirt that probably once belonged to his dad, based on how worn it is. In the short time he's been living here, I've never seen him study in the kitchen, or anywhere that isn't his room.

The fact that there's a box of Lucky Charms, a bowl, a spoon, coconut milk, and a canister of something I can't identify because it's half-hidden by the cereal box, tells me the studying is likely a ruse.

He looks up from his textbook when I open the cupboard to retrieve a mug. My nondairy creamer is already on the counter, along with the organic agave syrup and a carafe of pressed coffee.

"The coffee's fresh." His voice is a low, quiet rumble that pours over me like warm butter.

I don't respond, because it's not a statement that requires one. I fill my mug and add creamer and syrup, stirring for far longer than is necessary. I'm mentally fortifying myself for whatever is about to happen. Will he go back to being an asshole? Will he say something horrible about what I did last night? Or is he going to magically be the Kodiak I once loved?

I turn to face him, the mug raised to my lips, sort of like a shield.

"Hey." He pushes back his chair and stands. He runs his hand through his hair, eyes moving over me in a slow sweep that makes me feel as naked as I was last night. He licks his lips and motions to the bowl and cereal. "I thought you might be hungry."

"Yeah, I worked up quite an appetite last night." Normally

my sarcasm isn't this on point first thing in the morning, but I'm deflecting some fairly intense embarrassment.

Kodiak cough-chokes, but doesn't comment otherwise.

I move the bowl and spoon to the chair across from him, rather than the one beside him, to avoid any potential physical contact. I pull out the chair and sit, somewhat gingerly.

Kodiak looks like he wants to say something, or ask something, but doesn't know how or what so he sits back down and says nothing. He also looks tired, as though he didn't sleep well—unlike me, who slept like a damn baby. It was the same kind of passed-out-like-the-dead sleep I have post-extended panic attack. And I suppose in a lot of ways, it was, because I'd spent a lot of years believing one thing was true, only to be told something else entirely last night.

I figure blasé is pretty much the only way I can play this without having some kind of epic, girl-style fit that may or may not include screaming and possibly crying.

"Rough night?" I ask as I shake cereal into my bowl.

Kodiak is in the middle of a sip of coffee, which he sprays all over his textbook. He coughs a couple of times and wipes his mouth with the back of his hand. "Seriously, Lavender?"

I shrug and reach for the coconut milk. "You look tired."

"Yeah, well, I had a lot to think about." He pushes the other container toward me.

I spin it around so I can read the label. "Cereal marshmallows?"

"You eat all the ones out of the Lucky Charms, so it's pretty much Alpha-Bits by the time you're done. I figured this would make the boxes last longer, and you can adjust the marshmallow-to-cereal ratio." His cheeks flush, and the table shakes, likely because his foot is going on the floor.

"You think cereal marshmallows are going to make up for years of lies and you being a giant asshole to me?"

He flips his textbook closed and clasps his hands on the table. His expression is pained. "Are we unfixable?"

"I don't know, Kodiak."

He goes still and silent. His eyes fall closed, and I watch his chest rise slowly to the count of four, his breath leaving him even slower through slightly parted lips. It feels like all the air is suddenly sucked out of the room.

So much pain swims in his northern-light eyes when he opens them. "Can we try?"

"Try what exactly?"

"To be something again?"

"I won't go back to how it was. I don't want to be that girl ever again, and you can't undo damage that's already been done."

He nods. "I don't want it to be like it was before either. And I don't think it can be, because you're not the same. I mean, last night you were—"

I arch a brow, and he drops his head, blowing out a long breath before he shifts course. "Maybe we could try to be something better, something . . . equal?"

"Do you think that's possible?" I'm not asking to be difficult, or a bitch, but because I honestly don't know. I made him into a god as a child and never really stopped believing he was, when truly, he's as fallible as the rest of us.

"All I know is that it's torture being this close to you and feeling like you're forever out of reach. I wanted to get over you, but I can't, and I don't know if I ever will, so please, can we just try?"

"What are you going to say to Maverick?"

"Nothing he doesn't already know, even though he pretends otherwise."

He's not wrong. Maverick has always known there's something between us, and yet he's never once said anything. "And River?"

"I figure you can handle him." He bites the inside of his lip, fighting a smile.

I turn my head and huff a laugh. "Making coffee and pulling a box of cereal out of a cupboard doesn't erase all the awful things you've said and done."

"I know." He reaches across the table, palm up. "I'm so tired of trying to make you hate me. I just want to love you again, but better this time."

I line my fingers up with his, the tips touching. "I don't need to be saved anymore, Kodiak. I slay my own dragons now."

He curls his pinkie around mine and nods.

And we begin again.

26

Let Me Back in

LAVENDER

Present day

IRONICALLY, NEITHER OF my brothers is home this morning, so Kodiak and I end up driving in together in my car. It's weird at best. He doesn't make any snide, shitty comments. In fact, he doesn't say much at all, but I can tell by the way he keeps his hands on his knees that he's seriously anxious.

"Talk," I tell him.

"Huh?"

"What's eating at you?" I point to his legs.

"I don't know. Everything, I guess."

"Want to get a little more specific?"

"I don't know how to be around you. I want to touch you, but I don't think I'm allowed to yet." He runs his hands up and down his thighs.

"You would be correct."

He nods and blows out a breath. "I need to earn your trust again."

"You do," I agree. "And we don't even really know each other anymore, Kodiak. What if you don't like this version of me?"

"I already like this version of you. I like that you don't take shit. I like that you're strong and independent and that you know what you want. I like that despite knowing what's best for you, you still took into consideration what was best for River when you decided you were going to live in that house with them this year, and that you deferred declaring your major so you could get a handle on things first. I like that you won't just forgive me and let it all go. And even though I have no idea whether or not you'll ever really be able to forgive me, this is the most at peace I've felt in a lot of years."

That he's paid attention gives me hope that maybe we can be a better version of us. Something new and redefined. I pull into the lot and find a spot near the back, shifting the car into park and cutting the engine. "Why is it like this with us?"

"I don't know, but fighting it has been torture." He places his hand palm-down on the center console and splays his fingers out. I spot the small infinity sign tattooed into the webbing between his ring and middle finger on his left hand.

I trace the sign on the back of his hand. "When did you get that?"

"Christmas break two years ago." He flips his hand over again, his expression hopeful.

"Why?" I slide my fingers between his, and he curls them around mine, squeezing gently.

"I needed a reminder so I wouldn't make the same mistake again."

"Mistake?"

"Thinking I could handle being near you without fucking

things up." He stares at our twined hands. "I don't think I ever got over that night at the carnival. I knew we should've waited for you and River, and we didn't, and then you went missing. It was the longest hour of my life, Lavender, and after . . . none of us was ever the same. You weren't the same. But when I figured out I could help you with the anxiety, it felt like I got you back, that we were connected again, and I didn't want to lose that. So I did everything I could to keep you close, and by doing that, I screwed us both up. After we moved, I thought it would get easier, but it never did. And then you stopped answering my messages, and I figured you'd realized how bad I was for you."

"Except it was River blocking your messages." Talking to River about this isn't going to be pretty.

We sit in silence for a minute, eyes on each other, absorbing this new situation, until his phone chimes with an alert. He glances at the clock on the dash. "Dammit. I have class in fifteen minutes."

We untwine our hands. I feel off-balance after just that innocuous contact, because now that the walls are coming down, there's potential for so much more. Also, the shit I pulled in my bedroom sits between us like a fresh cum shot.

So I should not be surprised when Kodiak falls into step beside me as we cross campus and mutters, "Uh, about last night . . ."

"You really want to talk about that *now*?" There are people everywhere. Girls gawk openly, as if I don't exist. He's walking close, but not quite touching me.

He side-eyes me. "I was kind of wondering if that was, like, a one-time thing, or if maybe it was going to happen again?"

"Is that you saying you'd like it to happen again?" *How is this even a conversation I'm entertaining at nine in the morning?*

"I wouldn't be opposed, you know, until I earn the actual

right to be the one who does that for you." We stop in front of the theater, and he jams his hand in his pocket. He looks halfway between earnest and like he wants to devour me.

"I guess you better talk to Maverick, then." I turn and walk away, smiling to myself. It's odd to have the upper hand with Kodiak. Or maybe I always had it and never realized. Either way, he needs to know who he's dealing with now.

I could tell Mav, and I'm pretty sure he isn't going to make much of a fuss either way, but Kodiak has been his best friend our entire lives, so it's a conversation they need to have without me to mediate. Also, like I told him last night, Kodiak needs to nut the fuck up about this.

Besides, I'm going to deal with River, and that on its own is enough.

I don't see my brothers or Kodiak for the rest of the day, but I do meet the twins and BJ at the café for a dairy-free latte and one of their edamame salad things. I figure I can't exist solely on Lucky Charms and muffins, although I would like to try.

Lovey and Lacey jump up and hug me when I arrive. "How are you? How is everything?" they ask, nearly in unison. "You know you can always come stay with us, if you want to."

"I'm fine. Everything is okay. I appreciate the offer, but I can't live without my sewing machine." This is the truth. I was going through withdrawal by the end of the first twelve hours. The fact that my roommate was getting plowed outside my door added to my level of desperation.

I fill them in on the whole situation, since I haven't seen them since the guys came to get all my stuff. BJ doesn't add much, other than to say Bethany is a loon and any of the guys on the team who slept with her are idiots.

Lacey and Lovey have to go to class, which leaves me and BJ. He arches a brow. "So . . ."

I shove a forkful of salad in my mouth and wish it were a

blueberry muffin instead. I put a hand in front of my face and mumble, "So what?"

"What happened with Kody last night?"

"What do you mean what happened?" My voice is hella pitchy.

"Well, he went upstairs about ten minutes after you and your friend went to study and never came back down. So what happened?"

"Kodiak and I had a discussion." This is not untrue.

"What happened to your friend?"

"He went home."

BJ frowns and strokes his beard. "Huh."

"Huh, what?"

"Nothing. I must've been in the bathroom or something when he left." He makes a dismissive gesture and crosses one leg over the other. "Anyway, tell me about this discussion."

"Kodiak was a douche, I called him out, we exchanged a bunch of words, and now we're figuring things out."

"What does that mean? Figuring things out how?"

"It's complicated."

"It's really not, though. It's always been simple, and you two just make it complicated."

"What's that supposed to mean?"

He laces his hands behind his head. "He's been in love with you since you were kids. He just didn't know how to love you without taking over your entire world, or letting you take over his. He needed you to be strong enough to put him in his place, and you are, which means things are finally going to be as they should."

I stare at him for a few long seconds, waiting to see if he's going to continue or not. "Have you been reading the *Tao of Pooh* again or something?"

"Or something. It's been infuriating, fascinating, and damn

well annoying watching you two screw up this year. I mean, mostly it's been Kody fucking shit up and you sitting back and letting it happen, but man, it's nice to see you wearing your lady balls with pride."

I laugh and shake my head. "He's not yet forgiven for all the crap he's pulled."

BJ inclines his head, half acknowledgment, half consideration. "Kody is the best at punishing himself, Lavender. You don't have to forgive him quickly, but don't throw all his mistakes back in his face when he makes new ones. He'll carry that guilt for the rest of his life if you let him."

I nod. Kodiak wears his mistakes like scars that scratch up his insides. "I know better than to do that to him."

BJ smiles, and there's something wistful in it. "It must be kind of messed up to have found your soul mate before you even understood what it meant." He ruffles my hair and pushes out of his chair. "I gotta head to class."

I check the time. It's still early but I can head to the theater, so I gather my things and leave with BJ.

After I finish up at the theater, I check my phone. I have a message from Kodiak telling me he's been thinking about me all day. He doesn't elaborate, but I'm 1000 percent sure I know what he means.

I also have a message from River saying he's out for the night, but to text or call if I need anything. He's been doing that a lot lately—the not coming home part. So has Maverick, but that's not entirely unusual. Regardless, it means I won't have a chance to talk to him about Kodiak, since it isn't something I'm interested in doing over the phone.

I do, however, fill my mom in on the fact that I've moved back into the house with my brothers and tell her not to worry about Kodiak because I can totally hold my own. Thankfully she had yet to mention the dorms to my dad, so that was one freak-out neither of us had to deal with. I also drop a mention of the summer internship opportunity, but blow it off as unlikely since I'm only a sophomore and they pretty much always take juniors or seniors. But, I tell her, it doesn't hurt to submit an application so I'm familiar with the process. She agrees.

Before I can change my mind, I stop by my professor's office and let her know I'd like to apply so she can send me the forms.

It's after six by the time I get home. Maverick, BJ, and Quinn are sitting in front of the TV playing video games, a mostly empty pizza box on the table in front of them.

Maverick looks up for a second but doesn't bother to pause. I sort of expected an immediate confrontation of some kind. Instead, he goes back to furiously pounding on the controller. "There's a nondescript black package on the counter from Gigi."

"Awesome." I cut through the living room. Obviously she ignored my mom's request to stop sending me sex-positive items.

"Wanna grab me a beer?" Mav calls.

"Me too!" BJ adds.

"You all have legs. Why can't you get your own beers?" I drop my backpack on the kitchen island and check out the black bag on the counter with a set of cherries on it. So discreet. I tuck it in my backpack so I can open it later, when I'm in the privacy of my own room.

I pull three bottles from the beer fridge. It's actually supposed to be for wine, but no one in this house is sophisticated enough to drink that, so it's filled with beer and random girly coolers that I sometimes drink.

I take a few deep breaths, prepared for Maverick to come in here and say something about the whole Kodiak thing, but BJ pops his head in instead. He yells something toward the living room about wanting a snack.

"Who's telling Mav?" he asks as he opens the pantry door and grabs two bags of chips from the top shelf.

I had no idea they were there because I'd have to stand on a freaking chair to be able to see them. "Kodiak."

BJ arches a brow. "When's that happening?"

I shrug. "I figured he would've said something by now."

"Kody disappeared into his room as soon as he got home, and Mav seems oblivious as usual, so I'm gonna go ahead and surmise that's not the case."

I cross my arms, annoyed. "Well, I'm not going to be the one to tell him."

BJ snorts a laugh. "Might wanna give your boy some incentive, then."

"*My boy*." I roll my eyes. "You're going to have a field day with this, aren't you?"

"Hell, yeah. I've been waiting years for this to go down. I can't wait to see River flip his lid."

I grab my bag and head for the stairs, but before I get far, BJ pulls me into a wiry hug. "But seriously, Lav, you two belong together and always have."

I climb the stairs, my stomach flipping with a mixture of anxiety, irritation, and anticipation. I pause on the first landing and pull the black package out, tearing into it. There's a gift note inside.

Lavender,

Your mom told me you've been having a rough time lately, and I figured this might cheer you up!

~xo Gigi

I pull out the item meant to make me feel better and stare at it. I have always loved Marvel and DC Comics movies. They're my favorite. It's probably because my mom always had a weird thing about superheroes and passed it down to me. So I should not be shocked that I'm holding an Aquaman dildo. And yet I am. Being the thoughtful, inappropriate gigi that she is, it also includes cleansing wipes and lube. Not like she hasn't sent me that stuff a dozen times before.

I climb the rest of the stairs and pause in front of Kodiak's room. I'm annoyed that he hasn't said anything to Maverick yet, especially since they had practice this afternoon and he should have had plenty of opportunity to pull him aside.

I consider the pick-me-up gift Gigi gave me, the conversation Kodiak and I had in the car on the way to campus this morning, and BJ's incentive idea. Before I lose my nerve, I turn the knob—surprised his door isn't locked—and push it open a couple of inches.

Kodiak is sitting at his computer desk, his back to me, wearing headphones and bent over a textbook, pen poised in his left hand as he awkwardly tries to write without smearing the text. Being a lefty is a pain in the ass.

I slip into the room and close the door behind me, flipping the lock. I take a moment to check out his room, having never been inside since he moved in here. Everything is tidy and organized, bed neatly made, pillows arranged perfectly, the top of the comforter folded down, the flat sheet tucked tightly under the mattress. I bet it has hospital corners. It's almost like he's military trained, even though he's not.

But what steals my breath are the pieces of old art that hang on the walls. *My* art from when I was a kid—most of it splatter-painted silliness. On the desk beside him is the ratty, old pencil case I made when I was ten. I was so proud of that thing. I stitched the infinity symbol right into the black fabric in thread the same color as his eyes.

The music is so loud, I can hear it from across the room. He needs that sometimes to drown out all the other stuff that happens in his head. His heel bounces on the floor, and I can feel his anxiety from across the room. He always dealt with it so much differently than I did. Hockey is both a cure and a cause for him.

He tosses his pencil on the desk, and his fists clench and release three times. He clasps his hands behind his head and both knees start bouncing as he breathes. I count his inhale and exhale. In for four, out for eight, eight times in a row. His shoulders curl in, and he unlocks his hands on a low groan. He grabs for the mouse and double clicks. The screen flickers, and he quickly types in a password. A few seconds later, he opens a folder and hovers the cursor over an image. He remains that way for several long seconds before he finally clicks on it.

I appear on the screen.

It's a still shot of me sitting outside by the pool, wearing a huge hat and a cover up, while reading a book under an umbrella. Me and the sun have a love-hate relationship. Based on what I'm wearing and reading, it must have been taken at the beginning of the semester. One of his hands drops to his lap.

There's a distinct possibility he's going to whack off to a very PG and fully clothed picture of me reading a book, if I don't make my presence known.

That changes drastically the way I approach this situation and him. He has a second study table in his room that's home to some kind of project. It's the only part of his room that isn't perfectly neat. Among pieces of PVC piping and a bunch of tools is a roll of duct tape.

I nab it before I cross over to his desk and drop my bag next to his textbook, scaring the shit out of him. He scrambles to remove his earbuds—they're wireless, so he drops one on the floor.

"Lavender? Holy shit. How long have you been in here? It's not what it looks like."

I glance down at his lap. He's wearing gray jogging pants— why are they always gray?—and his erection strains against the fabric.

"Really? Because it looked like you were about to jerk off to that picture of me."

He opens and closes his mouth a couple of times, likely trying to come up with an excuse. "I was taking a study break."

I snort a laugh. "How often have I been the focus of your study breaks, Kodiak?"

"Probably more than you should," he admits.

"I see." I free a strip of duct tape, the zip ridiculously loud.

"What're you doing?" His voice holds equal parts curiosity and anxiety.

"That depends."

"On what?"

"On your personal restraint, and whether or not you think you can keep your hands to yourself. How in control are you right now?"

His pale, vibrant green gaze meets mine, wide with want, and he grips the armrests. "Not very."

"Hmm, I should probably help with that, then, shouldn't I?"

He nods. His chest rises and falls with uneven breaths as I wrap the tape around his wrist. I have no idea what I'm doing, apart from reclaiming the power balance in this fucked-up relationship we seem to have. I tear a second strip free and secure his other wrist to the chair.

I wonder if duct-taping my future boyfriend to his

computer chair so I can jill off on him without him putting his hands on me is going to be a thing for us. He seems into it.

Not that I don't want them on me, but he needs to deal with Maverick, and I'm still pissed that he's been a dick this year.

I lift my gaze to his. "Are you anxious?"

"Right now?"

"Yes, right now."

He shrugs, as though he's not entirely sure.

"Have I ever hurt you?"

His brow furrows. "No."

"Have you ever hurt me?"

He closes his eyes, and his full, perfect lips press together. "Yes."

"On purpose?"

His lids lift, and there's pain swimming behind his eyes. "Only because I didn't think there was any other way to keep you safe from me."

"You were always trying to save me." I give in and stroke his cheek, gently, exactly the way he used to do to me when we were young and loved each other in the simple, untainted way innocent soul mates do. His eyes slide closed, and his whole body shudders.

I drop my hand and rummage inside my bag. I'd say I can't believe I'm doing this, but I can, because I did it yesterday.

Except I'm taking it to a whole different level of messed up this time around. I pull out the Aquaman-inspired pleasure toy and the lube.

"What is that?" He sounds appropriately confused.

"A gift from Gigi."

"Oh fuck." Realization dawns, and it's laced with excitement.

I set it on his lap. If he's aware I'm not nearly as confident as I'm pretending to be, he doesn't let on. And regardless of how awful he's been over the past couple of months, I know I'm safe with him.

And sometimes I hate him for that. Because it's made loving anyone else impossible. Not that I've tried very hard.

Kodiak's knees are parted, so I slide the Aqua-D, complete with balls—just like the one from last night, minus the suction base—between his legs. I tear a strip of duct tape free with my teeth and tap his thigh. "Knees together."

He complies, no questions asked, probably because he knows where this is going and like me, he's fucked up enough to want it.

I tear off a couple extra strips of tape and fix them on either side of Aqua-D's base to hold it in place. This means I tape over Kodiak's actual cock, which twitches and strains behind the gray fabric.

I caress his cheek again. "You okay? Do you need me to stop? Because I can." And I mean it. I want to tease him, not maim him.

"No. I'm okay." He shakes his head, his voice choked with excitement.

I step back and pull my shirt over my head. Reaching behind me, I unclasp my bra and let it fall to the floor.

"Oh shit." Kodiak's fists clench and release as if he wants to be able to reach out and touch me.

The power is heady, overwhelming and addicting.

I slide my pants and underwear over my hips and kick them off.

Kodiak's gaze runs over my body, feral and needy. I grip his forearms and straddle his lap. It's not particularly comfortable. He has hockey thighs, and they take up most of the chair, so my shins rest against the metal bars that attach the armrest to the seat. But I'm not stopping now.

Kodiak angles his head down and nuzzles into my neck, his groan plaintive and desperate. His lips part, and his warm, wet tongue swipes over my skin. He mutters *oh my God*, burrowing in, trying to bow forward enough so he can shove his face in my boobs.

I slide my hands under his shirt and push it up, exposing his cut abs and defined chest. Kodiak pushes himself to the very limit of his capabilities in every single facet of his life. And it's clear he's worked incredibly hard on his body in order to excel at hockey.

If I'd planned this better, I would have taken his shirt off before I duct-taped him to the chair. Since I can't do that now, I pull the front over his head, the material stretching across the back of his neck and cutting into his shoulders.

I run my fingers through his hair, taming the mess. He leans in, as if he's about to kiss me, and I grip the strands gently. I shake my head, our lips almost touching. "You said you were going to talk to Mav."

"I am. I will. I'm going to." His breath is warm and sweet, like he's been sucking on a watermelon Jolly Rancher. He used to eat them all the time when we were kids and share them with me, but not anyone else—little gifts that meant nothing and everything.

I don't ask any more questions. Instead, I wait for him to offer the information I want.

"We have a game tomorrow, and we're playing on the same line. It's our biggest rival team, and I don't want to mess it up, so I was planning to talk to him after."

"Are you nervous?" I keep running my fingers through his silky hair, watching the strands sweep back over his forehead.

"About telling him?" His legs bounce, and I shift forward, my breasts hitting his chest.

"And the game." I trace an infinity symbol on the side of his neck, I can almost taste his watermelon Jolly Rancher I'm so close to his lips.

"Yes and yes. We've lost to them once already this year, and I don't want that to happen again. And Maverick is my teammate and my best friend; I don't want to lose that either. But you're integral to the fabric of my existence in a way that he's not, and I feel like I've been sitting out in space for the past seven years without a sun to circle."

I nod, and the tips of our noses brush with the movement, because I understand now, in a way I couldn't have before yesterday, exactly how much this has tortured him. Even with all the pain he's caused, I can see why he felt it was necessary.

"We're a little fucked up, aren't we?"

"Everyone's fucked up, Lavender. We just happen to be the right kind of fucked up for each other." He exhales a tremulous breath. "I'm sorry for all the ways I hurt us."

His words are loaded, an apology that carries the weight and burden of years of guilt and absence.

I tilt his head down and press my lips to his forehead. "I know you are."

I stay like that for a few moments, appreciating the calm it brings, despite how messed up this entire scenario happens to be—this heart-to-heart while I'm naked and he's duct-taped to his computer chair.

Eventually, I tip his head back and trace his lips with my fingertips. He parts them, and I slip two inside. "Suck, please."

His lips close, tongue sliding over the length of my fingers. The pulse between my legs flares to an almost unbearable level, but relief is coming soon. Not the kind either of us really wants, but it should provide the motivation Kodiak needs.

"Enough," I tell him and ease my fingers from between his lips. Edging back a few inches to make room for my hand, I rub my wet fingers over my clit before I slide them inside me.

Kodiak's mouth hangs open, breathing ragged, hands gripping the armrests. I pump slowly, finding the spot inside that's hard to reach but makes me feel the most relaxed and overwhelmed at the same time. When the tingle between my thighs becomes an ache, I withdraw. Keeping one hand fisted in his hair, I raise my glistening fingers in front of him. "Would you like to know what I taste like?"

"Please. Fuck. Yes."

I release his hair and he jerks forward, capturing my fingers in his mouth again. His teeth sink in at the third knuckle, locking them in place as he sucks hard. A low rumble comes from his chest, and he makes a thick, mewling sound.

I reach for the bottle of lube on his desk and prep Aqua-D. Then I rise up, position it at my entrance, and sink down.

It's my turn to moan, soft and low.

Kodiak's eyes pop open, and he releases me from his teeth. "Oh God. Holy hell." He struggles against the duct tape, the arms of the chair creaking.

"It's hard when you can't have what you want, and it's right there in front of you, isn't it, Kodiak?" I brace my hands on his shoulders, lifting and lowering.

He nods.

"You made me feel unwanted," I whisper.

"I know. I'm sorry. I'm so sorry." His voice is low and guttural.

"Such a terrible lie to tell, wasn't it?"

"It was. It is. I didn't know what else to do. I was scared. I still am. Fuck. Please. I lo—"

I cover his mouth with my palm. "Don't. You still don't get to say those words to me, not when all of your actions have told me the opposite."

I ride the stupid dildo, my clit rubbing against his shaft through his jogging pants every time I lower myself. I slip a finger into his mouth again, and he wets it with his tongue. I use it to circle my clit, the sensation building between my thighs. I come hard, mouth open in a silent scream, my entire body trembling.

Kodiak writhes under me, muttering *please, please, please.*

I slip my hand into his jogging pants and grip the hot, pulsing length.

My lips brush his, but he doesn't make a move to deepen the kiss, maybe understanding that it's not something he can have until he's done the thing I've asked of him. Either that or he's punishing himself, as he likes to do.

It takes all of ten quick, hard strokes before Kodiak's head snaps back, and he groans as thick spurts of cum cover his chest.

He's shaking and straining and magnificent. He jolts when I skim the wet tip with my thumb and bring it to my mouth.

We're both panting and sweaty. I wait for embarrassment or awkwardness to settle between us, but it doesn't. We just sit there, breathing, both half-sated.

I brace myself on his shoulders and lift myself out of his lap. Aqua-D is covered in my orgasm, which drips down the sides.

I clean myself up in his bathroom before I wet a washcloth and bring it back to wipe down his chest, then shimmy back into my clothes on shaky legs.

"You're not going to leave me here like this, are you?"

And there's the panic I've been waiting for.

"Of course not." I open his desk drawer and grab a pair of scissors. I set them on his lap and go about packing up my bag again, putting the duct tape back on his project table where I found it.

"Lavender, come on." He yanks against his arm restraints.

"Just a second." I zip up my backpack and slip my arms through. Once I'm ready to leave, I slide the scissors carefully between the tape and his right wrist. I tap the tip of the dildo still taped between his legs. "You can give that back to me tomorrow, after you've talked to Maverick." I set the scissors on the desk behind him. "Good luck with the game." I kiss him on the cheek and leave before he can free himself and stop me.

27

Balance

KODIAK

Present day

PREGAME ANXIETY IS magnified today. I sit on the bench in the locker room and focus on breathing. My stomach is a fucking mess. My head is almost as bad. The whole scene with Lavender coming into my room last night keeps playing on an endless loop, and my half-hard cock is bent at an uncomfortable angle behind my cup. Guilt weighs heavy on my shoulders for all the things I've done this semester when it comes to Lavender.

But I try to push through it and clear my head. I may not have the control I need, but Lavender isn't the same girl she once was. She's stronger and much more self-assured. We'll never be like we were before because she doesn't need me the way she once did. But I'm lucky as hell that she still seems to want me, despite me being an asshole to her. It's hard to reconcile my memory of her with this new, empowered version, so comfortable in her own skin, so very much a woman and not a meek, uncertain girl anymore.

"You all right, K?" Maverick asks.

I nod and still my jittery legs so I can tighten my laces again. For the third time. When the anxiety is particularly bad, my rituals amplify. I go over the same thing until it's nearly maddening—like making sure my laces are tied tight enough.

"We're not going to lose. We watched all the videos. We know their tricks. Stay on Bender's left side as much as you can 'cause that's where his shot is the weakest." He pats my back. "We got this."

"We got this," I repeat.

I compartmentalize the guilt and worries, box them up and set them aside so I can perform on the ice. I pop a watermelon Jolly Rancher and finish getting dressed. Tonight is a big one. My dad told me scouts might be here, and since this is the team we've struggled to beat in the past, I need to have my head fully in the game.

The arena is packed, and I spot my parents and Maverick's in the stands. They do that sometimes—show up at games just because they can. My dad is talking to some guy in a suit. My stomach rolls again, but it's empty, since I already tossed my cookies. It doesn't happen as much as it used to, but before big games, it's a thing.

In the first three minutes, Bender scores a goal, putting us at an immediate disadvantage. But instead of rocking our game, it pushes us to play smarter, and by the end of the first period, Maverick has tied it up.

At the beginning of the second period, Mav and I are sitting on the bench, watching our teammates dominate, waiting to get back on the ice.

"What is my sister doing here?"

I follow his gaze, noting Lavender, Lovey, Lacey, and BJ

sitting in the stands behind our parents. I don't know when they arrived, or if they've been there the entire time, but this is definitely a first for Lavender. Lovey and Lacey come to the occasional game, and BJ does too, when he isn't busy napping or practicing.

"Dunno. Maybe she has plans with the twins tonight." I hope not, though. I sort of had it in my head that tonight I'd get to put my hands on her. Finally.

I shift my focus back to the ice, but I can feel Mav's eyes on me. He chuckles quietly. I fight not to glance his way and fail.

"Looks like you finally got your head out of your ass, then."

I don't have a chance to respond to that, because we're called back out on the ice. The rest of the game is a blur, but I score two goals to their one at the beginning of the third, and we manage to keep the lead, giving us the win. Coach is happy with our performance, and I have to say, I am too.

Our parents don't stick around long after the game since it's late, and they have to drive home. My mom gives me a hug, despite my being sweaty and disgusting, and murmurs something about calling later in the week and being safe. Lavender's dad wears an expression that makes my balls want to crawl up inside my body, and her mom is smirking, like she knows every single thought in my head.

Lavender hangs back with Lovey, Lacey, and BJ, her cheeks flushing every time one of them leans in to whisper something to her. She's always been a different person behind closed doors, but now I'm learning exactly how different she is.

BJ says they're going out for something to eat because he's starving, which is always the case, so we wave goodbye for now.

The locker room is loud and rowdy with excitement over the win, and a bunch of the guys want to hit the bar and get their party on.

Mav pulls his shirt over his head and runs his fingers

through his wet hair. "When were you planning to tell me?" He doesn't sound angry, just conversational.

"Tonight. After the game."

"How long has this been going on?" He chuckles. "I guess that's actually a pretty pointless question, isn't it?"

"What do you mean?" I button my jeans.

He gives me a look. "Come on, Kody. You've been in love with Lavender since before you understood the concept. We all knew it, our parents knew it, and then they got paranoid and shit about it and messed things up for all of us. We've all been waiting for the two of you to figure it out and deal with it."

I'm a little stunned, since he's never once brought this up. "Why didn't you say anything before now?"

"Conflict of interest, man. She's my little sister; you're my best friend. And I didn't want to get in the middle of whatever it was, so I chose to stay out of it altogether. Not that it was easy, because you have to be the two most stubborn, obtuse people I've ever met in my damn life. Besides, everyone's always been up in Lavender's business, interfering when they shouldn't, and I wasn't about to be another one of those people. She's fully capable of managing herself and has been for a long time."

His expression turns serious. "I was never worried about her being able to handle you. It was *you* being able to handle you when you're *with her* that was always the issue. Just find the balance, Kody. And stop torturing yourself for the past. It doesn't help either of you move forward."

We finish getting changed and head out to the car. We drove in together, so the awkward ratchets up a couple of notches when I check my messages and find one from Lavender letting me know which diner they're at.

"You want me to drop you off at home, or . . ." I let it hang.

"And miss this epic moment in all of our lives? Hell to the fuck no."

"You really don't have to come," I tell him.

Mav slides into the passenger seat. "Like you're getting off that easy. Besides, I'm available. After that date-night fiasco, I called things off with Carly. I don't want her to think it's going to turn into something when it's not. I don't need the clinginess or the headache, especially with this being my last year."

"But you've still been out somewhere. So who have you been seeing if it's not Carly?"

"Just some chick. She's not into the party scene, though, so it's easier to keep it low-key."

The late-night breakfast place is ridiculously busy. It's midnight, and although it's not a weekend, this is still a popular hangout for the underage crowd who don't have fake IDs and can't do the bar scene yet, or those who don't like it. I happen to fit into the latter of those categories. I prefer my own home, or Mav's, and screw everyone else. Mav is the social one who likes all the people around.

At least three of his previous "girlfriends" can be found at various tables in the restaurant. Interestingly, despite the fact that he has a constant rotation of girls, he always seems to be on good terms with them.

I spot BJ sprawled across a booth in the back corner of the restaurant, the tops of two blonde heads barely visible on the opposing bench. My palms sweat as we make our way through the tables, Mav pausing every five seconds to say hi to someone. I don't bother acknowledging anyone, because the only person I really care about seeing should be with BJ and the twins. My heart rate picks up and my palms go damp when I finally reach the table. It's one of those round booths that's meant to seat six or more, and Lavender is sitting at the end, sipping on some kind of smoothie.

"Hey."

All four sets of eyes shift my way as I slide in beside Lavender.

She tips her head back so she can meet my gaze. Her expression is somewhere between amusement and low-level mortification. She whispers *hi*.

I don't think it could possibly get more uncomfortable until Mav drops down across from me and kicks me in the shin. Likely on purpose.

"The fuck?" I shoot him a glare.

He props his chin on his clasped hands and smiles like a lunatic. "Look at how awkward you two are. This is awesome."

Lavender slurps her smoothie loudly and turns her sharp gaze on her brother. "This is your one and only opportunity to be a dick about this, so make it good."

Mav's grin widens. "I'm not being a dick. I'm just being honest. You're like a couple of eighth graders trying not to make eye contact for too long. You're not even touching." He motions to the inch or two of space between us. "Kody is halfway out of the booth, and he looks like he's going to shit his pants. You look like you're trying to snuggle with Lacey."

"You're all staring at us like we're some kind of circus act," Lavender says. "What did you think was going to happen? Heart bubbles were going to magically appear over our heads?"

"Kinda, yeah. I mean, this storm has been brewing since this guy could get a boner." Mav points at me.

Lavender holds up her hand. "Stop right there. We are not having a conversation about Kodiak's boners in the middle of this diner. In fact, we are *never* having a conversation about Kodiak's boners, because you're my brother and there are some goddamn lines that should never be crossed."

"You're really intent on sucking the fun right out of this for me, aren't you?" Mav sighs. "So Kody never told me what you did that finally pushed him over the edge."

"Maybe I figured my shit out. Did you ever think of that?" I shoot back.

BJ snorts, and so does Lavender.

I give her the side-eye. "Whose side are you on?"

"My own."

The server comes and takes our order. It's a guy, and he keeps looking at Lavender, so I slide my arm across the back of the seat, trace an infinity symbol on her shoulder, and don't bother to drop it after he leaves.

"Look at you, being all territorial." Mav is still grinning. "You know, I figured that whole thong thing would've done it, and then Lav freaking moved out."

"Wait, you know about the thong?" Lavender's eyes are extra wide, and she glances from Mav to me and back again.

"Everyone knows about that. Mom called me the day after to ask a bunch of questions I sure as hell didn't want to answer," Mav replies.

"What kind of questions?" Lavender asks.

"The kind I tried to wipe from my memory forever." He shakes his head. "And don't look so surprised. She's got these freaking fake social media accounts set up, and she thinks she's being sly about it, but we all know it's her. She uses stock photography from cheap sites I've seen a million times."

"Your mom has sock accounts?" I don't know why this surprises me. Violet is basically insane. Awesome, but definitely not normal. Mav gets his sense of humor from her.

"I'm sure she's set your mom up with one too." Mav raises an eyebrow at me. "And yours." He points to BJ.

"How do you know it's your mom? I mean, there are loads of catfish accounts out there," BJ says.

Mav pulls his phone out of his pocket, pulls up his IG

account, and clicks on a post of him with some girl sitting in his lap from earlier in the semester. He scrolls through the comments, clicking on a profile of a woman wearing a tiny bikini top blowing a kiss at the camera. Every single post she has looks like it's from some kind of photo shoot, and there are captions like "Feeling pretty." Another says, "Just reading by the pool" with the same model sprawled out on a towel beside a pool with a magazine artfully placed by her head. The best one is captioned "I love pineapple," and the model is lovingly cradling a pineapple while wearing a pineapple-print bikini. "Now read the comment she left."

Lavender nabs the phone and barks out a laugh before she passes it to me. The comment reads: "So HAWT! Don't forget to wrap your sausage! XOXO #safesex."

Mav has liked the comment and replied with: "Thanks for worrying about my junk."

"Does she know you know?" BJ is basically doubled over with laughter.

"I don't think so, and I'm not going to ruin it for her." He slides his phone into his pocket when our food arrives. "So does River know?"

"Not yet." Lavender pokes at a chunk of pineapple floating in her smoothie. "I haven't seen him to tell him since he hasn't been home much lately."

Mav digs into his scrambled eggs. "Man, I hope I'm around for that."

"Guess it's a good thing we'll be able to move back into our house again soon, huh? Less chance of you being murdered in your sleep that way." BJ chuckles.

Lovey elbows BJ in the side. "I'm sure it'll be fine."

But everyone exchanges a look.

28

The Geyser

LAVENDER

Present day

I'M NOT PLEASED to see River's car in the driveway when we get home late that night—or early that morning, I guess. BJ wishes me luck, and Maverick is pretty much gleeful as he punches in the code. If River is in the living room, there's going to be a confrontation—one that has to happen if Kodiak and I are going to try to make this work.

I steel myself for the coming meltdown as Maverick opens the door and we follow him inside. Kodiak laces his fingers with mine and gives my hand a squeeze. I feel a lot like we're walking into an angry lion's cage.

River is right where I expect to find him, sitting on the couch. I *don't* expect him to be drinking one of my extra-sugary coolers and watching old episodes of *Vampire Diaries*, but then, this has been the year of the unexpected.

His gaze shifts away from the TV and immediately finds

me. His eyes narrow as he takes in Kodiak's proximity and our clasped hands.

His lip curls up, and he flings out a hand. "What is this?"

"Can you hold the meltdown for a minute? I need to get popcorn for this." Maverick is so excited, he's like a shaken bottle of soda, ready to explode.

I throw an unimpressed glare his way. "Not helpful, and you are not sticking around for this. I need to have a conversation with my brother without a bunch of gawkers."

"Sorry. I'll keep my mouth shut." Maverick looks appropriately chagrined.

"I think we need to have a talk, Lavender, in fucking private." River's gaze bounces between me and Kodiak, nostrils flaring.

"I fully agree that we need to have a talk, but there are some issues we need to address, and since they revolve around Kodiak, he should be involved."

River slams his bottle down on the table and pushes to his feet. "You can't be serious!"

He storms across the room, and I step in front of Kodiak, crossing my arms. "You need to calm down."

"And you need to get out of my way because I'm going to kick this fucker's ass! How are you with him? He put you through hell!" River yells.

"So have you!" I shout back.

"What?" River recoils as though I've slapped him.

"You keep blaming Kodiak for making a mess of things when we were kids, but you were just as bad. Look at what you're doing right now."

"I just wanted to keep you safe. I'm always going to want to keep you safe, especially from someone who's hurt you time and time again." River jabs his finger toward Kodiak. I can feel him behind me, but I don't turn to see his reaction.

"I love you, River, and I will always love you, but this blame game has to stop. It's not healthy for you, or me, and all you'll do is push me away if this animosity between you and Kodiak continues."

"He's been nothing but an asshole to you all semester, and now you're going to what, go right back to the way things were when you were kids? How is *that* good for you?"

"We aren't kids anymore, River. I'm not the same girl I was, and he's not the same boy. We're adults, and we're figuring things out. Holding on to the past is going to drag us both down."

"Can I say something?" Kodiak asks.

River's angry glare lifts. "You need her permission to speak now?" he sneers.

Kodiak sighs. "Look, River, you have every right to hate me for the way I've acted this semester. I was 100 percent a dick. But, in the interest of not making things more difficult, I think we need to clear the air so we can all move forward like Lavender has been trying to do pretty much her entire life."

"This isn't just about this semester!" River snaps.

"I know."

"You can't do to Lavender what you did to her before. I won't let that happen." His gaze shifts around, wild and panicked. "I can't watch her go through that again."

I consider what it must have been like for him, watching me fall apart, powerless to do anything about it, only to have Kodiak constantly come in to pick up my pieces. Until he left. The aftermath wasn't pretty.

"Lavender isn't the same person, and neither am I, River. She won't let me do that, and I would rather die than drag her down like I did back then. But you have to see that the way you're dealing with this isn't any better." Kodiak gives my hand a gentle squeeze. "We all feel bad about what happened when

Lavender was a kid. You and I the most, I think. And I won't pretend to know how hard it was for you to have me always in the way, but I do know that I carried around a lot of guilt for a long time, and the way I chose to atone for it did a lot more harm than good."

His jaw tics, but he says nothing.

"I haven't let it define me, River. You can't let it define you either. It was never your fault," I tell him.

River runs his hands through his hair. "I don't know how else to be. This is all I know." He motions to me. "It's who I am."

I finally see what the real issue is. Our entire lives have been about me—my anxiety, my struggles, my fears, and if we shift the focus away, where else can River look but inside himself?

I look him in the eyes. "Can I have a minute with River?" I say to Kodiak.

"Of course." Kodiak bows his head, and his lips brush my temple. "I'll meet you upstairs." He steps around me and pauses in front of River. "I know we don't have a lot in common, but the person we both love happens to be integral to our lives, so I hope we can at least be civil."

River nods, although he's still frowning. "I'll work on it. But if you fuck up, I'm probably going to kick your ass."

"I figured." Kodiak disappears upstairs, and Maverick claps River on the shoulder before he follows, leaving me alone with my twin.

"So, this is really happening?" He rubs the back of his neck. "You and Kody are a thing now?"

"We're trying to be." I nod to the couch, and we both drop down. I rest my head on his biceps. "This isn't really about Kodiak, though."

"What?"

"You. The protectiveness. Needing to make sure I'm okay."

"I'm your twin. That's my job."

"But it's not, River. Of course you're going to want to be there for me, but I think this is more than that."

His gaze darts away, and his jaw flexes. "I don't know what you mean."

"It's always been different for you. Maverick is like Dad, I'm like Mom, Robbie is like Gram-pot, but you're *you*, and sometimes I think you've struggled to figure out where you fit. And if you're not focused on me, you have to focus on *you*. I'd kind of hoped that my staying home last year would give you the chance to be your own person, instead of always trying to be *my person*. We will always be connected. You will always be the other half of me, but you need to live for you."

River drops his head. "Sometimes I don't feel like I know who I am."

"I think that's pretty normal at our age, but if you stop channeling all your energy into me, maybe you'll be able to figure out you and what you want."

"I'm sorry I've made things so hard for you."

My heart clenches for my poor twin. Our bond is unmatched. I love him as fiercely as he loves me, but sometimes we lack balance. "It's okay. Nothing worth fighting for should come easy. And I know it comes from a good place. You're my trampoline, and I'm yours."

"Safe to fall."

"Always."

29

Infinite

KODIAK

Present day

I WAIT, SITTING on the top step outside Lavender's door. She appears at the landing and gives me a small smile. "No breaking and entering this time?"

I grin sheepishly. I could've picked the lock, but waiting for her seems symbolic of this new version of us. "Figured it was better if you let me into your space, considering the conversation. Everything okay with River?"

"I think so. He's spent so much of his life focused on me that he hasn't looked enough at himself and what he wants. We had that year apart, which was good for both of us, but now that I'm here it's like we're right back where we started. He needs to figure himself out, just like we need to figure us out."

I nod. "I guess I never thought about it like that." But it makes sense. "Now that you don't need looking out for, everything has shifted."

"But he'll be okay. I think he probably needed someone to tell him it's okay to live for himself instead of everyone else."

She holds out her hand, her expression both expectant and the tiniest bit uncertain until I stand and thread my fingers through hers. The connection we've always had feels stronger than ever.

She unlocks her door, and we slip inside. The lamp beside her sewing machine is the only light in the room and casts shadows over her face, making it hard for me to read her expression. She links our fingers again and leads me over to her bed, flicking on the light beside it, which washes the pale purple comforter in its soft glow. She turns on her stereo, and the low tones of her favorite band fill the room.

Lavender doesn't speak as she moves me to sit on the edge of her bed. My heart pounds, and my palms are damp. I wipe them on my thighs and part my legs as she steps into the space. Those vibrant blue eyes meet mine as she sifts her fingers through my hair. I feel the contact through my entire body, all the way to the core of my guilty, fractured soul.

"I missed you so much," I whisper. "It's been hell being this close to you and still feeling like we were a million miles apart."

She nods and inhales a slow, steadying breath as she steps in closer, wrapping her arms around me. I mirror the movement, pulling her into me and feeling the pulse in her throat against my cheek, breathing in her familiar scent.

Lavender traces the infinity symbol up and down the back of my neck, along my spine, and I echo the pattern between her shoulder blades. Our breathing syncs, our heartbeats find a steady rhythm, and we hold on to each other, anchors and buoys.

I turn my face toward her, her pulse thrumming against my lips. We both make a soft, needy sound and chuckle at the same time. Lavender shifts to straddle my lap and begins the torturous process of tracing the contours of my face, her fingers, gentle and warm, skimming my lips and eyes.

I encircle her wrist and kiss the tip of each finger and the faded scars on her palm before I place it against the side of my neck. I brush my thumb across her bottom lip, over the scar that marked a beginning and an ending we never could have predicted.

"I want to take away every hurt I caused, but I don't know how," I admit.

She cups my face between her warm palms. "You can start by erasing all the little lies with truths."

It's Lavender who tips her chin up and brings my mouth to hers.

My entire universe shifts back into alignment.

Her lips part, and I breathe in her forgiveness as our tongues meet on a soft stroke. I catalogue this moment: the slight weight of her body in my lap, the way her breasts press against my chest, the arch in her spine, the hum of her need vibrating through me, the uneven texture of her bottom lip where the scar is, the taste of watermelon Jolly Rancher, the smell of her sheets, her lavender shampoo, and her vanilla body lotion.

Everything about this has been inevitable—our connection a wire stretched tight to the point of snapping, but with enough strength to survive the tension. We've been traveling in a figure eight, passing each other until we finally got the timing right and met in the middle.

The calm I haven't experienced in years merges with a desire so all-consuming, it feels like I'm melting from the inside. Lavender's hands slide under the hem of my shirt, pushing the fabric up. She breaks our kiss and tugs it over my head, then removes her shirt. Her bra is the color of her name. It's made of satin and lace, pretty, delicate.

She takes my hand and places it over her heart—which also means I'm palming her breast—and mirrors the action with her own hand. A small smile tips the corner of her mouth, and she whispers, "Your need is my need."

It breaks the heavy tension filling the space around us, but only for a few seconds, because we lean in at the same time, mouths connecting once again. I explore her curves, the dip at her waist, the swell of her breasts, and I reach between her shoulder blades to flick the clasp on her bra.

Part of me wants to rush, to get inside her and seal the connection that's never dissipated, no matter how hard I tried to build a wall between us. You can't keep out what makes your heart beat in the first place. But everything about the way she touches me is unhurried, slow and gentle, and I respond in kind, stripping down until we're bared for each other.

She pulls the cover back, and we stretch out on her sheets, legs tangled together, hands roaming as we sink deeper into our kiss. I smooth my palm down her stomach, and she makes the softest sound when I dip between her thighs. I lift my head, eyes on hers as I circle her clit and go lower, easing a finger inside.

Her brow pulls down, and her teeth press into her lip, so close to that scar. She places one hand against the side of my neck, and the other moves down to rest on top of mine.

"Do you want me to stop?"

She shakes her head.

"Keep going?"

"Please."

I curl my finger, watching as her eyes soften and her breathing grows shallow and ragged. Her nails dig into the side of my neck, little punishments I hope I get to wear tomorrow on my skin.

Her hips lift and roll, her hand pressing hard on top of

mine, urging me deeper. I kiss my way down her body and bury my face between her legs, licking up the length of her, desperate to swallow her down and have the taste of her orgasm on my tongue.

"Oh my God!" Lavender drags in a gasping breath, and her thighs clamp against my ears as I cover her clit.

I grip her hips to keep her from wriggling away. "Too much?"

She nods, and her fingertips skim my cheek. "Be soft for me."

I nuzzle in, lapping at her, learning her body and what she likes, what takes her higher and what pulls her away from the edge. I don't know how long I spend with my face between her thighs, but when she comes, it's on the sweetest sigh.

I kiss my way back up, and she wraps her legs around my waist. Pulling my mouth to hers, she makes a sound between a moan and a *hmm* before she breaks the kiss.

"Do you like the way I taste?" Curiosity colors her words and her expression.

I groan into a laugh. "Yes, Lavender, I like the way you taste. So much so that I will gladly eat you any time you want."

"That's good, because I think I'm going to want you to do that a lot." She captures my top lip between her teeth and bites gently. "I like how much softer your tongue is than my fingers. And those sounds you make, like you're starving for me."

I stroke her cheek. "That's because I have been."

She shifts under me and makes a needy noise in the back of her throat. "Will you be in me?"

I drop my forehead to hers. "Do you want me to?"

"It's a need, not a want."

I don't know why her words strip me down. "You're sure?"

"I've always been sure, Kodiak."

"Let me get a condom." I reach for my discarded jeans, hoping I remembered to put one in my wallet.

"I'm on the pill."

I freeze and meet her searching gaze. Questions I have no right to ask sit on my tongue.

She arches a brow in challenge. "Unless you think it's a bad idea."

"I haven't . . . there hasn't been—" I haven't been with anyone since she arrived in Chicago. And I've always used condoms, but I don't want to have to admit that to her and risk ruining this. "Condoms are safer," I grind out. But even as I say it, I ease my hips back, the head of my cock sliding over her clit and going low until I'm nudging at her entrance.

"Just this first time, then."

"Just this time," I agree. I lean down to kiss her, shifting until my fingers curl around her nape so I can feel her pulse against my palm. She mirrors the movement, her breath leaving her on an unsteady exhale, the same way mine does.

"Okay?" I ask.

She nods, and our gazes stay locked as I ease inside, inch by inch.

Lavender's eyes flare, her lips forming the words *oh God* as my hips meet hers. Her nails dig into the back of my neck, and her knees press into my sides.

I'm unprepared for the way it feels to be connected to her so completely. My entire body hums with foreign energy, lighting up from the inside like a neon sign. She's so warm and tight and wet and soft.

"Are you okay?" I grind out.

"Yes. Are you?" Her finger travels in a figure eight along the top of my spine.

I have to close my eyes for a second to block out her guile-less eyes and get a handle on the emotions and sensations. Sex with Lavender isn't just physical; it's every part of me and every part of her fusing into one.

We've always been connected in ways that defy reason, and now, in this, it's like a circuit completing. Emotions pass between us, thick with desire, electric and dangerously addicting.

"Kodiak?" Her thumb strokes along the edge of my jaw, and I open my eyes.

"I'm here."

"I know. I can feel you." She pulls my mouth down to hers. Every point of connection is another place we're plugged into each other. I hover in some odd state of anxious calm. The urge to shift my hips is hard to deny, but I wait until Lavender tells me she's ready for more.

"Show me your truth," she whispers.

I start to move, long strokes and a slow climb. Lavender tilts her hips, eyes locked on my face. Logic slips away, and primal desire takes hold. The need to claim and be claimed over-whelms as I move faster, go deeper, and try to get closer.

Lavender whispers words of encouragement against my lips, *more* and *yes* and *oh, right there.* I slide a hand under her and fold back on my knees, taking her with me so she's sitting in my lap and we're chest to chest, skin slick with sweat, breath coming in quick, hard pants.

"Do you think you can come?" I ask.

She grips my shoulders. "Maybe? I don't know."

"Help me get you there," I beg.

She palms the back of my neck with one hand and drops the other between her thighs. Her fingertips graze the base of my cock where we're joined. I groan, and we both look down as she makes tight circles over her swollen clit. I stay deep, rocking her over me.

A quiet moan bubbles up, and she contracts around me. As

soon as her eyes flutter open, I grip her hips and move her, lifting and lowering, hard and fast, slamming her down on my cock as my own orgasm rockets through me—a violent power surge that turns the world black before my vision returns in a vivid, colorful burst.

We stay wrapped around each other for long minutes, foreheads pressed against each other's necks as our hearts slow to calm. I feel equal parts sated and ravenous.

Eventually I turn my head and kiss my way back to her lips. I don't want to break the connection, but we can't stay like this forever.

I reach over to her nightstand and grab a handful of tissues, lifting her off me so I can clean her up. I drop a quick kiss on her lips and disappear into the bathroom to take care of myself and bring a warm washcloth out for her.

When I return, she pulls back the covers and I stretch out beside her. She runs her fingers through my hair, her expression pensive. "I understand now." Her voice is raspy and low.

"Understand what?" I can't stop touching her, my fingers trailing up and down the length of her spine, her soft, wavy hair tickling the back of my hand.

"Why you lied."

"I wasn't in control," I admit.

"Neither of us was," she replies. "They were right to keep us apart, weren't they?"

I want to disagree, but I can't. "This." I skim the contour of her face with a single fingertip. "The way it feels to be with you, I wouldn't have known how to deal with it back then. I needed you to need me. It was addicting, and I don't think I would've been able to find any sort of balance when we were younger." I kiss her forehead. "I overheard my parents talking one night, not long after they sat us down and told us we needed time apart. My mom said something about our relationship being toxic. She was worried about what it would look like when we were teenagers. I didn't get it then, but when I saw you again at that holiday party, it finally made sense."

Her palm rests on my chest, and I pick it up as I fall back in time, searching for the words to explain. "All the space, all the separation, all the time meant nothing. All it did was make the longing worse. And then there you were, looking so beautiful and resilient and whole. That's when I knew why they'd done what they did, because even then, I wanted you in a way that wasn't reasonable, and I knew if I acted on that, I'd only do more damage to us. There was too much distance. I could see the way things would fall apart. The way I would've shredded us."

"And now?"

"Now you're strong enough to hold yourself together, and I've realized that's even better. I'm strong enough not to tear you apart by loving you."

30

The Things We Know

LAVENDER

Present day

I'VE HAD AN embarrassing number of safe-sex conversations since Kodiak and I started officially dating. The worst is when my *dad,* of all people, asks me if I need him to contact his previous endorsement sponsors about prophylactics.

The best was when Kodiak answered a call from his mom literally two minutes after we'd finished having sex, and she went into a ten-minute lecture on safe sex and how it only takes one time without a condom to get pregnant.

Kodiak assures her we're being responsible, while I bury my face in my pillow and try not to laugh. But we are being responsible. I'm on the pill, and about 70 percent of the time we use condoms. The other 30 percent we start without one and put one on halfway through so he'll last longer and it's less messy.

Last week, Kodiak moved back into his house with the

guys. Not that it's really changed anything. We're still together a lot. Only now, we can divide our time between his bedroom and mine.

We go out on dates, we study together, we hang out with friends. It's a grown-up version of how we were when we were kids. The transition from fighting to stay away from each other to falling into a new kind of love all over again feels seamless.

Balance isn't always easy to find with Kodiak, because when he discovers something he's passionate about, he immerses himself in it completely. That's how he is with hockey and school. And now it's how he is with me. Sometimes we struggle to give each other space, but we manage.

In the back of my head, I often remind myself that he's graduating this year and there's a very good chance he'll be playing for the NHL come the fall. There's also that internship I applied for, but the chances of me getting it are virtually nonexistent, so I try not to worry.

I scan the library shelves, looking for the book I want, running my fingers over their spines. I love getting lost in books, and while I don't have a lot of time for recreational reading these days, I'm loving the course list for my psych class and I'm excited for next semester's contemporary lit course. Right now I'm searching for a textile resource book. It might sound boring to some people but I find it riveting.

My phone keeps vibrating in my pocket. It's Kodiak. He's not texting, he's calling, and he knows better than to think I'll risk getting caught answering in the middle of the library. It finally stops so I can concentrate again. It's distracting when he pulls this kind of shit for no other reason than he's probably bored and wants to talk about sex positions or whatever.

Or when I plan to duct-tape him to his computer chair again. It turns out Kodiak has a bit of a freaky side (to match mine), and he really, really likes being duct-taped to the chair and taunted while I get off on something other than his dick. It's a little fucked up, but then, so are we.

I find the book—of course it's on the top shelf—and push up on my tiptoes, reaching as high as I can. I'm about three inches too short. My phone starts buzzing *again*, and I roll my eyes. "I'm going to do a hell of a lot more than duct-tape you to your damn computer chair when I get home," I mutter.

An arm winds around my waist, and I suck in a shocked breath as I'm pulled back into a hard body. I breathe in Kodiak's familiar cologne and shiver when his lips brush my ear. "I hope that's a promise *and* a threat," he whispers.

I try to spin around, but he tightens his hold on my waist and drags his lips along the edge of my jaw. So warm and soft and *mine*. "What're you doing here and how did you find me?" I ask.

His other hand skims my hip, smoothing over the fabric of my dress. "I needed to see you, and lucky guess."

His voice has a slight waver to it. I cover the hand splayed out over my stomach, my body warming under his touch. "Is everything okay?"

"Mmm. I have a biochem test in forty-five minutes."

"Oh." Kodiak has a 97 percent in biochem. I'm sure the 3 percent he's missing is eating at him, but he'll survive. He could probably take the test blind-drunk, and high and still get a great mark. Besides, he's ridiculous about studying and requires rewards for meeting every single goal he sets. There are a lot of goals, and consequently a lot of rewards. Sometimes I have to give him IOUs for those when they interfere with my schedule.

"So you're looking to rub up on me for good luck?"

He burrows through my hair, lips finding my neck. "I mean, rubbing up on you is nice, but I was thinking I'd need a little . . . liquid courage."

"You want to go for a beer?" I'm confused, particularly

because he's rubbing his hard-on against my back and drawing figure eights on my thigh.

"Baby, no." He chuckles and sucks on my neck.

"Then what kind of liquid courage are you referring to, Kodiak?"

"I have a theory I need to test out." He slips his fingers under my skirt and drags them up the inside of my leg. I'm wearing tights, but we're standing in the middle of the stacks. It's not particularly private.

"Can you please explain this in a way that my peon brain will understand? What in the actual fuck are you talking about?"

"Do you remember the organic chemistry test I had last week?"

"Sure." I don't, but I'm hoping to hurry this along so he can get to the point.

"No, you don't." He nibbles my earlobe.

"You're right. I don't. What happened with the organic chemistry test?"

"I aced it."

"Awesome. You deserve to be duct-taped to your computer chair for that." I'm mostly serious.

Kodiak groans against my neck, and my skirt bunches up as he cups me, fingertips pressing against my clit through the layers of fabric.

"What're you doing? Anyone could walk by." I make no move to stop him.

"Does it make you anxious?"

"Well, yeah." The *duh* is in my tone.

"Me too," he admits. "But it jacks me right up. That's fucked, isn't it?"

I shrug, because honestly, it jacks me up too.

"Anyway, you know what happened right before I took that

test?" He rubs slow circles on me through my tights; it's delicious and not nearly enough.

"No clue," I whisper-moan.

"I ate you out, and you came all over my face."

I can feel my cheeks flushing, partly at the memory, partly at how insanely wet it made me then, and how wet I am now. Apparently being extra juicy runs in my family. Unfortunately I know this because my gigi told me.

"It's all I can think about, and I really need to be able to focus on this test so I can do well."

"We don't have time to go home for a pussy buffet, Kodiak."

"I got the key to a study room." He raises his hand, and a key on a chain dangles from his ring finger.

I spin around in his arms. "Are you serious?"

He bites his lip. "Please?"

"You got the key to a study room so you can eat me out?" I don't know why I'm flabbergasted. I mean, this is Kodiak we're talking about. He's slightly off-kilter when it comes to rituals. It appears eating my vagina before tests is now one of those things.

He nods. I don't know how he manages to look angelic right now, his wide, green eyes are doe-like. He's almost vibrating with excitement and anxiety.

I should probably say no, because this is kind of nuts. But at the same time, I don't want him to psych himself out and not do well on the test because he didn't get to go down on me.

That I'm rationalizing this is craziness.

Also, as nervous as it makes me, it's also kind of thrilling to have my boyfriend go to such extreme lengths to give me an orgasm. Obviously it's for his benefit, but I'll get something out of it too.

I nod once. "Okay."

"Really?" His eyes flare, as if my agreeing is completely unexpected.

I hold up a finger. "Just this once, though."

He nods vigorously. "Right. Yes. Of course. Just this once." He grabs my hand and tugs me down the aisle.

"Wait!"

His eyes flare with panic and something like disappointment.

"Can you grab that book for me?" I point to the top shelf. "I can't reach it."

"Anything for you, baby." He nabs it from the shelf, laces our fingers together, and drags me down the hall.

My heart rate skyrockets as we pass the group study rooms with the glass walls. There's no way he can do what he intends to in one of those.

He drops my hand halfway down the hall and pulls me around a corner as a security guard comes out of the stairwell. There are a lot of them in here, more than I realized up until now.

He shoves the key into my palm and wraps my fingers around it. "You go first. I'll follow when the coast is clear."

I take a deep breath, my anxiety spiking, but not the kind that usually results in a meltdown. This is a very different, very new kind of anxiety—one I don't entirely dislike.

I'm surprised to find the door is already unlocked, so I slip into room forty-four and set my bag on the desk, then pull the door closed, except it doesn't shut all the way, leaving a one-inch gap. It's not a lot, but it's enough that people can see inside. Maybe not much, but still. Not to mention the fact that the majority of the door is an opaque panel through which my silhouette is visible.

A minute later, Kodiak slides it open and pulls it shut behind him. He frowns when it doesn't close all the way.

I'm about to tell him this might not be a good idea, but he takes my face between his hands and bends to kiss me. It would actually probably be a lot easier for him and his neck if he dropped to his knees, but there's something about the way he's willing to suffer in the name of making out with me that's . . . almost sweet. Although, I think it's part penance for being a giant dick to me for a lot of years and also possibly because he enjoys being the big protector. Boy-men are strange creatures.

After several aggressive strokes of tongue, I finally bite his. It's meant to get him to stop, but instead, all it does is make him groan. Eventually I put a hand on his forehead and push. "You can see our profiles through the door," I whisper.

He glances up, his supercharged brain finally firing on more than just the sex-cylinder. He surveys the small space. "I have an idea." He drops to all fours and tucks his huge body under the desk, pushing out the single chair and giving it a pat.

I give him a look, because this is a seriously bad idea.

He tips his head to the side and mouths *please*.

I have no idea how he plans to make this work, but weird things are happening in my body, and I'm actually curious to see if he can pull it off. I shrug out of my coat and hang it on the hook by the door, which helps to cover the gap. I take a seat and pull out my binder, setting it up so it looks like I'm working on something. I drop my bag by the leg of the chair, to hopefully hide Kodiak's ridiculously large body tucked under the desk.

"This is insane," I mutter.

My face feels like it's a million degrees right now.

Kodiak slides his hands up the inside of my legs and under my dress. I feel something hard and cold moving along with it, which spikes my anxiety again.

"What is that?" I whisper-hiss.

I get my answer a few seconds later when I hear a faint snip and the tear of fabric as he rips the crotch of my tights open.

I kick him under the desk. What if he'd cut me? And why didn't he pull them down instead?

"Sorry. Easier this way." All I can see are his eyes, and they're far from sorry; they're full of a million other fleeting emotions, hunger the most prominent. He slides a finger under the crotch of my panties and presses his face against the inside of my thigh to muffle his groan. I grip the edge of the desk, working to control my breathing and the wild panic that makes my heart race.

He slides one finger inside me. It's callused and rough, but I clench around him, knowing that later tonight he'll be inside me, filling me, quelling the ache, feeding our new obsession, which happens to be the magical, calming properties of sex and orgasms. He pumps a few times, mumbling about how soft and wet I am.

I shush him, and he bites the inside of my thigh. His finger disappears, and I clench my teeth against the urge to complain. A slurping sound and a low growl follow. And then he pulls me to the edge of the chair, pushes my thighs apart, noses my panties out of the way and rubs his face all over my vagina, sort of the way a cat does to its owner to mark its territory. He laps at me, swirling his tongue around and around, dipping inside and swirling again. I grip the edge of the desk with one hand and drop the other to the top of his head, fisting his hair, guiding him to prevent me from moving my hips.

This particular act—so vulgar, so intimate, such a sensory overload—has to be one of my favorites. I love the feel of his tongue on me, the way he grips my hips, the sounds he makes, like he can't get enough, like he's been dying for my taste.

Except we're in a study booth in a library, so all the little noises he's making are a problem. "Shut the fuck up, Kodiak," I whisper.

He turns his head and bites the inside of my thigh so hard

this time that I clamp my legs shut on his face. He pries them apart and dives back in, this time using teeth and suction, and I nearly shoot out of the damn chair. As it is, I have to shove my fist in my mouth to keep from making sounds. And all the while my heart is beating frantically, aware that if one of the security guards should pass by and hear us, we will definitely be banned from the library.

Instead of that knowledge making it more difficult for me to come, it seems to push me right toward the edge. I don't even know how Kodiak can breathe with the way his face is buried between my legs. It's almost like he's trying to crawl up in there. There's a brief moment in which I almost laugh, except a wave of pleasure rolls through me, making it impossible to do anything but sink into the sensation and fight not to moan.

Kodiak's hand shoots up. He tugs my lip free from my teeth and shoves two fingers into my mouth. I suck automatically, eyes rolling up, aware I'm no longer in control of my body, and this is his way of reminding me to keep quiet. When the orgasm finally ends, I sag against the chair, a limp ragdoll.

We're both breathing like we've run up twenty flights of stairs while being chased by a damn demon. I should really offer to return the favor, but I don't think I can move, let alone unlock my jaw and blow him—from under a desk no less.

He rolls the chair back a few inches and pulls my skirt down, smoothing it out. My tights are ruined, my panties are soaked, and I'm far from coherent. I'd like to take a nap and then have Kodiak fuck me into oblivion—after his test, obviously.

I can't even manage words, so I hope I'm communicating that telepathically.

When his head pops out from under the desk, I put a hand on his forehead to prevent him from getting any closer. "Wipe your face."

He uses the bottom of his gray shirt to clean his chin, which is covered in girl jizz. Like, it's everywhere. He's going to need a serious shower. Kodiak is a bit of a germaphobe, so the fact that he willingly bathes his face in my vagina juice is crazy, and a big question mark. I'm the exception to his every psychosis.

"You should go first. I'll follow behind. Sorry about your tights." He's grinning, so he's obviously not sorry.

I slowly regain the use of my limbs, collect my belongings, and jam my stuff into my backpack. When I stand up, I'm appalled by the puddle on the seat. *Oh my God,* I mouth to Kodiak. I run my hands down the back of my skirt, and sure enough, it's wet. I can't tell if it's because Kodiak drooled all over me or my damn vagina drooled all over the chair. I'm thinking it's probably a bit of both, and how embarrassing is *that?*

Even worse, he looks absolutely gleeful over it.

I yank my coat from the hook and shrug into it jerkily. My legs still feel like Jell-O. I point at him. "Never again."

He shakes his head and nods once, smiling. "Never."

He's going to want to do this every chance he gets.

I sling my backpack over my shoulder, take a deep breath, and open the door enough to slip out, closing it behind me. I keep my head down and find the nearest bathroom. I'm a total wreck.

I do my best to make myself presentable, but I can't get rid of my red cheeks or the blotchy patches on my neck. Kodiak is waiting for me outside the bathroom, looking ridiculously smug and smelling a lot like eau de vagina. There is no way I'm leaving through the main entrance with me looking the way I do and him wearing that expression. I leave the book I was supposed to check out behind. I'll have to come back for it when I'm less mortified.

I brush by Kodiak, and he automatically links his pinkie with mine. "Where we goin'?"

"Out one of the side doors. It's closer to your class, which you need to be at in"—I point at the wall—"sixteen minutes if that clock is correct." The exit is also not frequently used, so we're less likely to run into people. Besides, I passed a group of girls who I know from my psych course before I ran into Kodiak, and I would like to avoid them post-orgasm.

I take the stairs as quickly as my short legs will carry me, Kodiak's pinkie still linked with mine. When we get to the last flight, I glance down between the railings and catch a glimpse of a couple in what looks like a very heated make-out session. And upon closer inspection, I'm pretty sure half of the couple is Josiah. They're so engrossed in each other, that they must not hear us.

"What time does your class end?" I ask rather loudly as we descend the final flight.

They jump apart, and I almost trip down the last four steps. Because the other half of that couple is my twin.

THE FOUR OF us stand there for a few long seconds, staring at one another. Well, I assume Kodiak is staring, but he's behind me, so I can't know for sure. He bends and kisses me on the cheek, whispering in my ear, "I gotta get to class. You gonna be okay?"

I nod, aware he has a test and can't be late.

"I'll see you at your place after class. Text me if you need me." He traces a figure eight on the side of my neck, tips my chin up, and presses his lips to mine. "Josiah, River." He gives them a nod and disappears out the door and into the sunshine, leaving me alone with my brother and Josiah, who both look cagey as fuck.

River begins, "Lav, it's not—"

Josiah's head snaps in his direction, and he pins my brother with the same look he gave Kodiak when he made it rain dicks in my bedroom and acted like a territorial asshole.

River's expression is pained and conflicted.

"I'm not going to be some secret you're ashamed of," Josiah says quietly. He turns to me. "I wanted to tell you, but River was adamant he be the one." He takes a couple of steps toward the door. "Call me when you're tired of hiding in your closet."

"'Siah." River reaches out, but Josiah shakes his head, and River's hand falls limply to his side.

"Sorry, Lavender. This is not how I wanted you to find out." Josiah pushes through the door, leaving me and River alone in a stairwell that smells like guilt, shame, desire, and cologne.

I lean against the railing and set aside my feelings about River and Josiah keeping this from me, so I can deal with my twin. "You do realize this isn't a surprise, right?"

River's gaze shifts to meet mine. How he manages to have a furrowed brow *and* wide eyes is beyond me.

I raise a finger and clarify. "I mean, the fact that it's Josiah is a surprise, but you being gay, or bi, or however you choose to identify, isn't."

His gaze darts around before it finally settles on me again. "Gay. I'm gay."

Based on Josiah's reaction, this isn't a random hookup. "You know you don't have to hide who you are from me, right? I'm always going to love and accept you, no matter what."

He nods, but the sound of a door opening somewhere in the stairwell above us prevents him from responding.

"Wanna get a coffee?" I ask.

"Shots would be better."

"I'm done with class for the day, so we can go home and *you* can do shots and we can talk?"

He nods.

Twenty minutes later, we're at the house. I'm no longer wearing ripped tights and damp underwear, and my brother and I are sitting on my bed, both of us drinking coolers even though it's the middle of the afternoon.

"So when did you and Josiah become a thing?" I figure I can start with the easier questions.

"A couple of weeks into the semester, I guess. I met him last year at some party, but nothing really came of it until I saw him again. He figured out pretty quick that you and I were related because my name isn't all that common." He takes a huge gulp of cooler and blows out a breath. "I'm sorry I didn't tell you. I felt shitty about it—I *feel* shitty about it—but it's so fucking complicated."

"Complicated how? As far as I can see, it's pretty simple. You like him, he likes you, and that's that."

"We live in a neighborhood full of hockey players and jocks, Lavender. How do you think it's gonna go over if I have a boyfriend and I'm on the football team?"

"Shouldn't we all be past that archaic line of thinking?" I'm not asking to be a jerk; I really don't have the answer.

"Should we? Yes. Are we? No. It's better than it used to be, but it's still not going to be easy."

"Nothing worth fighting for is easy, River."

"I know."

He holds his index finger out, and I link mine with it. "There's a but coming."

"What if our friends aren't cool with it? What about Mom and Dad?"

"If our friends aren't cool with it, they weren't good friends in the first place. And our parents just want us to be happy. Mom isn't going to care one way or the other, but I'm sure you'll get a talk on safe anal or something ridiculously embarrassing. And as for Dad, I think more than anything, he wants to understand you and find a way to connect with you. I know that hasn't been easy. Give him a chance to do that. Give us *all* a chance. We love you unconditionally. Let us prove it."

"I'm sorry I didn't tell you sooner."

"I figured you would when you were ready." So much makes sense about the past couple of months—the not coming home, his excessive reclusiveness, the distance between us. "And now that I know, maybe we can do the double-date thing. Or at least you can bring Josiah here." I bolt upright. "Oh my God. That night Josiah was here to help me with econ, were you two already a thing?"

River's cheeks go red. "Uh, yeah. I was kinda surprised to see him, to be honest—and worried he was going to out me."

"Wow." I relax back into my pillow. Part of me wants to feel hurt that they've been going behind my back this entire time, but I get why it's been difficult for River. He's always been guarded with our dad. I used to think it was because of me, but I realize there are far more layers to my twin that he's kept hidden all these years. "So are you, like, in love with Josiah?"

River shrugs. "I don't know. Maybe? I like him a lot, and he's been really patient with me. Up until now, anyway."

"Well, if you want it to work, maybe you should call him and invite him over so you can talk it through."

His finger tightens around mine. "You mean here?"

I squeeze back. "It's a good way to show him you're serious and that you care, don't you think?"

"You'll be around in case things don't go well?"

My heart breaks for my twin, aware that he carries

everyone else's perceived expectations and his own fear of failure and disappointment around like a burden he can't shake. And now, more than ever, I understand why it's been easier for me to be his focus. That way he didn't have to face his own truth and deal with it.

"Of course," I tell him. "But I'm thinking if he's been patient with you up until now, he'll be willing to hear you out."

"Okay, I'll invite him over." He pulls me into a tight hug and mumbles, "Trampoline."

"Safe to fall." I'm glad for once I get to be his soft place to land, instead of the other way around.

31

The Salty Sweet

LAVENDER

Present day

WEEKS BLEED INTO each other, the holidays quickly approaching. As excited as I am for the break, I'm not really looking forward to two weeks during which I won't be able to sleep next to Kodiak. We've gotten used to spending most nights together, other than his overnight away games or my occasional sleepovers at Lovey and Lacey's— which often coincide with each other.

Finals are coming up, and even with Kodiak's help, I'm barely passing my economics course. But at least I *am* passing, and I'll never have to take it again after this. It's a chilly December morning, snow swirling frantically in the biting wind as I head for the quad. Lovey and Lacey are already in the café, and Kodiak and BJ are supposed to meet up with us for coffee before we all go to our next classes.

I duck my head to protect my face from the biting wind.

My eyes water, thanks to the way my contact lenses are trying to freeze to my eyeballs. Because I'm looking at the ground and not where I'm going, I run right into someone and lose my hold on my backpack, which was slung over one shoulder.

"I'm so sorry." I bend to pick up my bag, but a foot comes down on the strap.

I'm looking at a very impractical, heeled boot for this weather. It's icy and salty everywhere.

"You're about to be, *bitch*."

The familiar voice sends a shiver down my spine, and I slowly push to a stand, reluctant to confirm what I already know. I'm about to have a long-overdue confrontation with Bethany, my very brief former roommate and one of Kodiak's bunny groupies.

Kodiak never came out and told me exactly what happened, but based on his sometimes voyeuristic and slightly kinky predilections, I have a pretty good idea.

I've seen Bethany a bunch of times on campus, but I've always been with other people. When I'm with Lovey and Lacey, she shoots me dirty looks, but when I'm with Kodiak, she pretends neither of us exists. Today she's with two of her friends. They're all wearing some kind of school gear—although their allegiance seems to have changed to the rugby team.

"You fucked things up for me, for all three of us." She motions to her friends.

I don't respond. Not because I can't, but because I have no idea what to say to that. I don't understand why anyone would want to be the communal fucktoy for a college sports team. I imagine low self-esteem has something to do with it, but pointing that out probably isn't going to help my case.

"Kody was mine first. I had dibs. There's a system here, and you messed with it, and now we're blacklisted from all the hockey and football parties. You're not special, you know.

They're all gonna get bored with you. And Kody's never going to stick with just you. He likes variety. Isn't that right?" She looks to her friends for confirmation.

They nod their agreement. "We'd know. We've all had a piece of him," the one on the right says.

"Okay, well, that's just . . . kind of gross, and also probably untrue." I shudder at the thought. While Kodiak is certainly no saint, he's also too much of a germaphobe to play pass-the-bunny.

"Are you calling us liars?" Bethany is unnecessarily loud.

I shrug. "If the shoe fits . . ."

"Whatever. Believe me or don't, he's going to get tired of you, and when he does, we'll all be there to make him feel better."

Her outburst is drawing attention—the embarrassing kind. I'm actually mortified for her, and also myself, because this is fairly horrifying as far as public self-humiliation goes. But I recognize that it's par for the course. And when Kodiak is likely playing professional hockey next year, the rumors will become infinitely worse. Things will be taken out of context; pictures will be manipulated. I know because my mother has never hidden what happened with her and my dad when they first started dating.

My relationship with Kodiak will most definitely be tested.

These are all the things I'm thinking about as Bethany rants and raves about how she's determined to get her team-bunny status back.

"What's going on here?"

Kodiak's voice brings instant relief and added anxiety at the same time. I don't want him to lose his shit publicly on these girls.

"Kody! Oh, hey! We were just talking. Isn't that right?" Bethany's smile is ridiculously fake.

I stare at her in absolute disbelief. As if I'm going to pretend we were having a fun, casual chat.

"Lavender?" Kodiak wraps an arm around me, going into overprotective mode. "Stay away from my girlfriend."

"We were girl bonding." Bethany flips her hair over her shoulder and motions between her and me. "Sharing stories, 'cause we know what you're like."

I can't even with this girl. "Look, Bethany, I've known Kodiak for as long as I've been breathing, so whatever chance you girls think you have with him, you don't. He's mine. He's always been mine, and he will always be mine. End of story."

I tug on Kodiak's arm. I need to get away from these girls and the scene they're causing before they say something even more humiliating, or expose either of us in ways I'd prefer they didn't. I'm so angry, I'm shaking.

Kodiak tightens his arm around me as we cross the quad toward the closest building. A student comes out of a stairwell exit, and Kodiak catches the door before it can close, tugging me inside. He pulls me against his chest, wraps me in a hug, and tells me how sorry he is while he rubs my back. I let him, because it's freezing outside, and he's warm, and it feels nice to be held.

Someone mutters *excuse me*, and he shuffles us out of the way, finally releasing me. He jumps back like I've turned into a poisonous spider, eyes wide with panic. "Shit. You're shaking. Are you okay? I'm screwing this up, aren't I? I shouldn't be doing this."

"Shouldn't be doing what?" I'm super confused right now.

He runs a hand roughly through his hair. "Falling into old patterns."

"Old patterns?"

"Trying to save you from a panic attack."

I roll my eyes. "I'm not having a panic attack, Kodiak."

"But Bethany was ripping into you, and you're shaking, and I thought maybe you were starting to panic because of all the people around."

"I'm shaking because I'm pissed off."

"At me?"

"No, at her and her asshole friends. I'm also highly disturbed by her lack of self-worth and how intent she seems on being a team fucktoy when you're done with me."

"Oh." He looks appropriately chagrined. "Well, that's never going to happen. Either of those things."

"I know. That's why I told her you were mine." I rub the space between my eyes. "I've learned how to deal, just like you have, Kodiak."

"I know you have. I just . . . I think it reminded me of that time with Courtney, and then everything got so messed up after that, and I lost you for more than half a decade, and I really can't go through that again."

I take his cold hand and press it against the side of my neck, doing the same with mine. "Who's panicking now?" It's half joke, half not.

He huffs a laugh. "Me."

"Don't forget that I've grown up with Mav being a giant playboy and River being a commitment-phobe. We're okay, Kodiak. You're not creating dependency by wanting to be there for me, and I don't need you to save me, but it's nice to feel safe and loved." I tug him closer, and he wraps his arms around me again.

I sink into the affection, aware he needs it as much as me.

Maybe even more.

Maybe he always has.

32

The Fears That Bind Us

LAVENDER

Present day

THE FALL SEMESTER ends—I pass economics with Kodiak's help, barely—and the winter semester rolls in, bringing colder temperatures, more snow, and the desire to hibernate. Hockey and studying takes up more and more of Kodiak's time. He has frequent conversations with his parents about making sure he's finding balance between sports, schoolwork, and friends—something he's never been particularly good at, and still isn't. I know when he's been talking to his dad, because those are the nights he's extra needy in bed.

River manages to patch things up with Josiah, and he even starts inviting him over, but he has yet to say anything to our parents. He wants to, but he says he's trying to figure out how to do it. As confident as I am that they'll support him, I know he needs to do it in his own time.

The parties from the beginning of the year dwindle to

almost nothing. Everyone's focus is shifting to studies, especially after Maverick barely managed to eke out a passing grade in two of the classes he typically excels at.

This also prompts a visit from my parents, during which my mom takes me and River out for lunch while my dad lectures Maverick on being responsible and not putting his dick before his studies. Actually it's my mom who makes the "study before sex" comment prior to ushering us out the door. She's never been one to sugarcoat things, except when she's dealing with me. I try to persuade River that now would be a good time to say something about Josiah, but he says he doesn't want to invite a *different* kind of safe sex and responsibility talk. The timing seems pretty opportune to me, but I don't push, so Mom sticks with her general "work first, party later" conversation during lunch.

I will say that's one thing Kodiak takes very seriously. Sex is always a reward for hours put into homework and studying. A very frequent reward. Despite his genius status, Kodiak spends an inordinate amount of time reviewing notes, always aiming for perfection. I don't envy him in that regard. It would be difficult to constantly strive for the impossible.

A few weeks into the winter term, my costume design professor asks if I'd like to help out with the winter production. Despite how busy my schedule is, there's no way I'm going to pass up the opportunity.

I also take on a very part-time job at the library. It's not that I need the extra cash. If I ask my parents, they will most definitely put money into my account, but I like the independence and the peacefulness that comes from being surrounded by books. I like that here, in college, I can shed the shy, tongue-tied girl of my youth, escape the past that defined me, and be a more confident, competent, less anxious version of myself. It's not easy, but it's empowering, and I feel like I'm finally coming into my own.

The job basically fell in my lap. I'd gone to the library to study between classes and noticed someone had left a stack of books on a table. Half an hour later, they were still there, so I took it upon myself to shelve them. Another student mistook me for someone who worked there and asked where she could find a book on biochemical engineering, so I showed her. It just so happened that the woman in charge of hiring watched it all happen and asked if I'd like a job. I said yes.

It's a Friday evening, and Kodiak has an away game. This means he won't be home until late tonight, which is good because I need time to work on one of the costume pieces for the upcoming production. The girl who's playing the lead has been stress eating, and last night she had a huge meltdown because her costume is too tight.

I took the blame and told her I must have miscalculated the seam allowance—I didn't—and could most certainly fix the problem. So that's what I'm doing.

It's closing in on ten when Professor Martin pokes her head in.

I pop out my earbuds. "I'm nearly done with the alterations."

She checks over her shoulder before she says, "You are a godsend for doing this."

I wave the comment away. "Can't have the star of the show feeling uncomfortable or it'll affect the entire performance." Besides, I like her. She has great respect for those of us who like to stay behind the scenes, and she's always been nice to me.

She nods her agreement. "I have some news for you."

I can't read her expression. "Oh?"

"It's about the internship we discussed."

"The long shot for the off Broadway company? I never

expected to get it since I'm a sophomore, but I love that you asked me to apply."

I mean that. Professor Martin has never coddled me. She's unaware that I've spent the majority of my life overprotected and sometimes over-loved by my family. It's nice to have someone assume I'm capable and competent. And now I truly feel that way.

She smiles slightly. "What if I told you they want you for the internship?"

It takes me several long moments to digest that news. "Seriously?"

Her grin widens. "Most seriously, Lavender."

"Oh, wow." I sink back into my chair and exhale a long, slow breath. Within seconds, my mind becomes cluttered with too many thoughts. *What if I'm not good enough? Where will I live? How am I going to manage the city on my own? Will I have to take the subway? What will my parents say? What about Kodiak?* "This is kind of a big deal, isn't it?"

Professor Martin sits on the edge of the desk. "You would be the youngest intern they've ever had, but if you don't think you're ready, we can try again next year."

"But there's no guarantee I'll get it next year."

"I'd like to say invariably you would, but I can't know that. Every year is different, and it's highly competitive. You have incredible talent, Lavender. There will most definitely be other opportunities for you, but this one is special."

"Wow, okay. I figured the chances I'd get it were slim to none."

My dad is going to shit a brick. I love him to pieces, but good Lord, he could barely handle me being an hour away while living with my brothers. And the whole freaking Kodiak thing has been another source of freak-out for him. Mom had to intervene and tell him that threatening one of his best friend's sons with castration was not a good way to manage us dating. I want to be ready for something like this, but there are so many unknowns.

"Why don't I email you all the information, and you can discuss it with everyone you need to? I don't want you to feel pressured, but they'll need to know either way by the end of next week."

I nod. "I'll have an answer by then."

THE HOUSE IS EMPTY. River is out with friends, and Maverick is at the game with Kodiak. Despite the fact that it's closing in on eleven, I call my mom.

She answers on the second ring. "How is my favorite daughter? And why in the world are you calling me on a Friday night? Shouldn't you be out breaking rules and doing things I don't want to think about?"

I laugh. "I took a break from the rule-breaking this weekend. Are you busy?"

"If you call listening to your dad sawing logs while I watch bad reality TV busy, then yes. What's up? Things still okay with you and Kody?"

"Things are great with Kodiak." And they really are. Loving him is so much easier than trying to hate him.

"I'm glad to hear that. And you're being safe and all that jazz, right?"

"Yes, Mom. We're being safe."

"I can literally hear you rolling your eyes at me. You know it's my motherly duty to ask. Anyway, I'm guessing you didn't call so I could ask awkward questions."

"You would be correct." I fill her in on getting the internship and remind her that it's in New York and I'd be there for two months. I finish up with, "It's a once-in-a-lifetime opportunity."

"It sounds like it. It also sounds a lot like you're unsure whether you should take it, despite it being so awesome. So why don't you tell me what your reservations are?"

I love how easy my mom makes it to talk things through. "Dad is gonna freak if I take it."

"Honey, I will deal with your dad. And I don't buy for a second that he's the real reason you're on the fence. Are you worried about being on your own?"

I sigh. "Maybe a little, and New York is huge."

"It's a bigger, grumpier, exciting version of Chicago, and nothing you can't handle. You've proven that this year."

"They have housing options where I'd be with other interns, so that would make it less scary," I tell her.

"For all of us, including your dad." Her voice softens. "If this is about Kody, just say so, and we'll figure it out."

"I don't want to leave him."

"Of course you don't. You've been absent from each other for a lot of years, and you're relearning how to be together. Not wanting to leave him makes perfect sense. But ask yourself this: What would be harder in the long run—two months of long distance where you get to live your dream and do something you're incredibly passionate about, or walking away from the opportunity and always wondering if it was a mistake you can't unmake?"

"They're both hard, for different reasons."

"You're absolutely right. And not to add another level of stress to this, but Kody is graduating this year, and they're ravenous to get him on a team. Would you want him to say no to his dream when the opportunity presents itself?"

"Of course not. When he's offered a contract, he has to take it."

"Don't you think he would want the same for you?"

She affirms what I already know but am having a hard time facing. If the shoe were on the other foot, I'd push Kodiak to take the opportunity. "I have to take the internship, don't I?" My stomach churns with excitement and anxiety.

"You don't have to do anything you don't want to do, other than make sure you're having safe sex. But in this case, I believe you want this very much, and I want it for you. I would say you're young, and that boyfriends come and go, but I don't know that's true for you and Kody. You two have survived a lot, and you can survive this too. Love is an amazing gift, but sometimes it hurts, and unfortunately, the two of you know that all too well."

33

Don't Let Go

KODIAK

Present day

I T'S ALMOST ONE by the time we get back from the game. Maverick hits the bar with some of the guys, but all I want to do is get back to Lavender. Despite winning the game, my body is still humming with nervous energy. There were scouts hanging around. There's been a lot of chatter lately about the draft picks and contract offers coming at the end of the year—things I don't want to think too much about, especially since Vancouver is a real possibility.

I stop at my place so I can hang up my hockey equipment and put a load in the wash. I also take a quick shower so I smell less like bus exhaust. Then I make the short trek down the street to Lavender.

The nights I don't sleep beside her are few and far between. Her bed is only a queen, but I don't mind the lack of space since it means she's always curled into my side. I climb the stairs, the pit in my stomach getting deeper instead of closing up the closer I get to her. It's late, and if she's asleep, I don't want to wake her, so I slip into her room without knocking.

I'm surprised to find the light beside her bed on, although sometimes she falls asleep reading. She sits up, and that heavy feeling in my stomach spreads through my limbs, making my cells feel like they're made of lead.

I cross the room in three quick strides. My skin itches with panic as I take in her red-rimmed eyes and the tremble in her chin. I cup her warm, damp cheeks between my palms, but it doesn't help settle the nerves, especially when two tears leak out of the corners of her eyes. "What's wrong? What happened?"

"I need to tell you something," she whispers.

A deluge of horrible thoughts come flooding in, over-whelming me. *She doesn't want me anymore. There's someone else. She's pregnant.* I drop down beside her, and have to remind myself to breathe. "Okay. I'm listening. Freaking out, but listening."

"I'm sorry." She covers my hands with hers. "It's not bad, but it's going to complicate things."

I nod and wait.

"I was offered an internship opportunity to work on costume design this summer for an off Broadway production company."

My eyes widen, but almost immediately, excitement and pride give way to understanding, and that heavy feeling I've been carrying all night finally makes sense. "In New York?"

"Yeah." She swallows thickly, more tears welling.

"The whole summer?" I don't need to ask why she's upset. We'd planned to spend at least part of this summer together. She was going to work at the library and take a course, and I'd coach kids' hockey, like I do most summers, and train. And now she's going to be hours away, too far to drive for a visit. We've been avoiding the other inevitability—finding out where I'll be playing—but there's no escaping this.

"It's two months. It starts basically as soon as we're done with exams, and I'd be there all of June and July."

I'm trying to figure out how often I can fly there to see her. Selfishly, I want her to stay here with me, to find something local so it's not as difficult. But I can't be selfish when it comes to her future. Lavender is insanely talented, and she's going to do great things.

"You have to take it." I shift her so she's straddling my lap.

"I know." She traces an infinity symbol over my heart. "But it won't be easy to go."

"What if I came with you?" I scramble for a way to keep us together.

"To New York?"

"We could get an apartment. I'll get a job, and then you won't be out there alone. Then we can still have the summer together." I don't want to deal with the thing that worries me most—what's going to happen *after* the summer. So many things are already up in the air, and I just got her back. I don't want to let her go.

Her eyes light up with hope, but dim quickly. "What about hockey? You play all summer."

"There are training camps in New York. I can talk to my dad and see if we can get me hooked up out there."

"What if that won't work?"

"Then we'll figure it out. But you have to go, Lavender." I force the words out, even though I feel the pain of them physically in my chest.

She runs her fingers through my hair, her smile sad. "I know I do. And I love the idea of you coming with me, if we can make it work. But even if we can't, I need this. I don't want to regret not going, and I don't want that regret to taint what we have, not when we've already been through so much to get back to each other."

"We'll make it work, no matter what."

I'm aware this conversation is one we're likely to have again, sooner than either of us wants. Two months in New York should be totally doable. But I worry about the inevitable distance we'll face come the fall.

But I don't say any of those things. Instead, I capture her mouth with mine and get lost in loving her.

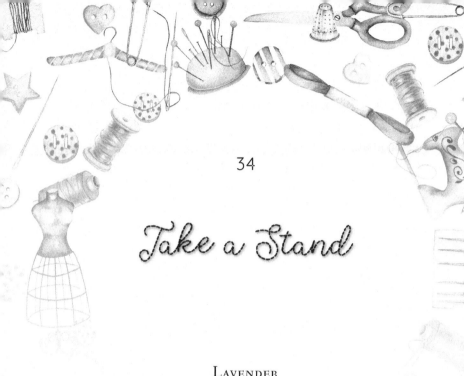

34

Take a Stand

Present day

THE NEXT MORNING, Kodiak broaches the subject of coming with me to New York with his parents, which spurs an impromptu parental visit. We have enough time to shower off the sex smell and tidy up the living room before the 'rents descend.

I fire off a warning to River, in case he decides to come home. He's been a lot better about things since he and I had it out, but that doesn't mean I'm not concerned about his reaction to me going to New York for the summer. He's still River.

Kodiak's parents and mine arrive together in a brand new giant truck at two in the afternoon. Lainey's behind the wheel, though. I freaking love Kodiak's mom almost as much as I love my own. She and I have a lot in common, minus being geniuses, and seeing this tiny woman get out from behind the wheel of a boss truck is awesome.

My mom engulfs me in a hug and whispers, "I promise it'll be fine. Just let your dad feel like he's being heard."

I figured this wouldn't be as simple as everyone thinking it was a fabulous idea for Kodiak and me to move to New York for the summer.

Lainey and my mom have brought enough food to feed an entire hockey team. They go about setting up a charcuterie board while our dads raid the beer fridge.

"Should we do this in the living room or at the dining room table?" my dad asks, draining half his beer in two long swallows.

Yeah, he's definitely stressed.

"I would say the living room, but that's where the guys hang out and play video games, so there's no telling what's stuck between the couch cushions." Two weeks ago, it stunk to high heaven in there. I forced the guys to clean their shit up because I couldn't even walk by the room without gagging. Turns out, it was a rotten hot dog that had ended up under the lounger.

"Dining room it is."

Kodiak grabs me a cooler, likely out of habit. Plus, it's the weekend. I take a seat beside him. His foot is tapping on the floor, and he keeps swallowing and blinking.

Our moms sit across from us, with a dad on either end. It reminds me a lot of the family meeting we had after the Courtney incident back when we were kids.

I link my fingers with Kodiak's under the table.

"Is that alcohol?" my dad asks, nodding to the bottle in my hand.

"It's a cooler, and it's, like, two-and-a-half percent. I'd have to drink a case to even get a buzz."

"You're underage." He glares pointedly at Kodiak.

"Pretend we're in Canada, Dad. And I'm going to go out on

a limb and assume you partook in some drinking when you were my age."

"I lived in Canada when I was your age."

"Exactly."

"She's not doing keg stands, Alex. Let it go," Mom says.

He leans back in his chair with a frown. "Is this what's going to happen if you go to New York? Is Kody going to be buying you alcohol? You know people make a lot of bad decisions when they've been drinking."

My mom snorts. "Like making out in public with hockey players where people can take photos that end up on the internet for all eternity?"

I bite my tongue so I don't laugh, or say something to make this situation worse.

My dad shoots my mom a look. "You're not helping, Vi."

She bats her lashes and arches a brow. "I'm not trying to."

My dad turns to Rook, like he's looking for him to weigh in. "Well, Kody has always proven to be fairly responsible, and Lavender has never gotten into trouble as far as I'm aware. So I can't really see my son going out and getting your daughter sloshed for shits and giggles."

My dad seems to realize this isn't a great argument to start with, so he switches gears. "Moving in together is a really big step, even if it's only for a short period of time. Merging your life with someone else's isn't seamless, and moving to a big city is another big change."

He laces his hands and rests his forearms on the table, leaning in and using his soft dad voice, the one he used to pull out when I was having a particularly bad panic attack. "Maybe it would be better to wait a couple more years until you're a little older, Lavender. This is the first time you've ever lived away from home, and New York isn't within driving distance. I don't want you to take on something you're not ready for."

I fully expected him to take this stance, and to pull the *you're-not-ready* card again. "I appreciate your concerns, Dad, but I feel like I am ready. This is a once-in-a-lifetime opportunity, and I may not have another chance to do it. As far as moving in together goes, Kodiak and I have pretty much been living together this entire semester. And if you remember, you all agreed that he could move in here with me and Maverick and River after the fire." I arch a brow.

"Well, that was before the two of you were involved," Dad argues.

Kodiak squeezes my hand, so I glance at him, thinking he's giving me some silent moral support, but he mostly looks like he's going to crap his pants.

I give him a look before I turn back to my dad. "I mean, come on, Dad. He lives down the street. We're adults, and we're being responsible. And let's be real, I stayed home last year because you and Mom wanted me to, not because I didn't feel ready to do this." I motion to our surroundings. "And I would have gladly moved into the dorms if I hadn't thought you and River would have had a coronary over it."

My dad crosses his arms over his chest. "You tried the dorms, and it only lasted two days."

Mom didn't say anything to him about my brief attempt at living in the dorms, until Dad noticed the bank transactions, the withdrawal and the refund. By that time I was back in the house and things with me and Kodiak had changed completely, but he still likes to try to use it as leverage of some kind.

"My roommate was a whack job. If I'd applied for the dorms right from the beginning, I could've gotten a single, and it wouldn't have been an issue. Anyway, that's beside the point. I've been successful at college. I'm dealing fine, and I still have monthly sessions with Queenie. I get that maybe you didn't expect this, but I think your hesitation is a lot less about me not being ready and more about *you* not being ready to let me go. I realize I'm always going to be *your* little girl, but that doesn't mean I'm still a little girl. You need to let me grow up and make my own decisions."

"She has a point, Alex," my mom says.

He glances at her, his brow pulling down in a furrow that makes him look so much like River. "I know you're not a little girl anymore."

"Then give me some freedom to be an adult."

Dad runs his hand through his hair. "I thought we were already doing the freedom thing. What happened to baby steps?"

"This was the baby step."

"Well, moving to New York with your boyfriend seems like a whole bunch of leaps all at once."

"I'm sure for you it is, but it's not like you don't know Kodiak. We grew up together. He's Maverick's best friend." I take a deep breath and blow it out, feeling my frustration grow. "I'm only having this discussion because I'd love to have your support. I'm not asking for permission, though. Neither of us is." I motion between Kodiak and me.

"We're not?" His eyes are wide.

I roll mine. "No. We aren't." I huff out a sigh. "Look, I get it. My childhood was traumatic for all of us, and I recognize you all did your best to manage things, but don't you think it's time to let us figure things out on our own?" I make eye contact with every adult at the table.

Rook and my dad slowly sink back in their chairs, and Lainey and my mom give me sad, but proud smiles.

"You know she's right, Alex. I think we've probably done enough interfering when it comes to these two. Maybe it would be a good idea to trust them and their ability to cope instead of finding reasons not to," Mom says.

My dad rubs his chin and mutters, "Ah hell." He nods slowly. "Does it have to be New York?"

"That's where the internship is, so yeah, Dad, it has to be New York. Why don't you look at it this way: You've done your job. You've helped raise a competent, confident young woman, and I want to take this amazing shot to pursue my dream. And I'm smart enough to bring along someone who is 100 percent behind me on this and will most definitely make sure I'm okay."

"I'm so sorry we've made it so hard for you," Lainey says softly.

"You were doing what you thought was right," Kodiak replies, his tone equally gentle.

"Rook and I have connections in New York. We'll see about getting you into a training camp out there for the summer," my dad says. "But only if you want us to make calls."

I look to Kodiak.

"Uh, yeah, that'd be great, Alex. I mean sir."

"I've changed your diapers, Kody. You don't have to start calling me sir." My dad gives me an apologetic smile. "I only ever want what's best for you."

"I know. You wouldn't have put all that money into therapy and sewing machines and an art room if you didn't."

That gets a chuckle out of everyone.

The house alarm beeps, a signal that either Maverick or River is home.

Everyone turns when River shouts, "Whose bomb-ass truck is in the drive—" He comes to a very abrupt halt the moment he enters the dining room with Josiah at his side. "What the hell is going on?"

River's eyes lock with mine, and I give him an apologetic shrug. "I texted you."

"Right. Okay. I didn't check my messages."

Mom stands and pulls him into a hug, then gives him a

questioning smile. "Aren't you going to introduce us to your friend?"

"Huh?" He glances at Josiah, and I can see the moment he decides not to disappoint him.

Kodiak squeezes my hand.

River clears his throat, gaze darting from me, to Dad, and then to Mom. "This is Josiah. And uh . . ." He looks at Josiah. "He's my boyfriend."

And just like that, me and Kodiak moving to New York together isn't the biggest news anymore.

Mom nods knowingly. "I figured. Well, let's get you two boys a chair so we can get to know Josiah better."

Three hours and a whole lot of yummy food and surprisingly easy conversation later, our parents gather their things and get ready to head home.

Dad pulls me into a hug. "You've grown into quite an incredible person, Lavender. It's hard to let you go."

"I know, and I love you for it, but I promise I can hold my own these days."

He kisses the top of my head. "I know you can, and I know Kody will be a good partner for you. Otherwise he'll have me to answer to."

I laugh, because what can I really say to that. He's my dad, and I'm always going to be his little girl.

Mom slips her arm around my waist. We're close to the same height. We watch as Dad and River have a whispered conversation.

"You knew River was gay?" I ask.

She lifts a shoulder in a slight shrug. "I suspected. I mean, whenever we went to the beach, it was never the girls he was staring at."

She has a point.

Dad puts a hand on River's shoulder, and his expression

shifts to one I'm familiar with. It's the one I called his marsh-mallow face when I was little, when he would go all soft and warm and compassionate. Whatever he says to River makes him duck his head. Dad pulls him in for a hug—and not one of those manly, back-pat jobs, but a real hug. I can practically feel the emotion in it.

They needed this.

We all did.

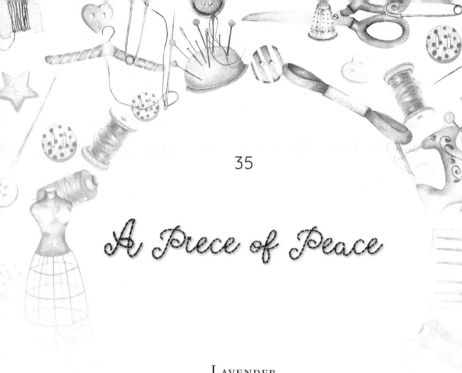

35

A Piece of Peace

LAVENDER

Present day

A S SOON AS finals are over, and Kodiak and Maverick graduate, Kodiak and I pack our things and move into a condo sublet our parents found in New York City. Although the internship offered accommodations, my dad and Kodiak's mom researched the most statistically safe location within walking distance of my internship and a short subway ride from Kodiak's training camp. Hence the sublet.

New York is busy and noisy and overwhelming. The bustle makes my heart race, but the internship is totally worth it. It takes all of twenty-four hours in the theater for me to come to the conclusion that this is my dream job.

My mentor, Priscilla, doesn't coddle me. And even better, everyone I work with asks for my opinion. They push my creative boundaries and test my skill set. I love everything about it. For the first time in my life, I understand what it means to feel truly comfortable in my own skin.

Kodiak and I are learning how to manage life together. It isn't seamless, or perfect, but it's real, and it's honest, and it's us. He's an excessive neat freak, and I'm less rigid about immediately putting everything away as soon as I'm done with it.

Regardless of our differences, we get each other on a level that feels soul deep. Sure, we're young, and we have our entire lives ahead of us, and so many things could change. But in those first few weeks, we carve out a hectic existence for ourselves, and I finally feel at peace with our past and how we managed to get here, to this place where we're wholly in love.

I stayed late at the theater tonight so I could finish a particularly tricky part of the costume I'm working on. Priscilla has been so supportive, always there to answer questions and teach me tricks to make things easier. It's almost eight o'clock by the time I get home to our ridiculously nice, two-bedroom sublet on the twentieth floor.

I'm hopeful that Kodiak is in the mood for a little fun and stress relief tonight. There are times when I worry I'm becoming a sex addict, but then I remind myself Kodiak is a twenty-two-year-old athlete—his birthday has come and gone— and there's nothing wrong with having a high sex drive. Besides, sex counts as exercise. Also, orgasms are a great, natural relaxant.

Kodiak actually looked it up when I made a joke about our slightly over-prolific sex life, paranoid that maybe we were having it too often. Then he read two books on sex addiction. And another one on bondage and voyeurism.

All they seemed to do was make him hornier and confirm that we were totally normal.

I let myself into the condo, and my excitement dampens

when I hear him talking. Maybe one of the guys he plays hockey with is over. He's made a few friends, as have I, but he never mentioned company tonight. I toe off my shoes and head down the hall, pausing when I catch him pacing the length of the living room with his phone in his hand.

He's wearing only a pair of athletic shorts, his heavily muscled back flexing as he runs a hand roughly through his hair. "I'm not going to Vancouver."

He's on speakerphone, but his dad's voice is low and muffled, so I don't catch his response.

"There has to be another option. That can't be the only team who wants me. Can't you get them to trade me? Maybe you should call my agent and ask about Chicago?"

"That's not how it works, Kodiak." Rook's voice is gentle, rational.

"You pulled strings for training camp this summer, though. You have to be able to do something! It's too far away. Lavender has two years of college left, and then we can go wherever."

"You don't know what things are going to look like two years from now, and you can't base this decision on one person. Just because Vancouver has you doesn't mean it's going to be the only option."

"It's the only one I'm hearing about! I'm not being separated from her again. You'll never understand what it's like. I'm not you. I can't walk away from the person I love and just deal for a year. I will lose my fucking mind!"

There's some muttering on the other end of the line, and suddenly it's his mom on the phone instead of his dad, her voice soft, but strong. "Kodiak, remember that your words have an impact on the people they're directed at, and throwing the past in someone's face is not a way to manage your emotions."

The shift in his demeanor is immediate. "You don't understand, Mom."

"You're right, I don't. I will never truly be able to understand what this is like for you, or for Lavender, because it's not *my* experience. You can be angry about the past, but at some point, you have to let it go and live in your present. I know you're worried about signing a contract that will take you away from Lavender again, but you can't tether yourself to her, or rely on her as the sole source of your happiness. Otherwise you're going in reverse."

"We're doing so good right now, though. I don't want to lose this."

"No one says you have to, Kodiak."

"How is it gonna work if I'm halfway across the country? I'll be traveling nine months out of the year." He rubs the space between his eyes.

"Have faith that your relationship is strong enough to withstand this," she tells him.

"What if *I'm* not strong enough?" he asks softly as I step into the living room. He catches the movement, and his face pales. "Lavender's home. I gotta go. I love you, Mom. Tell Dad I'm sorry. I'll see you in a few days." He ends the call and tosses the phone on the couch. "How much of that did you hear?"

There's no point in lying. "Vancouver wants you."

He shakes his head. "I won't do it. I won't take the deal."

I bridge the gap between us, link our pinkies, and guide him to the couch. He sits heavily and rests his forearms on his thighs.

"We knew this was coming." I run my fingers through his hair, pushing it out of his eyes, but he bows his head.

"I won't go to the West Coast. I'm not leaving you." His knees bounce, even though I know he's trying to force them to stay still.

"Kodiak, look at me." He glances at me briefly, and all I see is fear. These are the times I don't envy him and his massive brain. He unpacks every scenario in his head and runs it through, finding a fatalistic ending that drags him down into a soul-crushing abyss of terror.

I straddle his thighs and place my palm on the side of his neck. His pulse pounds violently. "I know you're scared, but you have to take the deal."

"I don't want to risk losing you," he whispers.

"Why do you think you'd lose me?"

"It's the other side of the country. I'll hardly see you." His face is etched with pain. "What if you decide it's too hard? What if I can't handle it?"

"Of course it's going to be hard, but have faith that we *can* handle it." I stroke his cheek, hating that I have to do this. "You have to promise me you'll take a deal, Kodiak, even if it's on the West Coast. You wouldn't let me walk away from an opportunity to live my dream, and I won't let you do that either."

"It's not the same. This is a two-month internship, not a contract that's going to lock you in for years in another country."

I sigh, weighing how best to approach this. "I will not let you waste your talent on fear of the unknown. And I refuse to carry that kind of guilt around with me for the rest of my life. We already know what that looks like."

His panic flares, and despite the fact that I'm sitting on his legs, they still manage a couple of bounces before they still. "What're you saying?"

"You can't put your life on hold. You *have* to sign with a team this year."

His eyes harden, and his jaw tightens. I sincerely hope we're not gearing up for a fight. "What if that's not what I want? What if I want to go to grad school instead?"

I make a face. "You would've applied if that's what you

wanted, and you didn't. Your mom posts the video of you playing hockey in your crib every year on your birthday. You played almost before you could walk. This is what you were meant to do, and you will be amazing no matter what team you play for or where. But you *will* play for a team this year."

Fear and anger twine together. "This sounds a lot like an ultimatum, Lavender."

I stroke his cheek; my anxiety mirrors his. "What do you think will happen to us if you throw away everything you've been working for just so you can be close to me? Isn't that us falling into the same pattern of dependency we've worked so hard to overcome? How do you think that will end?"

He puts his hand over mine, and his eyes fall shut. He inhales deeply and releases the breath slowly, seeking calm as he absorbs my words. I allow him to fall back into the past, reliving every instance in which he tried to save me from myself, but couldn't. He was great at calming the aftermath, but only *I* could ever save myself. Now it's my turn to save him from me.

When he opens his eyes, he whispers, "Badly. It would end badly."

I nod and give him a small, sad smile. "We'll make it work, wherever you go." I hope it's not a little lie, because in my heart I believe it to be the truth.

Otherwise, what was the point of all the suffering in the first place?

THE NEXT FEW days are tense and anxious. I try not to show my distraction when I'm at the theater, but it's tough. I'm watching the clock, counting the hours until I can be home with Kodiak.

The moment either of us walks in the door, we're on each other. We barely make time for dinner or sleep, too consumed with getting in as much togetherness as we can before he has to fly to Chicago for the weekend.

He'll only be gone a few days, but there's a sense of urgency that increases as the days dwindle into hours.

On Thursday morning, Kodiak watches me get ready for work. I pull on one of my light summer dresses and fix my hair in a ponytail. I don't bother with contacts these days, or makeup.

"Do you wonder if it would've been easier if I'd stayed in Chicago and let you come here on your own?" He's sitting on the edge of the bed, dressed in a polo and black pants, his suit-case packed and waiting by the front door.

"But then we wouldn't know what it's like to live together," I offer.

"You've become my definition of home, and if I get picked up by a team out west, I'll feel displaced."

Kodiak's way has always been able to filter the thoughts in his head and express only the ones he feels are most vital. I cross the room and step between his legs. We've been up since four and had sex three times between then and now, and still my body warms to his proximity.

I take his hand and place it against the side of my neck as he does the same to me. It will always be our thing. "We will adapt. How do you think our parents survived all those years with our dads on the road so much of the time? It's an adjustment. And to answer your original question, I don't know if it would've been easier or not. But we'll always have this time that was just ours to hold on to when being apart hurts."

"I wish it hadn't taken me this long to learn how to love you without consuming you."

I take his face in my hands. "You say it like you hold all the blame. We were equally complicit in our fall. Sometimes we have to break so we can recreate a stronger version of ourselves." I press my lips to his, but pull back before he can deepen the kiss. "Promise me you'll sign a contract."

"I promise." He makes an X over my heart and rises, sealing it with a searing, desperate kiss.

We walk down to street level together, and Kodiak makes a scene as he kisses me goodbye for far longer than is reasonable or appropriate. Afterward, I stand on the sidewalk, watching his cab disappear into morning traffic and feel the string that connects us pulling tighter the farther away he goes. It's something I'll have to get used to.

I manage to keep it together at work, but the moment I walk into the empty condo at the end of the day, I break down in tears. After stewing all day, I'm scared he might be right, and if he gets picked up by a West Coast team, we're not going to be able to handle the distance.

I'm home for all of two minutes when there's a knock on my door. The elderly woman down the hall sometimes has trouble with her key, so I wipe the tears away and try to get myself together enough to help her out.

Except when I open the door, it's not my neighbor.

"Surprise!" My mom does jazz hands and nearly hits Lacey in the face. She ducks out of the way and elbows Lovey in the boob. Behind them are River and Josiah, who, unlike the twins, are standing a safe distance from my mom.

There's a round of cringing and *sorry* before they all turn back to me.

"What are you guys doing here?"

"As if we were going to leave you here alone this weekend," my mom says.

And of course I burst into tears, because that's the kind of day it's been. I can't even speak I'm so choked up. They shuffle inside the condo and fold me into a group hug.

"We got you, Lavender." My mom squeezes me tightly. "No matter what, you're not going through this alone."

36

Go the Distance

Kodiak

Present day

MY DAD PICKS me up from the airport. He surprises me by pulling me into a hug. And not a back-slap man hug—a full-on, rib-crushing hug.

"Is everything okay? Where's Mom?"

He releases me and smiles wryly. "Yeah, everything's fine. Your mom had to take Dakota to his track meet, and Aspen is at robotics, designing some kind of fighting robot, but they should all be home by the time we get there." He gives my shoulder a squeeze. "It's good to have you home, son."

I nod and blow out a breath. "I'm ambivalent about being home, if I'm going to be a 100 percent honest."

He laughs. "I know, but your mom misses you, and so do your brother and sister. So feign enthusiasm when you see them."

"Don't worry, I'll drop the morose BS by the time we get home."

We head for the exit. "Things okay with Lavender?"

"Uh, yeah. Mostly." I rub the back of my neck. It took all of my resolve not to hook into the plane Wi-Fi on the two-hour flight and try to negotiate some sort of new deal with her. Logical? Nope. Desperate? Definitely.

"Mostly?"

"She overheard the conversation we had the other night."

"Ah. So she's aware Vancouver is looking at you?" my dad asks.

"Yeah."

"I'm sorry I can't make this easier on you, son."

"I'm sorry I lost my cool."

He puts an arm around my shoulder and gives it a squeeze. "If anyone should be apologizing, Kody, it's me. Sometimes I forget you and your mom are so much alike in the way you process things. But at the same time, you're also a lot like me, just a whole shitload smarter."

"I do a lot of stupid stuff for someone who's supposedly so smart."

"You're twenty-two. You're supposed to make mistakes. It's how we learn from them. But I'm still sorry I can't make this easier on you."

"I'd feel a lot less conflicted if I weren't looking at being so far away." I rub at the webbing between my middle and ring finger on my left hand, where the infinity symbol is tattooed. In hindsight, it's not a great spot for a tattoo, but I was also not in a great frame of mind when I got it.

"Because you don't want to be away from Lavender?" His voice is laced with concern.

He unlocks the back of his SUV, and I toss my bag in.

"She kinda gave me an ultimatum." I round the passenger

side and slide into the seat.

His brow furrows. "What kind of ultimatum?"

"She basically threatened to break up with me if I don't sign with a team while I'm here."

My dad's focus shifts to my bouncing legs before he meets my gaze, nodding slowly. "She's not a meek little girl anymore, is she?"

"She was never meek. She just went through more than most kids and experiences the world with overwhelming clarity. We didn't know how to deal with it then, but we do now."

"And apparently she knows how to deal with you." He shifts the SUV into gear and pulls out of the parking spot.

I have to look away, because a million really inappropriate images pop into my head—like how things went down last night and the fact that I'm missing a strip of hair on both forearms thanks to the duct tape. I clear my throat.

"Apparently." I'm still about two octaves higher than usual, and my face feels hot.

My dad laughs. "Oh, son, you are in trouble, aren't you?"

"What's that supposed to mean?"

He smirks and reaches over to ruffle my hair. "Just make sure you're being safe."

"Jesus, Dad. We're being safe. Mom says the same freaking thing every time I talk to her."

"All it takes is one time without protection."

"Yeah, well, you would know, wouldn't you?" I point to myself.

I'm the product of an unplanned pregnancy. My parents had what they refer to as a "whirlwind romance" one summer in Alaska. Basically that means they had an extended hookup. My dad had to leave because of a family emergency, and they lost contact, but managed to find their way back to each other. By that time, I'd already been born.

"And I don't regret it for a second, because if it wasn't for you, there's a good chance I wouldn't have your mother in my life. But we were both older, and not just starting our lives. You and Lavender are young and finding your way, so don't go complicating it with unplanned pregnancies."

"Okay, can we change the subject, please? Because talking about how my existence came to be is really damn awkward."

"It's only awkward if you make it awkward, son."

"No, it's awkward because you're talking about my mom in ways I'm not interested in thinking about."

"Noted. How are you feeling about tomorrow?"

"Anxious. Excited. Terrified that I'll have to sign with Vancouver and be halfway across the country while Lavender is back here. Just thinking about it makes my brain feel like it's frying itself."

He's quiet for a minute before he finally says, "It isn't easy, is it? Being able to see all the sides at the same time?"

"It's maddening. Paralyzing. I run through every possible future path, and I can see exactly what could happen if I make the wrong choice. The only time I can shut everything else off and just exist is when I'm on the ice or with Lavender. I don't want to have to give up one so I can have the other, but she's not giving me an option. I feel like I'm going to lose her either way." I rub my chest, trying to ease the ache.

"I know your tendency is to go to the worst-possible scenario, but let's wait and see what happens tomorrow. Just because Vancouver has designs on you doesn't mean there won't be other options."

I nod, but I don't want to get my hopes up.

The house is a flurry of activity as soon as I walk in the door, with Aspen wanting to show me the robot she's been designing and Dakota showing me all the ribbons he won at the track meet. I'm a full hybrid of my parents, both physically and mentally. But my sister is 100 percent a miniature version of our mom, and Dakota is my dad. They're both a lot younger than me, Aspen a freshman in high school and Dakota in seventh grade.

Aspen is having a sleepover, so when her friend arrives, they rush up to her room, giggling and whispering. Dakota decides he needs to take his second shower of the day since he smells like four-day-old socks. My dad has to run out for a business meeting, but promises he'll only be a couple of hours.

Once it's just me and my mom, she goes into feed-the-growing-boy mode. I don't mind the doting. She and I have always been tight—having the same kind of brain and the same worries can do that.

She leans on the counter across from me. "How are you doing?"

I shrug. "I should be excited, but mostly I'm scared." I fill her in on Lavender's ultimatum. Threat. Whatever it is.

My mom covers my hand with her much smaller one and squeezes. "She's a smart girl."

I nod. "I know she's right, but I don't want her to be."

She props her chin on her clasped hands. "Life is not a series of all-or-nothing decisions, Kody. If the roads we travel were all straight with no bumps or twists and turns along the way, we wouldn't appreciate the ups between the downs and the easy-to-navigate stretches."

"What if I'm only allowed to have hockey or Lavender, not both?"

"Why would you think that?"

"I tried so hard not to love her." I look down at the counter. "It's like she engraved herself on my heart when we were kids. I couldn't *not* love her. So I tried everything I could to make her hate me. I said and did such horrible, hurtful things."

"Has she forgiven you for that?"

"Yeah."

"But you haven't forgiven yourself?"

I shrug.

My mom pats my cheek and forces me to look at her. "You're a good person, with a good heart, and you love intensely. Sometimes that level of love can be confusing and frightening, and we fight against it as a result. But Lavender *sees* you, just like you see her. She's already granted you grace. It's your turn to do the same."

THE WEEKEND IS PRETTY DAMN stressful, but at least I'm not in it alone, since Maverick is in the same position. Interestingly enough, the fact that I'm now living with his sister hasn't affected our friendship. Obviously there is absolutely no locker-room-style talk, but I was never really one to do that anyway, and neither is he.

By the end of the weekend, I've done what I said I would and signed with a team.

My dad is all smiles, and if rainbows could shoot out of his ass, they would.

"We'll be in touch soon with all the details for training camp, and we'll set up a time for you to come out and see the facilities in the next month," the general manager tells me. "You're going to be a great addition to the team."

I shake his hand and mumble a bunch of nervous nonsense about how I'm looking forward to being part of the team and can't wait for training camp, but what I'm mostly thinking is that at least Lavender won't have to make good on her threat to break up with me.

37

Concede

LAVENDER

Present day

ME AND MY mom are always up at the crack of dawn, no matter what time we go to bed, so on Sunday morning, we leave everyone else to sleep in, and I take her to the theater so she can see where I work and what I'm involved in. We grab coffees and pastries on the way. I point out all the places Kodiak and I like to go, and where some of the other interns live.

My mom makes a face. "Kinda reminds me of the apartment I lived in before your dad convinced me to move into his place."

"I thought you lived in Gigi's pool house."

"For a while, so I could save up enough money to get my own place, but you know Gigi. She's well-meaning but has zero concept of personal space and does not know how to knock."

I can only imagine what that would be like. Gigi is inappropriate at the best of times, and when she gets together with Grandma Daisy, they're a total train wreck. "Thank you for trying your best not to mortify me on a regular basis."

"I save it all for Maverick, since he deserves it."

"Where do you think he'll be next year?" I've been so focused on what's going on with me and Kodiak that I've totally spaced on the fact that my brother is in the same position.

"Hard to say. Your dad seems to think there's a chance he'll end up in Nashville, but you never really know. And Mav is all about going with the flow, so he'll be fine with whatever team wants him. Honestly, my biggest concern for your brother is the decadent lifestyle."

"You're worried the fame is going to go to his head?" I ask.

"He just . . . likes to have a little too much fun, and he doesn't take things as seriously as he should."

He buckled down after my dad called him out on all the partying and his poor grades in the first semester and managed to graduate with honors. "He was better second semester, though. Maybe he'll do some growing up once he's playing professionally."

"We can hope."

Rehearsal isn't scheduled until later in the day, so the theater is quiet and basically empty when we arrive. I take her behind the stage to the back rooms where I work and show her some of the costumes I've completed since I started, as well as the one I've been working on for the past few days. I'm in the middle of explaining how fabric colors and textures work together with the set to make the actors really pop on the stage when she pulls me into a tight hug.

"Mom?"

"I'm so proud of you." When she releases me, she dabs at

her eyes. "You've come so far from that shy girl who didn't speak above a whisper."

"I had a lot of therapy and support and *you*, so that definitely helped."

"I know we were super overprotective, and having three brothers did not make it easy, but you've always been your own person, and I'm so happy to see you shine the way I always knew you were meant to."

I wave my hand in front of my face. "Stop with the mushy stuff! If I start crying, it's your fault."

Priscilla pops her head in the room. "I thought I heard voices in here! Lavender, I didn't expect to see you today. But your timing couldn't be more perfect. I have something I wanted to discuss with you. Oh! Hello." Her gaze flits between me and my mom.

"Hi, I'm Violet. Lavender's mother." She holds out her hand.

"Oh, I can most definitely see that." She smiles warmly and shakes my mom's hand. "You must be incredibly proud of Lavender. I have to say, she is hands down the best intern we've ever had, which is what I wanted to talk to you about, although it can wait until tomorrow, if you prefer." She looks from me to my mom.

"Now is fine with me." I'm flustered by the praise.

Her smile widens. "The production team has been talking about how wonderful you've been, and we'd like you to stay on with us."

"Stay on with you?" I feel like an idiot for echoing her, but I've only been here a few weeks. I had to have misheard that. "As in, you want to keep me on as an intern after July?"

"Not as an intern, but as a member of our company. You have an incredible skill set, Lavender. I know you've been studying in Chicago, but there are amazing programs here in New York you could transfer to, and many accept part-time students. That way you'd be able to continue your education while working with us."

"Oh. Wow. That's . . . very humbling." That I manage to get any words out at all is amazing, considering my level of shock is pretty damn high.

"You're a rare talent," Priscilla continues. "I would love to help you foster that. Of course, I understand that it's something you'll need to think about. I wanted to give you time to consider it."

"It sounds like a wonderful opportunity." My mom threads her arm through mine and gives it a squeeze. "And it sounds like Lavender has some pretty big decisions to make for the fall."

I'm not sure if she actually thinks it's a wonderful opportunity or not, but I appreciate her speaking, because I don't think I can right now.

"She certainly does, and of course there's no rush. I just wanted to put it on the table. Regardless of your decision, Lavender, there will always be a place here for you."

My mom waits until we're outside the theater before she grabs my arm and turns me so we're facing each other. "Gut reaction, no thinking—do you want to stay in New York?"

"Yes, but—"

She raises a finger. "Hold the *but*. What makes you *want* to stay in New York?"

"I love what I'm doing, I love this theater, everyone has embraced me, and I've found my people. I'm not weird or different. It's okay that I'm quiet sometimes. People like my ideas, and we spark as a team. And surprisingly enough, I like the city. But the subway sucks." I prefer walking over using public transit.

My mom wrinkles her nose. "Exhaust and urine are not a winning combination of odors."

"So true. Besides that, I've made friends who aren't my relatives, I feel like I've gained some real independence, and I've found something I'm really good at. Robbie has botany, River is great at school and football and being angry at life, and Maverick is great at hockey and one-month relationships."

"Is that actually a thing for Maverick? You know what? Don't bother answering that. It's irrelevant to this discussion, and we can come back to it later. Or maybe never. Now, tell me the *but* side to this." The right side of her mouth quirks up at the way she stresses the word *but*.

"Stop being such a twelve-year-old boy."

She taps her temple. "My maturity level is at least fifteen. What's holding you back?"

"It's far from home and my family and friends."

"We're a plane ride away, and I love shopping, so I'll come visit all the time and bring the people you love and miss with me."

"Kodiak will have training camp in August, so I'll be out here on my own."

"But you've made friends, and he was always going somewhere, honey. So the way I see it, you have two options. You come back to Chicago and finish school there, or you stay here and take this amazing opportunity to do something you truly, wholly love."

"What do you think Dad will say?"

"He'll say the real estate is a good investment once I calm him down. Don't worry about your dad, Lavender. He wants you to be happy, and he realizes that in order for that to happen, we can't helicopter-parent you or smother you. You came here for a reason. It looks to me like the universe is giving you something else to stay for."

MY MOM, Lacey, Lovey, River, and Josiah leave for the airport midafternoon. Kodiak isn't due back until later in the evening, so I sit in front of my sewing machine, unable to relax. We made a deal that he wouldn't tell me where he was going until he got home. But he did message me a picture of his very neat signature written on a contract.

Which brings with it equal parts relief and terror.

Now I just have to prepare myself for what's coming next, which is a lot of change for both of us.

It's almost nine when he walks in the door, looking exhausted. He drops his bag on the floor and opens his arms. I'm wearing socks, so I skid across the slippery hardwood into his hard chest.

He folds me into his embrace. "I missed you so goddamn much."

"Same." I breathe him in—his cologne, the scent of his laundry detergent, stale airplane, and possibly some kind of pizza. His heart thunders, and mine matches the frantic rhythm.

He cups my face between his palms, tips my head back, and covers my mouth with his. I sink into the kiss for a few minutes, allowing myself the fantasy that this isn't going to come to an end in a month, that every day he's going to walk through that door and kiss me like this for the rest of our lives, that I won't have to go weeks at a time without him.

Eventually I pull away. "You signed with a team."

He nods. "For three years."

My heart skips a few beats. That will feel like an eternity. "We'll make it work."

"We'll have the off-season, and the flight to Chicago isn't that long. We'll be able—"

"I won't be in Chicago."

"Wait. What?" His brow furrows.

I swallow my fears. "While you were away, I got an offer from the production company. They want to keep me on."

"Here? In New York?"

I nod. "I really love it, Kodiak. I love what I'm doing, and if you're already going to be all the way across the country, it makes sense." I run my hands over his chest, working to find some calm when my nerves are going haywire. "New York and Chicago are pretty close to the same distance from Vancouver."

"I won't be in Vancouver." He sweeps a thumb across the hollow under my eye, wiping away a tear.

My heart stutters. "Where will you be?"

"Close." A massive grin breaks across his face, popping the dimple that makes him look so boyish. "I signed with Philly."

"Philadelphia? That's really close."

"Drivably close," he agrees and lowers his voice to a whisper. "We're gonna be okay, Lavender. We can make this work."

I break down in tears, the relief overwhelming. "I was so scared you were going to be on the other side of the country."

He wraps his arms around me and carries me over to the couch, arranging me so I'm settled in his lap. "I was fucking terrified." He brushes my hair away from my face. "I didn't want to be that far away from you."

"Me either, but I couldn't let you walk away from your dream."

He nods, eyes soft and warm. He wraps me in his safe, strong embrace, dips his head and kisses me breathless. "Thank you for making sure I didn't mess this up for us."

"I love you too much to let something like distance break us, but I'll admit, I'm so glad you won't be far away."

"Well, I'm always right here." He draws a figure eight over my heart. "But I prefer when I can feel it beat for me."

EPILOGUE

Keeper of My Heart

KODIAK

Eighteen months later

IT'S AFTER MIDNIGHT when I get home. And home isn't Philly anymore. The planets aligned, and I was traded at the end of last season. But home isn't a spot on a map for me anyway. It isn't the two-story brownstone with a garden full of purple flowers in the summer and a door the color of my girlfriend's name.

Home is the feeling I get when the plane touches down in New York City. It's the spike of anxiety mixed with anticipation as I slide into the back seat of the cab, knowing with every passing mile, I'm that much closer to the one person who makes me feel whole.

Home is wherever Lavender happens to be.

And currently, she's curled up on the couch, having fallen asleep while crocheting. Her brother Robbie's girlfriend is due any day, and Lavender decided before I left for my away series that she was going to teach herself to crochet because *so many cute things*!

One of her favorite albums is playing, probably on repeat. She does that sometimes, plays the same album on an endless loop when she's trying to concentrate. She says she stops hearing it, and it drowns out the noise in her head.

Based on the rainbow of bunnies populating the arm of the couch at her feet, the mission was a resounding success—either that or the crocheted bunnies have learned how to multiply on their own.

I take a moment to appreciate that Lavender is willing to deal with the insanity that is my life, and sometimes me. I love her so fiercely, it can be overwhelming at times—for both of us. But we've learned how to find our own version of balance. It isn't always easy, and the long stretches during my away series test me more than they test Lavender, but we manage. She's proven to be the stronger and more resilient of the two of us in that regard.

I pad back to the kitchen to gather the items I left on the counter, and I arrange them carefully on the end table before I kneel on the floor beside her.

Her lips are parted slightly, the scar from her childhood forever a reminder of the night that cemented our souls together. No matter how far away I am, I feel that connection, like a tripping switch, an invisible energy that only seems to grow stronger the longer we're together.

I brush my thumb across her bottom lip, and she sighs, head turning in my direction. She swipes at her face with an uncoordinated hand, and when it connects with mine, she finds my pinkie and curls hers around it.

"Baby, you wakin' up?" I kiss her temple and down her cheek.

She hums softly, and her palm comes to rest against the side of my neck. "Kodiak."

"You talking to me in your sleep?" I hover over her mouth.

Her lips turn up. "I tried to stay awake."

"You and the bunnies?"

"Mmm. Me and the bunnies." She licks her lips. "I need a mint before you kiss me hello."

"No, you don't." I slant my mouth over hers and part her lips with my tongue.

She makes a slight noise of protest that turns into a sweet moan. She tastes like watermelon Jolly Rancher, so she must not have been asleep all that long. We kiss until it's clear Lavender wants it to become more. She kicks off the blanket and tries to shove my hand down the front of her sleep shorts.

"Not yet." I smile against her lips. "I have something for you."

"I'd rather have an orgasm than whatever it is."

I chuckle. Lavender is always a little surly when she's woken unexpectedly, and now is a perfect example of that.

"I promise you'll get what you want *after*, but I have something special for you since it happens to be your birthday." I pull back and tilt my head toward the end of the couch where helium balloons and a bottle of champagne are set up. "No more underage drinking for you. Gonna be hard to give up your badass, deviant ways."

"If we lived in Canada, I'd have been legal for two years already." She grabs the front of my shirt and tries to pull my mouth back to hers. "Thank you for the balloons and champagne. Let's drink that after you've been inside me."

"That's not the present." I kiss the end of her nose.

"I missed you," she whispers huskily. "The sun isn't as bright when you're not here for it to shine on."

"I missed you too." I indulge her in a short, chaste kiss while

I produce a small box from behind my back. "Happy twenty-first birthday, baby." I shift so I'm on one knee and swallow my anxiety as I flip the box open.

Lavender shakes off the residual sleepiness and sits up in a rush. "Kodiak?"

The diamonds sparkle in the dim light. "You've had my heart your entire life, Lavender, and even when I bruised yours, you still took care of mine. I'm sorry it took me so long to be able to love you like I was supposed to, and I don't know if I'll ever truly deserve you, but I want to try. I want this life with you. Please let me keep your heart."

She strokes my cheek gently. "It's always been yours."

"Bind your soul to mine." I lift the ring from its satin box and slide it on her finger. The center is set with a pale purple diamond, and on either side are two diamond-encrusted infinity symbols.

"They're already long bound, but I'll marry you anyway." Her smile softens as she takes my face between her palms. "It's beautiful and perfect, and I love you more than is rational most days."

"And I love you beyond comprehension."

"So much we nearly broke us."

Her kiss is my grace. Lavender is the keeper of my heart. She's the only truth that matters.

THE END

A NOTE TO MY READERS

Thank you for coming on this journey with Lavender and Kodiak. For jumping in with both feet and making it to the end. I know it wasn't easy, but this story came right from my heart and I couldn't let these characters go until I reached their happily ever after.

Anxiety is such a beast.

One I'm familiar with. I couldn't name it as a kid and didn't understand why my heart would race, or I sometimes felt like my mind was spinning and I couldn't get it to stop. I wanted off the roller coaster ride, but it was hard to escape when it was inside my own head. It took time, and a lot of practice, falling down and getting back up, but I learned how to live with the fears and worries and not let them rule me. Running and writing have been my best coping strategies.

I once had the very rare privilege of working with a young woman with paralyzing anxiety. She didn't speak above a whisper when she was in public places, if at all. I was one of the few she talked to, but even I didn't get to see her truly come out of her shell, and to this day it haunts me. Because I've seen

e people she is most comfortable with
d vital and amazing. But the world was
· her.

ivender I put pieces of this young
ind resilient parts.

ister and a weed. It can grow and become
-, and suffocating. But there are ways to cope.

If you've found yourself anxious this year in ways you haven't before (you're not alone), know there are resources and help available. There are places and people you can connect with.

You can tame the beast. It isn't easy, but you can be a Lavender. You can find your voice and take control.

This story is for everyone out there who experiences life with overwhelming clarity. And still pushes through every day and makes the most of this beautiful, terrible world.

Much love,

~Helena

OTHER TITLES BY HELENA HUNTING

LIES, HEARTS & TRUTHS SERIES

Little Lies

Bitter Sweet Heart

All IN SERIES

A Lie for a Lie

A Favor for a Favor

A Secret for a Secret

A Kiss for a Kiss

PUCKED SERIES

Pucked (Pucked #1)

Pucked Up (Pucked #2)

Pucked Over (Pucked #3)

Forever Pucked (Pucked Book #4)

Pucked Under (Pucked #5)

Pucked Off (Pucked #6)

Pucked Love (Pucked #7)

AREA 51: Deleted Scenes & Outtakes

Get Inked

Pucks & Penalties

SHACKING UP SERIES

Shacking Up

Getting Down (Novella)

Hooking Up

I Flipping Love You

Making Up

Handle with Care

SPARK SISTERS SERIES

When Sparks Fly

Starry-Eyed Love

Make A Wish

LAKESIDE SERIES

Love Next Door

Love on the Lake

THE CLIPPED WINGS SERIES

Cupcakes and Ink

Clipped Wings

Between the Cracks

Inked Armor

Cracks in the Armor

Fractures in Ink

STANDALONE NOVELS

The Librarian Principle

Felony Ever After

Before You Ghost (with Debra Anastasia)

FOREVER ROMANCE STANDALONES

The Good Luck Charm

Meet Cute

Kiss my Cupcake

ABOUT THE AUTHOR H. HUNTING

NYT and *USA Today* bestselling author, Helena Hunting, lives on the outskirts of Toronto with her incredibly tolerant family and two moderately intolerant cats. She writes contemporary romance and romantic comedies, and when she wants to dive into her angsty side, she writes new adult romance under H. Hunting.

Scan this code to stay connected with Helena

Made in the USA
Las Vegas, NV
27 December 2022

64214638R00214